Bracelet of the Morning

-A novel of Africa-

Jerold Richert

Bracelet of the Morning

by Jerold Richert

This book is for my wife
Lorna Rose
with all my love

BRACELET OF THE MORNING
Part One

The land breeze arrived at dawn. Warm as a lion's breath it wafted across Table Bay like an awakening sigh, bringing to the weary passengers lining the rail of the barque, *Avocet*, their first scent of Africa, and they stirred anxiously, as if preparing themselves for what lay ahead.

The ship too, stirred and came reluctantly round to the wind, her ancient timbers groaning as if in protest at being aroused from her well-earned rest

'Hands on deck!'

The Bosun's bellow was echoed several times below amidst the grumbling of sleepy men and the thumping of bare feet.

'Foresail and mizzen for a starboard tack, Mister Franks.'

'As you say, Cap'n.'

The passengers moved hastily clear of the rail to give the crew room, standing in a tight group amidships, and strangely silent now as they peered into the gloom ahead for the first sight of the famous flat-topped mountain.

Charles Atherstone stood apart from the others. Seasickness and the resulting loss of appetite had pared him down to the extent his trousers bagged at the seat and the pale skin of his elbows showed through the threadbare sleeves of his coat. Much of his time had been spent shivering on deck, where he could at least inhale fresh air and receive forewarning from the waves of the otherwise unpredictable motion of the ship, and the equally unpredictable heaving of his stomach. Despite his exposure to the elements, they had done little to improve his sallow complexion. It came as no surprise to his fellow travellers when he informed them he was not joining the diamond rush as were they, but intended to take up employment in the colony as a clerk.

It was approaching noon by the time the barque finally docked and the wharf was in chaos. From one end to the other it was cluttered with dirty unpainted wagons, tangled mules, and hordes of blacks, all of whom seemed intent on shouting louder than the next man as they carried the bales and barrels from the ship to the waiting jumble of wagons.

After disembarking Charles lingered to watch

the activity with astonishment from beside the security of a wagon. The blacks did not look at all like the dangerous savages he had been led to expect. They carried no spears or shields, and wore a strange mix of cast-off settler clothing in place of animal skins and feathers. Some even wore top hats, while others donned ladies' bonnets worn back to front, and one, sporting only the brim of a Derby, wore also a pink gown that had been hacked off at the hips, presumably to better display the frilly lilac bloomers. An overseer, wielding a short length of tarred rope, charged into a group arguing over a fallen stack of barrels, one of which had broken and spilled its contents. The blacks scattered hastily, leaving the overseer engulfed and cursing in a white haze of flour.

The sudden crash of a cannon sent Charles scurrying and diving for cover under the wagon. He peered out anxiously. It did not appear to be an uprising. As if it had been a signal, the labourers surrendered their bundles to the ground where they stood and sauntered cheerily away towards the nearest shade.

Sheepishly, Charles retrieved his bag and picked his way warily through the deserted wagons and onto the streets of Cape Town.

Fleetwood Erskine Tucker was a gentleman. It was evident in the the stylish quilting of his brocaded satin waistcoat, the fashionable yellow and brown check of his taylored trousers, and the perfect twin curls of his waxed moustache.

On a hot humid morning in the summer of 1870, he sat with his polished boots atop the balcony railing of the *Hotel de Europe* in Cape Town, smoking a cigar and watching the boatload of newly arrived hopefuls as they passed below on their way to Yorky's Bar.

Fleetwood had been watching them arrive for the past year; lured to the colony - as he himself had been - by the promise of easy riches. But having a cynically practical turn of mind when it came to easy money, Fleetwood, unlike most, had quickly assessed the situation for what it was. Only an imbecile, he believed, could be sucked in by the stories of diamonds lying on the ground simply waiting to be picked up, and the gullibility of the dreamers who believed the stories was a source of never ending amazement to him.

He knew that the vast majority of the new arrivals would fail, of course, like many had before, and those lucky enough to stumble over a gem would be forced to sell it at a bargain price to the first illicit diamond buyer - or kopje walloper as they had become known – that came along, so they could then buy supplies at grossly inflated prices to avoid starvation.

Fleetwood had learned that only the large consortiums, merchants, and registered diamond buyers made money, and the latter was an avenue he had explored thoroughly before rejecting. Authorised diamond buying required too large an outlay of ready cash, and illicit buying was too risky.

Not that the illegality of illicit dealing deterred Fleetwood - if anything that was a challenge - but wandering around with bags full of money and diamonds in a camp overflowing with the world's riff-raff was a little too adventurous for his liking. A safer, more rewarding means had to be available other than scrabbling in the dirt or fighting off ruffians. A way more suited to his own particular talents, and which would also allow him to enjoy the luxurious hospitality of the *Hotel de Europe* rather than the primitive conditions at the diggings.

To Fleetwood's unending delight and astonishment, it had proved to be not that difficult. The vast majority of diamonds found at the Vaal River eventually passed through Cape Town on their way to

London, conveniently parceled and well guarded, but there was always a weak link, Fleetwood believed, and it had not taken him long to find it.

Despite the oppressive heat, Fleetwood was thoroughly enjoying himself. A bottle of the best French champagne nestled in the ice tub at his side, and the smoke from his cigar drifted slowly heavenwards in the still air, leaving behind a rich enveloping flavour of well-being.

He ran his fingers lovingly over the front of the waistcoat, once again enjoying the sensuous feel of the satin. He was immensely proud of the garment, which he had designed himself, and the diamond pattern of the quilting appealed hugely to his sense of humour.

Mister Mooljee, the renowned Indian tailor who had made it, would have been horrified had he known that the black silk lining he had sewn on with such meticulous care had been unceremoniously ripped out and replaced with coarse red sail cloth. He would have been even more alarmed had he known that before the lining was replaced with such a common and garish substitute, at least one carefully wrapped diamond had been pushed into each segment of the quilting.

Excluding the inflated fee for tailoring, Fleetwood estimated its worth at around fifteen thousand pounds; enough to set him up comfortably in Mayfair - where his former associates seldom ventured - for the rest of his life. He patted the quilting affectionately. It was a trifle bold perhaps, and rather warm in weather like this, but still a great comfort to have close to his skin.

That the contents were stolen did not bother Fleetwood in the slightest. The diamonds would no doubt be well insured, so the diggers - or more likely the buyers who had cheated them - would lose nothing. If anyone were to lose, Fleetwood reasoned, it should be the Department of Customs who had shown such criminal disregard for the safety of the diamonds while in their posession.

Smiling with contentment, Fleetwood silently toasted His Majesty's Department of Customs and Excise with the last of the champagne. Then, with the Derby tilted forward against the glare, he settled lower in the canvas chair with a contented sigh and gave himself over to day-dreaming about the furore that would erupt when the package supposedly containing the gems finally reached London.

Tugging at his ear in indecision, the Chinese Malay stood hesitantly on the balcony behind the sleeping man. He had tried coughing politely, noisily shuffling his feet, and even a tentative 'Suh?' But the man in the chair snored on.

He reached to shake him by the shoulder, then paused. Such familiarity may provoke anger. Instead, he redirected his claw-like hand to the tilted Derby and rapped sharply on the crown as if it were a closed door.

With a snort of alarm, Fleetwood snatched the Derby from his face at the same instant as his feet clattered off the railing to the floor. Startled, he looked wildly about, and the Malay took a precautionary step back, glancing towards the open French doors.

'Ha!' Fleetwood caught the movement at the limit of his vision. 'What the devil do you think you're doing?' He reached quickly for the reassuring feel of the waistcoat and started to rise, then abruptly changed his mind. His head throbbed abominably. He shook it experimentally. The effect was not encouraging.

With a groan he dipped his handkerchief in the now tepid water of the ice tub and dabbed gently at his forehead. Noticing that a mouthful of champagne still lingered in the bottle, he swigged it back, grimacing at the sour flat taste. He turned his head cautiously to peer once more at the waiting Malay.

'Good Lord! What a wretched fellow you are... what the devil do you think you're doing waking me in such a manner?' He squeezed the handkerchief dry then held it to his face. 'What the blazes do you want?'

He lowered the cloth to squint suspiciously up at the Malay. 'Me no gottee money. Me no givee money Chinee... understand?'

The Malay bobbed his head and smiled, the action causing his eyes to disappear into the folds of his yellow skin at the same time as his lips split wide to reveal foul-looking purple gums. He shuffled forward and held out a soiled scrap of paper.

Fleetwood recoiled slightly, eyeing the paper suspiciously but making no move to take it, and the Malay shook it as if to reassure him it was quite safe.

Fleetwood took it warily by the corner, as if it may suddenly come alive. It was so tattered and grubby as to be barely recognisable as a note but, with a final accusing look at the Malay, he turned it the right way up and began to read.

Fleetwood read the note three times.

The first time he was inclined to believe he was still dreaming and things had simply taken a nasty turn.

The second time he snorted in derision as if it were some cheap practical joke, and was barely able to restrain himself from tossing the note over the balcony in disgust.

On the third reading, a sufficient quantity of information penetrated the champagne fog to make sense, and Fleetwood began to melt into his chair.

Blisters of sweat broke out on his forehead and dripped from his nose to splatter on the note, further blurring the words, which his shaking fingers caused to swim before his eyes. His shoulders slumped as if a heavy chain had been draped around his neck. The wax on his moustache had become a victim of the heat and the once proud upward sweeps had uncurled into forlorn droops. They began to twitch spasmodically.

Fleetwood fumbled in his waistcoat pocket for a coin and held it out without looking, and the Malay clasped it with both hands then backed away through the doors.

Fleetwood sat for a long time staring vacantly at the note, his eyes clouding with self pity. All he had needed was another two days. Two short days before the ship sailed for England, taking Toby Hollings with it and out of his life forever. But the imbecile had not been able to wait even that short a time. Like all his low criminal class he had to get himself drunk and arrested at the first opportunity. And there was no doubt whatsoever he would squeal at the first glimpse of the cat. It had been a mistake to give him the money so soon. He should have made him wait until the very last moment, then escorted him to the ship himself.

Fleetwood eased slowly out of the chair to pace the balcony, cursing Toby Hollings with as much vigour as his throbbing head would allow.

He would have to leave Cape Town immediately, that was certain. By now, not only Hollings, but also most of the inmates of Newmarket Gaol would know where he was living. It was little comfort they knew him by a false name. Even the most simple-minded clod in the police force would be able to trace him to the hotel.

Fleetwood lit a cigar with a trembling flame and tried to think. It was not the first time he had been in a tight spot. It was only the first time he had been in a tight spot in the colony, and he had hoped to avoid such unpleasantness in his fresh start on life

He made a concerted effort to evaluate his situation. As yet, no diamonds had been reported missing. At least that was something in his favour. But eventually they would be, and to save his neck, Hollings would lead the police directly to him. It was only a matter of time.

The waistcoat pressed heavily against Fleetwood's chest, and for the first time he regretted having had it made in such a heavy and ostentatious style. He loosened the buttons and took a deep breath, dabbing at the beginnings of a heat rash on his chest with the handkerchief.

A cannon thundered from the fort on the hill,

signalling noon, and the flock of pigeons dozing overhead on the ornate facade of the hotel exploded in a panicky flapping of wings. Fleetwood also started, then automatically checked his pocket watch. Thinking on the run was a prerequisite of his profession. He took another deep breath then gave his full attention to solving his latest predicament.

What he needed, he finally decided, was a red herring; someone to lead the police astray and keep them amused while he was going in the opposite direction. And if the police were going to be looking for a parcel, it seemed only right that he should provide one. It would have to be obvious, of course, so their limited intelligence would not be unduly over-taxed - and he would need a sucker to carry the parcel.

Fleetwood tossed the cigar over the rail with sudden purpose. That should not be too difficult. An entire boatload of suckers had arrived only that morning from England.

Yorky's Bar was Cape Town's unofficial staging post for all new arrivals. It was not the sort of place Fleetwood usually frequented, being too common and rowdy for his tastes, but it attracted an interesting cross-section of the population and provided a valuable pool of information not obtainable elsewhere. Advertising posters of the local ballet and theatre groups vied for space on the walls with colourful descriptions of some of Cape Town's less inhibited ladies, alongside blander notices for bullock sales, transport company rates, second hand goods, and help wanted.

Fleetwood saw his mark almost immediately; a scrawny, pale-looking individual clutching a battered travel bag in one hand and a grubby white cap in the other. Seemingly oblivious to the clamour going on around him, the young man was moving slowly from one transport poster to another; carefully scrutinising those dealing with coach fares to the diggings. When he reached the last poster, he went back to the beginning and read them again, his face bearing a worried frown. He looked perfect.

Fleetwood waited until the man reached the end for the second time before approaching.

'Deuced expensive, wouldn't you say?' he greeted pleasantly.

The young man turned towards him. His face was blotchy and his nose flaky and pink from freshly discarded skin. 'I heard it was only four pounds to the Vaal River,' he answered disconsolately.

'Ah!' Fleetwood exclaimed brightly, almost happily. It was even better than expected. 'Positively scandalous the way they keep increasing the price simply because they have so many passengers. Should be the other way round, if you ask me.' He smiled sympathetically 'Recently arrived?'

'This morning.'

'Well then. Allow me to buy you a refreshment and welcome you to the fairest Cape and all that.' He offered his hand. 'My name is Smythe.'

'Charles Atherstone... most kind of you, sir, but I shan't be able to return the favour, you see I....'

Fleetwood interrupted by placing a fatherly hand on the young man's shoulder. 'Not necessary, my boy.' He steered him through the crowd to the bar, giving the help wanted section of the wall a wide berth.

'So, Charles, my lad,' he boomed heartily. 'Off to seek your fortune, hey? Lucky fellow. I would be doing the same thing if I was your age.' Fleetwood heaved a great sigh. 'By jove! I do envy you. They say you can walk along the river and simply pick the diamonds up off the sand.'

While the newcomer sipped dolefully at his drink, Fleetwood questioned him skilfully, soon confirming what he already suspected. Charles Atherstone had foolish dreams and little money. Four pounds seven shillings and sixpence, to be exact, which, in Fleetwood's book, was the equivelent of penniless.

'Hmm... not a great deal to start with, really, ' he mused.

'I suppose I could walk,' Charles Atherstone suggested tentatively. 'I should have enough to buy food on the way, and I once walked from Brighton to Hastings. If I follow the signs, and if I can...'

'Good Lord!' Fleetwood was genuinely astonished. He laughed - a series of short nasal implosions that attracted several curious glances. 'Of course there are no signs! This is not England you know.' He gave a few more snorts. 'It's over seven hundred miles to the Vaal, and most of it through desert. If you didn't get lost you would die of thirst or get eaten by wolves.'

'Wolves?'

'Nasty spotted beasts with jaws that can take your leg off with a single bite. No, my boy, walking is quite out of the question.' Fleetwood snorted again with laughter, unable to restrain himself. 'Especially with only one leg.' affirmative action had completely disolved his earlier dispondency.

'I will have to get work then,' Charles Atherstone stated positively, missing the joke, and the drink apparently beginning to strengthen his resolve. 'You wouldn't perhaps know where I could find...'

'Afraid not, old chap.' Fleetwood waved his cigar at the surrounding crowd. 'Half the foo...er... folk here are in the same boat, so to speak.' He paused to wipe the foam carefully from his moustache and give the ends a tweak before delivering the final blow.

'And there are so many of them. By the time you had saved the money all the diamonds will have been picked up.'

Charles gulped at his drink. He looked despondently around the room as if hoping a solution would somehow materialise from the haze of tobacco smoke.

With his sucker well and truly hooked, Fleetwood decided there was no point in delaying things further. The heat in the crowded bar was playing havoc with the rash and he urgently needed to remove the waistcoat.

Fleetwood thumped suddenly on the counter with his hand, feigning surprise. 'I say! What a fool I am.' He gripped the startled youth by the elbow. 'My boy, I have just had the most stupendous idea.' He pointed to the package he had been carrying under his arm, and which now reposed prominently on the bar in front of him. 'I had intended giving this to Yorky to put on the mail coach to Hope Town.' Fleetwood lowered his voice and leaned closer to whisper conspiratorially. 'Important personal papers, you understand, belonging to a dear friend of mine whose uncle has recently passed away. It may be his inheritance, you see, and it has occurred to me that if I were to give the package to an honest young fellow such as yourself to deliver personally... well, it would be in much safer hands, and could save me a great deal of trouble.'

He paused to let the information sink in, watching the boy's owlish expression furtively, and wondering if perhaps he hadn't been overly generous with the drinks.

'Quite honestly, Charles, you can't trust the mail these days. I would really be most awfully obliged if you would consider taking it for me.'

'But how can it... I mean, how will I?' Charles Atherston's frown deepened and he lapsed into confused silence.

'Naturally,' Fleetwood said, waving an expansive hand, 'I will pay your fare... although not by mail coach,' he added hastily. 'Bullock wagons are much more comfortable. Yes, indeed. A bit slower but well worth it in the long run. Gives you time to adjust to the climate.'

Fleetwood did not feel it necessary to mention

that it took more than six times as long and cost only a third of the usual price. The fellow had enough to think about already. He carefully clipped a cigar and lit it, squinting through the smoke as he watched Charles Atherstone's expression change from one of owlish bewilderment to that of open-eyed wonder. Fleetwood quickly subdued the twinge of guilt. After all, there was nothing illegal in the package, only a bundle of worthless newspaper and, when questioned, the lad had only to tell the truth - that he had been given the package by a Mister Smythe to deliver to a Mister Sylvester in Hope Town. By then he should be well on his way to England. A few pounds for the fare was a small price to pay for peace of mind.

'Well, what do you say, old chap?'

Charles Atherstone opened his mouth, then closed it to grin foolishly, and Fleetwood held up a deprecating palm, 'No need to thank me, dear boy. It's the least I can do for a fellow countryman.'

The formalities were straightforward. As agent for most of the transport companies in the area, Yorky wrote the details in the ledger himself and issued a receipt. In return, Charles Atherstone was given a rail ticket to Wellington, where he was to meet the wagon owner, a Meneer Steyn.

Fleetwood drew attention to the package on

several occasions, stressing its importance to be certain Yorky would remember it. He could hardly have not. It was wrapped in bright, almost luminous, red sailcloth.

Marthinus Steyn was checking the harness chains of his oxen when his passenger arrived. Unlike many owners, Marthinus preferred to drive his own team, and amongst the transport drivers of the Cape his name was legendary. No score marks showed on the sleek hides of his cattle, and their eyes never rolled in fear at the crack of his whip; as had the eyes of a few wagon boys who had been foolish enough to mistreat his prize team.

Toughened by years of coping with the myriad disasters common to wagon transporting in the Karoo, not much could ruffle his calm, but the sight of his passenger came close. He removed his greasy bush hat to run his fingers through his hair as the Englishman introduced himself and asked if he was at the right place.

'Ja... I am Marthinus Steyn,' he replied cautiously. Ignoring the proffered ticket he studied his passenger while scratching thoughtfully at his beard.

He grunted, giving an almost imperceptible shake of his head, as if not quite believing what he was seeing. He sighed and hung his hat on the long horn of the ox standing alongside before taking the ticket and reading it in a grudging manner. He gave it back and shook the outstretched hand with a grip that crackled the Englishman's fingers.

'You understand I don't usually take passengers.' His voice was deep and thick with accent. 'It is a long way and mostly you will have to walk. Maybe it is not such a good idea, ja?' From his screwed up, questioning expression he made it obvious that he thought it was a terrible idea. 'It would be a good thing for me to give your money back, I think.'

'Oh, I'm not worried about walking,' the Englishman responded. 'I'm used to it. I once walked from Brighton to Hastings. I'm sure I won't be a trouble to you.'

Marthinus frowned, then shrugged philosophically. The money would certainly be useful. 'As you wish, meneer. Give your bag to the Zulu.' He turned away with a further shake of his head to continue his interrupted checking of the oxen.

A fierce-looking African with naked torso glistening, tossed the bag on top of the loaded wagon beside a reed cage full of nervously alert chickens, and Charles sat in the shade of a tree to watch and wait. The wagon owner's attitude did not concern him. He was looking forward to doing a bit of walking after the months at sea, and the Boer looked well over fifty - twice his own age, and with a pot belly to boot. It could not be that bad.

The thirty-foot-long whip rose in a wide looping figure of eight against the clear blue of the sky. For a moment it seemed to hang motionless, then it swooped down with the speed of a striking snake to snap the *voorslag* with a crack like a rifle shot.

The piercing whistles of the Zulu followed immediately, and the span of eighteen oxen leaned heavily into their yokes. The wagon creaked and groaned against the four-ton load, then heaved forward in a sudden rush and clatter.

The juvenile Herero, Timisani, led them onto the track, and the two experienced lead oxen set the pace, knowing the feel and weight of the load and what their team mates were capable of.

Charles walked behind, staying far enough to the side to avoid the worst of the dust and freshly splattered dung that steamed in the cattle's wake. The weather was warm and sunny, the air filled with strange vibrant smells and the chirping of exotic birds, and he walked with a spring in his step, feeling alive again after the months of inactivity and sea-sickness. He knew he had lost weight and was not as fit as he had been before the voyage, but the wonder of being in Africa and on his way with money still in his pocket sent his spirits soaring. He could barely restrain himself from bursting into song with the birds.

Occasionally he was joined by the Zulu, whose brief visits always seemed to coincide with the appearance on the road ahead of young African women. The Zulu shouted loud greetings to them as they passed with their precarious loads balanced gracefully on their heads; straight backed and bare footed, hips and buttocks swinging under colourful drapes of cloth.

Although the Zulu never spoke to Charles directly, he would look at him and roll his eyes, white teeth flashing, whenever a particularly buxom girl walked by. Charles enjoyed the visits and tried to encourage the big African by laughing at his antics, but the Zulu never stayed long, resuming his place alongside the team of oxen to await the arrival of the next distraction.

Their way led past thatched white houses and clusters of huts cluttered about with chickens, children and dogs. The dogs barked and the children waved excitedly as the wagon passed, and when Charles gave them a bow and waved back, they danced about and shrieked with glee. It gave him the feeling of being back with the carnival he had grown up in, trouping through the crowded streets of Brighton in the summer with the Shetland ponies gaily decked in ribbons and balloons. All that was missing was the clamour of the brass band and the clashing of cymbals.

The feeling brought with it a pang of nostalgia for the friends left behind, but Charles quickly shrugged it off. Everything had changed, and the carnival was finished. Gone with the changing times; starved out then swallowed by the larger circuses', all his friends dispersed. For the first time in his life he was truly on his own, but it felt good to be doing something new and exciting, and he had never had that many friends there anyway.

The attitude of the Boer remained distant. He was neither rude nor friendly, and for the most part simply ignored Charles. All his attempts to engage the Boer in friendly conversation failed.

'Do you mind if I have a try at cracking the whip?' Charles asked during one of the rest stops.

The Boer gave him a startled look and answered brusquely. 'It is not a good idea. It will take your eye out. Better you save your strength for the climb.'

The white houses with their orange-flowered hedges disappeared as they began to climb through the foothills and into the passes of the mountains. The stony track narrowed and the sides fell away steeply into deep gullies, and Charles stayed closer to the wagon, keeping a wary eye open for the wild animals he had heard so much about.

Towering ragged peaks loomed over the track, in some places seeming to overhang and threaten their progress. More frequently the crack of the whip and the whistles that invariably followed it echoed amongst the barren cliffs, and the heavy snorts of the oxen sounded almost in unison, like the puffing of a steam engine.

The Boer walked beside his oxen, talking to them, calling them individually by name, and giving encouragement where needed with gentle prods from the butt of his whip-stick, and they responded faithfully, neither shirking nor lunging as their hooves slipped and rattled on the stony ground.

At times they came perilously close to the edge as the long span swung out wide to negotiate the tight bends, the wheels coming within inches of the inside wall of the cliff on the turns. The wagon stopped more frequently to give the oxen a rest, and Charles was happy to stop with them. In the flat country the ten-minute stops every hour had seemed unnecessary, but the trapped heat of the pass and the steep climb was beginning to exact a toll. He developed a grudging and uneasy respect for the Boer who, after leaning heavily on his whip for only a few moments to catch his breath at the stops, would methodically check all the oxen for chafing and loose harness, running his hands smoothly over each beast in turn, as if to gauge the strength and courage that flowed through their giant frames.

They made the final stop for the day on a small bare plateau beside the road. The oxen were outspanned and given water from buckets filled from the wooden barrels in the wagon, then a sack of white corn was emptied onto the ground and the beasts gathered around to munch on the cobs.

After giving Charles a short and unnecessary warning not to go wandering off by himself, the Boer disappeared up the road with a gun.

Charles was quite content to rest and observe the chickens. Released from their coop, they scrambled noisily from the wagon like children let out of class, darting about after insects and led importantly by a red rooster devoid of neck feathers.

Charles took a piece of charcoal from the fire and made a sketch of the rooster on the smooth side of the wagon, trying to capture the comical attitude of self importance. He had done no animal sketching since the last batch of posters for the carnival, and was pleased to note he had not lost the touch.

The Boer returned at dusk with a large hare, which the two Africans skinned and chopped up with enthusiasm, throwing large chunks into the black three-legged pot that stood in the fire. When Meneer Steyn walked past and saw the sketch, he stopped and gaped in astonishment.

'It's only charcoal.' Charles offered defensively, expecting to be rebuked for drawing on the wagon. 'I can easily wash it off.'

The Boer did not reply. After giving the sketch another long look, he simply shook his head and walked away.

The Zulu and young Herero seemed more impressed, clicking their tongues in appreciation. The Herero did a strutting imitation of the rooster that was so typical Charles laughed until his eyes watered.

With a full day of exercise behind him, he ate the hare stew ravenously, wiping the bowl clean with a thick wedge of solid bread, but he was unable to drink the coffee. Black and bitter, it clawed at his throat, so he tipped it out when no one was looking.

'Better to get some sleep,' the Boer told him as soon as it became dark, 'tomorrow we start early.'

The Zulu brought Charles his bag and indicated

he could sleep under the wagon, but was to stay away from the wheels. He explained with sign language, first pointing to the wheel, then grinning as he drew a finger across his throat and made choking sounds.

For a long time Charles was unable to sleep. The events of the day, the strangeness of the blacks and the attitude of Meneer Steyn all crowding his mind. He was sure the Boer would be happier without him. The men on the boat had told him that all Boers hated Englishmen, calling them *rooineks* because their necks burned red in the sun - just as his own was beginning to do. It seemed they were right.

Charles came to the conclusion he would have to learn the Boer language. He had always been good at languages, and he would then learn more about their ways and customs and fit in. He would start right away and try not to act like a *rooinek*. That was his first word.

The morning began badly. It was still dark when Charles's foot was shaken vigorously. Tired and half asleep he failed to respond It was shaken again more urgently, a few moments later.

'Trek, Baasie, trek!'

Charles yelped and jerked his foot away. Visions of wolves trying to bite it off brought him fully awake. He sat up quickly and banged his head on the bedplate of the wagon. Pain sliced through his skull as he clasped his head in both hands, fighting the dizziness.

'Trek Baasie!'

Charles became aware of the sound of hooves and rattling chains. Scrambling from under the wagon in panic, he collided with the oxen and was forced to scramble back to avoid being trampled. Clutching his head with one hand, he dragged his bag and blanket out the other side and stumbled away.

They stopped for breakfast at sunrise - cold left-over stew thickly congealed in grease. Charles drank water instead, then lay on the ground until it was time to go.

For the next two days they twisted through one rocky pass after another, and each was more nightmarish than the one before. Like the fantasy castles of a fairy tale, the stark orange crags reached higher and pushed in closer. Thick red dust rose from the hooves of the oxen to fill Charles's nose and eyes until he could barely see or breathe. He felt as though he were entering the gates of hell.

The sun beat down remorselessly, the heat reflecting back from the naked cliffs in stifling waves, sucking at the moisture in his body until it became as dry as the small dusty bushes that bordered the track.

A canvas sail was hung over the rear canopy frame of the wagon to give the chickens shade, and Charles wished with his whole being he could join them. His head throbbed in time to every laboured footstep. The soles of his inadequate shoes had worn thin, and every pebble sent shock waves pulsing through his body.

The top of his head baked under the thick felt of the cap, and the back of his exposed neck turned from red to scarlet. He took a spare shirt from his bag and hung it over his head, but although it gave some relief, the damage was already done, and he was reminded at every touch. The sweat trickling down on the inside of his chafed thighs seemed like streams of molten lava.

Incredibly, none of the others showed any sign of hardship or fatigue. The Africans laughed and sang in monotonous falsetto voices, while the Boer, despite the size of his belly, walked effortlessly beside his oxen while smoking his pipe. Charles began to feel they were deliberately ignoring him and making fun of his plight, trying to show him up for what he was; a redneck Englishman who should have stayed in England where he belonged. His foolish boast about having walked from Brighton to Hastings ran repeatedly through his mind like a taunting jibe.

'You can ride on the wagon,' the Boer offered

after one of the stops. 'We don't usually allow it on the hills, but you look tired. Maybe it would be a good idea, ja?'

'No, I'm all right,' Charles heard himself say. He would have given the rest of his money to be able to climb on the wagon. 'It's just that I'm not used to the heat. How far is it to the top?'

'Not so far, only another two days.'

Charles refused the offer of dried meat to chew on, which he was told would be good for energy, and forced himself to keep up. He also refused to limp, though his feet ached and the blisters grew then burst with a sharp sting. At the stops he deliberately took his time about sitting down, although he longed to fling himself on the ground and remain there forever.

The morning starts were the worst; an agonising test of will that took all the strength he had to drag his stiff, pain racked body from the blanket.

He no longer took any interest in the countryside, and heard nothing but the constant rumble of the wagon. He fixed his eyes a few paces ahead, no thought entering his throbbing skull but the achievement of the next step.

When they outspanned at the end of the fourth day, Charles collapsed on his blanket and knew he was beaten. He would tell the Boer he could walk no farther and would have to ride in the wagon or stay behind. He no longer cared what they thought of him. He would return to Cape Town and look for a job.

Charles awoke next day to the warmth of the sun on his face and an urgent churning in his stomach. He lay for a while, listening for the rattling of harness, but all was still, only the subdued voices of the Africans talking nearby.

He crawled stiffly from under the wagon and stood blinking in the sunlight, slowly becoming aware that something was different. Then he realised it was the colour green. Green grass, green bushes, and tall, flat-topped green trees. A narrow stream wound its way through all the green. It seemed like a miracle had occurred. He was also surprised to note that it was late in the day.

The Boer was cleaning his rifle in the shade of one of the trees and looked up as Charles approached. 'Are you better, meneer? I think you had too much of the sun, ja?'

Charles tried to detect a note of disapproval, but couldn't be sure. 'Is that why we have stopped… because of me?'

'We are at the top now. For two days we must rest the cattle before we go down.' He returned his attention to the rifle. 'There is plenty of water if you wish a bath.'

Water! Charles looked down at himself. His skin was coated in thick red dust. A bath sounded like heaven. But first there was a more urgent need.

'Do you have any paper?'

'Paper?' The Boer looked up in surprise. 'What is it you want with paper... you wish to make a picture?'

Charles shook his head, his expression blank as he tried to think how to express his need.

The Boer held the rifle up to the sky and squinted through the barrel. He gave a grunt of satisfaction. 'I am sorry, meneer, but we have no paper.'

After some hesitation Charles patted his stomach, screwed his face up into an expression of what he hoped looked like urgent need, and pointed to a thick clump of trees.

The Boer's puzzled expression changed and he nodded. 'Oh, ja... I see...' He turned towards the two Africans squatting over a pile of harness and spoke to them briefly in their language, and Charles started to gather his dignity, expecting laughter.

There was none. The Zulu's face showed no expression as, still squatting, and barely pausing in his conversation with the Herero, he reached to the side and pulled out a clump of grass. Knocking the sand off against his knee, he gave a brief but graphic description of how it was to be used. He tossed the clump aside with casual indifference, and Meneer Steyn added his endorsement by shrugging, giving all his attention to the rifle.

With the feeling they were laughing at him behind his back, Charles walked into the trees trying not to show his discomfort. His tired muscles still ached and pulled, and the rash on his thighs continued to smart and burn with the intensity of smouldering lava, but thankfully, the throbbing in his head had eased.

He followed the shady stream as it twisted through the rocks into the mouth of a narrow gorge, looking for a pool. He had not forgotten the Boer's warning about straying too far from the camp, but it looked safe enough, and he wanted something larger than a bucket to wash in. Preferably something in which he could submerge his whole abused body.

He found one where the cleft of a gorge opened out to a small, almost sheer-sided valley; a pool of clear enticing water bordered with ferns and trees. Four or five paces wide and less than knee deep, it was more than adequate for his needs.

Quivering with anticipation, Charles removed his clothes and waded in, but had gone only a few steps when his stomach growled, warning him of his more urgent need. For a moment he wavered on the brink of surrender. The water felt even better than it looked. Not even champagne could have felt so tingling good. But it would have to wait.

He searched the undergrowth for likely looking material. No grass grew in the shade of the trees, and the ferns were too coarse for his liking, but he found an abundance of soft downy leaves growing on a vine that looked just right in size and texture. After peering around carefully to be certain he would not be disturbed by unwelcome intruders, he gathered a handful and settled down comfortably on a fallen branch.

It took some moments after the satisfactory completion of his ablutions for the minute hairy spines of the leaf to transmit their poisonous message to his unsuspecting brain. At first, it was merely a warm tingle, almost indistinguishable from the burning of his inflamed inner thighs, but the tingle blossomed rapidly into a flicker of flame, then, with no further warning, into a full blown furnace blast that made him gasp.

The burning came in waves, almost subsiding entirely before being replaced by another wave even more ferocious than the one before. They built rapidly into a wall of flame that sent Charles stumbling, straddle-legged, towards the water.

He lowered himself gently, then lay on his back with his forearms supporting his weight, allowing his body to float free and well clear of the shale, and slowly the salving effect of the water began to ease the burning that seemed to cover his body from the lump on his head to the soles of his blistered feet.

For a long while he wallowed happily, groaning with the ecstasy of relief. He put his head under and gently washed the dried blood and dust from his scalp and hair while he snorted and blew bubbles.

Charles washed cautiously all over, carefully inspecting the damaged areas. The redness had gone from between his legs, replaced with a becoming shade of pink, and although his sunburn looked similarly raw, he much preferred it to the fish-belly colour of before. Being blessed with dark hair, he knew a healthy-looking tan would follow.

He lay in the water staring up at the blue sky through the green leaves of the trees, wondering at the circling vultures, reduced to mere specks by their height. Everything seemed so strange and wild compared to the softness of England.

His thoughts turned again to diamonds. He had never had much chance of making a secure life for himself working for the carnival, and had it not been for the poster drawing, he would not even have been able to save enough to buy the ticket. Sketching was the only thing he had ever been any good at. If he could find a few diamonds, enough perhaps to buy a studio in London, he was sure he could make a good living as an artist.

The wild fig tree with its lacework of roots and thick branches spreading wide across the face of the cliff was the ideal sleeping place for the baboons. Water was always available, and the pool was a favourite place for the young to frolic in the afternoons before the sun dipped behind the cliffs and the shadows deepened in the gorge.

    The troop approached warily, the big males leading through the narrow clefts and ridges that fractured the face of the cliff. Intruders seldom encroached on the area. The troop was large and more than capable of defending itself, even from leopards, but driven by hunger or foolishness, the large cats were still an ever present threat to the unwary straggler.

    The oldest male, grizzled and battle scarred, sensed immediately that something was wrong. He paced the ledge beside the fig tree with indecision, stopping often to crouch with his head close to the ground so he could peer under the canopy of leaves sheltering the pool below.

Noticing his agitation, the troop became silent and closed in around him and, encouraged by their support, the old male descended the cliff to the base of the tree, with the troop crowding impatiently behind.

He barked a warning challenge, loud and booming, and the troop responded on all sides, their cries echoing throughout the narrow confines of the gorge.

Charles sat up in the water with an urgent thrashing of arms and legs. He had not seen or heard anything until then, yet suddenly there they were - so close he could clearly see the wizened pink faces of the babies clinging to their mother's bellies.

He scrambled to his feet and made a dive for his clothes, slipping and stumbling over the algae covered rocks, and had almost reached them when his foot slipped and he fell with a heavy splash.

'Wahaw!' The challenge, deep throated and resonating, caused the hair on the back of Charles's neck to stand on end and his stomach to clench with fear. The sound hung threateningly in the air, like the rumble of distant thunder and, as the first echo was thrown back from the cliffs, the challenge was repeated by the barking of a dozen other baboons.

Shivering with fright, Charles rolled in the water and watched with growing alarm as the baboons closed in. They seemed to materialise from the cliffs and trees in ever increasing numbers, and the noise they made clamoured inside his head and set his mind to spinning.

Charles abandoned all thoughts of reaching his clothes. He looked frantically for the way out, but movement in the trees behind told him they were there too. He was surrounded.

In a frenzy of panic, Charles pushed his way backwards through the shallow water to the far edge of the pool and hard into the fern-covered bank. He looked around for something with which to defend himself, but found only the rotting debris of the pool bottom and slimy boulders.

He watched fearfully from behind a veil of fronds, trying to keep his body hidden under the water. His only hope was that they would ignore him and go away, although there seemed little chance of that happening.

The old male, tail arched high, swaggered arrogantly on the far side of the pool, stopping every few paces to lower his head and bark, throwing his head forward at the same time, as if to hurl the challenge with greater force.

The clothes had attracted the attention of the younger members of the troop. They made short, rushing charges at them, only to stop at the limit of their courage and walk away on stiff legs, looking back with threatening grimaces. The rushes were getting closer each time, as if it were some sort of daring game.

With his curiosity aroused by their antics, the male went to investigate for himself. He cautiously flipped the clothes over, as if expecting to find something lurking beneath, then sat down to probe inside a shoe. He suddenly ripped it apart with a powerful wrench and sniffed inside, tasting with a cautious flick of his tongue before dropping it to pick up the other shoe, his eyes constantly busy, shifting rapidly back and forth to where Charles lay behind his cover of fern. The male lost interest when the shoes yielded nothing to eat. He moved away, and there was an immediate rush as the younger members swooped in to snatch the clothes.

It was too much for Charles. Seeing his only pair of shoes destroyed was bad enough, but now his clothes were being stolen as well.

'Shoo!' he yelled. 'Leave them alone! Get away!' He threw a handful of rotten leaves and mud, which splattered harmlessly over the water.

His voice sounded weak and ineffectual in his ears compared to the shouting of the baboons, but his actions provoked an immediate and terrifying response.

The big grey male bounded around the pool to

a slide of rock and shale below the fig tree and, with underhand scraping motions, showered the pool with loose gravel and dirt. He gave a terrifying roar that brought several other males to his side. Shoulder to shoulder, and growing in number by the second, the baboons loosed a tirade of abuse at the intruder.

Behind the line of males pandemonium broke out. The young baboons, alarmed by the loud challenging roars, ran into the trees and bushes screaming in panic, filling the lower branches until they sagged almost to the ground. The shaking of the trees, the snapping of sticks and branches, the roars, bellows and screams, filled Charles with an overwhelming dread.

The baboons at the water's edge grew until they almost circled the pool. Foot by foot they came closer, each gaining courage from the advance of the others and, as they advanced, they roared their defiance and showered the pool with debris.

Whimpering and gulping with fear, Charles slipped under the water in a last desperate attempt to hide himself. But he knew even as he was doing so that the defence was futile. It could only be a matter of moments before the baboons attacked and ripped him into pieces.

Quabe Mapepela gave the heavy boulder atached to

the saturated strips of raw hide a gentle spin and they twisted together, squeezing out the water until they were almost dry. He let them unwind freely to hang and stretch. In the morning the strips would have shrunk tightly together and be strong enough to replace the broken reim on *Stompie's* yoke.

Quabe turned his attention to the small antelope hanging alongside, expertly slicing it with the sharp blade of his axe, then scooping the entrails into the bucket with his hand, turning his head to the side as the foul gases of the stomach cavity were released. Roasted over the fire, the entrails would make a tasty delicacy. He cut the rest of the meat into strips and laid them in another bucket with a handful of coarse salt between each layer. Tomorrow, when the salt had drawn out most of the juices, he would hang them in the thorn tree to dry.

Quabe sang as he worked. The Zulu songs of wars and triumphs his ancestors had sung, and he sang them proudly and with gusto, for he was a descendant of Malendela's Rainbow Indunas, and was named after the brother of Zulu himself.

He also sang nostalgic songs, for he was far from his homeland and no longer a proud warrior with ostrich feather plumes and ox-hide shield. Now he was only a wagon boy who drove the oxen.

With his work completed, Quabe spat on the flat stone beside him and sharpened the blade of his double-headed axe, restoring the edge dulled by the skinning.

'I hear the great lion of Nguni singing,' called Timisani. 'But he has more the sound of the mating hyena than of the lion.'

'Hau! Is it the chee-chee-chee of the desert rabbit that I hear?' Quabe retorted. 'The one that has the colour and smell of dung? I hear him and I smell him, but he is too small to see.'

'There are some who cannot see even the spoor of the elephant though he walks in the mud after the rain.' Timisani replied, laughing and shuffling his feet in a victory dance, pleased with his joke.

'If the rabbit does not hurry and clean this skin, I will remove what it is he calls his manhood and eat them.' Quabe raised the axe in a threatening gesture, and Timisani hastened to obey. He knew just how far he could joke with the Zulu without overstepping the bounds of respect. There was many a crushed skull to attest to Quabe's lack of humour when it came to insulting jokes from inferiors.

Marthinus Steyn smiled as he listened to the banter. As long as they were laughing and joking he knew the work would get done. A sulking black was as much use as a lame ox.

Marthinus had chosen his two Africans with care. Zulus made the best wagon boys, for they took immense pride in their work and had the strength and courage to handle big teams in dangerous conditions. The young Herero had Bushman blood in his veins and the same tracking ability as that mysterious tribe - a vital skill when the cattle took to wandering.

'When you have finished,' Marthinus called, 'you had better see where the Englishman is.' It was not really dangerous country, maybe the odd leopard, but he did not want the *rooinek* to get lost and have to go looking for him.

When he was sure that he couldn't be seen, Quabe sliced off a chunk of the raw liver and popped it into his mouth. It was known to have special properties that enhanced manhood. He hoped the next woman appreciated the sacrifice, for he did not relish the taste of it all that much.

'I think it must be a leopard.' Marthinus said suddenly.

Quabe gulped, almost swallowing the raw liver whole. He looked anxiously toward the bush.

'The baboons, you fool, the baboons. They are making too much noise...listen!'

The barking of baboons was commonplace in

the high crags of the berg in the late afternoons, but this was more than the normal calling of the males. When the entire troop was involved, as it appeared to be in this case, Marthinus knew it spelled trouble.

'Ja, *Nkosi*. It seems they have big trouble with meneer leopard, as you say.'

'Where is the Englishman?' Marthinus asked.

'He went into the bushes to make the kak.' Timisani replied.

'Ja, I know that, but it was a long time ago. Which way did he go… did you see?'

Timisani was looking in the direction of the noise with a worried expression. No further explanation was necessary.

'*Magtag*!' Marthinus jumped to his feet. 'Quickly, bring the shotgun.'

They forced their way through the overgrown stream in single file, Marthinus leading, but it was not long before he came to a halt. 'Which way dammit?'

Timisani pointed the way with the barrel of the shotgun, waving it about dangerously, and Marthinus snatched it from his hands and pushed him ahead.

'Quickly, follow the signs'.

As they approached the opening of the gorge the noise of the baboons suddenly intensified and Timisani halted.

'What is it?' Marthinus demanded.

'Eh, eh, eh.' Timisani shook his head in dismay and pointed.

Marthinus climbed up beside him. A short distance ahead almost every tree was shaking as if caught in a whirlwind. He had never seen such a large troop of baboons. The surrounding cliffs were black with them, and the Englishman's spoor was heading straight in their direction. Marthinus suddenly felt as if the blood in his veins was turning solid.

'I think the English Baas is now dead,' Timisani said with finality. 'They make the sound of the kill. Very big danger here... better we go.'

'Hau!' Quabe scoffed. 'The rabbit wants to run.' He pushed contemptuously past. With big purposeful strides he ran forward, waving his axe and blowing a series of his short, piercing whistles. The same whistles he used to stir the cattle.

Marthinus fired two shots in the air to distract the baboons, then reloaded quickly, cursing as he realised the only cartridges he had in his pocket were birdshot.

At the sound of the shots, the baboons fell from the shaking trees like over-ripe fruit. The screaming and barking stopped suddenly and there was a frantic scramble for the cliffs.

'Bekizwe!' Quabe yelled the Zulu war cry at them. 'Run from the Zulu!' He whistled some more, then charged aggressively towards the startled baboons, leaping over boulders and tearing through bushes without slowing, screaming his Zulu war cries and brandishing his axe. 'Bekizwe! Bekizwe! He threw rocks and sticks and challenged them to return and fight like men.

'Stop! Come back here!' Marthinus bellowed, but the fighting fever had taken over and the Zulu ignored him.

'Stupid bugger!' Marthinus swore as he followed hastily after him.

They charged into the pool together, stumbling over the rocks, shouting and whistling as loud as they could to reinforce their aggression, hoping to make up for in sound what they lacked in numbers.

The main body of baboons had scattered, but a group of agitated males had rallied at the top of the rockslide to voice their protests and make short, rushing charges. Quabe shook his axe and threw rocks at them, and they responded by showering down loose gravel and sand with their awkward underhand motions.

'Leave them be!' Marthinus yelled. 'Find the bloody *rooinek*.'

A spluttering and choking sound from behind

made him turn quickly to see a head disappearing under the water. The Englishman's eyes were shut tight and his hair was plastered with rotten leaves and mud.

Marthinus splashed through the pool to take a handful of the hair and pull him up. 'Jesus man! We thought you was dead! What the hell do you....'

He was interrupted by a violent thrashing in the water. Two naked legs appeared from the froth and lashed out, catching Marthinus in the stomach. He fell over backwards with a cry of surprise, losing his grip on the shotgun, which disappeared under the water.

Distracted from his on-going war with the baboons, Quabe surged past Marthinus and felt around under the water with one hand while the other remained firmly clasped around the shaft of his axe. He gripped the Englishman by the upper arm and, with a heave of his powerful shoulders, lifted him naked and struggling clear of the water. The eyes shot open to stare at the face of the Zulu only a few inches away. They flicked to the raised axe and, for the space of a heartbeat, registered stark terror before glazing over and rolling back as the Englishman fainted.

'Baas! Baas!' Timisani screamed, his voice breaking into adolescent squeaks. 'Bobo! Bobo!'

Struggling to his feet Marthinus saw the big grey baboon rushing down the rockslide towards them. It came in great sideways bounds with shoulders hunched and head lowered, as if intending to launch himself feet first. His tail stood out stiffly to the side, his fangs bared in a ferocious grimace.

Marthinus scrabbled urgently under the water for the shotgun.

'Hai! Hai!' With a blood-chilling cry, Quabe dropped the Englishman back in the water and shoved Marthinus roughly aside. 'Come! Come to the Zulu!' He splashed directly towards the charging baboon.

In a shower of loose shale the baboon suddenly changed direction, leaping from boulder to boulder around the edge of the pool, attempting to attack from behind, and Quabe turned to follow it. The baboon switched direction again then, using the side of a boulder for leverage, he launched himself bodily at the Zulu.

Quabe stepped to the side and swung the axe underhand with casual, almost contemptuous ease, and the baboon seemed to stop for an instant in mid air as the spiked end of the axe thudded into his chest. The momentum of his charge threw them both back in the water.

Screaming with pain and rage, the baboon clutched at the handle, trying to pull away from it as if not aware he was attached to it by the deadly spike.

Quabe did it for him, wrenching it free with a jerk that flipped the baboon over in the water. It sat stunned and unmoving, white-lidded eyes rolling and yellow-fanged mouth gaping.

On his knees in the water, Quabe reversed the axe. With an overhead swing that left an arc of sparkling water high in the air, he sank the blade up to the handle in the baboon's skull. It fell back in the water with its fangs still bared, its eyes tightly closed and screwed, as if they had been slammed shut.

'Bayede! Bayede Zulu!' Quabe used a foot on the dead animal's bloodied chest to lever the blade from the skull.

The screams of the baboon had brought several other males close to the water's edge. With menacing roars and feinting charges, they continued to shower the pool, while Quabe shook his bloodied axe at them and yelled abuse in return.

Hands shaking with urgency, Marthinus emptied the water and wet shells from the barrels of the shotgun. He knew about baboons. He knew they would not easily abandon a member of the troop, and he knew they would risk their lives if they thought the troop was in danger. He had seen them attack leopards, and seen them being killed by leopards. He had also seen what was left of a leopard once the troop had finished with him. Scraps of fur and not much else.

Marthinus had no intention of ending up like that. The shotgun was useless, and not even Quabe and his axe could withstand a concerted attack for more than a few seconds. The most he could hope for was time to retreat.

He replaced the cartridges with dry ones from his breast pocket and fired a shot into the air, hoping to keep them confused while they were still without a leader, and the pack fell back a short distance. Before they could rally, Marthinus fired the second barrel into their midst to encourage their retreat.

They screamed as the birdshot peppered their hides, beating and pulling at their fur as if being attacked by bees.

'Quick! get the Englishman... I have no more ammunition'.

They pulled the rooinek from the water and Quabe lifted him effortlessly onto his shoulder. The shot had given them the respite they needed, but Marthinus prayed there were no reckless and aspiring leaders in the troop to take the initiative. Quabe shouted abuse and waved his axe defiantly as they stumbled from the pool.

The baboons clamoured and followed until they were well out of the gorge, then barked and roared their dissent well into the night.

Marthinus Steyn's camp was also noisy that night. He was angry, and gave Charles a tongue lashing that, had it been a whip, would have left his flesh raw and bleeding. Even the two Africans were quiet, their high spirits after the day's exciting events quenched by the ferocity of the Boer's attack.

Fortunately, most of what he said was in the Afrikaans language, so Charles never understood, but the actions spoke clearly for themselves.

Marthinus could not stand in one place. He stalked around the camp with heavy-footed agitation, so everyone had to crane and turn to follow his movements. At one point he lifted the whip from the wagon and shook it in Charles's face.

The action initiated some quick shuffling as the two Africans moved out of range, but Charles stood his ground. His dignity had suffered enough, and he was not going to stand and take a whipping as well. At least not without trying to defend himself. He raised his fists and adopted the classic stance of a boxer. The effect was somewhat spoiled by his spare trousers, which, having no braces, had a tendency to slip down.

Marthinus threw the whip on the ground in disgust and continued stalking and shaking his head. The word *rooinek'* was mentioned several times.

'We could have all been killed, do you understand nothing?'

'I really didn't mean to...'

'You can't fool around with baboons, meneer,' Marthinus stormed. 'If it wasn't for that bugger there,' he pointed at Quabe, 'we could all be dead. Do you know what I'm saying?'

Marthinus turned back to glower at Charles, hands akimbo, and behind him, Quabe flashed his teeth in a smile and picked up his axe, waving it triumphantly in the air.

'I can tell you, meneer...' Marthinus stopped when he saw Charles was not paying attention and turned to see the Zulu waving the axe. 'What the hell are you doing?'

Quabe hesitated guiltily, then his body stiffened and he became trance-like. Holding the axe in the air, he started to dance. A slow shuffling on stiff legs, his bare feet thudding on the ground, and he began to sing in a quavering falsetto voice - singing the victory song of the Zulu women as they welcomed their warriors home from battle.

Marthinus and Charles watched in bemusement, their argument forgotten; captivated by the serious intensity of the Zulu's actions and the nostalgic tone of the song.

Finally Marthinus shook his head, a strange smile threatening. 'Man!' he exclaimed to no one in particular. 'What a silly bugger that is.'

Ten minutes ought to do it, Fleetwood was thinking. An hour or two would be more satisfying, but the way he was feeling, he would not be able to restrain himself for that long. In a few minutes he could inflict permanent damage, even death. Of course, being such a weasel, there was a good chance Toby Hollings may not last even that long, which would be a pity, so he would have to be careful and not rush it. He would take his time and enjoy thinking about it while waiting for the iron spikes to get hot. Then he would tell Hollings what he was going to do with them and watch the little rat grovel and squeak for mercy.

But even the satisfying thoughts of Toby Hollings's slow and painful demise could not compensate Fleetwood for the torture he had been made to endure himself over the past week. He had been choked and coated with red dust, persistently assailed by swarms of flies, squeezed dry by the merciless heat, jostled, chafed, bruised and battered by the constant jolting of the ridiculous coach, and had suffered the company of eleven imbecile passengers and two lunatic drivers.

He had been vomited on by a Greek sailor, threatened with physical violence by an arrogant Boer who refused to speak English, and had undergone the distasteful and embarrassing experience of having the overweight moron sitting beside him take a fit. Altogether, it was the worst week of his life, and it was all due to Toby Hollings.

The knowledge he had another four days to go before reaching the Vaal River sank Fleetwood further into despair. He was not sure he could survive that long without taking a fit himself.

The coach seldom stopped for more than the few hours it took to change the team of mules, and he was desperately short of sleep. Any form of rest was impossible in the rattling contraption, for they were crammed together onto three wooden benches like convicts being transported to prison.

The waistcoat too, was becoming a problem. He could not risk removing it in the company of so many ruffians, and the heat-rash had developed into a malevolent imitation of smallpox. The strong sailcloth lining had the insulating qualities of asbestos, and his entire chest was affected to such a degree that, even with the waistcoat unbuttoned, he had to sit hunched forward in order to keep a small gap between his tender skin and the cloth of his undershirt.

Not being able to secure a berth on a ship to England for at least a month had been a devastating blow. It was far too long a wait when he could be arrested at any moment. Even so, perhaps his decision to go to the Vaal River and lose himself in the rabble had been made too hastily. He could as easily have taken a coach to Port Natal, or some other God-forsaken colonial backwater.

Fleetwood used some of his brilliantine on the rash and, surprisingly, after some initial stinging it seemed to help. He tried to overcome the discomfort of the journey by thinking of what he was going to do at the diggings, and how he could turn the disastrous trip to some advantage. Digging for diamonds was obviously out of the question, as was shopkeeping. It looked as if illicit buying was the only option. At least then he would have a means of laundering the contents of the waistcoat.

But mostly Fleetwood thought about Toby Hollings, and what he would do to him should the opportunity ever present itself. Ten minutes, that was all he needed.

'Worms, Meneer Hollings. Worms is what the game is called. It is a good name, I think.'

With the flesh of his upper torso quivering like disturbed pink blancmange, Toby Hollings sat hunched and mute on a stool set in the middle of the interrogation room of Newmarket Gaol.

Other than the stool and a complicated wooden contrivance hanging from spikes on the wall, the floor and walls were bare and damp. Green slime seeped from the joints of the sandstone blocks. There were no windows. Had it not been for the open doorway, it could easily have been mistaken for a room designed to store water.

Senior Police Sergeant Koos Erasmus circled Toby Hollings like a shark, prodding him at random intervals with the tip of his swagger stick.

'Ja, that's it!' he exclaimed as Toby jerked away from a particularly vicious jab. 'Very good! What a nice little wriggly worm you are. I think warder Gysbert who does the fishing will be very pleased with such wriggling.'

He continued to circle menacingly, tapping on his leg with the stick in rhythm with his pace. He stopped in front of Hollings and traced a circle around his naked left breast, and Toby flinched at the cold touch of the brass tip.

'Sit still!'

The command rang out in beautifully crisp parade-ground tenor, rebounding from the walls of the interrogation room, then reverberating through the long stone-walled corridor to startle the corporal dozing at the enquiry counter. It filtered onto the street, where passers-by cocked an appreciative ear at the splendid operatic quality and turned their heads in curiosity.

Toby sank even lower on his stool, looking as if he had been struck on the head with a gong.

'The time...' Sergeant Erasmus said conversationally, tapping against his palm with the stick. '...the time to wriggle, Hollings, is when warder Gysbert puts his big fish hook in here...' He gently placed the tip of his stick to the side of Toby's left breast, 'and then pushes it out here.' He moved the stick in a graceful arc to the other side of the breast.

Toby Hollings sat frozen, his eyes glassy. He had been intimidated before. Whitechapel was no schoolyard, but this was different. The big Afrikaner filled him with so much terror that every breath he took wheezed painfully in his constricted throat. From the policeman's pale metallic eyes - visible only as glints under the glossy peak of his cap - to the gleaming toes of his leather boots some six and a half feet lower down, Sergeant Erasmus was a towering, ramrod-stiff, mind-numbing experience.

'The best part, Meneer Hollings,' the sergeant continued pleasantly, as if recounting an excursion to the beach, 'is when they take you out in the rowing boat and throw you over the side.' He paused to reflect, then shook his head in disagreement with himself. 'No, Meneer Hollings. My apologies. That is not the best part at all. The best part is when they start pulling you in and the race begins with the sharks. Ja, absolutely! That is by far the best part.'

He paused to allow the full implications to filter through the spongy tissues of Toby's numbed brain before continuing.

'That is the time to wriggle, meneer. The sharks like the worms to wriggle a bit on the end of the line. It makes it much more interesting for them, you see. Nice, fat, juicy, wriggling limey worms like you, meneer Hollings.'

He prodded Toby sharply about the body with his stick, laughing as he jerked away. 'Ja, that's it! See how well you can do it? Very good indeed. I think I might even make a small wager myself. Yes, of course I will. But tell me who I should wager on, meneer? Tell me who will win the race? Will it be the sharks, or the ones who are pulling you on the line?'

Sergeant Erasmus did not wait for an answer. He placed a hand on Toby's shoulder and gave it a conciliatory pat. 'Don't worry, meneer, they tell me there is not much pain. The water is very cold, you see.' He continued slowly around in a circle, tapping.

'Sometimes, it does not go too well though,' he explained apologetically. 'Sometimes the hook rips through the flesh when the pullers are too keen to win their bet, especially when the worms are fat and heavy like you, meneer, and sometimes the sharks are too lazy and only bite off some leg.'

Sergeant Erasmus paused and clicked his tongue with dismay. 'Then we have to do it all over again. But it is never the same. There is not enough wriggling left and the sharks get bored. I think they much prefer wriggly worms, meneer Hollings.'

He prodded Toby again. ' Ja, I think they will like that. Now, tell me, meneer, who would be so stupid as to give twenty pounds to a worm like you?'

Toby Hollings wanted desperately to talk. He opened his dry mouth and managed a faint croak.

Sergeant Erasmus gave Toby another vicious jab in the belly. 'Speak!'

Toby squealed in pain and fell from the stool. He scrambled back on it hastily and, in a voice made tremulous and halting with fear, told Sergeant Erasmus everything he wanted to know.

When Sergeant Erasmus informed the Chief of Customs that a package had been placed in his safe without anyone's knowledge, the chief, with an ill-concealed smirk, called in all his office staff and asked the sergeant to repeat what he had said.

A brief silence greeted the repetition, followed by some subdued sniggering, and the back of the sergeant's clean-shaven neck turned pink.

'Now why would anyone want to do that, sergeant?' the chief asked, his smirk extending to a smile. Little love existed between the two, and the chief was clearly thoroughly enjoying his adversary's discomfort. 'What was supposed to be in this package anyway?'

After some distracted twiddling of his stick, Sergeant Erasmus decided it was time to get his own back. Not only did he dislike the customs officer, he also resented having to remove his cap every time he entered the building simply because of some stupid limey naval tradition.

'Perhaps it was a bomb,' he said with a sneer.

The giggling stopped abruptly as all eyes turned towards the safe in the corner. A slight shuffling of feet and a perceptible movement towards the door prompted a quick reaction from the chief.

'Impossible!' he exclaimed. 'The contents of the safe are checked every day and registered.' He consulted his pocket watch and added the clincher. 'Why, I checked it myself less than four hours ago when I came on duty.' Then, as an afterthought. 'When was this package supposed to have been deposited?'

Sergeant Erasmus hesitated. 'About a week ago.'

The tension in the office dissipated rapidly and the smiles returned.

'Ah then! No cause for alarm, is there? You see, sergeant, at present there are no packages at all in the safe.'

Nevertheless, after Sergeant Erasmus had gone, the chief dismissed his staff then checked the safe carefully. He poured himself a good nip of rum and watched the policeman's departure from his window.

'Blasted ape!' he muttered. 'Should be yardarmed for trying to scuttle us like that.'

When Sergeant Erasmus entered Yorky's bar the noise

level fell by half, which roughly approximated the number of customers who had reason to remain silent in the presence of the law. The sergeant was well aware of the effect his entrance caused and, still smarting from his brush with the Chief of Customs, he capitalised on it to the full.

Standing in the light of the open doorway with the stick tucked under his arm and his eyes masked by the visor of the cap, he slowly inspected the crowd while he unbuttoned his breast pocket and removed a notebook.

When the chatter had subsided to a suitably respectable level he strode purposefully towards the bar and the patrons parted hastily. He came to a halt in front of Yorky.

'I am looking for a man,' he stated crisply, glaring down accusingly at the flustered bartender. Although he did not raise his voice, it carried to every straining ear in the room. It became even more hushed. 'A gentleman, I believe.'

A communal sigh, hinting of relief, rustled through the customers.

'A well-dressed gentleman by the name of...' the sergeant consulted his notebook, licking his finger to slowly turn the pages. '...Smythe.'

'Ah...'

'So you know this gentleman?'

'No!' Yorky responded quickly, obviously unwilling to associate himself with anyone the policeman had an interest in. 'Well, that is, I believe a gentleman of that name did call in some days ago.'

'And would you be able to tell me where I can find him?'

Yorky screwed his face up in the semblance of thought, acting for the benefit of those listening and watching. 'If I remember correctly, the gentleman said as how he was leaving for England and wanted a package delivered to Hope Town.'

Sergeant Erasmus stiffened and rose even higher. 'A package?'

'Yes.' Yorky gulped and shrugged defensively. The question sounded more like an accusation. 'A young man was to take it for him personally because he said as how it was too important to send in the mail.' Yorky suddenly remembered the register and pulled it out from under the counter. He ran his finger shakily down the columns until he found the entry he was looking for.

'There you are, officer.' Yorky stabbed triumphantly at the name. 'All put down nice and legal like.' He smiled, displaying a large amount of gold filling. 'The gentleman was most anxious I write it all down nice and legal like.'

The policeman was not overly impressed. 'What was in the package?' he demanded.

Yorky looked blank. 'It was a red package.'

'Ah!' The sergeant copied the details from the ledger carefully into his notebook while Yorky stood nervously wiping invisible stains from the counter. When the transfer was completed the policeman returned the book to his pocket and buttoned it down carefully.

'Thank you, sir, you have been most helpful.'

As the policeman strode out Yorky shrugged and smiled weakly at his customers. Being helpful to the law was not exactly the sort of testimonial he wanted bandied around. It was bad for business.

Sensing danger, the bushbuck stood perfectly still, all but invisible in the tangle of thorny scrub. Only the twitch of a fly-tickled ear had given him away.

Marthinus steadied the rifle against the tree and fixed the notch of the rear sight where he estimated the point of the shoulder to be. Then as his finger tightened on the trigger the bushbuck turned its head to look directly at him.

For long moments Marthinus held his aim, then his finger relaxed and he lowered the rifle. Catching the movement the bushbuck melted into the scrub with only a faint rattling of stones to mark his flight.

Marthinus slung his rifle and turned towards the camp. The bushbuck had been a magnificent specimen, but they had more than enough fresh meat, and making more *biltong* would mean another delay when there was really no good reason to stay longer. The oxen were well rested and grazed, and all the gear had been prepared for the trek down the berg to the Karoo. The incident with the baboons had been a good excuse to spend a few extra days in the krans camp while the Englishman recovered, but now it was time to leave.

Marthinus took his time returning, stopping frequently to rest and enjoy the solitude of the bush. Reluctantly he was coming to the conclusion that his age was beginning to tell. The treks were becoming harder and the rest stops seemed to be getting longer and more enjoyable.

Since Hester's death, being on the road with his oxen had been a reason to stay away from the farm and all the memories it held, but it was a selfish reason, and he knew he should be at home with Aneline and Jurie. They would be finding it hard now, with the drought.

Perhaps it was time to think of something else. The team and wagon would bring a good price. Enough to pay off the bank loan and keep the farm going, maybe even until the drought broke.

But Marthinus also knew in his heart he could not do it. He had worked hard to build his team into the best in the Cape, and a subtle bond of trust had developed that he could not see betrayed by some ignorant whip-happy driver. He would rather shoot the cattle first.

By the time he reached the camp, Marthinus had come to a decision. He would not sell the team. Somehow, he would have to find another way. But this would be his last trek.

At first, Charles put it down to his imagination, but as the day progressed he became certain. The Boer was not only more friendly, he seemed almost happy. Since returning empty-handed from his morning hunt he had laughed and joked with the Africans, and, at times, even included Charles in his banter. He had dug around in the wagon and produced a pair of well-worn soft leather boots, which he first soaked in water then handed to Charles with a terse explanation.

'*Veldskoen*. Put them on without stockings and wear them until they are dry.'

Dubiously, Charles did as he was told. Anything was better than bare feet, and the problem had been nagging him. Without boots he was as good as crippled, but he had been reluctant to mention that he had no spare pair, even though his cautious mincing on the stony ground with his bare feet made it obvious.

He squelched around in the boots and was surprised at how comfortable they became after they had dried and moulded to his feet.

Then he was relieved of his only pair of spare trousers.

'Do not worry,' Marthinus reassured Charles as he protested, 'you will get them back. But first we have to change the colour. It is frightening the cattle.'

He dropped the mustard-coloured trousers into a bucket of water simmering on the fire, then emptied the old coffee grounds on top, along with a handful of salt and some bark and leaves stripped from a tree.

Quabe and Timisani watched the proceedings with amused interest. When Marthinus produced a spare bush hat and Charles pulled it well down over his ears, they nudged each other and giggled surreptitiously behind their palms.

Charles forgot his embarrassment at wearing only shirt and boots and entered into the spirit of the occasion. He took his useless white cap and threw it far into the scrub.

An immediate scramble followed as, pushing and shoving, the two Africans raced after it. Timisani won by a hand, diving on it, but the big Zulu fell on top of him, knocking the wind from the Herero's small frame and snatching the cap from his grasp. Complaining bitterly, Timisani brushed the dust from his body as the Zulu tried the cap on. Unfortunately it was too small, so he handed it back reluctantly and, grinning self-consciously, Timisani put it on. It became his most cherished possession.

As usual, they left early, and Charles surprised himself by being awake and ready to go. His muscles still ached and his sunburned skin remained taut and touchy, but his spirits were high.

He had wanted to express his gratitude toward the Boer the previous evening, but did not know how. He suspected the tough old man was not the sort of person who showed his feelings easily, so he decided he would be the same. He waited for the right opportunity and it came when he put on the subdued trousers. He simply smiled his thanks, and the Boer, after looking steadily at him for a few moments without expression, nodded in return.

Jurie Steyn could stand the discomfort no longer. He stopped the mules under the sparse shade of a thorn tree and sat on the ground to remove his boots.

An expression of ecstasy slowly replaced the frown that had been etched on his face for the past several hours.

'Ja,' he muttered to himself, 'much better.'

With eyes closed, he enjoyed the feeling for a few moments before beginning a careful examination of his feet.

The toes, normally wide and splayed from constantly walking barefoot, were red and bunched up, as if cowering together for protection. Tenderly he prised them apart and examined each one individually for signs of mutilation.

Finally satisfied that no risk of permanent disability existed, he gave them a tentative rub and wriggled them experimentally. They responded lethargically. He stood up and walked around.

'Ja, much better!' It felt as though he was walking on air. 'Man! Only a *rooinek* could make such boots.'

He looked at the discarded footwear accusingly. The foot part was too narrow and the leg part was too long. The heels were so high he had been forced to walk while leaning back with knees bent to avoid falling forward. The posture had given him the unpleasant sensation of creeping away to the bushes after of having done something nasty in his trousers.

The boots no longer gleamed with the sheep fat so energetically rubbed into the leather. The fat had softened and attracted a thick coating of red dust. Now they looked more like a pair of dead jackals that had been dragged behind the wagon than a pair of English riding boots.

'Jurie, what's the matter... why have we stopped? And who are you talking to?'

'It's all right, sis, it's only these *bliksem* boots have been killing my bloody feet.'

A clatter came from inside the wagon, then the canvas curtain was thrown open and Aneline Steyn came onto the fore-carriage.

'Jurie! You know better than to talk like that.' She broke off to wave at a fine cloud of disturbed dust. 'Especially about Oupa's gift.'

'Sorry, sis, but they're just too bloody small. And anyway, oupa never used them.'

'Rubbish! They only need a bit of wearing in, that's all. What do you think people will say at Pniel if you don't have any boots on?'

Jurie opened his mouth to answer but wasn't

quick enough.

'They'll say… look at that big ignorant Boer with no boots on. He's worse than the savages… now come on, please, we can't wait around here all day. The meat will go bad and I want to get there before dark.'

Jurie sighed. Although two years older he knew better than to argue with his sister. She was like their mother had been, bossy and always nagging him about how he looked. As if it mattered. He picked up the boots and threw them under the driving bench, then he climbed up and took the reins. At the first opportunity he promised himself, he would drop the boots down an antbear hole.

Inside the covered wagon, Aneline sprinkled water over the sacks covering the meat to keep it cool. It was almost two months since their father had returned to Cape Town for another load, and in that time things had got steadily worse on the farm. Marthinus usually provided sufficient money to last longer than his time away, but there had been some heavy expenses this time, and Aneline had spent many a sleepless night trying to figure out where the money should go.

Her accounting system was simple but effective, consisting of seven preserving jars in the pantry. Each jar was allocated a specific responsibility. The house jar took care of the household expenses, including food, clothing and paraffin for the lamps, the bank jar paid off the loan they had taken to build the slaughter house, and the stock-feed jar, wages jar, medicine jar, repairs jar, and emergency jar divided what money was left.

Because of the worsening drought, all the jars had been emptied within the first month, and Aneline considered it her responsibility to find a way of filling them.

Reluctantly she had come to the unhappy conclusion that the few remaining head of breeding stock had to be butchered. She realised it was the only asset they had left, and would take years to replace, but she had no other choice, and they could easily die because of the drought anyway.

Jurie had butchered them one at a time as the need arose, and Aneline had flinched every time she heard the shot and prayed again for the rains to come.

They sold the meat in Pniel where the demand was steadily growing with the influx of people coming to look for diamonds, and they stopped at Hope Town on the way back to spend the money on grain and feed to keep the remaining herd alive. They used little on themselves, but despite the sacrifice and sleepless nights, most of the jars on the shelf remained empty.

Before she had died Hester Steyn had given instructions that she was to be buried under the wild mulberry trees at the bottom of the garden. It was where she had insisted, despite opposition, that her father should also be buried.

'Why should he be stuck up there on the hill with all those strangers?' she had argued. 'Who cares what they say about consecrated ground? That's nonsense. Oupa will be buried next to the mulberry trees where he can be close to his family. It is what he would want, and it's what I want too when my time comes, so that's it.'

As usual, Hester got her way, and Oupa was buried under the trees with a simple cross of whitewashed stinkwood from an old wagon to mark the spot.

Since then, the number of crosses had increased by two.

Hester's own grave lay in the middle, between her father and the smaller grave of the stillborn child that had been the cause of her own death. No flowers were ever put on the graves. Hester had never liked the forlorn effect when they wilted, which they did quickly in the heat, and only the carefully swept area showed it was a special place. That and the simple white crosses splattered with pink and black stains from the mulberries.

On the Sunday following their trip to Pniel with the load of meat, Aneline and Jurie stood under the trees as usual to pay their respects. The area had been freshly brushed clean that morning by Kobe, the old Zulu servant, and the dust still lingered in the air, catching the morning shafts of sunlight as they filtered through the branches and giving an ethereal sense of peace to the area..

Aneline began the service in the usual way. 'Lord, you are welcome in this place.' She paused, and they stood silently for a few moments with heads bowed.

'Hello, Mamma. Hello, Oupa. Well, here we are again.' Aneline always spoke informally, and never read from the bible as her father did. She did not understand, or care much for the strange language used. It did not seem right that she should speak differently to her mother and oupa simply because they were dead. She held the bible under her arm though, in case anyone should be offended.

She spoke conversationally to them for some time, telling them of the events, large and small, that had occurred during the week and, as usual, she ended with the drought.

'If you happen to meet anyone there who can help with the rains it would be a good thing, Mama. We really need it bad.' She nudged Jurie who had been standing silently at her side. 'Your turn,' she whispered.

'Amen,' Jurie intoned solemnly.

'Not now!' Aneline hissed. 'Tell oupa about the boots.'

'Hey?'

'Tell him about his boots like I told you.'

'Oh, ja,' Jurie murmured. 'Sorry I threw the boots away, oupa. It's only that they were too damned small and were killing my feet.' Jurie became aware that Aneline was glaring at him so he finished off with a lame, 'thanks anyway.'

'One more thing,' Aneline said, continuing her one-way conversation with her mother. 'Pa will be here next Sunday to speak to you. The coach passed them near Proud's and they were short of water, so we are going to meet them. *Totsiens* for now.'

'Ja, goodbye,' Jurie echoed his sister's farewell.

As Jurie and Aneline were leaving the farm to meet up with their father, Mbalifu Kumbemba was approaching the confluence of the Orange and Vaal Rivers, some fifty miles to the west.

Already thirty-five summers old, Mbalifu was as yet unmarried. It was not a shortage of suitable women in the area that had delayed him, there were plenty. It was only that his tastes always seemed to include those with excessively greedy fathers.

The source of his latest frustration lay a good eight days' walk to the north, in a dusty cluster of huts on the edge of the Kalahari desert. The village was presided over by a belligerent headman with a beautiful daughter and a desire for more wealth. He had sneeringly refused the generous offer of a lion skin blanket, and stubbornly insisted that nothing less than ten goats would secure her release.

Despite the high price, Mbalifu would willingly have paid it - if only he had it. Unfortunately, he had nothing. He had the single cloth he wore around his middle, an axe for protection and chopping wood, two water calabashes, and a lion skin blanket. No goats, not even a chicken, and certainly no money.

So desperate had Mbalifu been to be with his love, he had even considered abducting her - a crime punishable by instant head splitting if caught. He had been delayed only by the awkward mechanics involved with carrying her plump body into the bush at the same time as trying to keep her quiet.

Fortunately, he had been spared from taking such drastic measures - and of risking the dire consequences - by his cousin. It seemed his cousin had heard first hand from his uncle, that a friend of his cousin's uncle had gone to the meeting place of the two great rivers. He had returned not long after with enough money to buy two wives and still have enough left over for a third if he wished.

His cousin was not able to find out exactly how his uncle's friend had earned the money, only that it had something to do with small stones that the white men were looking for near the river.

It was not much to go on, but it was enough. Many small stones lay on the ground, even big stones, and the thought of being rich and able to afford two wives was all the encouragement Mbalifu needed to get him going.

He informed his beloved of his intentions and was gratified when she giggled demurely and wished him a safe journey.

Carried away by the promise in her eyes and an urge to boast, he had stupidly informed her father that he intended to give him not ten goats, but twelve. He had regretted the impulse immediately, but the surprised look on the old fool's face had almost been worth it.

Mbalifu smiled to himself and broke into song every time he thought of his beloved, which was often, and he was thinking of her when he passed an antbear hole and noticed something inside that looked oddly out of place.

He broke off singing and peered into the angled hole to see what it was. It was not a dead antbear as he had first thought, rather it looked like two dead things.

Curious, he hooked them out with his axe, and his puzzled frown turned to a broad smile. Boots! And boots such as he had never seen before.

Mbalifu talked to the boots as he brushed away the dirt. Unlike most people, he believed that *all* dead things, even if their bodies had been turned into something else, still had a spirit of their own.

He told the boots to show him what they were like under the dust and, revived by spit, the boots gleamed at him. He instructed them to turn over so he could see what was wrong with them underneath, and they did, but he could find no fault. They were almost perfect.

But Mbalifu had a feeling something was not right. No one would throw away such valuable boots. He peered farther into the gloom of the hole and called out persuasively in case someone was hiding there, but the hole remained silent. He searched the ground and saw the faint barefoot marks of someone who had walked up to the hole then walked away again.

Mbalifu spoke to the footprints and told them to show him where they were going. He followed and stopped when the prints disappeared at some wagon tracks. He considered following them for a while too, then decided against it. They were going in the wrong direction.

He stripped some bark from a sapling and made a sling for the boots, then he hung them around his neck and set off in the direction of the big river. Only one more day and he would be there, but already he was getting rich. The boots must be worth at least one of the extra goats he had promised.

Encouraged, Mbalifu quickened his pace and, with a yodelling falsetto, broke into another of his favourite songs.

Magnificent as they were, the oxen were showing signs of exhaustion. They plodded mechanically with heads lowered and eyes showing too much white, and their flanks were speckled with brown foam snorted from the dust-clogged nostrils of their team-mates.

Even the stalwart *Witbeen* was affected, and he tossed his head angrily against the downward and sideways pull of the yoke, his great hump quivering with the strain. His partner reacted sluggishly to the signals, jerking his head up and forward, but he could hold for only a few moments before exhaustion dragged it down to slump once more against the securing reim.

It was twenty miles and twelve hours since they had last had water, and they would not have it again until they reached the scheduled outspan, some eight miles ahead. It was one of the last, but also one of the longest stretches of the journey, and although Marthinus had done the trip many times before, he had never known it to be so bad.

The large beasts drank water by the bucket-full, and even with valuable space on the wagon already taken up by extra barrels, Marthinus was unable to carry sufficient to satisfy their gargantuan thirsts.

The dry north-westerly sucked the moisture from their bodies almost as fast as it went in and, to make matters worse, the borehole at Proud's Coach Station had dried to a trickle, so water had to be rationed. It was the first time it had happened.

Marthinus could not even wash the dust from the clogged nostrils of his oxen for fear of what the scent of the water would do. He coaxed them along as best he could, calling encouragement, but their pace was slowing. They needed to rest badly, but he also knew the dangers of outspanning without water. Even hobbled, the thirst-crazed animals would wander by instinct in search of it, and it could take days to round them up. By then they would either have perished or been torn down by prowling hyenas.

He kept the team going on through the night, believing they would make it, but also aware it would take days, maybe even weeks, for them to recover, and a few might not and would have to be shot. It was a terrible price to pay for the sake of a few barrels of water, and something Marthinus was finding hard to accept.

The scheduled outspan was more a sip-well than a spring. Situated in the bend of a dry stream it was covered with sand, and invisible. Few knew of its existence other than the local tribesmen, and Marthinus knew of it only because Timisani had shown it to him one day on a previous trip while they were hunting.

Marthinus sent the two Africans ahead with shovels and instructions to start digging. He did not want any delay when the oxen arrived, and he prayed the spring had not dried up like the borehole.

With the two Africans gone, Charles offered to spell Marthinus on the leading reim, and was pleasantly surprised when his offer was accepted. The track ahead was straight and clearly visible in the moonlight, and Marthinus assured him the oxen were so tired the worst they could do was stop. He instructed Charles to wake him in an hour, then climbed into the wagon and went to sleep.

Charles thoroughly enjoyed his new responsibility, although it seemed to him that no matter what he did with the lead-reim the oxen did as they pleased anyway. He tried experimenting, tentatively at first, by pulling forward on the reim to speed them up, but it was like trying to pull a train. When he pulled to the side in an effort to turn them, they remained doggedly unturnable, as if they were on rails, and when he slowed down they simply blundered into him and he was forced to skip ahead or be trampled. Their awesome power unnerved him, and he learned a measure of respect for the seemingly simple way that young Timisani handled them.

Charles set his pace to that of the oxen and sauntered along in front with the reim slung casually over his shoulder. When the hour was up he decided to keep going and let Marthinus sleep. The old man was obviously exhausted and needed the rest, while he was wide-awake and feeling fitter than he had in a long time. A month of walking had begun to harden and shape his muscles, and the simple diet of lean meat, vegetables and maize-meal porridge had replaced the weight lost on the voyage from England. His dry skin had mostly peeled away and the exposed layers were beginning to brown under the cloudless sky.

Towards dawn it darkened and become cooler, but with his eyes well accustomed to the dark Charles could see the trail ahead clearly; a webbed pattern of thin silvery lines stretching into the veld. A cool breeze sprang up to fan at his cheek and he inhaled deeply, filling his nostrils with the clear sweet smell. Far to the north the sky flickered with light, and above the clatter of the wagon Charles fancied he heard the rumble of thunder. He wondered if it heralded the end of the drought. He hoped it did, if for no other reason than to provide a fresh topic of conversation around the campfire.

Charles switched his attention from the lightning to the pebble lodged in his boot. It was proving difficult to remove. He tried taking the boot off while hopping, and when he eventually managed it, he found he was unable to put it back on again without stopping. After some minutes of limping along with one bare foot, he slipped the coiled reim over one of

Witbeen's long horns and moved out of the way, the wagon trundling slowly past as he sat by the side of the trail replacing his boot.

Feeling expendable, he walked beside the oxen, running his hand over their warm hides as he had seen Marthinus do, feeling the powerful rippling of muscle beneath, and it was some time before he realised he was walking faster than before. He was pleased. Obviously, the oxen had sensed they were nearing the camp and were keen to get there. The riding ponies at the carnival had been the same, tossing their heads impatiently and quickening their pace when they knew they were on the way home.

It was only when the pace increased further that Charles felt the first twinge of concern. He ran to the front to take up the reim, but it had been thrown off and was trailing on the ground between the oxen's legs.

He was further disturbed to see they were no longer on the trail. Small bushes loomed up at him, forcing him to run around or jump over, while the oxen ploughed straight through. Then, alarmingly, they broke into a slow, lumbering trot. Warm mucus from their blowing nostrils splattered on his arms when he grabbed at the yoke between the two leaders and tried to push back. Horns flashed dangerously close to his face and he abandoned the idea hastily. He ran forward then turned and waved his arms.

'Whoa there! Whoa there!' he yelled, but they kept coming with heads lowered and eyes wide, straining and snorting, and picking up speed with every step. He may just as well have been another bush waving in the breeze for all the attention they paid him, and again he had to leap out of the way or be run over.

'Meneer Steyn! Wake up!' In a panic, Charles grabbed at the side of the wagon as it went past and, by kicking and clawing, managed to scramble up. He was making his way precariously over the load towards the rear canopy where the Boer was sleeping when the wagon lurched violently through a ditch and Charles became airborne. He saw a blur of bushes, and heard the pounding of hooves and thunderous clatter of the wagon, but the last thing he heard before his face smashed into the hard ground was the terrified squawking of the chickens.

Marthinus was jolted awake when the wagon hit the ditch. He realised immediately that the oxen were stampeding. Branches ripped and screeched at the canvas canopy, and the chicken coop had broken loose and turned upside down, sending the birds into a flapping frenzy.

Marthinus lunged for the front of the wagon, crawling precariously over the bouncing load, clutching wildly at anything he could get a hold on to stop himself from being thrown off. He lay sprawled in the centre of the wagon, watching helplessly as they careered through the scrub toward a dark ribbon of trees.

The veld suddenly lit up as though a light had been turned on and, for an instant, a crack of thunder drowned out the pulverising clatter. But Marthinus did not have time to reflect on the event. His sole preoccupation should have been with survival. He knew that his best chance was to jump off and hope for the best, but he could not bring himself to do it. Like the captain of a sinking ship he was determined to stay on until the last moment in case a chance arose of somehow saving the wagon.

Marthinus watched the trees grow large and start to flash past, and he prayed they would not hit one. And even had he been able to think of something to do, there was no time. A bank appeared suddenly in front and the leading oxen reared up as they tried to slow down, but the momentum of the four ton load was too great. They were forced over the edge by their team-mates behind in a bellowing sprawl of falling bodies, clashing horns and tangled harness.

With a sickening lurch the wagon dipped over the bank and careered down, pushing the falling oxen ahead of it. The *disselboom* snapped with a loud crack and the broken end dug into the sand, bringing the wagon to a jarring halt.

Marthinus was hurled forward, into the bunched up, sprawling bodies of the oxen. He landed amongst the forest of horns with such force that had any one of them been angled in the wrong direction he would have been impaled. As it was, he did not remain unscathed. The sharp point of a broken yoke ripped at the inside of his thigh, leaving an eight inch gash, and a horn grazed his cheek, narrowly missing his eye.

Marthinus felt neither of the injuries. He lay stunned between two large beasts that were scrambling to get to their feet, and even in his dazed state he knew he would have to get out fast. He took hold of the nearest horn and tried to pull himself up, but the beast was on its knees and off balance, and the sudden weight pulled him over so that he fell half on top of Marthinus.

He heard his ribs crack under the weight and felt the pain knife through his chest, and he thought it was the end. He felt the bile rise in his throat to choke him, and he gulped for air that was thick with dust and the stench of cattle.

The fallen ox was also trying to rise. Marthinus could see the powerful shoulder only inches from his face. The big knees were quivering with the strain of trying to unbend against the weight of the twisted yoke that was keeping him down. Marthinus covered his head with his arms, aware it would do little good if the beast managed to rise up and his head got in the way of the stumbling hooves.

With a strained bellow of panic, the beast on top of Marthinus rolled away, and the movement seemed to help the ox on his other side. It rose, also bellowing, and Marthinus saw his opportunity. Fighting against the pain in his chest, he turned onto his stomach and, in a desperate gamble, crawled through between the animal's legs.

Gasping and retching, he rested his forehead against the cool sand and fought the dizziness that threatened to overcome him. He lay for a long time trying to assess the extent of his injuries, steeling himself against the bawling of the cattle needing his attention.

Finally, he could stand it no longer. He climbed unsteadily to his feet and stood swaying, holding his broken ribs and bending almost double against the pain.

Vaguely aware that it was dawn and the sky

was leaden with storm clouds, Marthinus observed the shambles.

Half the team was still down, unable to move in the tangle of harness, held by the weight of the others. Some had turned and were facing the wrong way. The luckier ones had broken free. Trailing scraps of harness they were drinking what they could from the small trickle of water that had flowed down from the storm farther north.

Marthinus cut the remaining beasts free with his pocket knife, being careful not to be in the way as they scrambled impatiently away. He hobbled slowly and painfully among them, trying to soothe those waiting by calling their names with as calm a voice as he could manage.

Several were injured, and five were beyond any help, with broken legs or gored flesh. A few were blown with exhaustion.

Marthinus shot them where they lay, wincing as each recoil of the rifle ripped painfully at his broken ribs. But it was not the physical pain that brought the sharp sting of tears to his eyes.

Charles was aroused by raindrops the size of ripe

gooseberries splattering on the back of his neck. He lifted his head cautiously and opened his eyes, focusing on the pool of bloodied water lying a few inches from his nose. For a horrifying moment he thought he was bleeding to death. Stupefied, he stared as the drops increased in intensity and the pain in his face began to make itself felt. Beside the pool of blood, the large drops thudded into still dry ground, sending up spurts of dust like miniature volcanoes. They rattled on the leaves of the trees, then the sound swelled steadily until it became a roar.

Charles scrambled into the meagre shelter of a nearby bush and covered his head against the stinging onslaught. It pulverised his body until it became numb, the roar changing to a steady hiss as the ground became sodden then sheeted with water.

Then suddenly it stopped. Charles lay waiting, almost cringing in anticipation for it to start again, and when it didn't, he sat up hesitantly and wiped the water from his eyes. His body tingled from the pummelling. His face hurt, especially the nose, and he wondered if it was broken. He probed gently with an exploratory finger and winced at the pain. Maybe it was. He stood cautiously, but apart from a few wobbles and some stiffness that soon passed, most everything seemed to be in working order.

He looked around, taking stock of his situation. The veld glistened with a sheen of water, covering whatever signs the wagon may have left in its passing. It took some time before he could work out which way to go.

Cautiously, through nostrils partly clogged with dried blood, Charles took a few deep breaths of the freshly rinsed air. Then he set off toward a dark line of trees.

As he picked his way through the claggy red soil, Charles reviewed the previous night's events and considered his situation. Marthinus would be furious with him for not waking him as ordered. But even if he had, what good would it have done? Nothing could have stopped the oxen once they had started to run. He had been unable to control them even when they were walking.

Surely Marthinus would understand that it was not his fault. He had done everything he could. Still, Charles could not shake off the feeling it was his fault. He hoped nothing serious had happened. Maybe the oxen had simply stopped when they reached the river. Anyway, he was almost there and would soon find out.

He heard the running water some time before he reached it, and was surprised to find it was not a river but a shallow creek, through which tumbled a foot of frothy red storm-water. He could see no sign of the wagon.

He stood in the rushing stream to remove the layers of mud from his boots, then splashed water over his face. The heavy cloud had dispersed and the sun shone brightly, drawing the moisture back into the air and turning it damp and sticky. Insects fluttered and buzzed about and birds swooped on them from every direction.

After giving it some thought, Charles decided to follow the direction of the flowing water. It was obvious he must have veered off slightly, but by following the creek he was sure to reach the river. It could not be far.

He walked for at least an hour before stopping at a fork in the stream. The water ran both ways, and had subsided considerably, but he paused for only a moment before crossing over and following the larger one.

A few minutes later he realised he had made a mistake. The stream ended in a large shallow pan of water less than an inch deep. Muttering under his breath, he retraced his steps and tried the other branch, only to discover that it ended in the same place, less than twenty paces away from the first one.

Cursing with more imagination, Charles

walked back the way he had come until he reached the place where he had washed his boots. The water had subsided to barely a trickle. After deliberating on it for a while he came to another conclusion. The water was coming *from* the river, not going to it. He had been walking in the wrong direction.

For another hour at least, Charles followed the creek upstream, but instead of getting larger as he expected, it gradually became smaller, until finally it disappeared in a confusing network of corroded channels.

He walked doggedly back to the boot-washing place to start over. Marthinus had told him stories about how easy it was to get lost in the veld and he was determined it was not going to happen to him. As long as he kept his head and thought logically he would find the way.

Charles followed his footsteps in the mud back to where he had fallen off the wagon and saw immediately where he had gone wrong. He had walked in a wide arc instead of straight across, and had been too far to the left. His suspicions seemed to be confirmed when he set off again towards the north and came upon some broken bushes. They must have been damaged when the wagon ran over them during the night.

Feeling more confident, he looked up to note

the position of the sun in order to keep a check on his direction, but it was directly overhead and of no use, so he followed the broken bushes as best he could. They were leading towards another, darker belt of trees that could only be the river, so he was not too concerned.

At times the bushes were so widely spaced, it was difficult to find any that were damaged, and he cursed the heavy rain that had obliterated all the tracks. Without the rain, it would have been simple to follow a team of stampeding oxen and a heavy wagon.

By late afternoon he had still not reached the dark line of trees. When he stood on a small anthill and looked around, he was alarmed to see several dark lines of trees. Not only on all three sides, but also behind – in the direction he had come.

For a moment, Charles almost panicked. He stood for a while, breathing deeply to calm himself. It was essential to stick to his plan of following the damaged bushes until he found the wagon. It could not be that far. The oxen would never have been able to run for more than a few miles.

He came on the footprints only a few minutes later, and the sight of them brought a heady rush of relief. With the relief he was able once more to look realistically at his situation. He was surprised at how close to despair he had come without even realising it.

With renewed energy, Charles set off briskly. The tracks were obviously recent for the imprint stood out sharp and clear in the soft ground. Although they were going in the opposite direction, it did not concern him. It was probably Marthinus, or one of the Africans looking for him. They must have realised by now that something had happened and would be out searching. They would not have gone this long without trying to find him. It was already almost dark.

The backbreaking task of unloading, splinting the broken *disselboom*, then hauling the empty wagon up the bank took most of the day, and Quabe accomplished the majority of the task on his own.

He and Timisani had heard the shots Marthinus had fired as he put his injured cattle out of their miseary, but had not immediately associated the sound with any of their business. The shots had not been spaced like a signal and had been coming from the wrong direction, about two miles downstream and, as they were only a few days away from the busy diggings, it could have been anyone. They discussed it at length, then built up the fire so Marthinus wouldn't miss them and went back to sleep.

It was not until after the rain had woken them that they became concerned and went to look, and they had found the oxen walking up the river bed, still trailing broken harness.

Marthinus directed the operation from the shade of the wagon canopy, which had been removed and set up on the bank, and his inability to help put an impatient edge to his voice.

Around him, the chickens clucked happily as they chased after insects and flying ants flushed out by the storm, seemingly unperturbed by their rough and confusing tumble.

Timisani had bound Marthinus's ribs with strips of blanket, and the gash on his leg was treated with iodine then also bound. He was forced to walk doubled over and as slowly as if he were stalking game, but he considered himself fortunate to have survived.

The tough wagon had suffered little damage apart from the broken *disselboom* and a splintered wheel, which was easily replaced. Had it not been for the loss of the cattle, Marthinus would have considered it a minor accident. He had suffered a lot worse over the years. And it was his own fault, he told himself, for leaving the wagon in charge of someone with no experience.

As soon as his injuries had been tended, Marthinus sent Timisani to look for the Englishman, concerned he may also be hurt.

'If he is all right, show him where we are,' Marthinus instructed. 'Then go and fetch the rest of the cattle before they walk all the way back to Cape Town. And don't be long, we have a lot of work to do here.'

Timisani tried not to look too pleased and left quickly before Marthinus changed his mind. He had not been looking forward to the task of unloading - and of having to listen to the Zulu's jokes about his size and strength.

He cut across the Englishman's tracks within half an hour of leaving the camp, and followed them for a short distance before noticing with surprise they were going the wrong way. He followed them in the opposite direction, and found the place where the man had fallen off the wagon. The rain had washed away many of the tracks, but the signs were still clear to see.

The Englishman must have seen them too, for he had followed the trail of broken and trampled bushes, and by now, would surely be at the wagon. Timisani was surprised he hadn't seen him on the way. He shrugged it off. It was pointless going back to the wagon now. It would be better to go after the cattle instead.

Timisani was in no hurry. He knew the cattle would not stray far from the stream, so he cut across a shallow pan to where he thought they would be. He found them resting contentedly in the shade and drove them back slowly, even taking time off to stop at an anthill and fill his shirt with drowned flying ants to suplement the evening stew. He bundled them up and continued his pleasant stroll along the river, timing it so he would arrive an hour before dark, by which time the wagon should have been unloaded.

When he finally arrived, Marthinus was angry, but was relieved to know the Englishman was still alive and unharmed, even though he had not arrived. Timisani was threatened with a whipping, then given the task of inspanning *Witbeen* and his yoke partner, and hauling the dead oxen a hundred yards downwind where they were to be burned. Marthinus never allowed any of his oxen to be eaten. A fact which both Timisani and the Zulu accepted philosophically as simply another strange and impractical quirk of white men.

Timisani was kept busy far into the night collecting firewood to fuel the pyre. At first light he was sent once more to look for the Englishman. He returned two hours later with Aneline and Jurie in the mule wagon, and the search was temporarily forgotten in the excitement of the reunion.

When questioned later, Timisani explained that the Englishman's tracks were heading upstream towards the diggings, and Marthinus decided that, with so much else to do, it would be a waste of time to go after him right away. With the help of Jurie and the extra wagon to split the load, they would soon be close behind. If the man had any brains he would realise his mistake and either wait for them or return.

At least, Marthinus reassured himself, the *rooinek* was following the stream and wasn't lost out in the veld where he could die of thirst.

Charles's every muscle ached from the effort of maintaining his precarious perch in the tree. Sniffing and grunting sounds during the night, the whining of mosquitoes, and dark shadows moving below the tree had kept him awake, and his eyes were gritty from lack of sleep.

By the time it was light enough to see, he was cold, stiff and lumpy with bites, but he stayed in the tree until the sun came up, wanting to see the tracks he was following clearly, but also wanting to be sure that all the wild animals had returned to their hiding places.

Despite the discomfort, he resumed his journey in a buoyant mood, feeling positive it would not be long before he was back with the wagon.

The suspicion that something was not quite right came slowly. It started when he remembered that the two Africans always went barefoot, and the footprints were of someone wearing boots. The suspicion grew when he realised it was unlikely the Boer would have come looking by himself. Almost certainly, he would have sent Timisani. So who was it he was following?

Charles stopped. With a sinking feeling he turned to look closely at the footprints behind him - both his own and the ones he was following. They were identical. When he placed his boot in either print it fitted exactly. The final realisation stunned him. He had been following himself, and was now hopelessly lost.

Charles experienced a variety of emotions in quick succession. The feeling of doom gave way to disappointment, followed by dismay that he had walked all day with a thumping head to no purpose. Then came fear, for he was lost in this strange and desolate place without water, any means of making a fire, or a weapon. Although he had not actually *seen* any wild animals, he knew they must be there. Especially the hyenas everyone seemed to talk about with such loathing.

Anger was the last emotion Charles experienced. Anger at his stupidity for getting lost, anger at the oxen for their obstinate behaviour, and anger at the Boer for not bothering to look for him.

When Charles was mad, he kicked things. Anything within range, and was not fussy about what he kicked so long as it wasn't solid.

It was unfortunate that the flowering shrub he chose to vent his fury on was a camel-thorn bush. It retaliated aggressively by depositing a two-inch thorn in his big toe.

The pain was sudden and acute, and when he attempted to pull it out while still hopping around,+ it broke off inside the boot.

The pain did not subdue his anger, it inflamed it. He picked up a dead branch and hacked the camel-thorn bush into a pile of shredded leaves, flowers and sticks. Only when his anger was spent did he allow himself to sit down and remove the boot. He discovered the thorn had broken off under the skin and he had no way of removing it.

Carrying the boot, feeling disconsolate and sick, he limped awkwardly on one foot and one heel towards the north.

At midday he finally found the stream, but was too exhausted to feel any elation. He spent a few hours resting in the shade with his feet in the cool water, then reluctantly continued his slow journey along the bank.

Although he saw increasing signs of activity, he met no one, and by dusk was preparing himself for another night in a tree. For a while he searched for one that looked as though it would be more comfortable than the last, then, in a sudden fit of obstinacy, he abandoned the idea and scraped a comfortable hollow in the sand. If the wolves wanted his foot they were welcome to it – especially the sore one.

The night was bad, and the following day worse. All that kept him going was the increasing signs he was getting closer to habitation. He crossed several paths and a few old camps littered with scraps of paper and rusty tins. The empty tins made him realise he hadn't eaten for two days.

His nose was sore and swollen, and his toe felt ready to burst. He used a branch as a walking stick, but progress was slow and painful. He bathed his foot in the stream every few hundred yards and drank the muddy water freely.

He came upon a fresh camp in the afternoon. The first clue to its freshness was the smell of food cooking. It came from a large black pot suspended over the embers of a fire. Around it lay an untidy jumble of blankets, clothes and tools. He could see no sign of the occupants.

'Hello there!' he called, his voice sounding strange. He coughed and tried again. 'Hello... is anyone here?'

A dog growled from the shade of a tree and Charles started nervously. 'Good dog,' he coaxed. 'Where's your master?'

The dog panted heavily. It gave another short growl, then whined and grovelled with its tail between its legs. Charles looked at it curiously. It was a nondescript black dog, and was tied to a tree with a short length of rope. Its bowl of water had been placed out of reach.

'Are you thirsty?' Charles hobbled towards it and warily nudged the bowl forward, and the dog crawled towards it, shivering with fear. Still on its belly, it lapped greedily at the water.

Charles turned his attention to the pot. The smell was making his mouth water. He lifted the lid with the end of his stick. A ladle hung on the wire above and he dipped it into the stew. If he took only a spoonful, no one would know. He lifted it to his lips, blowing cautiously.

'And what the bejasus do you think you be

doin'?'

Charles dropped the ladle as if it were red hot and spun round. Three men stood at the edge of the camp watching him. He smiled guiltily.

'Sorry, I wasn't doing anything. Only having a look at your stew. Smells good.'

The largest of the three smiled back. Apart from a bowler hat, he was naked from the waist up, his hairless belly pale and bulging. A towel hung around his neck.

'Not doing nothin' he says. Hear that, Clance? He says he's not doin' nothin'. Jus' stickin' his dirty nose in our lovely stew as we be takin' a bath. Now what do you think of that then?'

'Bad manners I think it is, Horry,' replied the smaller of his two companions. He wore a knotted red handkerchief on his head and his pink face was ringed with ginger curls. 'Sure he should be beggin' our pardon.'

The third member of the trio was much older than his companions. Scrawny, with long, wispy grey hair sticking out from under his bowler hat like the hair of a scarecrow, he had several days' growth of silvery stubble and appeared to have no teeth, for his cheeks were sunken and his mouth rubbery.

Charles was somewhat taken aback by their

menacing attitude, his smile frpoze, but he kept it on his face as he tried to explain.

'I called out but no one answered. I've been sort of lost for two days and haven't eaten. But I haven't touched a thing, honest.'

'Honest is it? Are you hearin' it right, Seggy? And what would an honest man be doin' snoopin' around other peoples things?'

'I gave your dog some water,' Charles explained, hoping to appease them by his charitable act.

'An' meddlin' with the mongrel dog what is bein' taught a lesson for his thievin' ways,' the one called Clance added.

'Poor wee lamb's been lost,' the old man said in a thin voice. 'Lucky he found us then.'

'Thievin' limey prig should be taught a lesson same as the mongrel.'

'Now, Clance, you ought not to be callin' the thievin' gentleman such dirty names as that. You ought to be apologisin' to him.'

'Aye, with me boot.'

'Pretty wee lamb, isn't he then.'

'Fancy him do ya? You're a dirty old bugger, Seggy.'

The big man called Horry laughed, then

suddeny pushed the old man forward. 'Go get 'im then.'

Charles backed away, then turned to run, but his sore foot slowed him, and the three men pounced on him before he had gone more than a few paces. His arms were clamped to his sides as the big one caught him in a bear hug from behind and lifted him clear of the ground.

Charles kicked and wriggled ineffectually. 'What do you think you're doing? Put me down!'

'Now why would you be runnin' off so quick then, me poor lamb?' the man breathed over Charles's shoulder. 'Without even a toodeloo to your new friends.'

He spoke to his companions who were dancing around and looked to be on the verge of laying in with punches and kicks. 'Now hold on there, boyos. Fetch something to tie him up with... and Seggy, you pull his trousers down so he can't be runnin' off an' gettin' himself lost again.'

Frightened, Charles yelled as loud as he could in the desperate hope someone would hear. He struggled violently, but the grip around him remained as firm as if he were clamped in steel bands.

'Hurry with the rope, will ya? Poor lamb's gettin' tired with the waitin'...'

Two of them tied Charles's hands behind his back while the other pulled his trousers down around his ankles. They looped a rope around his neck and the big Irishman led him towards the tree, jerking on the rope.

'Come along, wee lamb. I'll tie you up with the mongrel so you'll not be gettin' lost again.'

Humiliated, Charles was forced to hop and shuffle to avoid being pulled over. The other two men laughed and jeered.

'Giddup, will ya?' The old man lifted Charles's shirt and gave him a stinging slap on his bared buttocks.

'Now don't be gettin' sparky with poor lamb just now, Seggy. We haven't et our dinner yet.'

The dog growled as he was being tied to the tree, and the big Irishman gave it a kick. 'Ungrateful mongrel. Is that the thanks you be givin' me for bringin' a nice friend to play with?'

They made Charles lie on the ground while they ate their food. He was offered a bowl of stew, then it was snatched away and given to the dog. Charles had lost his appetite anyway, but was happy to see the dog ignored the food, even though it looked half starved. It sat at the end of the rope with ears drooping, shivering spasmodically, and he guessed its life was not a pleasant one.

Charles remained silent, ignoring the jibes. He could see no future in trying to reason, and he did not want to antagonise them and give them the excuse of doing more than they had already. Their behaviour terrified him. Particularly that of the old man.

After the men had finished eating they talked quietly among themselves for a while, and Charles strained his ears to hear if what they were saying concerned his fate. He heard the word `safe' spoken once by the short man, and the other two immediately shut him up and glanced towards Charles. He pretended not to be paying attention.

Finally the big man came over and untied the rope from the tree. 'Come, wee lamb,' he said, leading Charles away. 'The mongrel don't like your company and nor do we. You can go get lost some more.' He paused, then added with a laugh. 'Soon as that dirty ole bugger is done havin' his fun.'

He suddenly jerked hard on the rope and, with his feet restricted by his lowered trousers, Charles fell face down on the ground. Before he could move, the other two pushed him flat, forcing his face and sore nose into the dirt. Pain, revulsion and despair took hold of Charles. He struggled and thrashed about.

'Why are you doing this?' he yelled. 'Leave me alone, you swines!'

'Keep the bastard still, Horry.'

Suddenly, Charles's ears were gripped viciously and he was head-butted from behind. Coloured lights flashed before his eyes, and waves of darkness began to wash over him. He was dimly aware of his shirt being pulled over his head, and faintly heard their voices.

'There, Seggy, you old bugger, he's all yours. But you won't be mindin' if we watch now, will ya?'

Timisani studied the shredded camel-thorn bush from several different angles, but was still unable to make any sense of it.

The Englishman's footprints circled the bush, and were scuffed and blurred, as if he had been dancing around it. But why, Timisani pondered, would he do such a strange thing? And why was the bush all broken, like he had jumped on it as well? No animal he knew of could break up a camel-thorn like that. No, it was certainly no animal, or he would have seen their spoor, so it must have been the man.

Timisani widened his area of search and found the dead branch with shreds of leaves and yellow flowers still clinging to it, and he nodded sagely to himself. The Englishman had obviously beaten the

113

bush with the stick, and there could be only one reason for doing that. Something had been hiding in the bush, and the man had tried to kill it. Maybe a tortoise or snake.

Timisani returned to the shredded camel-thorn but could find no snake or tortoise spoor. He did, however, notice something peculiar about the footprints leading away. They were much closer together than before, and one was fainter than the other, as if the man had been limping.

Timisani smiled in sudden enlightenment. Something… most likely a snake… had bitten the man on the foot and he had killed it in the bush. Then his frown returned. But where was the snake? Could he have taken it with him... maybe to eat?

Timisani removed his white cap and turned it over to mop the top of his sweating head. The man's behaviour was very puzzling. First he walked this way, then he walked that way, going almost in a circle before turning back, as if he were looking for something he had dropped on the way.

And Timisani could still not work out what had happened at the tree.

Footprints led up to it and then away from it again, but the prints approaching up were older than those leading away by many hours, and there was clear jackal spoor on top of the old footprints, but not on the new ones. It looked as if the Englishman had spent many hours, if not the whole night, in the tree, for that was the only time the jackal would have been wandering around. But why would he be in the tree? It had nothing edible in it, and they were far from lion country, so what other reason could there be to climb it?

Timisani replaced his cap and continued following the sign of the limping Englishman, the mystery nagging at him, then he shrugged it off. If he remembered he would ask the Boer's son, Jurie, about it when he saw him. Only a white man could understand the odd behaviour of another white man.

Timisani saw where his quarry had camped the night in the sandy hollow by the stream, and also that he was using a stick. The snake could not have been a poisonous one or he would be dead by now. Still, it must be a bad bite for him to be walking so slowly and stopping so often for water.

The tracks were now fresh, only a few hours old, and Timisani was happy to see they were going in the same direction as the wagons. They may even meet, for the wagons had left before dawn and would make good time with the lighter load, even though they were five oxen short, and he had wasted much time walking in circles after the Englishman.

When Timisani saw the Boer's wagons outspanning in a grove of trees within calling distance a short while later, he whistled to attract attention, then gave the hand signal of all fingers pointing down to show that he was following tracks.

Jurie and Quabe came quickly, and Timisani showed them proudly what he had deduced from the signs. He went into a lengthy explanation of the broken bush and the snake that disappeared, and they listened to him patiently with puzzled expressions, but when he began telling them about the mystery of the tree, the young Boer cut him short, then, much to Timisani's disgust, sent him to the wagons to carry on with the outspanning and watering of the animals.

Jurie and Quabe followed the tracks on the run. They had less than two hours of daylight remaining in which to find the Englishman and bring him back to the camp. Then they still had other work to do.

Quabe was happy to let the young Boer take the lead. He had never been able to master the Bushman art of tracking. Although he did not consider this a shortcoming. Jackals and hyenas followed spoor too. Zulus and lions simply waited for the right moment and pounced.

Nevertheless, he held a grudging admiration for the young Boer. He ran barefoot like a Zulu, and spoke the language like one. He was also big, with muscles that moved easily. It was told he had killed his first lion when the hair on his face was still like that of a woman, although Quabe found this hard to believe.

They heard the yelling from some distance away and stopped briefly to listen. Only one voice.

'It is the one we follow,' Quabe said, recognising the strange accent. 'Maybe he faces the lion.'

'No lions here,' Jurie answered, and charged ahead.

Their sudden arrival caught the men by surprise. For some moments no one moved as each side glared at the other, taking stock of the situation. Quabe had understood immediately what was about to happen, and was shocked. He did not think white men did such things. Zulus did it openly only to degrade a chief or important indunas they had defeated in battle, presuming, that is, the vanquished leaders were still alive and fully able to appreciate the indignity of being raped by the herd-boys.

It seemed the young Boer could not believe his eyes either.

'What's going on here?' he demanded.

'That is the one we look for,' Quabe explained,

pointing to the Englishman lying face down on the ground with his exposed buttocks in full view.

'What are you doing to him?' Jurie looked at the old man who was hastily replacing his braces.

'None of your business, Boer. This is our camp. Bugger off.'

Jurie strode forward and shoved the old man in the chest, sending him stumbling backwards. He collided with the big man behind, who was hunching his shoulders and raising his fists in preparation for attack. Jurie didn't give him a chance. Following up quickly, and while the man was still off balance, he punched him solidly on the nose. The blow made a dull but satisfying meaty sound.

The man's head snapped back and he dropped to his knees. He shook his head, splattering blood from his nose onto the dust.

Quabe grunted in satisfaction, as though he himself had landed the blow. He was pleased to see that the young Boer had the courage and acted quickly, but was a little surprised that he didn't immediately kick or find something to club the man with while he was still crouched on his hands and knees. Had he brought his axe he would have offered it.

'I said what's going on here?' Jurie repeated.

The old man and the short one only stared at

their fallen comrade with their mouths open.

Still invitingly on his hands and knees, the subject of their disbelief hawked and spat blood onto the ground, then he suddenly lunged forward, catching Jurie around the waist in a tackle. His charge propelled them both backwards through a jumble of blankets, pots and buckets. They fell in a tangle of limbs, clutching wildly at each other to get an advantage.

Ignoring Quabe, the other two men rushed to help their friend, and Quabe realised he would also have to lend a hand somehow or see the young Boer overpowered. He was reluctant to fight with white men. Not through fear, or the way they fought, for fighting was in his blood, but because they were white. Different rules applied. In this place he was only one of the wagon boys - a servant. It was simply the way it was. It had not always been that way, and one day it may change again, but that was the way it was right now. The white man was master - any white man. Even, sadly, white men like these, who would already have been jackal food had he been the one doing the fighting.

Compromising, Quabe moved to block the men with his arms, feinting from side to side as if he were protecting the open gate of a pen to prevent the goats from escaping. He smiled apologetically, using the few

English words he knew. 'Excuse, please.'

The two men stumbled to a halt. 'Out of the way, darkie.'

The old one tried to dodge around. Quabe caught him by the collar as he went past and stopped him with a jerk that lifted both the man's feet off the ground. Quabe spun him around and flung him back.

'Excuse, please.'

Quabe contemptuously brushed away a vicious kick from the one with red hair, then caught him around the waist with his left arm.

'Git off, kaffir! I'll kill ya!'

With a powerful heave, Quabe lifted him, cursing and kicking like an unruly child, and dumped him face down in the dirt. The cursing stopped abruptly as the wind was knocked from his body.

While the man was still gasping for breath, Quabe left him to collect the old man, catching him again by the collar as he turned to run. With the other hand, he took him by the seat of his baggy trousers and lifted him horizontally.

'We're goin' ter kill you, kaffir!' he screeched. 'We're goin' to kill the bejasus outa ya! Let me be... ya black heathen...!'

Quabe carried him back and dumped him on top of the other man, then he sat astride them both to watch the fight.

It was not going too well. Although the young Boer had the strength and the speed, he did not have the experience. It was taking all his skill to avoid the fingers, feet, teeth and head of his opponent.

Quabe had never seen white men fighting before, but he thought it was an experience he was going to enjoy. He had heard from others that they fought with their hands and feet, and not with clubs and spears the way men were supposed to fight - the way Zulus fought.

They rolled and tumbled through the camp in a welter of arms and legs, grunting and cursing between clenched teeth. They smashed through anything in the way, including the frame holding up the pot of stew. It collapsed into the fire, sending up a hissing cloud of steam and ash.

From his squirming perch Quabe waited for an opportunity to help, but the rolling bodies did not come within range. He was tempted to leave his two charges and put an end to it with the aid of a shovel he had noticed nearby, but curiosity held him back. He wanted to see how the Boer handled himself. A day may come when the information would be useful.

His attention was diverted briefly by the two men below, who began kicking and bucking violently in an effort to throw him off. Quabe reached out and picked up a solid-looking pot. After glancing around guiltily to be sure no one was watching, he struck both men on the head in quick succession. The iron pot made a hollow but satisfyingly firm sound, and the bucking stopped abruptly. After waiting a few moments with the pot raised in case it started up again, Quabe returned his attention to the fight.

If the Boer didn't do something soon he would be in danger of losing an ear, or even an eye. He had already had a finger bitten when he tried to employ some of the other man's tactics. Then, apparently in desperation, he attempted something else. Instead of trying to break away from the man, he went with him, both of them rolling and flopping along the ground, still clutching and pulling hair, and Quabe could not resist a knowing chuckle. He had seen Zulu women fighting in exactly the same fashion.

Then they rolled into a tree and stopped short.

'Now, I've got ya.' The fat man panted, shifting his body around to get leverage. 'Good as dead... Boer bastard...'

Exhausted, and with his back against the tree, Jurie was unable to move. It would soon be over. The man had him by the hair and was slowly pulling his head back while trying to bite him on the neck, snuffling and snorting as he apparently searched for something to clamp his teeth on, and the Boer's eyes bulged as he strained against the slow and relentless pulling.

Quabe was about to go to his aid when he noticed the dog. Tied to the tree it had been unable to move out of the way, and the rope had become caught up in the struggling bodies, pulling its head in close to them. Its lips were drawn back in a snarl, yet its whole body and head trembled, as if afraid. In rapid succession it alternated its snarling with whining, its ears first cocking, then drooping, giving it a curious flapping motion. Its eyes moved constantly from side to side, as if looking for a way out, but its head remained perfectly still - except for the trembling.

Whether driven by fear, instinct, or some spur of the moment urge, Quabe was not sure, but the dog suddenly darted its head forward and bit the fat man on the ear. It was so fast that Quabe was not even sure it had actually made contact until the man bellowed in pain and pushed away from the Boer. He stood up to clamp a hand to his ripped ear, and Jurie acted quickly. He rolled onto his hands and kicked out with both feet at the same time, like a mule, catching the man square in his belly, and sending him reeling backwards towards where Quabe was sitting astride his two captives.

Quabe grinned in anticipation as he raised the

pot with both hands.

'*Bekizwe!*' he roared, and brought the vessel down with such force on the man's head that, had the handle not snapped off, his skull would have split like a dropped melon.

'Hau!' Quabe exclaimed in satisfaction. 'Hau, Zulu!'

Still grinning, he left the three squirming but otherwise docile men and, while Jurie washed his bloodied face in a bucket of water and untied the dog – which immediately slunk away into the bush - Quabe went to attend to the Englishman.

He untied him then stood the dazed man on his feet while he hoisted up his trousers. When he looked as if he was going to fall again, Quabe lifted him onto his shoulder as he had done once before.

Without waiting for the young Boer, Quabe set off for the wagon with fierce, determined strides, well pleased with the way things had turned out.

'*Donderkop*!' Aneline Steyn sat on the ground and reproached herself in a quiet but most unladylike manner. 'Stupid bitch.'

She rubbed vigorously at her shoulder where the heel of the shotgun had bruised it. The two guinea fowl had been perched high in the tree, settling down to roost, and they had been almost directly above. She had been too quick with the second shot, forgetting, in her haste, to pull the butt firmly back into the shoulder, and the kick of the recoil had slammed her backwards, tumbling her over a bush and sitting her down hard on the ground.

She reloaded both barrels with birdshot before getting up, thumping the cartridges home angrily then slamming the breech shut. She jabbed on the safety catch then, rubbing at her rear and still muttering under her breath, went to examine the birds.

Both had been shot cleanly, with the heads taking most of the blast. Two from the one barrel, she surmised, for they had been close together. The second shot had been wasted. Somewhat appeased by her good marksmanship, she tied the legs together then set about adjusting her clothes, which had come adrift during the tumble over the bush.

She untied the cord holding up the oversize trousers, and tucked in the brown calico shirt, pleating the waistband of the pants in handfuls before replacing the cord and rolling the excess of material down.. She fastened the leather thongs above the knees that shortened the legs, and also stopped the squishing sound when she walked, then tested the result by stamping her feet and jumping up and down a few times.

Although acquired from Jurie's wardrobe some years previously, the trousers were still several sizes too large, but more practical in the bush than long dresses, which, although cooler, snagged on every bush, and allowed insects to fly up inside. One day, she promised herself, she would sit down with the sewing box and alter them properly.

Aneline slung the trussed birds over the barrel and set off jauntily towards the camp, humming one of her favourite Afrikaans folk songs. If she hurried, she would still have enough time after cleaning and roasting the birds to make her father's special desert of goat-milk tart.

Still humming, Aneline swung into camp and stopped short, the tune dying on her lips. The fire had not been lit as she had instructed, and the camp seemed deserted, although a pile of wood lay ready and the animals had been outspanned. She presumed they were still tending to them or had gone for a wash, but her father should know better than go walking around. She had told him to rest. Clicking her tongue in annoyance, she set about making the fire, stacking it high, so as to get plenty of coals for the roasting.

She was on her way to the wagon for some utensils when she saw the stranger lying asleep on her bed-roll, with his dirty head propped up by her own pillow.

Stifling a cry of alarm, Aneline ran back to the fire for the shotgun.

She approached the sleeping man cautiously with her finger ready on the trigger. The diamond field was not far away and had attracted a lot of rough characters. She was not about to take any chances.

She stopped a few feet away to study him. He seemed quite young, although it was hard to tell. He was unshaven, but not enough to make a beard, and his hair was tangled and greasy-looking. He had a blotchy face that was streaked with dirt and what looked like dry blood. His nose was red and swollen, and his clothes filthy. He looked like a drunken tramp, and Aneline felt a wave of revulsion and anger that he should choose her clean blankets and pillow to lie on.

'Mister... what are you doing here please?' she called out.

When she received no response she moved closer and prodded him on the leg with the barrel, stepping back quickly.

'Meneer? Wake up! You are not allowed here.'

A low growl answered her from the deep shade under the wagon, and Aneline started. She spun around, pointing the gun in the direction of the sound. 'Dammit!' What is going on here?'

She crouched to peer under the wagon. '*Voetsak* dog!' she ordered. 'Who do you think you are growling at?' She pushed the barrel forward threateningly. 'Get!' The dog whined softly and she could hear its tail thumping on the ground.

'Stupid dog.' She turned back to the stranger.

Aneline considered firing one of the barrels. That would be sure to wake him up. It may also alert the others. She raised the gun high, but before she could pull the trigger the stranger groaned. Hastily she lowered it again, pointing at his stomach. After some hesitation she moved it down lower. No point in killing him, she thought. If necessary, she would shoot him in the legs. She waited for the man to open his eyes, but he seemed to have gone back to sleep.

Becoming exasperated, Aneline looked towards the stream, hoping to see some sign of the others, but could see nothing. Not even a mule or an ox. She was on her own, and beginning to feel a trifle jittery. The feeling made her angry with herself. It also made her angry with the man who refused to wake up. Boldly she stepped forward and kicked him on the foot.

The response was startling. For a moment the man only stiffened, then suddenly his whole body seemed to go into convulsions. His legs jerked about as if they were trying to run on their own, and his body thrashed from side to side as if trying to follow. His eyes remained shut, but squeezed tight, and a long, high pitched squealing sound came from between his bared teeth.

Alarmed, Aneline moved back to a safe distance from the thrashing body.

The man took a long time to quieten down. The rolling and thrashing finally stopped, but then the squirming began, and then, after that stopped, he began rocking and gasping, as if he was about to be sick on her blanket.

Aneline watched and waited with increasing impatience. When the man finally stopped rocking she moved forward purposefully, the gun pointing straight at his chest. His eyes were open, but were bloodshot and glassy, and although he appeared to be looking at her, he seemed not to see either her or the gun.

'What are you doing here?' she demanded. 'On my bed.'

He continued staring with a stupid expression on his face and did not seem to have heard, then he groaned and lay back again on her pillow.

'Meneer! I am speaking to you. Are you drunk?'

When she still received no reply, Aneline shuffled forward cautiously and raised her foot for another kick. This time she would make it a good one.

But before she could land it the man jerked his foot away with a short cry and held it in both hands.

'Do not play games with me, sir,' Aneline warned, her voice menacing. 'I am a very good shot. Now you must go. This is not your camp, and that is my bed you are lying on. You have made a mistake.'

She moved back again as a precaution in case he made a grab for her when getting up. 'Go quickly, please, and take your stupid dog with you.'

Instead of getting up as she expected, he sat and looked at her, the dazed expression slowly being replaced by a frown, then he looked down and hid his face behind his hands.

'Meneer?' He must be drunker than she had thought.

He spoke from behind his hands. 'What am I doing here?'

'I beg yours?' Aneline was not sure if she had heard right.

'How did I get here?'

'You must be very drunk not to have remembered. Don't you know it is a sin to drink? And I do not care how you got here, I just want you to leave.'

'Who are you... where are they?'

'It is not your business who I am. Just take your dog and get!'

'What?'

Aneline's patience finally ran out. It was time he knew she meant business and that he should not try and be smart with her. She lowered the barrel in the direction of his feet and fired.

'Perhaps we should offer a reward,' the appraiser ventured timidly. Mister Hoffmann was not the sort of person who took advice easily. Especially when it involved spending money.

'Hmmph! Why should we pay to get our own diamonds back? That's why we have insurance.'

'Of course, you are quite right, Mister Hoffmann. 'It was only a thought.' The appraiser twisted distractedly at the chain of his watch. 'Do you think the insurance company will pay a reward? I mean, there is over twenty thousand pounds involved.'

'Hah! Some hope.'

The appraiser had run out of ideas. He pulled

out his watch and checked the time once more with a sigh. It had been a long day.

From early afternoon, the plush red carpet in the foyer of Hoffmann & Co. London, had suffered a continuous procession of official footwear, the like of which it was never designed to withstand.

First there had been the two officers from the fraud squad. Bowler-hatted and puffing from the climb up the stairs, they had congregated all the staff in the foyer and questioned them at length, chewing thoughtfully on their pencils and writing in their notebooks.

They were still at it when the representative of the Department of Customs and Excise arrived, gold buttons twinkling and with his cap tucked correctly under his left arm. He had examined the broken seals of the opened package carefully, and was barely able to suppress a smile when he saw the contents. He gave the officers of the Fraud Squad his details then left, promising to `look into the matter further.'

On his way out he held the door open for the agent of the Castle Shipping Line. The agent polished his glasses and, after peering through them at the package for a few seconds, remarked that, although the contents appeared to be suspicious, the seals looked authentic.

He produced a copy of the bond ledger and pointed to where the customs officer involved had duly signed for receipt of said package in good order and condition.

The office boy was hastily dispatched to recall the customs official so he could verify the signature and establish that the correct procedure had been adhered to.

They arrived back at the same time as the wife of the representative of Golden Globe Insurance. She swept through the foyer in a dazzle of mauve tweed and dropped a stack of forms on the bookkeeper's desk with a terse instruction that they were to be filled out in triplicate. She departed without looking at the package, leaving in her wake a strong smell of violets.

Late in the afternoon, the two officers of the fraud squad left. They returned an hour later to continue the investigation with a more relaxed and jovial approach to their questioning. They also brought with them a reporter and photographer from the *Clarion*, whom they had just happened to meet by coincidence as they were passing the Bell and Whistle.

The photographer arranged the package and its contents of glass beads, shells and pebbles artfully, giving them the 'spilled out' look, before photographing them.

Early in the evening the office staff were allowed to leave. They were followed soon after by the officers, yawning and squinting at their watches.

At the eleventh stroke of Big Ben, Mister Hoffmann also yawned and came to a decision. He would do nothing. The blasted insurance company could take care of everything. After all, he told his appraiser, that's what he paid his premiums for.

'Lucky she didn't blow his foot off,' Marthinus remarked, 'shooting from the hip like that. A bit higher and she could have got him in the bollocks.'

'Put some lead in his pencil, hey, Pa?'

'Can you see any pellets?'

'Only a few, just under the skin. She was close. The shot wouldn't have had time to spread.'

'After you dig them out you will have to cut around the thorn to remove the poison.'

Marthinus sat hunched over on a barrel with his arms folded across his injured chest, watching critically as Jurie probed at the Englishman's foot.

'Ja, I think you are right,' Jurie agreed. 'You can't even see it for all that yellow stuff.'

'Make two cuts, one on each side, and maybe one in the middle to make sure.'

'Better to get it all the first time. Remember Frik Joubert? That's why he lost his foot. Because they didn't get it all out the first time.'

'Should have been his head... get the razor, Jurie, and the strop. You need to get it good and sharp.'

Charles listened to the consultation over his foot with philosophical indifference. The traumas he had suffered over the past few days had immunised him against such minor assaults. A full stomach and tumbler of Cape Smoke had induced a pleasant state of euphoria. He endured the operation without complaint, although sweat popped out from his forehead and his teeth ached from the clenching of his jaw. He was determined not to disgrace himself further.

'I think I have it all,' Jurie commented finally.

'What about the thorn?'

'It will have to wait until morning when there is more light.'

'Pack some wet meal around and bind it to draw the poison,' Marthinus advised.

Another tot of brandy guaranteed Charles a good night of sleep.

In the clear light of morning his foot was propped up on a flour bag and examined again more carefully. It smelled strongly of carbolic soap.

'Not bad at all,' Jurie observed after removing the binding. 'See how the swelling has gone down? You can even see the end of the thorn.'

'Be careful not to break it,' Marthinus cautioned. His cracked ribs had prevented any direct involvement in the proceedings, but his advice had not been withheld. 'It is better to get down as far as you can and get it all at once.'

Despite his resolve of the previous evening, Charles could not help but flinch at each prick of the needle. With Jurie's right forefinger bandaged and swollen from the Irishman's bite, his clumsy probing was less than delicate.

'You must try to keep from moving,' he repeated for the fourth time. 'You are only making it worse.'

'Sorry,' Charles apologised shakily. He steeled himself as Jurie bent forward once more, but before he could begin, the girl suddenly appeared and pushed him aside.

'Men are such babies,' she said disdainfully, glancing at Charles without smiling. It seemed she had not yet forgiven any of them for allowing her to make a fool of herself. After spending a long time at the stream the previous evening, washing her blanket and pillow, she had silently directed them to the guinea fowl baking in their clay jackets and left them to it, sullenly ignoring Jurie's explanations and Charles's attempts to apologise.

Kneeling in Jurie's place, she ignored the needle he offered and gripped Charles's foot firmly in both hands. Spreading the wound apart with her thumbs, she examined it briefly, then lowered her head and probed for the tip of the thorn with her tongue.

Charles lifted up on his elbows to watch, fascinated – and pleasantly surprised. He had not realised how pretty she was. The baggy men's clothing of the night before had not entirely concealed the promise of a slim figure beneath, but the bush hat pulled down low had hidden her face and hair.

Now in the sunlight, wearing a dress, and with her blonde hair shining and tied at the sides with red ribbon, she looked stunningly attractive.

Charles felt no pain as she probed, only the smooth tickle of her tongue and the soft warmth of her breath. Compared to the clumsy digging of Jurie it was bliss, and he smiled as he let out an involuntary groan of relief and pleasure. Almost a giggle.

The tongue stopped its probing. Without lifting her head, she raised her eyes to flash a warning look. For long seconds she stared at him over the top of his toe without moving, daring him, and Charles froze.

He saw no friendliness in the look. It seemed as if she was staring right into him. Caught by the sun, flecks of gold flashed within the green depths of her eyes like goldfish in a pond.

Without warning she suddenly jerked her head back and the inch-long thorn was clamped between her teeth. Charles jumped, as much in surprise as pain, then lay unmoving as she wiped away the watery blood that had followed the thorn.

She removed it from between her teeth and examined it briefly before tossing it aside as if it was of no consequence.

'Ointment and clean bandage,' she declared to no one in particular. She stood quickly and, without giving Charles a chance to thank her, strode busily away.

Charles and the Steyns parted company at the Hope town junction later that day.

'Just stay on the track,' Jurie advised him. 'It is only a few miles to Pniel... on the river... you can't miss it.' He sounded dubious.

'Don't worry,' Charles reassured him. 'And thank you for your help, and... everything.'

Jurie laughed it off. 'It was nothing. I think the Zulu gave them a bit of a sore head. You had better watch out for them.'

Marthinus was sitting in the shade of the canopy where he had been ordered to rest, and Charles reached into the gloom to shake his hand.

'I hope your ribs are not too bad… and terribly sorry about the oxen. I really don't know…'

Marthinus shrugged. 'It was not a good time, but it is life. You are not to blame, meneer.' He smiled. 'I think you did all right for a *rooinek*.'

Charles was not sure if he was to take this as a compliment or not.

The girl and Timisani had gone ahead with the mule wagon so he did not get a chance to say goodbye to them.

Quabe was flustered when Charles offered his hand. It was not the custom. He shuffled uncomfortably, glancing around distractedly, then held his hand out limply and allowed it to be flopped about.

Charles moved his bag to the shade of a tree and watched as the wagon trundled up the road. There had been many times when he would have been glad to see it disappearing in the dust forever, but now he experienced the same hollow feeling he had when the ship arrived in Cape Town.

Marthinus and the two Africans had made a big impact on his life, making him aware of things about himself he had not realised were there. He would probably never understand their strange ways but, as men, he had come to admire them, and he felt a sense of frustration that he had lost the opportunity to prove he was not the complete idiot they obviously took him for. He wondered if he would ever see them again.

Charles lifted his bag and made his way along the track towards Pniel. He felt none of the expected excitement he thought he would feel at reaching the diamond fields. He felt strangely as if he should not be there at all.

He noticed the dog following him when he stopped for a rest. It also stopped, then sat in the road, looking at him.

Charles groaned. The last thing he needed was for the Irishmen to find him with their dog. He tried to discourage it.

'Shoo, dog!'

It remained where it was, head, tail and ears drooping.

'Come here then,' Charles repented, slapping at his knee in invitation. The dog sank lower and swept the dust with his tail.

'Have it your way then,' he told it, and walked on. More important things had to be considered. He had a little under four pounds left and no idea how long it would last. If he didn't find a diamond within the first week he would be in trouble.

'A little to the left... and down a bit,' Fleetwood directed the two men balancing precariously on the stack of barrels. They struggled to move the sign into position. It was made of solid stinkwood - the side of a wagon that had not survived the journey from Cape Town.

'No... perhaps a little more on the right,' Fleetwood corrected. 'Hold it there.'

He sauntered across the road to stand in the doorway of Frankie's barbershop, from where he could get a better view.

'Splendid! Fix it there.'

As the men nailed the sign in position, Fleetwood admired it with pride. It was the first time he had ever felt the need to advertise.

TUCKER & Co.

Diamond dealers and safe depository.

Est.1831 (Eng.)

Painted in red lettering on the varnished background, it invoked just the right amount of distinction and stability one would expect of an important company. That the establishment date was his birth date, could hardly be construed as untruthful.

He particularly liked the gold curlicue bordering, which added a touch of elegance and style. It was by far the most impressive sign in Pniel.

'Open for business today, Mister Tucker?' the barber called from inside his shop.

'As soon as I have paid the men and you have trimmed my whiskers, Mister Franks.'

'It will be a pleasure, sir. I have a new line of pomade just in from France that I'm keeping especially for discerning gentlemen such as yourself.'

'Excellent! Brilliantine can be a trifle bothersome with all this dust about.'

Fleetwood went to pay his men, then returned to amuse himself by reading the magazines while Frankie attended to another customer.

Nobody minded waiting at Frankie's. The longer the better, in fact. It was not every day that one could call in to have a haircut or shave, and Frankie had the largest collection of dirty magazines anyone had seen. Collected from around the world during his previous occupation as a ship's bosun, the magazines contributed more to the success of his business than his uncertain talent with scissors and razor. He was constantly being offered considerable sums of money for the collection, and had been forced to erect a small sign of his own declaring they were not for sale.

'Money can't buy the pleasure they give to my esteemed customers,' he told Fleetwood as he tied the cape around his neck. 'Works of art they are, same as your lovely waistcoat, Mister Tucker. Quite stylish if I may say so.'

'Yes, quite,' Fleetwood replied, not keen to dwell on the subject.

'By the way, sir, excuse my ignorance, but what exactly *is* a safe depository?'

'Well, Mister Franks... may I call you Frankie?'

'Please do, sir. Everyone does.'

'You see, Frankie, it's a place where you deposit your valuables for safe-keeping in return for a very small commission... mere pennies really.'

'You mean like a bank?'

'Good God no!' Fleetwood snorted with laughter. 'Banks are far too risky. Haven't you heard how many have had their safes stolen lately?'

'I believe I have, sir.'

'It's where I got the idea from,' Fleetwood explained. 'What we need here is a safe that is impossible to steal. I have one coming from Germany. A Braun. Best in the world, they say, and so large and heavy it needs an eighteen-span ox-wagon all of its own. That ought to solve the problem. Should be here in a few weeks. I think our hard-working diggers deserve some sleep at night, don't you?'

'Indeed I do, sir, and very thoughtful it is of you to think of them. Why, I myself have been robbed twice in the last month, even though I sleep in the back of the shop.'

'There you are then. Perhaps you should make use of my depository when it arrives. No charge to you, of course, Frankie... except maybe the odd free haircut.' He winked at Frankie in the mirror. 'Us businessmen should stick together.'

'Unfortunately I don't have many valuables, Mister Tucker. Leastwise nothing you would want to put in a safe. Certainly no diamonds. Barely make enough here to keep myself alive. Although...' Frankie's voice took on a menacing tone, '...a few of my magazines have gone missing, and when I find out who has taken them....' He held the razor to his throat and made a slicing motion. 'It will be goodbye Mister Thief.'

'And a jolly good show too,' Fleetwood applauded half-heartedly.

'It's only a matter of time before I find out,' Frankie continued. 'I do hear things you know, sir.

Amazing what you learn in this business.'

'Oh...?' Fleetwood raised an eyebrow at himself in the mirror. 'Like what?'

'Well, sir, it would be most unprofessional of me to repeat confidences, you understand, but I have heard a thing or two about these so-called kopje-wallopers. Quite illegal they are, as you know... care for a splash of bay rum, sir?'

'Thank you... what things?'

'It seems the latest trick is encouraging the blacks to steal diamonds from their masters, then paying them a pittance for the gems. They know the blacks won't say anything for fear of being flogged.'

'Really?'

'A poor show, if you ask me, sir. It's the buyers who should be flogged. It's about time we had a police force here.'

'Oh, I don't think we have to go to that extreme.' Fleetwood was quick to squash the idea. The law may have its place, but for the moment he would rather that place was somewhere else.

While Frankie applied the bay rum, Fleetwood thought about the package. No doubt the police would soon be sniffing along behind the red herring, and if the young fool carrying it was to find him here and squeal, the game would be up.

'Can I talk to you man to man, Frankie?'

'Certainly you can, sir.'

'Well, there's a certain er... shall we say... husband? Brutish, insensitive swine by all accounts... Anyway, I have reason to believe he is on his way here to er...meet with me, if you know what I mean.'

'Ah! Say no more, sir, been in the same predicament myself. It's why I went to sea. If you point him out to me I shall tell him you have left. Or would you prefer I told him you were dead, sir?'

'Oh, no.' Fleetwood gave a slight shudder. 'Nothing like that. He doesn't know my name, only what I look like. I think it would be wise to change my appearance.'

'Hmm... ' Frankie studied Fleetwood's reflection in the mirror. 'Well, let's see now....'

'The moustache, Frankie?'

'Oh dear, surely not that, sir. It's so...splendid.'

Fleetwood sighed. 'Yes, but I'm afraid it must go, it's too distinctive.... and the hair, can you make it look... well, sort of more... businesslike?'

When Frankie produced his scissors and took the waxed tip of one of the moustaches delicately between finger and thumb, he paused to give Fleetwood a sympathetic frown in the mirror. 'Best to close your eyes, sir,' he advised gently. 'You won't want to watch this.'

The rumours had been wrong. Charles had suspected it the moment he saw the seemingly endless sprawl of tents and piles of rock from the brow of the hill above Pniel. His suspicions were confirmed later by the bartender at Jardine's hotel, who was also, Charles had discovered with relief, the unofficial postmaster.

'If they were lying on the top, my friend, I'd be out there picking 'em up myself instead of slopping drinks and licking stamps. What was that name again?'

'Sylvester.'

'Can't say I've met the gentleman. Should remember a name like that. Mind you, I get a lot of folk come in here. You can leave the package if you wish, I'll send it to Hope Town in the bag. Two pence should cover it, thank you.'

Having fulfilled his obligation, Charles limped without direction around the village wondering what to do next. The single dusty street was busy with mule carts and ox-wagons coming and going, and many more people than he had expected. Nearly all were men, and all seemed to have a purpose. The buildings were ramshackle affairs of wood and iron, and supported a surprising variety of businesses.

Charles stopped at a store where a large pile of implements and tools were being off-loaded from a wagon. If he had to dig for diamonds, he would need something to dig with.

'We have these kits already made up for new chums,' the storekeeper informed him. 'Three pounds two shillings excluding the cradle. That's an extra three pounds.'

Charles came out feeling more despondent than ever. He was going to need a lot more money than he had.

He walked to the edge of the village to look at the famous Vaal River. It was wide - at least two hundred yards wide - and was bordered by thick vegetation and tall trees that looked out of place in the otherwise barren and rocky landscape.

He counted at least a hundred tents spread out on one side alone, and there must have been close to the same amount on the other side, if not more. Some were set amongst the trees, but most were out in the open, standing guard beside piles of gravel and rocks. Two ferryboats moved between the banks, and a steady stream of men walked the paths to the landings.

It was not at all what he had thought it would be. Some of the claims were large, with several tents and heavy machinery, and looked as though they had been established there for quite some time.

How could he have been so gullible, Charles wondered, as to think the diamonds would be lying on the ground waiting to be picked up?

He sat morosely on the rock trying to make some sort of plan, but his mind stubbornly refused to cooperate, preferring instead to dwell on the happenings of the past few months, especially the long wagon trek.

Not only had he been gullible, he had also been weak and stupid. Had it not been for the competence of the Boer and his two Africans, he would not have survived. It was no wonder they had treated him with such reserve. He had been nothing but a dangerous liability and he was lucky they hadn't dumped him after the first week.

Even the girl had treated him with disdain. She must have been told what had happened, or nearly happened, in the Irishmen's camp and, being a woman, had been embarrassed for him. He not only owed them his life for saving him from the baboons, but also his self respect and dignity, and in return he had caused an accident with the wagon and killed five precious oxen.

He could never hope to repay them. He had not even thanked them properly. Perhaps that was what the Boer was getting at when he told him he had done all right for a *rooinek*. What he *really* meant was that he didn't expect anything better from an Englishman.

Rebelling against his depression, Charles went back into the village and paid two shillings for the luxury of a roast beef dinner and a bed for the night at the hotel. The bed was simply one of a line of straw mattresses laid out on the floor under a flimsy lean-to at the back of the hotel, but it was the first he had been on since leaving England.

He lay on it, unable to sleep, listening to the sounds of revelry coming from the bar. When he could stand it no longer, he went through and, for the first time in his life, got thoroughly drunk.

Fleetwood was dubious. 'And you are certain it will look exactly like metal?'

'Please, do not worry, Mister Tucker,' Hans Struben replied patiently. It was the third time in the last half-hour he had been forced to reassure the gentleman. 'The new technique is excellent. You see, when the second coat of lacquer is almost dry, we take a fine....'

'Yes, yes, you told me all that,' Fleetwood

interrupted. 'What about the lock and the brass label, have you found them yet?'

Herr Struben shrugged in apology. 'I have only been able to find one Braun safe, and it is already in use. The owner says you can buy it for twelve pounds.'

'Twelve pounds!' Fleetwood was aghast. 'That's robbery. Are you sure there is nothing cheaper?'

Hans Struben shook his head. 'Nothing. Of course, we may be able to get one cheaper in Cape Town, if you care to...'

'No. It will take much too long. I suppose I have no option. Seems a pity though to ruin a good safe for only the handle and label. Will you be able to remove them without causing damage to the safe? Maybe we can replace the lock with a cheaper one.'

'My friend is a blacksmith. He says he can do it quite easily.'

'Good. And it will be ready in about two weeks you say?'

'Ja, as you can see, it is almost finished. There is only the back and the final coating to be done.'

Fleetwood had to admit it looked impressive. It stood six feet high and three feet across, and the wood was as smooth as glass. When painted as Hans Struben promised, and fitted with the solid brass handle and plaque, it should pass as the real thing to anything but the closest and most suspicious scrutiny, and Fleetwood was not going to allow anyone that close to it anyway.

His confidence in Herr Struben's ability to produce the goods was not restricted to hearsay alone. Besides being the most sought after coach builder in the district, the converted stable was filled with fine examples of his work, from gleaming buggies to a full blown barouche, complete with crest on the doors and crimson and yellow lines on the wheel spokes. It was rumoured that his presence in an agricultural backwater such as Hope Town was due to his romantic involvement with the wife of a Prussian count while demonstrating a new carriage, but Fleetwood held no stock in the rumour. Hans Struben was far too common a man to have become involved with a countess.

'You will have to keep it under cover from now on, Struben. We can't take the chance of someone finding out it is only a dummy. If word gets about the scoundrels will simply carry it off like they have all the others.'

'Don't worry, I will keep it hidden under blankets.'

'And I suppose I can trust you to keep our business a secret as well?'

'Mister Tucker, please! I am an honourable man. I would never...'

Fleetwood held up a placating hand. 'My apologies, Hansie. I did not mean to offend you. I'm only concerned for the welfare of the diggers, as you know. Do you think you can put some curly bits on like you have there?' He indicated the barouche doors. 'Say in red?'

'Gold is more traditional for a safe,' Hans Struben countered, a little huffily.

'Gold then,' Fleetwood agreed. 'But nice and curly, if you wouldn't mind.'

Charles spent his first month at the diggings discovering how little he knew. Driven by a subdued and sullen anger at himself, he stubbornly resisted the temptation to start digging until he knew what he was doing. He went from claim to claim, asking questions and, if not treated with suspicion after volunteering to work for only food and sent packing, learned the different operating methods, what sort of ground was most likely to yield diamonds, what diamonds really looked like, and how to tell if they were real. He also learned that they were not that easy to find.

It had become tradition that when a stone was

discovered, the lucky digger fired his gun in the air, then retired to one of the canteens with his friends to celebrate. It was an encouraging signal that served as great incentive for those still searching, but always initiated for Charles another battle with his resolve to learn before leaping. On a few occasions he was invited to join in the celebrating, but he resisted that temptation too, the memories of his first and, as far as he was concerned, his last hangover, still lingering.

He kept a wary eye out for the three Irishmen in his wanderings, but fortunately saw no sign of them. The dog, however, followed him everywhere, stopping when he stopped, lying in whatever shade was available nearby until he moved off again. Charles rather enjoyed its strange companionship, and fed it when he could, although the dog seemed more than capable of looking after himself, which he discovered one day as he was passing a claim. A man had removed a loaf of bread from a pot and placed it on a table to cool. As he turned to replace the pot, the dog appeared from behind the tent and, in a lightning-quick dash, removed the bread and disappeared back behind the tent.

Charles was still gaping in astonishment when the man turned to discover the bread missing. He stared at the empty space for a while, scratching his head in puzzlement, then he looked under the table and all around it. He checked in the pot in case he had forgotten to remove it, and even looked up in the air, perhaps in the expectation of seeing it being carried away by a crow. Arms akimbo, he glared accusingly at Charles, who was standing some distance away, hastily pretending to be tying his bootlace.

Charles didn't see the dog for the rest of the day, but it was back the next morning, following behind, and looking well satisfied.

By the end of the month, with judicious rationing of his remaining funds, Charles had acquired two second-hand buckets, a three-legged pot, and all the digging tools he needed. By being at the right place at the right time, he was also given a leaky tent by a disillusioned digger who was leaving.

He also adopted an abandoned mule that he found wandering along the river near where he had made his camp. He was unable to discover who owned it, but soon guessed the reason it had been abandoned. It was half blind, and also the most stubborn animal he had ever encountered. He named it One-way.

All he needed to become fully operational was the essential cradle for washing and sifting, and enough supplies to keep him going for at least another month. Applying the knowledge gained from his meandering should, he believed, net him at least one diamond in that time - presuming he chose the right spot and officialdom didn't begin charging for claims as they were threatening to do.

'Three shillings and one meal a day,' the owner of one of the larger claims answered in response to a query from the group gathered around the 'men wanted' sign. 'Take it or leave it.'

The men expressed their opinion with groans and some derisive laughter.

'I pay my blacks more than that,' one of them complained.

'Like I said, take it or leave it.'

'I'll take it,' Charles said. He was in no position to be choosy. 'What do I have to do?'

'See the sorter over there. He'll get you started.'

Charles made his way through the piles of gravel and rocks to where a man was standing over a sorting table. He looked up as Charles approached. 'New chum?'

'I've been here a while.'

'You'll have seen how it works then. Turn about on the cradle and haulin' the buckets. Will you be needing something to eat?'

'Wouldn't mind,' Charles replied, seeing no

reason to refuse a free meal.

'Help yourself from the pot then. As well to start on a full belly. When you've finished you can fetch two buckets and join the line.'

The work was hard and tedious. The buckets were filled with the diamontiferous gravel being dug from a large hole by a group of five Africans. It was then carried down to the water's edge where it was placed in the cradles and washed. The screened residue was then carried back up the bank to the sorting table.

Compared to hauling the heavy buckets of gravel up and down the bank, working the cradle was a pleasure. Charles was able to stand knee-deep in the cool water and duck his head under whenever the relentless sun and heat became intolerable, which was most of the time.

The cradle stood on legs close above the water. When the gravel was dumped in the top and a bucket of water thrown on, it was shaken vigorously by means of a long handle to sift the material through a series of three wire sieves of different size mesh . Once the washing was completed the bottom tray was removed for sorting and the remainder tipped into the river.

As Charles had discovered the day he arrived, cradles were the most expensive item of a digger's basic equipment, and perhaps the most necessary. It was going to take a few weeks at the measly rate of three shillings a day for him to get the one he wanted. It was the best available, made from heavy, water-resistant hardwood, and with a riffle tray that many others lacked. The old digger he had seen using one had been keen to recommend it.

'Even small diamonds are worth money,' he had told Charles, 'so why chuck them away? Comes to pieces easily too for carrying. Worth every penny, I say.'

The sorter drove everyone hard. Work started at daybreak after mugs of coffee sweetened with condensed milk, and ended at sunset with the same. The men were allowed a two-hour break during the heat of the day, when food was supplied - the inevitable stew.

As soon as he had eaten, the sorter usually returned to his table, and the hired men rested in the shade, gathering strength for the gruelling afternoon ahead, when the heat was at its worst.

Thinking he may be able to pick up a few extra tips, Charles asked the foreman during his break if he could help with the sorting. He was also curious to know how many diamonds were being found. No wild yells or gunfire had come from the claim, yet they must be finding something, or why else would extra labour be hired?

The sorter was reluctant. 'No offence, but I can't take the chance,' he responded to Charles's offer. 'Not that I don't trust you mind, but they're too easy to miss if you don't know what to look for. See that?' He removed a small, almost transparent pebble from the tray and held it up to the sunlight. 'Worthless crystal, though many a false hope has been raised by their looks.' He tossed it contemptuously aside.

'I heard you can tell if it's real by hitting it with a hammer,' Charles ventured.

The sorter laughed. 'Aye, heard that same one myself, but never been foolish enough to try. If I had all the diamonds that have been shattered that way I'd be a rich man. No, take it from me, lad, the only thing it proves is that there is a fool on the other end of the hammer.'

'How do you tell then?' Charles persisted. He had also been sceptical about the hammer theory.

'By the way it's formed if you know what to look for, and by the scratch test if you don't.'

'Can you show me?'

'Course I will...' the foreman replied, smiling secretively, '...if I ever find one.'

Charles never did get to see if any were found, but he knew they were there. A piece of broken glass at the end of the sorting table was almost opaque with the number of scratch marks marring its surface. He returned to work with renewed vitality.

It was after the lunch break on the fourth day that the owner of the claim reappeared. He rode into the section on a lathered grey horse and dismounted near the sorting table.

With a swarthy complexion and small goatee beard, he looked more like a Spanish grandee than an Englishman, and the white shirt and jodhpurs, tall polished riding boots, and silver spurs added weight to the comparison.

He talked with the sorter for a while, then sauntered around the claim, stepping carefully, and idly twirling a plaited leather *sjambok* looped to his wrist, as if overseeing the slaves on his plantation. He was obviously not one to get his hands dirty.

Charles was standing in the water, rocking the cradle, when a commotion started at the top of the claim where the Africans were digging. He looked up and saw one of them slithering down the bank towards him, yelping and covering his head. Close behind followed the owner, slashing at the man's naked back with the *sjambok*.

Charles heard the vicious whistle and fleshy smack as it connected, and stared in bewilderment as the black stumbled past him and flung himself into the river. The owner took one last swipe, which missed the African, but almost struck Charles. Ignoring him, and offering no apology, the claim owner stopped at the edge of the water.

'Thieving black swine!' he shouted after the man. 'I hope you drown!'

After ducking away from the whistling *sjambok,* Charles turned to look, expecting to see the man swimming across the river, but saw instead two wildly thrashing arms only a few yards away in the deeper water. The man's head was already submerged. Charles jumped forward into the deeper water and grabbed one of the arms. He towed the spluttering African back to the bank.

'Pass the black swine here,' the man ordered. 'I haven't finished with him yet. When I have, by God, he'll never steal again.'

Charles released his charge in the shallows. Flicking water from his eyes, he looked up at the man on the bank who was leaning forward with hand outstretched.

'What?'

'I said pass him here.' He clicked his fingers impatiently.

Charles could feel the African cowering close

behind him, still gulping for breath. He had no intention of handing him over

'I think you should cool down a bit, sir. He almost drowned. I think he's had enough.'

'I did not ask for your stupid opinion, you lout. Pass the kaffir here immediately.'

Charles became aware that everyone had stopped work and was watching with interest. But even had they not been, he was not going to be spoken to like that. Not any more.

He felt the anger build inside him and, almost without realising it, found himself wading the few steps through the water towards the bank. He glared up at the swarthy face, made even darker by anger, and he noticed a flicker of uncertainty crossed the man's eyes. Charles's confidence blossomed.

'I don't believe you have the right …' Charles began, then saw the *sjambok* lift to strike him. He snatched up an empty bucket from the bank and threw it and, bending forward at the waist in a reflex action to avoid the missile directed at his middle, the owner lost the power and direction of his swing. The *sjambok* landed weakly on Charles's shoulder, but even that light blow was enough to draw a sharp breath at the sting in its tail. Brushing it angrily aside, Charles suddenly found the snake-like end of the *sjambok* conveniently in his hand - at the same instant as the muddy bucket struck the man in the centre of his white shirt. With his arm still outstretched, teetering on the edge, and with his hand securely attached to the loop in the handle, the owner could offer no resistance when Charles jerked on the *sjambok* and pulled him head first into the river.

With a strangled cry the terrified African took the opportunity to scramble up the bank and run.

Charles stood and waited, determined to finish it if necessary, but the owner was floundering around after his hat and obviously had no intention of taking Charles on.

'I told him he needed to cool down,' Charles said out loud for the benefit of the onlookers, and was pleased to hear their laughter.

'Serves the bugger right,' someone said, and Charles grinned with relief.

He climbed the bank and went directly to the sorter.

'Four days it is,' he told him. 'That makes it twelve shillings, and I'll have it now if you please.' It wasn't quite four days, but he thought he had earned it.

The foreman did not argue. Looking uncomfortable, he went into the tent behind and returned with the money. 'No hard feelings, lad,' he said, handing it over.

'And none for you, sir,' Charles replied. 'But the owner needs to keep out of my way.' He felt good. Then, curious, he asked, 'How did the black manage to steal a diamond anyway?'

The sorter was surprised. 'Who said he stole a diamond?'

'He didn't? What did he steal then?'

'Boots,' the sorter answered, shaking his head in disbelief. 'An expensive pair of English riding boots. Now what would an ignorant savage be wanting with *them*, do you suppose?'

Later that evening, Charles was sitting by his camp-fire, reflecting again on the satisfying events of the day to compensate for his money worries, when the dog growled and he looked up to see the African he had saved standing at the edge of the light.

Startled, Charles moved his hand closer to a hefty piece of wood in the fire, not prepared to take any chances. The African came forward hesitantly, in a half crouch with his hands held out in front, looking almost as if he were creeping up on something with the intention of taking it by the throat, and Charles lifted the burning log from the fire and stood up. The black stopped and squatted down on his haunches; less threatening, but he continued to hold his hands out in front, one atop the other, thrusting them forward with palms uppermost, offering something.

More puzzled than concerned now, Charles moved towards him, holding the burning log aloft to spread its flickering light. He noticed the raw cuts and heavy welts on the African's shoulders and, lowering his eyes, looked to see what what the man offered in his open palm. At first he thought it was empty, then, catching the light, the tiny object he held gave a small, but brilliant, flash in return.

The African prodded himself in the chest with his finger. 'Mbalifu! Mbalifu!'

'Bally fool? I suppose some digger called you that, hey?'

The wide smile and vigorous nodding confirmed yet again that the fellow couldn't understand a word, and Charles gave up. Not that names – or any words, for that matter - were really needed. The slightest gesture on his part seemed more than adequate. The man hovered at his heels like a shadow, embarrassingly eager to help, and more than once Charles found himself having to execute a nimble side-step to avoid collision.

Bent on escape, Charles gathered the dirty plates from the previous evening and made a move towards the river, but it was not to be allowed. Frowning with apparent disapproval, his new helper all but snatched the utensils from his grasp and scurried away to wash them himself. On his return he propped the clean items carefully amongst the twigs of a bush to dry, all the while talking to them, in what sounded to a bemused Charles, like the gently admonishing tone of a mother with freshly bathed children. Ordering them to sit still and behave themselves until his return. When the tin plates were arranged to his satisfaction and it appeared they would obey, he looked around eagerly for something else to do.

It soon began to dawn on Charles that he had a problem. He had a stolen diamond in his pocket - which the African had insisted he take - and a mad thief who seemed determined to become his slave, and he had no idea what to do with either of them.

He had considered returning the diamond to the sorter at the claim he had recently departed, but could not be certain it had come from there, and even if it had, he did not want to put the fellow in jeopardy of another flogging.

How the diamond had come into the man's possession in the first place was a mystery to Charles.

No blacks had been allowed near the sorting table, so it could only have been found while digging in the gravel at the bottom of the hole, although that also seemed unlikely. Before being washed, every stone was coated with sticky clay and indistinguishable from the myriad pebbles. Still, it was the only explanation he could think of.

Finally, Charles decided the only thing he could do was to sell the gem to the first kopje-walloper that came along. No one could know the diamond was stolen, and if it did belong to the dandy in white, the swine deserved to pay for his arrogance anyway.

Charles sold it for twenty pounds - which he thought was probably only a quarter of its worth - then he spent a few pleasant hours shopping; revelling in the unique experience of having more money in his pocket than he needed.

Besides some new clothes and enough provisions for a month, he bought the cradle, some ointment for his new servant's back – which also helped to salve his conscience - another tent and more blankets, for the nights were surprisingly chilly close to the river. On impulse, he also bought a second-hand shotgun, and pondered over what type of ammunition he needed.

'Hunting or protection?' The storekeeper asked.

'Hunting, I think,' Charles replied, unwilling to admit he had never fired a gun before. 'That is, if there is anything worth shooting,'

'Nothing hereabouts,' the storekeeper shook his head. 'All shot out long ago. Gong Gong is the place to go. Quite a ways down the river, mind. Twenty miles or so, but a lovely spot once you get there. Good fishing too. Not many diamonds though, which is a blessing, I suppose, or it would soon be spoiled as well. Birdshot or buckshot?'

'Not sure…'

'Birdshot will be more useful, I'd say. And you'll be needing a cleaning kit to go with it.'

Overloaded with equipment, Charles hired two passing Africans to help carry it back to his camp.

As soon as he saw them approaching, his eager slave rushed to relieve the two strangers of their bundles, and a loud argument ensued that threatened to escalate into tribal warfare until Charles intervened with an extra sixpence apiece.

He changed into his new clothes. Tough khaki trousers with a broad leather belt and sheath-knife, light tan shirt and, to top and bottom them off, a new wide-brimmed bush hat and pair of *veldskoen,* bush shoes, made by a local Boer.

After applying the ointment - which treatment

was received with suspicion but not the slightest flinch - he gave the stunned African his old clothes, along with a pound note as his share of the spoils. Any more, Charles reasoned, would only encourage more theft and, as it was obvious the fellow had no intention of leaving, it was better to take no chances.

When the handclapping and obsequious grovelling had ended, Charles tried once more.

'Bally fool, hey?'

Enthusiastic nodding and an amiable grin was his answer.

'I don't think so, somehow,' Charles murmured. ' Fancy a trip to Gong Gong, Bally?'

Fleetwood orchestrated the arrival of his safe into Pniel with all the flamboyant flair of a circus ringmaster introducing a prize act. He wanted to provide the maximum amount of entertainment for the diggers, and thereby gain the most publicity for his new venture.

After considerable thought, he chose late on a Sunday morning as the most promising time. The impromptu church services would be over, the washing of clothes, repairing of tents and equipment completed, and the consumption of alcohol well enough advanced to ensure a jovial reception.

He decided a river crossing at the drift below the ferry would be ideal. It was a favourite place on Sundays for swimming and lounging in the shade of the tall trees, so he would be guaranteed an audience.

The wooden safe - filled with bags of sand to increase its weight - was loaded on the empty wagon late at night in the secure confines of Hans Struben's shed and covered with blankets under a canvas sheet to conceal its identity and protect the delicate paintwork.

At dawn, the full team of eighteen oxen Fleetwood had requested were inspanned by the owner, a Meneer Du Plooy and his wagon boy, then taken through the Hope Town drift, and down the river-track towards Pniel, where they had been instructed to wait out of sight near the landing.

Meneer Du Plooy was more than happy with the arrangement. He was getting paid double what he had expected, and the wagon was so light that even four oxen could have pulled it easily. Nevertheless, the agreement was for a full team and he had received his money in advance, so he had not complained.

He did complain however, when he arrived at the agreed meeting-place and beheld the assemblage that awaited him.

'What for are all the blacks here, meneer?' he enquired suspiciously of Fleetwood. 'Are they drunk?'

'Only to the limited extent of a shared bottle of Cape Smoke, Dupey, old chap,' Fleetwood replied lightly, waving his cigar in expansive dismissal. 'Have to set the stage, so to speak. Care for a drop?' He wiped the top of an open bottle of champagne on his sleeve and held it out.

Meneer Du Plooy eyed the bottle with disfavour. 'No, sir. It is a sin to drink on a Sunday.'

'Forgive us our sins, Dupey.' Fleetwood was in too good a mood to be offended. 'Today is a special occasion.' He offered the bottle to the short, bandy-legged man beside him. 'Time to whet the whistle, Scotty, afore we hit the high road.'

The Scotsman also viewed the bottle with disdain. He produced a bottle of whisky from a bag at his feet and took a healthy swig, grimacing with appreciation, before replacing it carefully in the bag and withdrawing a garment patterned in a glorious mix of fiery red and midnight blue. With aloof indifference to the stares and sudden hush that had fallen upon the onlookers, he removed his trousers and put on the kilt.

Some speculative nudging and whispering passed through the group of Africans as he fixed the sporran in place, but when he stuffed the discarded trousers into the bag and took from it what appeared to be a curiously deformed, headless goat of unusual colour, the assembly became still and silent. In breathless expectancy they gaped as he tucked the strange animal under his arm and adjusted the legs. When he placed one of the feet in his mouth and gave the stomach a tentative squeeze, and it made the plaintive bleating and wheezing sounds of a goat having its throat cut, they fell back with gasps and exclamations of astonishment - almost of fear.

One of the group, a wizened old man with his already jaded vision further impaired by Cape Smoke, was the first to intrude on the stunned silence. Holding a polite hand over his mouth, he stifled a giggle, then immediately coughed to cover the slip.

In ones and twos, like the tentative warming-up of an orchestra, there came from the group a series of strained whines, suppressed groans, thin squeals and nasal honkings that built rapidly into a prolonged caterwauling.

When it became too much to hold in, it exploded into snorts, howls, and screeches that caused the Africans to fall and stagger about helplessly.

Some ran doubled over to the nearest bushes, where they could release their pent-up mirth freely. They clung to trees and each other for support against the weakening effects of their hysteria and, when sufficiently composed to stumble back, it was only to start the whole process again as soon as they saw the convulsed antics of their comrades.

'Bloody heathens!' the Scotsman swore, his bushy eyebrows fixed in a fierce scowl. 'They dinna ken.'

'Not in a thousand years, Scotty, m'boy,' Fleetwood agreed. 'Not even sure I do myself.'

Meneer Du Plooy refused to go any farther.

'I have a reputation to keep,' he stated with finality. 'I cannot be seen with drunken blacks and such on the Lord's day.'

Not even more money would change his mind. When Fleetwood reminded him he had already been paid, and that going back on his word was also a sin, he reluctantly agreed the wagon boy could take charge of the crossing, then strode stiffly back the way he had come.

Promptly at eleven, to the accompaniment of whistling, whip cracking, and the uncertain strains of Scotland the Brave, the wagon skidded down the embankment and splashed into the drift.

Resplendent in white drills, top hat and lilac waistcoat, Fleetwood stood precariously atop the safe and, with an ivory-headed cane, conducted Scotty through his limited repertoire of stirring marches.

The accompanying retinue, still suffering from sporadic bouts of contagious hysteria, and spurred on by the lingering influence of Cape Smoke, performed far beyond expectations. They pushed and tugged at the wagon - often in opposing directions - whistled, yelled and sang, and a few of the more athletic even tried to climb on the oxen, much to the consternation of the wagon boy who had to discourage them with his whip. It was fortunate the water at the drift was only waist-deep or several casualties would have resulted to spoil the festive crossing.

Snorting with alarm at the excess of encouragement, the oxen heaved out of the water and up the far bank in a rush, leaving behind a sprawl of bodies, and almost causing the captain to abandon ship. Luckily, the wagon boy managed to bring the team to a halt in a thick patch of sand, where they stood with wet flanks steaming as he hurried to calm them down.

Fleetwood retrieved his top hat and breathed a great sigh of relief. For one moment as the wagon had careered up the bank, he had suffered horrifying visions of his safe sliding off the rear and floating away down the river.

He gathered his composure as the diggers started arriving to see what all the hullabaloo was about.

'Play something lively, Scotty,' he encouraged his one-man-band. 'Give them a jig or two.'

'Tis nae a bloody fiddle,' the Scot retorted frostily. Nevertheless, he filled his lungs and began another shaky rendition of the Gay Gordons.

'It's awful cruel you are to the cat, Geordie!' Someone called, and the predictable joke brought a smattering of laughter.

'Shut yer gob, Olsen.' Scotty broke off in mid-tune to rebuke the offender. 'You're nae better than the bloody savages.'

Loud groans and more laughter stirred the swelling audience.

'Keep playing, keep playing,' Fleetwood exhorted.

'Where are the dancing girls, Tucker?'

'He could only afford one,' someone answered, 'but she's a mite hairy for my taste.'

The crowd erupted with hoots and whistles, and Fleetwood had to forcibly restrain the irate Scotsman from leaping off the wagon to assault the offender.

'Is it grog that you have hiding under there, Mister? You should be sharin' it around with your friends.'

'Gentlemen!' Fleetwood held up a hand to still the gathering. 'This is no grog-box I have here. This is...'

he paused, uncertain of how best to hold the buoyant mood of the diggers. Then, perhaps because it was Sunday, he was struck with inspiration.

'This...' he cried, pointing to the safe with his cane, '...is a revelation!' Fleetwood whisked the cover off the safe with a showman's flourish. 'Behold, my friends! Your salvation is nigh.'

Encouraged by the curious looks and speculative comments, Fleetwood expanded on his evangelistic theme.

'Though he be evil of thought or deed, no man... nay...' He allowed his voice to rise and quaver with religious fervour, liking the effect. '..nay... nor even mortal man, shall smite asunder the portals of this here er...revelation... to reveal its innermost sanctums.'

'Holy moly,' a man cried out. 'Tis the blessed remains of Robbie Burns hisself in the box.'

The crowd erupted in applause, and the joker was slapped gleefully on the back by his appreciative comrades.

A little miffed at being upstaged, Fleetwood pounded on the safe with the head of his cane to regain their attention. He stopped abruptly when it made a hollow, wooden sound.

When his audience had quietened down, Fleetwood abandoned the religious angle.

'This, gentlemen....,' he patted the safe gently with the palm of his hand, '...is the largest and most secure safe in the whole of Africa.'

After some cynical jeering, and a few derisive comments, such as, 'Tell us another one,' the crowd began dispersing. But many were interested, particularly the buyers. Safe stealing had reached epidemic proportions, and only a few weeks previously a buyer without a safe had been bludgeoned to death for his bulging money-belt.

'Made in Germany,' Fleetwood continued, 'by the finest steel craftsman in the world. Guaranteed to be burglar-proof, completely unbreakable and, as you have witnessed, folks, much too large and heavy to steal. For a modest fee, Tucker and company will hold anyone's valuables, including diamonds, in this safe depository as from tomorrow.'

'How do we know you won't scarper with the goods, Tucker?'

Fleetwood recognised the speaker as one of the small group of adventurous buyers who continued to carry their stash on their persons. 'Well, I'm surprised and deeply shocked at your mistrust and slander, Mister Hiam. But the fact is, there are two doors to the safe and I have the key to only one of them. The other will be held by my good friend, Mister Franks, the barber.

Perhaps you would like to share the honour with him, Mister Hiam. Then you will have more time to spend with the dirty magazines you are always reading there.'

The remaining diggers cheered and whistled appreciatively at mention of this notoriously popular pastime, and Ikey Hiam retreated. His wife followed close behind, a certain stiffness in her bearing indicating that the matter was not yet concluded.

Fleetwood knew a curtain call when he saw one. He covered the safe and gave his final pitch. 'Open tomorrow, folks. Eight o'clock sharp.' He waved his cane at the wagon boy. 'Tallyho, boy.' And when the African looked at him blankly and made no move, Fleetwood waved again in forward motions. 'Giddyup, boy! There is work to be done.'

Later that night, when the side wall of his office had been replaced, the safe unwrapped and carefully inspected for damage, and the bags of sand stowed away under his bed for removal at a later date, Fleetwood invited Frankie over to admire his new acquisition and celebrate with a glass of champagne.

'Very handsome it is,' Frankie complimented. 'A credit to you, Mister Tucker.'

'Thank you, Frankie. I am rather proud of it. Nobody is going to run off with *that* in a hurry.' He gazed fondly at its gleaming bulk standing in the corner, seeming to fill the small office. It looked, thought Fleetwood, almost imperial with the lamp reflecting from the dark metallic green and glinting on the brass fixtures and gold curlicue bordering.

'Must have cost you a pretty penny, I'd say, Mister Tucker, coming all the way from Germany.' Frankie raised his glass. 'Here's to hoping it will pay its way.'

Fleetwood raised his own glass thoughtfully, recalling the exorbitant sum Hans Struben had charged for its construction. 'Yes, I'll certainly drink to that, Frankie,' he said.

Freshly doused with clean water to bring out their colours, the glistening stones were scattered along the sorting table. Bally's fingers fluttered over them like gulls searching the sea for fish, flicking swiftly over the spread of agate, quartz and pebble, pausing occasionally to probe or pluck out a likely-looking specimen, then moving on quickly again in tireless search of the pellucid gem.

Bally talked to the stones as he worked, ordering them to move aside and allow any unseen diamonds to reveal themselves for inspection.

Charles had discovered by accident that Bally had an uncanny ability at sorting.

He had spent more than an hour one day going through a batch on the table, and finally convinced there was nothing of value, had left the stones there while he took a break, despondent after weeks of failure to the point of giving up altogether.

Bally, with nothing to do while he waited to throw on the next batch, had run his fingers through the rubbish and plucked out a large crystal. Streaked with the sticky yellow clay, Charles realised he must have mistaken it for one of the many agates, and although a scratch test proved it was only a rock crystal, he was alarmed. If he had passed it over so easily, he wondered how many diamonds he had missed.

The hole they were now working was the fourth in the six weeks they had been at Gong Gong, and so far all they had to show for it was a few sapphires and a lot of blisters.

The current hole had yielded the precious stones, and looked to be the most promising, but they had been digging there for only a week, so it was too early to tell. Charles had a good feeling about it though, and from what he could gather by the frequency of his singing and the way he talked to the stones, so did

Bally.

The colour of the clay in the new hole was also different to the others; more yellow and blue, and it was much closer to the water - barely five yards - which made the washing easier and quicker. He was worried they would go below the water level and the hole would flood, but for some reason the clay level was higher, and seemed to be on an angle, as if the whole section had tilted over. Also, the hole had fewer of the big finger-squashing rocks that had plagued the others.

Charles sorted the next two batches himself, then invited Bally to check them, and was humiliated when each batch produced semi-precious stones that he had missed.

From then on, he made sure the washing was done more thoroughly at the river before the batch was brought up, and they sorted together at opposite sides of the table – each checking the other.

What previously had taken Charles an hour, now took less than fifteen minutes, and the speed at which Bally sorted left Charles dumbfounded. It was as if the long slender fingers had eyes of their own.

At first Charles refused to believe it could be done so rapidly. When Bally indicated to him that a batch was finished and should be tipped out, he would not agree, and insisted they do it again, and often a third time. But it made no difference. No matter how many times they sorted through, if Bally indicated that nothing of value was left on the table, that was how it turned out.

Production increased dramatically. In a week of sorting by himself, Charles had found only the sapphires, but with Bally helping, they found three diamonds in only two days.

Barely able to believe his luck, and stifling his battered pride under the excitement of the finds, Charles gave up the early-morning digging sessions, and for a week they went through the discarded waste-pile. He was further humiliated, although ecstatic, when they found another four diamonds, two sapphires and a ruby. All plucked out by the nimble fingers of Bally to the accompaniment of much triumphant giggling, which did little for Charles's self-esteem.

Vowing he would never sort by himself again, he gave Bally a one pound bonus for every stone he found – more than the average two month's pay for African labour. He considered it as insurance against temptation. The usual payment for stolen diamonds was only a few shillings, if anything at all, and he believed the added incentive would be a good antidote for carelessness. He wrapped the stones in cloth and put them in a coffee tin, which he then buried under his bed-roll.

Charles remembered the tight-lipped sorter at his last job and kept the news of his finds to himself, although at times the temptation to tell of his good fortune was almost overpowering. Especially so, as he was becoming friendly with a few of the nearby diggers, none of whom seemed to be having any luck. When they stopped by and asked how he was doing, he showed them two of his smallest diamonds and accepted their sympathy with a blank face.

'I don't think it's a good idea to have your black do the sorting,' one of them advised after just such an occasion. 'How do you know he isn't stealing from you?'

'I keep a close watch,' Charles replied.

The digger was sceptical. 'Well, I don't let mine anywhere near the table. Mark my words, give them a chance and they'll rob you blind.'

Charles resisted the temptation to enlighten the diggers for another reason. He did not want a sudden rush to his beautiful camp-site.

It was the beauty of the place that had attracted him in the first place, more than any potential for finding diamonds. He had no idea what a potential place looked like anyway, and there appeared to be no general rules to follow. He had simply started digging where it was not too steep or too far from the river for washing gravel. And he did not begin until he had run out of excuses for putting it off. Fear that he would find nothing to keep him there had kept him constantly busy elsewhere.

Set in a secluded grassy glade overlooking a bend in the river, the camp was sheltered on three sides by willows and tall, yellow flowering trees. The dense undergrowth rustled with pheasant, quail, and the occasional small buck, and guinea fowl clinked nearby in the early morning and evening.

Fifty yards upriver, opposite a stretch of shallow rapids, a jumble of large boulders and thorny scrub concealed a deep sandy pool adjoining the bank that was perfect for washing and sunbathing. Inaccessible except by crawling through the dense undergrowth, he had found it when searching for a pheasant he had shot, and had subsequently hacked a narrow path to it.

The camp was not plagued by mosquitoes, and his closest neighbour was a good ten-minute walk away. Only a few diggers were camped in the area, a large proportion of them families with children, for although it was not rich in diamond yield, it was healthier and more pleasant away from the dust and bustle of Pniel.

With his future becoming more secure by

the week, Charles saw no reason to rush things. He reorganised the schedule to provide more spare time. Instead of digging in the morning and washing in the afternoon, one day was spent digging and half a day washing. And although he could now afford it, Charles decided against taking on extra labour. He and Bally worked well as a team, and Bally would not have appreciated the competition. Besides, he rather enjoyed the hard digging that was making him fitter than he had ever been.

In his spare time, he practised with the shotgun. To such an extent that not only did his and Bally's diet improve dramatically, but so did that of the neighbours. When the ammunition ran out, Bally taught him how to build a fish trap and make snares, how to make string from bark, and what was edible or medicinal in the surrounding bush. In the evenings, he struggled with Bally's strange language, providing endless entertainment for his tutor.

With plenty of bones to gnaw on, the dog, which had followed them from Pniel, took less to wandering and stayed close to the camp, and even closer to the mule, to which it had formed an even stranger attachment than the one accorded Charles, following it around as it grazed, rolling over submissively when being sniffed and nudged for several feet along the ground - yet neither Charles nor Bally could get closer than a few yards without it slinking away with reproving growls.

Cocooned in this peaceful environment of domestic harmony and financial security, Charles put on weight, his skin darkened to the colour of the walnut butt of the shotgun, and his scraggy beard grew thick and dark. He was delighted when he called on a neighbouring family one Sunday and the old man commented jokingly on his appearance.

'I don't know, Charles, but you're beginning to look more like a Boer every day. Can you speak the language yet?'

Charles laughed, taking it as a great compliment. 'Not yet, Oupa, but I'm working on it. Why don't you teach me?'

Every Boer over fifty, Charles had discovered, was invariably referred to as either Oupa or Ouma, depending on their sex.

Although the claim was yielding less than before, Bally still continued to extract a diamond from the sorting table almost every week, and the number in the coffee tin grew to twenty three, excluding the larger number of semi-precious stones.

Charles had no idea what he was worth, and a stubborn quirk in his nature precluded him from finding out. He knew he was doing extremely well compared to most, and was probably wealthy enough to stop if he wanted to and return to England, and, having the choice, removed the yearning. He was enjoying himself and not ready to leave. He sold one diamond to a kopjie-walloper for his ongoing expenses, and bought a rifle from the old Boer. He roamed farther in search of new experience, often remaining out overnight, and Bally was hard pushed to keep up with his continual barrage of questions about the plants and animals. And the more he learned about it, the more Charles began to love and understand the strange veld, which only a short while before had seemed so threatening and foreign.

He began sketching some of the animals he saw, and when Bally viewed them for the first time his expression was one of profound, almost superstitious awe. Bally was at first reluctant to touch the sketches. When he was forced to pick one up after it had blown away in a gust of wind, his hand shook as he retrieved it, and he held it out in front and away from his body, as if afraid of contaminating it in some way. And he never spoke to the sketches in anything but the softest and most devout whispers.

Charles could not imagine himself as being any happier. He wanted nothing to change; would have been quite content to let it go on as it was forever.

The few leaves left on the mulberry trees were curled from the dry heat, the small white flowers and hard berries lying crisp and shrivelled on the ground; too dry even to rot.

Aneline Steyn swept them into a pile with the stiff, bound-up bundle of dry twigs that served as the yard broom, then scooped them up in her palms and tossed them clear of the swept area. She dusted off her hands, then used the hem of her wide skirt to mop at the tiny beads of perspiration above her lip.

Pushing back the strands of hair that had fallen loose, she went to her mother's grave and sat facing the white cross, hugging her knees and rocking while she gathered her thoughts. It was not right to hem and haw on such occasions.

She coughed to clear her throat and began talking quietly.

'Hello, Ma.... it's me, Anna. I'm sorry to disturb you. I know it's not yet Sunday, but I need to talk about... things.' Aneline paused to gather more thoughts before going on, not wanting to undermine the importance of the occasion with the usual trivialities.

'There is no good news for me to tell. The idea

of the vegetable garden for making money is no good, Ma. It is too far away from the diggings so they don't last in the heat, and the guinea fowl keep scratching out the seedlings. Then the oxen broke the fence and ate what was left. Jurie and Pa hate doing it anyway. They say it is work for Chinamen.'

Aneline sat quietly again, pulling reflectively at the loose strands of hair and tucking them in behind her ear.

'Pa says we should go on the trek again. He says he has contacts in the north who will give us good loads and rates, and it is the only way we can make the money to keep the farm. He refuses to sell the oxen to pay the bank. You know how he is, Ma, even better than me. He has the trek-fever again, even though he can't walk too good now after the accident. But this time I think he is right, Ma, there is no other way we can turn....'

Aneline paused to noisily clear her throat and frown at the bare branches above.

'Oh, Ma... I don't think it was such a good idea to be buried here. What will happen if we lose the farm and you have to stay with strangers...?'

Later that evening, Aneline informed her father and Jurie that they were right and she was wrong. Transporting was the only way they could survive, and they should plan to leave as soon as possible. She would try and get another extension from the bank.

'And what will happen if they won't give it?' Jurie asked, and her father nodded in support of the question. Neither of them looked overly concerned, Aneline thought. In fact, Jurie looked positively happy.

She shrugged. 'There is nothing we can do. We will have to leave.'

They sat in silence, toying with their tin mugs of coffee, each with their own thoughts as they contemplated this burdensome eventuality.

'Don't worry,' Aneline told them finally. 'I explained it all to Ma. She understands.'

Wearing only a pair of short trousers - the same ones Marthinus had dyed, but now minus the legs - Charles set out early on the Sunday morning to clear the fish traps Bally had set the day before.

He started at the top of the rapids, working his way down towards the camp, checking the traps as he went, enjoying the chill morning air and the compensating warmth of the sun on his bare skin. It was his favourite time of the day.

Bally had set the cone-shaped reed baskets deep into the rock crevices, where the water was channelled but not flowing too swiftly, and had placed the openings facing downstream so the traps did not fill with debris. Each was baited with scraps of rotten meat, but only one was deep enough to yield a catch, for Bally still held a pessimistic regard for deep water.

Charles gill-skewered the three fish onto a length of reed, and reset the trap, weighting it down with a rock and checking to see the marker stick was still securely wedged. Then he continued on through the shallow water, close to the bank, stepping cautiously on the slippery rocks.

The rustle and splash of the rapids covered any sound he made, and with his eyes down to watch his footing, he was unaware, until a movement in the bushes alerted him and he looked up quickly to see her.

She was kneeling beside a small wooden tub, screened on all sides by bushes except the front, and she was naked from the waist up. Below she wore only a pair of white pantalets with frilled edges that came a few inches below the knees.

Oblivious to Charles's presence, she was leaning forward over the tub, eyes screwed tight as she twisted her long dark tresses to squeeze out the water.

Her skin was the glistening cream of freshly peeled bark, her breasts full and firm, their size and shape accentuated by her uplifted arms and the sculptured hollow of her stomach. The dark nipples had firmed to points from the chill of the water trickling over them.

Mesmerised by the vision, Charles gaped. The thought of announcing his presence did not even enter his head. He stood and ogled openly and silently at the beautifully sensuous body, imprinting every voluptuous curve, every pale blue vein and brown mole, every quiver and tremble of her magnificent breasts, deep into his brain.

She tilted her head back to let the hair fall behind, smoothing it away from her face with slender fingers. She wiped the water from her eyes and opened them.

For a moment she looked almost calm, blinking, as if the sudden light was playing tricks on her, then they widened in alarm. Her arms shot down to cover her breasts, and she clamped a hand over her mouth to stifle a scream. Hunched forward in an effort to conceal herself, she stared at him over the top of her hand, her eyes wide and frightened.

Charles stared back, and for long moments they looked at each other, frozen with shock and surprise.

Removing one hand, she snatched at the blue dress hanging on a nearby branch, but it snagged, and when she gave it a frantic tug, it ripped. She left it there and quickly returned her covering hand.

Charles suddenly realised he was still staring and turned away, stammering an apology.

'You filthy swine.' she whispered hoarsely 'Why are you spying on me?'

'I'm sorry,' Charles repeated. 'I didn't know you were there. I wasn't spying on you. I was only collecting my fish.'

'Get away before I call my husband. You have no right to be spying on people.'

'I told you I wasn't...' Flustered, Charles turned back, holding up the fish to explain, 'I was ...'

'Don't turn around, damn you... just go!'

Turning quickly, Charles stepped too hastily on the rocks and slipped. He slid clumsily down the slimy shelf to the bottom, and the fish came slithering down after him. Wincing at the sting of a scraped elbow, he gathered them up quickly.

He looked back defiantly before he was out of view. She was still sitting as he had left her, leaning forward to cover herself with crossed arms, glaring after him, clearly waiting for him to disappear around the bend.

For the rest of the morning Charles wandered dreamily around the camp, poking absent-mindedly at the unlit fire, rearranging what Bally had already neatly tidied before going off to visit with friends, and standing, statue-like, for long periods gazing at nothing in particular as he recalled the sensuous images scorched on his brain.

He felt no guilt at not speaking out, only a sense of wonder enveloped in awe at what he had witnessed. He had not seen that many women in the past few months - at least not young, pretty ones - and certainly no half-naked ones. He had been too preoccupied with other things to even think of women at all, but now he could think of nothing else. The peculiarly feminine manner in which she had wrung the water from her hair and swept it back, the tilt of her breasts and hollowed stomach, the undoubted softness of her ivory skin, all rushed to make up for the lapse, and his aimless meandering around the camp slowly intensified to become the libidinous prowling of a young lion.

By noon Charles could stand it no longer. He had to see her again.

He dressed in clean clothes, brushed his over-long hair as best it allowed, and set off with the fish as a peace-offering. The worst that could happen, he surmised, was that he'd get chased away or beaten up, and either was preferable to not seeing her.

He thought of the way she had whispered. Even though in anger, it had given a secretive flavour to their meeting. No matter what happened, or what she thought of him, nothing could change the fact they had shared a few intensely personal moments together. They were no longer strangers.

He had not been upriver in the past few weeks, so was unaware that someone had taken over the Greek's claim, if indeed they had. She had mentioned a husband. Could she be the Greek's wife? She had dark hair and dark eyes, so it was possible, but the thought of the fat Pappas having a wife like that was too bizarre to contemplate.

A sandy-haired man wearing glasses was sitting at a table in the shade of the tent-fly. He smiled and lifted a hand in greeting as Charles approached. 'Hello, there.'

In a way, Charles was disappointed it wasn't Pappas. He would have felt less threatened – and less troubled by his motive for being there – had it been the Greek. Nevertheless, he was somewhat relieved by the man's friendly greeting.

'Good-day, sir.' He offered his hand. 'Charles Atherstone, your neighbour. Sorry I haven't been along sooner. Didn't know you were here.' He held up the fish. 'Brought you a welcoming gift.'

The man stood up to shake his hand. 'Sandy Johnson. Jolly kind of you, sir.' He turned to call out behind. 'Willa? Come… we have a guest.'

Without asking, Sandy Johnson poured a hefty tot of brandy into a mug and pointed to a canvas water-bag hanging from a pole. 'Help yourself, and take a seat. Excuse the furniture, but the drawing room is being redecorated.' He laughed.

Charles laughed with him, liking the man's easy manner. Apparently she had not mentioned their meeting. Watching anxiously for her arrival, he took a sip of the brandy and almost lost his breath. He had forgotten to add the water.

She appeared from behind the tent, dusting flour from her bare arms, and her step faltered when she saw him, almost stopping. Then she came forward, glaring at him from behind her husband's back, seemingly unimpressed by Charles's disarming smile.

'Willy, this is our neighbour, Charles. Look at the nice fish he brought us. You should bake him some of your bread in exchange.'

'No, really.' Charles was quick to get her off the hook. 'It's not necessary. Pleased to meet you… Willy.'

She did not acknowledge his greeting. She

continued to glare at him for a few moments, making her disapproval clear before shifting her gaze to look over his right shoulder and folding her arms across her stomach to further emphasis her displeasure.

She was smaller than he had imagined, and looked a little older with her hair dry and full, but the wide dark eyes and skin was as he remembered.

The hair had been thickly plaited into braids that reached down to her waist, the ends casually tied with strips of white cloth. The dress was the same faded blue one she had ripped on the branch, but he saw no evidence of repair. It pulled taut across her bust, and swelled provocatively over womanly hips before descending to almost cover her sandals.

Charles became suddenly aware that he was staring again, and attempted to cover up. 'I'm sorry if I disturbed you in the middle of wash… baking.'

She shot a quick, sideways glance at him, holding his eyes for a heartbeat before looking away. A flush of rose darkened her cheeks and throat.

'Willy doesn't mind, do you, dear?'

'I had better get back,' she murmured. 'My bread…'

'Willy's been feeling a bit off today,' Sandy Johnson excused. 'Woman get like that sometimes.' He grinned knowingly and winked.

Charles sat on the upturned barrel and tried to concentrate on what her husband was saying. The table was strewn with pebbles and the man had obviously been attempting to identify them with the aid of a ragged-looking reference book.

'Not much use I'm afraid.' He slammed the book shut and poured himself another drink. 'Bottoms up, Charles. Tell me what you know about these rocks. They all look the same to me.'

For a long few hours, Charles tried to share what limited knowledge he had with Sandy Johnson, but the man seemed to have little grasp, and even less interest. He drank steadily, and his words became more slurred as the afternoon progressed.

Charles sipped his own drink slowly, not wanting it, but not wishing to offend either. He became sombre and gloomy, a feeling he did not normally have when drinking, and the more he tried to regain his good spirits, the more gloomy he became. She was obviously keeping herself busy and out of sight, and the knowledge she was deliberately avoiding him did nothing to better his mood.

He tried to get as much information from her husband as he could without appearing to be nosy, and learned they were from Cape Town. Sandy Johnson had worked in a bank where he had met Willa, who also worked there. They had been married for five years and had no children.

So far, they had found no diamonds, although he was still hopeful. The Greek had shown him several good diamonds, and they had bought the claim for twenty pounds.

It took Charles a few moments to comprehend what the man had said. 'You paid twenty pounds for this claim?'

Sandy Johnson looked smug. 'Not bad eh? They're paying five times that much in Pniel now.'

Charles was astonished. Nobody bought claims at Gong Gong, and he doubted Pappas had found any diamonds at all. More than likely he had borrowed them from a friend to show so he could get a sale. The Greek had only been on the claim for little more than a month, and had always grumbled about how the ground was no good.

The longer he talked to Sandy Johnson, the more Charles realised the man had little idea of what to do, and even less chance of success, yet he seemed to think it was only a matter of a few weeks before he would be returning to Cape Town a rich man.

In a way, Charles felt sorry for him. He remembered feeling much the same in the beginning. But it was for his wife he felt most concerned. The camp was rough and poorly organised, with little in the way of comforts. He had peeked around the back of the tent on the pretext of stretching his legs, but really in the hope of catching a glimpse of her, and had seen nothing but bare earth and an open fire – not even a table. He had seen a tub though. It was full of pots, apparently used as a container for them, but he was almost certain it was the same one in which she had been washing, and his earlier respect for her husband began to diminish further.

And with his waning regard, Charles's despondency began to lift. They needed help. She needed help.

Charles saw her once more that afternoon.

When Sandy tottered unsteadily into the bushes to relieve himself, she appeared suddenly to confront him, but Charles's sudden exhilaration was short-lived.

'Why did you come here?' she demanded, her voice low and menacing. 'Are you trying to embarrass me?'

Bewildered, Charles could only offer as a defence the first thing that came into his head. 'Embarrass you? God, no. I only came to see if I could help.'

'We don't need any help, and my husband certainly doesn't need any help with his drinking. I want you to leave. I don't like the way you keep staring at me.'

Shocked by her tone and the implied insults, it took a few moments for Charles's awe of her to be replaced with outrage. 'I beg your pardon, madam,' he said coldly, but you presume too much, and you *do* need help. Your husband has no idea what he's doing, and should never have paid money to that crooked Greek for this worthless claim.'

'What do you mean?' she said, her face paling.

'I mean you were tricked. Nobody buys claims down here.' In the light of her obvious dismay, Charles's attitude softened. Also, he found it impossible to look at her and feel anger at the same time. 'If you want to find anything,' he said reasonably, 'you should let me help.'

'We can manage,' she said, but with a hint of uncertainty, and Charles found the courage to push his advantage.

'No you can't,' he said firmly. 'You don't even have a place to bath in private. I am not the only person to fish in the river, you know.'

Having made his point, he was about to leave it there and go, but her silence, and something almost forlorn in her expression, forced him on. 'Look, why don't you come and use my pool? It's completely private and there is only one way in. You'll be perfectly safe… even from spies, I promise you.'

She remained silent, her expression bleak, not meeting his eye as she twisted her fingers absentmindedly through one of the long braids and chewed on her lip, looking like a young girl quietly but defiantly taking a scolding, and Charles's resolve slipped further, beaten into submission by the intense aura of all things feminine that she exuded by the wagon-load.

Gaining courage from her silence, he spoke her name. 'Willa?' He liked the sound of it around his tongue, and it brought a certain intimacy. He waited for her to look at him, and when she did, and he saw no animosity in her eyes, only the uncertainty, the remnants of his resolve vanished, and with it went his courage.

'I was not spying on you this morning. Please believe me. I'm sorry if I frightened you...' then, recklessly, because he desperately wanted her to know how he felt about sharing that intimate moment with her. '...but I could never be sorry about seeing you there. You are so beautiful… I couldn't help staring. Please, don't be offended.'

He turned quickly and left before she could respond, acutely aware that her dark eyes would be following.

He did not see her husband as he left, but judging by the painful retching sounds coming from the bushes, he suspected he would not be missed.

Charles could tell by Bally's muttering as he sorted through the gravel that his own suspicions were correct. The stuff simply didn't look right. The yellow clay was the wrong texture, and it had no traces of blue, as in his own gravel. Bally tipped the rubbish out with a few eloquently disparaging clicks of his tongue and threw on the next batch.

'Are you sure he knows what he's doing?' Sandy Johnson queried. 'He does it much too quickly for my liking.'

'Check if you want to, but believe me, if any diamonds are there he'll find them.'

'I still don't see how you can trust a black to do it.'

Charles sighed. They had been through it before, and his patience with the man was wearing thin, yet he could understand how he must be feeling. Every day for the past week it had been the same. He had offered to help with the sorting, and they hadn't come up with anything but the occasional crystal.

'I think you should try nearer the river,' Charles advised.

'But the Greek said he found them where we are digging now.'

'If he did,' Charles said shortly, 'I'd be surprised.' He had not repeated what he had told Willa about his suspicions and, apparently, neither had she.

'Where, exactly?'

'I'll get Bally to show your two labourers where to start. I'll bring my cradle along and see if it makes a difference.'

'Very well, here's hoping. Will you stay for a drink?'

'No thanks, I have to get some more work done.'

'How about Sunday?'

Charles hesitated. He did not want to be accused of encouraging him to drink again, but did not want to miss the opportunity of seeing her either. He had seen her only twice during the week, once when she had watched Bally sorting a few tables, standing quietly by and saying nothing except when spoken to, and although she had not glared at him, still she seemed intent on keeping her distance and, wary of staring, Charles had studiously ignored her. An exercise in eyeball manoeuvring that had given him a headache. The second time was when he had brought Ouma Theron over and introduced them. An act of kindness he was beginning to regret, for now she spent most of her time with the old Boer couple.

'Only if you let me bring the lunch,' he told Sandy Johnson. 'I'll see if I can bag a few guinea fowl.'

When the last of the gravel had been sorted without success, Charles showed Bally where the new holes were to be dug, and left.

He was almost back at his camp when he met her on the path.

Caught unawares, he thought feverishly of something to say that wouldn't get him into more trouble, but seeing her coming towards him, the sensuous movement of her hips as she propped a basket on one of them, drove everything but desire from his mind. He stepped to the side of the path to let her pass, smiling pleasantly, and hoping he did not look too gawkish.

For a heart-tripping moment he thought she was going to ignore him and walk past, but she stopped and hoisted the basket more comfortably on her hip. Incredibly, she returned his smile.

'Been to Oumas', I see,' Charles ventured, staying on safe ground.

She nodded. 'Look at all the preserves she has given me.' She lifted aside the cloth to show him. 'Would you like some? We could never get through all these.'

'No, thanks. I already have more than a year's supply.'

She laughed, captivating him with an alluring set of dimples, and he grinned back, defenceless against their appeal. It was the first time he had heard or seen her laugh.

'I must thank you for going to the trouble of bringing the old woman to meet me,' she said. 'It was very thoughtful of you. She's a dear.'

'No trouble, glad to help,' Charles mumbled.

'There is something else.' Suddenly serious, she paid careful attention to replacing the cloth over the jars and tucking it in before glancing up. 'I want to apologise for my rudeness.'

'Oh? No... you mustn't. I probably deserve it.'

'I don't normally talk that way, it's only that you did give me a scare.'

'Of course...'

'And you have been kind to us. I'm sorry.'

Charles shuffled uncomfortably, not knowing what to say, and for a while they both stood in awkward silence. She shifted the basket on her hip, seeming about to move off, and Charles almost snatched it away from her. 'Here... let me carry it.'

She relinquished it gracefully. 'I've been wanting to ask. What you said about the Greek. Is it true?'

'I'm afraid so, yes.'

'Do you really think the claim is worthless?'

'I really don't know,' Charles lied. 'We'll find out next week when we try the new holes closer to the river.'

She sighed. 'I hope so. We can't last much longer than that. Poor Sandy, he wants so badly to make a go of it, but he's not really cut out for this sort of thing. I think I may have made a terrible mistake by spending all that money.'

Charles was confused. 'What... you mean it was you who bought the claim from the Greek?'

She nodded. 'I had to get Sandy away from Pniel. He has a drinking problem, as you will have guessed. Not that it has made much difference.' She sounded bitter.

'I'm sorry. I didn't realise...'

Suddenly she smiled, bringing sunshine to the sombre mood. 'I talk too much.'

'No, you don't. I promise not to encourage him.'

'Thank you. Well, I suppose I should be going…'

The thought of her leaving when everything was going so well inspired Charles further. 'While you're here, why don't you let me show you my pool?'

She seemed reluctant, frowning and chewing reflectively on her lip.

'It's less than a minute away,' he pleaded. 'Surely it won't do any harm to look? I know you will like it.'

'Well…' she demurred. 'I suppose…'

He led the way, showing her how she could go past his camp to the track he had cut without anyone seeing her, not even himself, and when they arrived he waited for her reaction as anxiously as a child showing off a new toy, and was happy to see the pleased look of surprise on her face.

'Well, what do you think?' he asked, grinning foolishly.

'What a lovely place. How lucky you are to have found it.'

He waded into the water, not bothering to remove his boots, impatient to show her the various depths; from the place where it was only knee-deep, to where it almost came over his head. He showed her where he had moved two large boulders into a fast moving channel of water to create a small whirlpool.

He lay down in it to fully demonstrate the soothing effect she could expect from the swirling water.

'Well... what do you say?' he called, 'Have I tempted you yet?'

She smiled. 'You've wet your clothes.'

Charles waded back to point out the flat sunbathing rock, and the soft sandy entrance he had created, then he made a sweeping gesture with his hand.

'It is all at your disposal, madam, any time you wish, at no charge whatsoever.'

'Are you sure?'

'I would be honoured. You don't have to tell me when you are coming. Leave something across the path to show you are here, and stay as long as you like... all day if you wish. You won't be disturbed, and you can't be seen from the river.'

She showed her dimples.

'You'll use it then?'

'I'd love to... thank you... Charles. The tub *is* a little on the small side.'

Charles's grin threatened to split his face in two. It was the first time she had spoken his name.

He walked with her until they were close to her camp, but still out of sight of it, when she stopped to retrieve the basket, smiling her thanks. Then she became serious again.

'Charles... why are you doing this?'

'Doing what?' he answered quickly, flustered, but instinctively knowing what she meant.

'Going out of your way to be nice, even though I was rude. Trying to be so helpful.'

Charles frowned with concern. 'You don't approve?'

'I don't know if I should, Charles,' she murmured and, as he stood nonplussed, she lifted up and kissed him swiftly on the cheek. 'But thank you.'

'Can't really say I've tasted better.' Sandy Johnson made small circles in the air with a guinea fowl drumstick and winked at Charles. 'How many more talents are you hiding from us, Charlie?'

'I'm afraid Ouma Theron and her Dutch oven will have to take the credit,' Charles replied evenly. Sandy was getting on his nerves. The man had been drinking steadily all through lunch, ignoring Willa's disapproving looks and not too subtle comments. And his own refusal to join in had served only to encourage him further.

'Now there's an idea, Willy. Why don't you get one of those? Maybe Charlie will show us how to make one.'

'Charles has done more than enough already,' said Willa quietly, and Charles glanced at her, but she was paying close attention to her food - which she had barely touched.

'No, I wouldn't mind at all. It's quite simple. The clay from...'

'It's not necessary,' she said. 'Ouma has offered me the use of hers whenever I want.'

'Ah, yes... the old Boer woman. Nice people down here, Charlie. All so helpful.'

'Which reminds me,' Charles said, standing up, 'Ouma is going to cut my hair this afternoon, so I had better get going.'

'No need.' Sandy waved him back down impatiently. 'Willy is an expert haircutter, aren't you, Willy?'

'No, and I'm sure Charles would rather have Ouma do it.'

'Nonsense. Get the shears. It's only fair that he allows us to return a favour.'

Despite her obvious reluctance - saying nothing as she pushed aside her plate and left the table without a glance in his direction - Charles proffered no objection. It was not the sort of opportunity he was about to miss out on.

He sat on the upturned barrel as she worked, eagerly anticipating her every touch as her fingers moved over his scalp, although he could sense her reluctance. It seemed to radiate from her body in seething waves. When she moved to the side and brushed against his protruding leg, the soft warmth of her thigh was a shock that almost caused him to jerk away, and the feel of it lingered, as if it had scorched an impression.

He tried to make light conversation, joking about the length and awkwardness of his hair, but his comments fell flat, receiving only a murmured denial from Willa, and no response whatsoever from her husband, who watched owlishly from the opposite side of the table. When he began to lean sideways and doze off, Charles suggested she wake him in case he fell.

Her response was curt. 'Let him.'

Charles retreated. If she was angry and embarrassed by her husband's drunkenness, so be it. He was not about to jeopardise his chances by interfering. Yet the continuing atmosphere confounded him. It should have eased without Sandy's sarcastic participation, but it seemed to have become even thicker. He wished she would say something to reassure him. Anything. He himself could think of nothing to say, and he began to regret not having come to her aid by refusing the haircut. In fact, it was a mistake to have come there at all.

Her silence gave him a bad case of the jitters. From the time he had arrived she had been withdrawn, treating him with reserve, and refusing to meet any of his glances. The warm pressure of her parting kiss had kept him in a state of dreamy euphoria ever since she had given it, and he had assumed that things would be different between them. But the friendliness seemed to have gone. Now he had the distinct feeling she didn't want him there.

She stooped low to snip around his ear, bringing the swell of her right breast – the one with the two small moles close together on the underside – into view. He could not be certain if it was his heightened sense of awareness, or simply his imagination, but her breathing seemed rapid and unsteady, fluttering warm on his ear, and he was sure her detected a trembling in the scissors as they pressed against his neck.

He made a point of trying to catch her eye, and when he did, she looked away quickly, unsmiling, and moved position.

No doubt remained for Charles. She was nervous, and he was embarrassing her.

The knowledge came as a shock. Then suddenly he understood the reason for her confusing behaviour. It was not her husband, it was him!

Charles felt the despair in the slump of his shoulders. It was obvious. She would have realised by the way he had been acting that he was infatuated with her, and it had put her in an awkward situation. She was married. She had every right to be concerned. He had gone out of his way to help, and she was sensitive enough not to want to hurt his feelings, even confiding in him, trying to treat him like a friend, but he had responded by acting like a lovesick fool instead. It was no wonder she was nervous and embarrassed.

It would also explain why she had not used the pool, even though she had said she would. She was simply trying to tell him in a nice way that she wanted to keep her distance. And now she was cutting his hair only because she thought she owed him a favour. And, like the fool he was, he had allowed it.

Thoroughly depressed, and vowing not to bother her again, but also knowing deep down that he would never find the resolve to stay away, Charles sat in morose silence until she had finished.

He stood and shook the hair from his shirt, making a bigger thing of it than was necessary, then thanked her politely. Equally polite, she murmured her thanks in return for the lunch he had provided. He left abruptly, before he had the chance to make a fool of himself again.

Almost out of view, Charles turned to look. She was standing in the shadow of the tent opening, facing his way. Unable to help himself, he waved, and was desolate when she did not wave back.

As Ouma Theron turned away with the coffee pot, the old man lifted his eyebrows at Charles. With the stem of his pipe, he made urgent tipping signals towards his mug. However, before he could comply, Ouma turned back and moved the bottle out of reach.

'You two have had enough,' she declared.

'What's the harm of a little drop in the coffee?' Oupa protested.

'One drop, two drops. Just because you put it in your coffee doesn't mean you are not drinking.'

Oupa shrugged apologetically at Charles and clamped his teeth on his pipe.

'And besides…' Ouma continued, changing to the Boer language, '…drinking doesn't stop woman problems, it starts them... not so, Charles?'

'I don't know what you are saying, Ouma,' Charles replied slowly in the same language.

'Very good, Charles. You learn quick. Too bad you don't learn about women as quick.. especially married ones.'

'Leave the fellow alone, *vrou*, he came to visit, not to listen to your lectures.'

'Rubbish!' Ouma snapped. 'And don't you *vrou* me, Danie Theron. I know what I'm talking about, believe me. After four sons and three daughters you think I know nothing? Charles came here because he is feeling sorry for himself... not so?' She ruffled Charles's hair. 'What's the matter? She tell you to jump in the river? Or was it her husband?'

Charles was flabbergasted. 'What do you mean, Ouma?'

'You know what I mean all right.' She rapped him gently on the head with her knuckles. 'It is what you must expect if you go sniffing around a married woman, young fellow.'

'That is enough!' Oupa struck the table with the palm of his hand, defusing the reprimand somewhat by forgetting he still held the pipe. 'You must not say such bad things,' he finished lamely. 'You don't know it's true.'

'Ja? And what do you know about it? You are

as big a fool as he is in these matters.' She retrieved the pipe from the floor and placed it calmly back on the table. 'But for once you're right, it is not my place to interfere. I'm sorry, Charles, I don't mean to be rude.' She ruffled his hair again. 'I don't think of you as a guest. We are friends, hey? But I don't want to see you get hurt... or her either, for that matter.'

Charles sat in a bewildered daze as Ouma fetched the bottle from the shelf and, ignoring Oupa's outstretched hand, poured a good slug of brandy in his coffee.

'You have the poor girl very confused, Charles. She tells me all the things you have been doing to help, and she asks questions. Too many questions, if you ask me.'

Charles looked up quickly. 'What questions?'

Ouma shrugged off the query. 'She tells me lots of things about herself too. Dear me...' Ouma shook her head and clicked her tongue sympathetically. 'She is not a very happy girl, I think.' She sat down and gave Charles a squeeze on the arm. 'It would be a sin to take advantage of her, my boy. She has enough problems already with that dronky husband. You should find yourself a nice single girl. A good-looking young fellow like you will have no trouble at all. They will come running from miles.'

She gave Charles's arm a final conciliatory pat, as if the matter was now decisively settled, and spoke to Oupa. 'You know that clay-pan you were talking about the other day, Danie? Why don't you take Charles there and show him some real animals? I think you both need some bush time.'

Oupa, who had been listening with a dour expression on his face, suddenly brightened. 'You think so? Man! I would give a lot to see that pan right now with some water in it.' He paused, thoughtfully. 'It's only three days to get there on the horses, but that still means we'll be away more than a week.'

'So?' Ouma raised both eyebrows. 'What of it?'

'Maybe Charles can't leave his claim for that long. And what about you, Hettie?'

'I've been looking after blacks all my life. Don't you worry about me.'

'Charles?' Oupa leaned forward, eyes gleaming. 'What do you say, man? You'll see more game than you've ever seen before. Not just rabbits and guinea fowl, but gemsbok, eland, springbok, maybe even lion or buffalo, if the grass is good.'

Still a little stunned by Ouma's knowledge of his feelings for Willa, Charles had not been listening too attentively. He was more confused than ever. What questions had Willa asked? And what did Ouma mean by saying she asked too many? Was he the one who was making her unhappy? He wished the old lady would tell him more.

'Well?' Oupa repeated. 'What do you think, man?'

'Sorry... yes, it sounds good, Oupa, but I haven't ridden a horse before. Only ponies.'

The old man chuckled. 'Same thing, only farther to fall. You'll have a sore backside for a few days, but you'll soon get used to it. What say we leave at first light tomorrow, hey?'

They spent the next hour planning what food and equipment they were going to take, and when Charles got back to his camp it was almost dark. Knowing he wouldn't have time in the morning, he went to the pool for a swim and saw immediately that she had been there. He had been carefully brushing the sandy entrance to the water with a branch before leaving each day, and there was no mistaking the small imprints of her bare feet.

He experienced a rush of exhilaration. She had come at last - and alone. That was a good sign. Maybe she wasn't trying to avoid him after all. He lay in the water trying to recall every word Ouma had said about her. That she was unhappy, and especially that she had asked too many questions, and he suddenly wished he had not committed himself so hastily into going away with Oupa. What if she had gone by the time they returned? She had told him if they found no diamonds soon they would have to leave. It would be quite possible he would never see her again.

The thought almost threw Charles into a panic, and he had almost made up his mind to go and see her when he remembered Ouma's advice and reluctantly accepted that she was right. Willa was married, and that's all there was to it. He would have to try and forget her.

But he couldn't forget her. Much of that night he lay sweating on top of his blanket with the image of her so strong he could almost believe she was there.

Finally he woke Bally, and threw a log on the fire to warm the coffee and give some light, then he explained to the bleary-eyed little African what he wanted him to do while he was away; especially in regard to the claim next door and the new hole closer to the river.

It took a long time, and included much pantomime, but finally Bally understood and took the small diamond Charles gave him, placing it carefully into the corner of a piece of cloth and tying a knot around it, then he looked at Charles and giggled, rolling his eyes knowingly.

Charles scowled, trying to look stern. 'Shut up, Bally, before I break your skinny arms.'

Bally rolled to his feet and shuffled away to his tent, still giggling, and Charles returned to his own bed, also smiling, but for a quite different reason. She had come.

'Keep walking steadily,' Oupa Theron advised in a whisper. 'If you stop, they get curious, then the ones behind push the ones in front so they can have a better look. If they get a sudden fright you could get trampled on by mistake.'

Charles walked as steadily and unconcernedly as his thumping chest and shaky legs permitted, and tried not to tread on Oupa's heels.

The moon had waned, but the stars were bright, and their eyes were now well accustomed to the dark, so the shadowy mass of animals around them was clearly visible. Charles had no idea what animals they were. Most of Oupa's whispered comments were lost in the rustle of grass and soft stamping of hooves. And the names he did hear were strange Boer ones, like hartebeest, bontebok or blesbok, which he couldn't remember anyway. He made a mental note to write them down the next day in his notebook, and to draw the shape of the horns and other unusual features so he would learn more quickly.

As they approached, the animals ahead would lift their heads and, after a quick, startled glance, would move aside, horns glinting in the pale light. He recognised a herd of zebra, which turned to look casually over their shoulders at them as they passed. Also the comical looking wildebeest mingling with the zebra, which stamped their feet rapidly, as if the ground was hot, their peculiar, metallic snorting reminding Charles of a toy bugle.

No animals ran from them in panic. They were accepted into their midst with the same degree of reserved tolerance given to the other animals, and Charles found it an exhilarating and humbling experience being a part of them.

Oupa kept his rifle slung casually over his shoulder, with his thumb hooked into the strap, and Charles, after some hesitation, cautiously followed his example, although it took a concerted effort of will not to have it pointed out at the ready with the safety-catch off. He fervently hoped they didn't meet up with any lions or elephants.

They had passed through the zebra herd when Oupa suddenly stopped. 'Listen… what do you think it is?'

Charles began to unsling his rifle, then relaxed when he noticed Oupa was still unconcerned. He listened. From the darkness around came an eerie clicking and whistling sound that made his scalp prickle. It seemed to be coming from all sides, some of it close and loud, some of it faint, as though far in the distance.

'What?' he whispered. 'Is it birds?'

Oupa's teeth flashed white in the dark bush of his beard. 'Springbok. And plenty of them by the sound of it.'

Charles had watched a group of the beautiful gazelles performing at dusk, leaping in the air as if jerked suddenly upwards by strings, their heads down almost between their knees, bodies gracefully arched. They did it time and again, some going straight up, others springing off sideways, crossing over each other in mid-air, like a troupe of acrobatic dancers, and doing it, apparently, for no other reason than an inability to keep still.

Oupa continued on and the herd parted as they went through, then closed in behind to surround them completely. Some of the younger and more curious followed for a short distance with daring, yet hesitant steps. White faces looked at them from the gloom on both sides, as if they were spectators lining a street and he and Oupa were odd-looking foreign dignitaries on a state visit.

The unearthly whistling sound, Oupa explained, was their calling to each other, and the clicking noise was made from the constant touching of thousands of horns.

'I would never have believed it.' Charles enthused when they were back at their camp. 'I didn't see even one of them run.'

'I didn't believe it either, the first time,' Oupa replied. 'It's as if they know when you're not a threat. I've seen a pride of lions walk that close to them as well, and all they do is look.'

Too excited to sleep, Charles kept Oupa awake until well after midnight with his questions, then was up before dawn, waiting for the sun to reveal more of the magical place.

Oupa had purposely planned their approach to the pan to keep it out of view behind the small flat-topped hill until the right moment. During the first two days of their journey, the ground had been dry and sparsely covered with stunted trees and thorn-bushes, but on the third day, small patches of wildflowers began appearing out of the seemingly barren earth, and a hint of green showed on the few blades of grass.

'This is as far as that big storm reached,' Oupa had explained, sounding pleased with himself. 'There should be at least a foot of water in the pan.'

It was late in the afternoon when they arrived at the foot of the hill, skirting around a carpet of yellow flowers, Oupa explaining that the pods were thorny and sharp.

Charles had not been sorry to see the end of the trip. He had experienced no real problems with the horse, but although he had taken the old man's advice on keeping his stirrups long, his backside ached and his legs felt like rubber.

He had followed stiffly behind Oupa as they climbed the hill, somewhat disgruntled by the fact the old man showed no effects whatsoever from the long ride. Then he stood beside him at the top and instantly forgot his discomfort.

'Better than I expected,' Oupa mused. 'Much better.'

The pan was at least a half-mile long. A perfect shining oval bordered by a fringe of lime-green. Behind the fringe lay vast irregular carpets of multi-coloured flowers. It looked as if gigantic pots of different coloured paint had been dropped from high to burst and splatter and mingle on impact with the landscape. The splashes of colour stretched for as far as Charles could see. From brilliant red, blue and orange, to white, yellow and purple.

But as breathtaking a sight as it was, it was not what caused Charles to gasp with wonder.

Thousands of antelope browsed peacefully around the pan, or stood drinking on the edges in the shallow water, all gathered into herds of their own kind, like sporting teams waiting on a playing field for the game to begin. Many animals looked bigger than oxen, and Charles searched eagerly for elephants, but there were none.

They sat on the hill and watched until the sun went down, Oupa pointing out the various species with his pipe, then Charles was back again on his own at sunrise. It looked more than ever like a fairyland, with a light mist floating above the water, and even more animals than the evening before.

He watched until the sun burned off the mist, then woke Oupa with coffee and stood around impatiently while he sipped at it slowly.

'Relax, Charles. We'll be here for a few days yet, and I'm not so young as you.' He took another tentative sip and grimaced. 'Too bad you forgot the brandy.'

For the next two days they meandered haphazardly about the pan and surrounding bush on the horses, Oupa explaining while Charles wrote notes and made rough sketches.

For each animal, Oupa had a story to tell from his earlier days as a hunter, and his knowledge of their habits seemed inexhaustible.

'Those fellows are nearly always here first,' he said, pointing with his chin to a herd of zebra. 'Most animals have to smell the water first, but not him, he's is on his way even before it rains.'

'How do they know?' Charles asked, pencil at the ready. He had been trying to write down some of the explanations as well, although it was proving near impossible on the jolting horse.

Oupa chuckled. 'Simple. He looks up at the sky. If he sees a storm, or even lightning, he follows it, just like the little Kalahari Bushman.'

Charles was puzzled by the fact he had not seen this sort of game near the river.

'They go there sometimes,' Oupa informed him, 'but farther down, where there are no people. They don't come here only for water, they come for the limey taste of it and the salts. They much prefer it to the fresh water in the river.'

At night, Oupa identified as many sounds as he

could, and Charles heard the deep, resonant wheezing of a lion for the first time. It sounded so close that he glanced quickly to where he had propped his rifle against a nearby tree, but Oupa reassured him.

'It's the ones you don't hear that you have to worry about, *boetie*. This one is at least a mile away, and probably wouldn't harm you anyway. Too much juicy game about.'

Still, that night Charles slept close to his rifle, and developed a new respect for the Africans like Bally, who wandered through the wild veld with nothing but a small axe for protection.

In the morning they found where the lions had made a kill. They had to dismount, then lead the reluctant and snorting horses in order to take a closer look at what was left of the carcass.

'Blesbok,' Charles announced proudly, after leafing quickly through his notes.

'Ja, that's him all right. The hyenas have had their share too. See how that big bone has been crunched? They are the ones you have to worry about, son. Once I had a saddle snatched from under my head when I was asleep. When I got it back there were teeth marks in the stirrup-irons. Friendly fellows, hyenas. Best to sleep with your head against a tree, or you could lose it.'

Charles remembered only too well his uncomfortable night in the tree when he was lost after the wagon accident with Marthinus, but he didn't bring the subject up. He had too many memories of that trip he would be happy to forget.

Although they carried their rifles with them, they never fired a shot, preferring to eat the tinned food they had brought rather than disturb the animals with gunfire. The Eden-like setting, and their acceptance amongst the herds, invoked a sense of primeval belonging that neither of them wished to spoil.

'We'll try for a warthog on the way home,' Oupa promised. 'You won't find anything better than his leg covered in clay and baked in Hettie's oven.'

Charles was reluctant to leave after only three days, but they had already stayed longer than planned, and Ouma would start worrying if they were too long away. As a compromise, Oupa suggested they make a slight detour to another, much smaller pan some ten miles away. From there, he explained, they could cut back across to the river and Gong-Gong.

At sunrise, Charles climbed the hill for a final look at the pan and the animals as they came to drink. He watched the wispy tendrils of mist drift between their legs and then slowly disappear as the water turned gold in the sun, and he knew he would never return to

England.

He turned in a circle, looking out at the blurred horizon and breathing in the crisp air that had the taste of wildflower in it, filling his lungs with the wonderful smell, holding it in, as if to soak up and retain every last bit of the vitality it contained.

He looked far to the east, to the unseen mountains where Oupa had spent most of his life hunting, and he made up his mind he would go there one day and discover it for himself. He would discover many places for himself. He felt so filled with life it became too much to hold in, and he yahooed and whooped at the top of his voice.

Around the pan, a tremor rippled through the herds as they lifted their heads to gaze in the direction of the unusual calling.

'Man! I thought it was a bloody mating hyena up there,' Oupa chided when Charles returned. 'What were you up to?'

Charles could not keep it to himself. 'Oupa, I've decided that Africa is the place for me. I'm not going back to England… ever.'

The old man looked strangely at him for a moment, then slowly shook his head. 'I think Ouma is right, that woman has mixed up your brain.'

'Why?' Charles was nonplussed. At the very

least he had been expecting encouragement. And mention of Willa had not helped.

'We have always known it, Ouma and me. You don't think I would bring a bloody *rooinek* out here and listen to all his stupid questions, do you? At least not without shooting him.'

Relieved, Charles grinned. 'But I am one,' he said. 'And proud of it.'

'Ja? Is that so? Well, in that case, you had better get on your horse while I fetch my rifle. Even bloody *rooineks* should get a sporting chance.'

The antelope herds thinned out as they rode farther from the pan, then suddenly they were gone. With still good grazing, and plenty of sign they had been around, it was puzzling. And what little game they did see, they couldn't get close to.

'Something has frightened them,' Oupa observed, stopping to stroke thoughtfully at his beard.

'Lions?'

The old man answered with a shrug, and the puzzled expression remained on his face as they continued, but a short while later he came to a stop again and pointed to the sky ahead. 'Look.'

Charles looked up at the cloud of dark spiralling dots, then clearly heard the spasmodic popping of gunfire in the distance. 'What's happening?'

Oupa frowned. 'It does not sound like a normal hunting party to me. It sounds more like a bloody war. I think we should take a look.'

Because of the flat terrain and squat thorny acacia scrub, they saw nothing until they began to emerge onto the outer perimeter of the pan, when Oupa suggested they leave the horses and go on foot. The sound of gunfire had dwindled to only an occasional shot every few minutes, but the sound of voices was loud.

They made their way forward under the cover of a densely covered anthill, then climbed it to get a view.

The pan was much smaller than the one they had left, barely three hundred yards long, and narrow, with only a light splatter of the colourful flowers. The bank on the far side, and for some way into the scrub, was littered with the bodies of dead and dying animals. Some floated, half-submerged, in the shallow water, and were being dragged to the edge by groups of noisy Africans. Several white men on horses rode amongst the animals on the ground, firing at close range into the heads of those still kicking.

As Charles viewed the bizarre spectacle with an astonished outrage so overwhelming he was finding it hard to accept that what he was seeing was real, two men on horses galloped from the trees behind a terror-stricken wildebeest calf, trying to herd it into the water. It managed to dart between their mounts at the last moment and, bugling pathetically, ran back toward the scrub.

One of the men dragged his horse to a halt and fired a few wild shots after the calf with a pistol, but it was impossible to tell if he hit it. Jeered at good-naturedly by his friends, the man, who was dressed all in white, and with a thin, snake-like *sjambok* dangling from his wrist, dismounted to fire several shots from close range at a kicking ostrich, finally killing it.

A low sound rumbled from deep within Charles's throat.

'Take it easy, *boetie*'. Oupa put a restraining hand on his arm as he moved to get up.

'I should have drowned the bastard when I had the chance,' Charles growled.

'You know them?'

'The one in white. He's the one who flogged Bally. I've a good mind to shoot the swine right now.'

'Ja, I know how you feel, but it won't do you any good to be hanged.'

'Who are they, Oupa? What the hell do they think they're doing?'

'I think they are all business people from Pniel

on a little shooting holiday.'

'What can we do?'

'Nothing.' Oupa turned away and started back to where they had left the horses, and Charles stormed after him.

'There has to be something we can do. They can't just shoot anything they like. I'm going to see them.'

'You'll only get yourself into trouble. There is no law against it.'

They remained in heavy silence until they reached the horses, then Oupa pulled out his pipe and began stuffing it with his strong tobacco.

'It's a bad thing, Charles, but I've seen worse. About ten years ago. Only a few hundred miles from here.' Oupa lit his pipe and puffed several clouds of soothing smoke. 'A big hunt was arranged for your Prince Alfred. They had Chief Moroko's people herd over twenty thousand head of game into a valley and circle them. Then the Prince and his friends had a good time shooting at anything that moved.'

Charles was appalled. 'Why would they do it? How could anyone do such a thing for fun?'

Oupa shrugged. 'Who knows. Maybe they thought they were big white hunters. Anyway, they killed more than three thousand, and many more were wounded by spears and bad shots.' He paused to drag on his pipe and study Charles's face. His own looked unusually calm, but his tone belied his expression. 'It took me and some of my friends a long time to track down all the wounded animals and finish them off.' He rapped the bowl of his pipe against his heel and stamped out the ashes. 'It is only one of the reasons I don't like *rooineks*.'

Dismayed by the story, and by what he had witnessed, Charles remained silent until they had mounted and were riding away.

'Do you think the same will happen here… lots of wounded animals running around in the bush?'

'No. I think these people only had a few beaters chase them into the pan, then they charge in on their horses and start shooting. The animals don't like to run through the water so turn back. They had them more or less trapped.'

'Bastards!'

'Ja, exactly.'

'I wish there was something we could do.'

'There is, we can go home.'

They rode wide around the pan and set a course by the sun for Gong Gong. Although unspoken, both understood there could be trouble if they met any of the hunting party, so they remained well out of sight.

When they came unexpectedly upon two outspanned wagons, Charles, still seething with frustration, and with no fixed purpose in mind, suddenly veered off and rode towards them. The story of the Prince Alfred hunt still rankled, and the similar performance they had recently witnessed evoked in him a deep sense of shame for his countrymen. He had to do something to prove, as much to himself as to Oupa, that not *all* Englishmen were the same. He could not simply ride away from it.

He saw no oxen, and presumed they were out grazing somewhere under guard, but two Africans were setting up tables and chairs under a large canvas awning. Charles ignored their hesitant greeting and curious stares, and rode towards the wagons. Behind him, he heard Oupa talking to the two men, and was relieved the old man had followed, but he would have come alone anyway.

One of the wagons was uncovered, and contained tents and camping equipment. The other had the canvass sides rolled up and he could see it was stacked with provisions. He dismounted to take a closer look.

The hunters believed in doing things in style. The best imported tinned foods, cartons of champagne and imported French brandy, caviar, boxes of cigars, and crystal glasses packed in straw. Even silverware. One section was devoted entirely to neatly stacked boxes of ammunition and several gleaming rifles.

Except for the weapons, it looked more like the equipment for a garden party, and he turned away from it in disgust.

Oupa had been talking at length to the Africans in their language, and he broke off to explain when Charles joined him.

'They're Sothos. Come from the same area as I do. I recognised the greeting.'

'What did you say?'

'I asked them what was happening.'

Charles waited for him to continue, but Oupa remained silent, and Charles knew him well enough to know something was bothering him.

'You were talking to them for a long time. What else did they say... that you don't want to tell me about?'

'They said that from here they are going with the wagons to little *Verneuk*.'

'Isn't that the name of the pan we just came from?'

Oupa nodded, and Charles looked at him in disbelief. Then he glared at the two Africans accusingly, as if expecting them to provide further explanation.

'They want to shoot more? What about all the game they shot here this morning? What are they going to do with it?'

Oupa's expression was disdainful. 'Like I said, who knows what these sort of people do.' He began to turn his horse.

'No. We can't let it happen. There's no reason for it.'

'What can we do? It is asking for trouble.'

'I don't know, Oupa, but we can't allow it. Maybe if we went back to little *Verneuk* and chased all the game away by shooting in the air, or making fires... or something.'

'No, it won't work. The grass is too green and there is too much game. They will only come back the next day.'

'Well, I'm going to talk to these people and tell them they can't do it.'

'They are important men, Charles. You will only get arrested if you try to stop them.'

Charles glared at Oupa, feeling the frustration and anger coming to boiling point. The few days he had spent at the pan had changed his life, and he felt a strong proprietary interest in the fate of the animals there. He was firmly committed to preventing their wholesale slaughter for the sake of light entertainment, no matter what risk was involved.

'Tell the blacks to go,' he instructed Oupa. 'Tell them they had better run. And you too, Oupa, I'll catch up.'

'What are you going to do? I think maybe I should stay.'

Charles turned back towards the wagons without answering, and heard Oupa talking again. By the sound of his voice, and the alarmed responses, he guessed they were getting the message. He did not wait to see if they obeyed. He swung from his horse onto the covered wagon and ripped open a carton of French brandy. One at a time, he smashed the bottles against the barrels of the rifles, ensuring that a good amount spilled over the ammunition. He smiled grimly as he inhaled the scented fumes. It was going to be a sure-fire success.

Sitting astride his horse, Charles lit a safety-match and carefully applied it to a twist of paper torn from his notebook. When the flame was at its largest, he tossed it into the wagon. The fumes ignited with a dull, but satisfying thomp.

When the explosions came, Charles was too busy holding on to the galloping horse to see the spectacular effects. But when he finally managed to slow up and turn, the sight of the narrow column of dark smoke reaching high in the blue sky was almost as satisfying as the sight of his first diamond. Without ammunition and fancy food the hunters would have no choice but to return home. The party was over.

They used the incoming tracks of the hunters for some miles before swinging away, hoping it would confuse any attempts to follow. When they eventually stopped to rest the horses, Charles removed a bottle of French brandy from inside his shirt, and Oupa grinned with anticipation. 'So you didn't forget after all.'

'Sorry, meneer, but it is *rooinek* brandy. I don't think it would be right for you to drink it.'

Oupa smacked his dry lips. 'Just pass it here, *boetie,* and I'll do my best not to choke on it.'

Ouma scowled. 'Are you sure they didn't see you?'

'They wouldn't have recognised us anyway.' Oupa was confident. 'Man, Hettie!. You should have seen that wagon go up. Like a Chinese picnic.'

'Well, I still think it was stupid of you to take such a risk,' Ouma scolded as she heaped more scones on the plate. 'Come on eat up. You both look half-starved. I suppose you ate nothing because you were too lazy to cook. Mind you, I can't say as I've done much myself... there's more honey if you want.'

Charles blinked dazedly. Ouma had been talking non-stop since they had arrived an hour earlier, a little after dawn, and he had been following her confusing blend of two languages with extreme difficulty.

The trip home had been hot and they had pushed hard for the last two days, cutting almost a day off their time, and stopping only to rest and water the horses. Every muscle protested against even the slightest movement. All he wanted to do was relax them and sleep.

Oupa pushed his plate away, coming to the rescue. 'Enough, Hettie. Save it for later. We have to rest now.'

Charles didn't bother with his bed-roll. Promising to send Bally for it later after he had finished his sorting at the Johnsons', he ambled stiffly and unsteadily back to camp and sprawled on a groundsheet in the shade of the trees.

He woke early in the afternoon, and stumbled down to lay dozing and wallowing in the therapeutic swirling of the whirlpool.

He heard no sound above the hiss and gurgle of the water around him, but suddenly Charles knew he was not alone and sat up quickly.

She stood on the small sandy beach, only a few yards away, a basket propped on her hip and the trace of smile on her lips, looking down at him sitting there, barely covered by the clear water.

'I'm sorry if I disturbed you,' she said mildly, apparently unconcerned by his nakedness, although it was impossible for her not to have seen it, floating head-up on the surface like a dead fish trapped on a clump of seaweed.

Charles quickly hugged his knees and struggled to contain his whirling thoughts. He could only gape at her with his throat going dry.

Her hair had been brushed out, but the unruly twists and curls from the braiding still showed. She had thrown it forward over one shoulder, possibly to keep it clear of the spiky branches on the path, and it fell in dark rippling cascades over the basket, almost concealing it.

The intriguing knowledge that she must have seen him, and the fact of her being there, vibrant and real, and so intensely feminine, combined to bring every pulse-quickening sensation rushing back stronger than ever, and he clamped his arms even more firmly about his knees. His determination to forget her evaporated under the sunshine of her smile like the mists had vanished on the clay-pan

Her smile faded under his lengthening silence. 'I think I had better go,' she said, and turned away.

'No!' It was almost a shout. 'I'm sorry, Willa, you surprised me. I forgot to leave something on the path... I hope you don't think I forgot on purpose...'

'Oh, no. I don't think that at all.' She seemed surprised. 'You have nothing to apologise for. I'm sorry if I've embarrassed you, I really think I should leave.'

'No, please... I need to talk. If you turn your back, I'll get dressed.'

'But your clothes are lying in the water.'

'Oh, yes... I was going to wash them... just arrived back.'

'Do you have a towel?'

'No, but if you wait, I can run to the camp and get one... I mean dressed.'

'You can use mine, if you wish.' She removed one from the basket and tossed it to him, then turned her back and removed her sandals while he stood to cover himself, wrapping the towel hastily around his middle, ensuring that the excess below the tuck hung straight down in front.

Hoisting her wide skirt above her ankles, she stepped lithely onto the flat rock beside the whirlpool and sat down, tucking the skirt under her legs and arranging it to cover her knees. She tossed her hair out behind, and leaned back on her hands, looking up at the trees and swinging her feet in the water.

Thrilled that she had come to sit close, Charles followed her every move, unable to take his eyes off her for even a moment, enthralled by her graceful actions, and how she looked with her hair loose and wild and falling.

'It's such a beautiful spot here,' she said. 'All these lovely yellow flowers... so calm and peaceful. I come to sit here often to listen to the birds and the water.' She looked down at him, her eyes questioning. 'What is it, Charles?'

'What... what do you mean?'

'You said you needed to talk to me.'

'Oh, yes. Well...' Charles couldn't think of anything. 'It's not important... not really...'

'Am I making you uncomfortable... being here?'

'No, of course not, why do you say that?'

Her foot stopped swinging. 'You left so suddenly that Sunday... when you came to lunch. I knew you were uncomfortable with me cutting your hair. Was it because Sandy was rude? Or was it because I offended you with that friendly kiss?'

'God, Willa!' Charles gaped at her in dismay. 'How could you think that? I thought it was you who was offended. What makes you think I didn't want you to cut my hair? Don't you know I'm...can't you see...?'

Lost for words, Charles looked down at the distorted vision of her feet in the water, berating himself for his cowardice. He wanted desperately to tell her how he felt. How she excited him as nothing ever had, but was afraid that if he did, she may leave and he would never see her again. The few brief encounters he had experienced with the carnival girls had not prepared him for this. He felt so inadequate and doltish in her company. Her sensuality awed him. Yet he knew he would have to do something. He may never get another chance.

He reached down and took hold of her one foot, firming his grip as she let out a small gasp of surprise and instinctively tried to pull it away. Holding it in both hands, he lifted it up and kissed it.

She giggled nervously. 'What are you doing...?'

'Just a friendly kiss... are we friends, Willa?'

'Yes, of course...'

'Can I kiss it some more? It's so beautiful... you are so beautiful.'

Not waiting for an answer, he kissed each toe in turn, while she sat with a bemused smile, unresisting, and encouraged, Charles shifted his attention to her ankle, then started on her leg.

'Charles? Enough…let go, please.'

He released it and she drew both her legs up sideways beneath her and tucked them away under her skirt, refusing to meet his eye.

Undaunted, he took her hand instead. 'Are you angry with me, Willa?'

She gave him a quizzical smile. 'Are you flirting with me, Charles?'

'No, It's more than that, Willa.' He paused to take a deep breath. It was time. 'I'm crazy about you… can't you tell?'

She gave a slow, pensive sigh and removed her hand. 'Yes, Charles, of course I can. And I think I should go now… really.'

'No, please, I want you to stay.'

'I'm married, Charles.'

He nodded. 'Yes.'

'It doesn't bother you?'

'Of course, but I cannot help myself. I love you for what you are… everything about you.'

She laid an apologetic hand on his arm. 'If things were different...'

She made a move to rise, but he held her back. 'Ouma told me you had found a diamond.'

'Yes. Bally found it. Only a small one, but Sandy is sure we'll find more, now that he knows where to dig. It was good advice, what you said about being closer to the river.' Her tone was matter-of-fact, as if she was not really interested and wanted to get it over with quickly so she could leave.

Charles had other ideas. He felt only mild guilt at having salted the claim. Even a salted diamond was better than none, and he was quite prepared to have Bally find more if it would mean keeping her from leaving. Meanwhile, he had to think of something to change her mood and keep her from leaving him now.

Willa herself solved the dilemma. 'How was your trip?' she asked.

Charles started from the beginning, drawing it out. He told of the animals in great detail, and about the colour and mystery of the wildflowers, how it had all combined to change his life. He spoke mundanely at first, as she had done, preoccupied and not really interested in repeating it, but was soon encouraged by the intensity of her expression and change in her demeanour as she became intrigued, and suddenly he found he was enjoying telling her about it.

She giggled when he told her how he and Oupa had felt like royalty walking through the herd of curious springbok in the dark, then laughed out loud when he told how Oupa had jokingly threatened to shoot him for admitting he was a *rooinek*.

When he spoke about the hunting party and the slaughter of the animals, her face crinkled in sympathy, then bloomed with delight when he told how he had smashed the bottles of expensive French brandy to set fire to the wagons.

'Oh, how wonderful, Charles! What a perfect thing to do.' She clapped her hands in approval. 'Oh, I *am* so proud of you!'

He beamed at her. 'Are you really?'

'Oh yes! It's the most marvellous story. It serves them right for being such swines.'

'Don't tell anyone, will you. I could end up in the Breakwater.'

'I promise not to tell a soul. It will be my very own special story. Oh, those poor creatures. It was a wonderful thing you did, Charles.' Her eyes suddenly filled with tears.

Charles was instantly alarmed. 'Willa… what's wrong?'

'Nothing.' She looked at him, unblinking, eyes bright, and he couldn't resist it. He leaned forward and kissed her quickly on the cheek - as she had done - trying not to give the wrong impression.

She caught his arm as he lifted away, holding

him there. Then her fingers tightened and she drew him back.

She kissed him full on the mouth, her lips parted, and she allowed them to linger softly, and when he thought she was about to remove them, she slipped an arm around his neck and pressed harder.

Charles responded with the eagerness of a doomed man being given a second chance. He enveloped her with both arms and pulled her close and hard against him. Too close.

With her legs tucked beneath her, trapped there by the skirt, she overbalanced and fell forward, pushing both of them away from the rock.

Charles tried to recover, but the uneven bottom and the resistance of the water around his legs was too much. He fell back into the whirlpool and Willa sprawled on top of him. Caught by the water and filled with air, her wide skirt billowed up to almost cover her head.

With a squeal she scrambled to her knees, grabbing at the cloth, trying in vain to clamp it between her legs, so it was a few moments before she noticed Charles.

He floundered helplessly on his back, hampered by her weight as she straddled his legs, sitting on them, and he was trying to reach the towel that had come undone and been whipped away by the swirling water.

They both became aware of his exposure at the same time. It was no longer a dead fish. It had miraculously come alive. And not only alive and well, but seemingly ravenous.

Willa gasped and covered her face quickly with her hands, but Charles could see one startled eye peeping from between spread fingers.

He made a sudden lunge for the towel, missing it, and knocking her off balance for the second time. The skirt came free again as she fell forward, ballooning up, but this time she did not bother to restrain it.

She lay straddling him, supporting his head to prevent it going under, and they stared at each other in shocked surprise. Then her face turned pink and she began to giggle.

Charles grinned foolishly back at her, feeling the tingle of blood in his own face. But also feeling something far more disconcerting. She wore no pantalets beneath the skirt, and even against the coolness of the water he could feel the heat of her thighs pressing against his hips. It was almost there. Only inches away from a feast fit for kings.

'Well... I suppose... we're even now...' he managed to blurt out.

She nodded several times, biting her lip as she

tried ineffectually to stifle the laughter, then she must have felt it too, for suddenly her expression changed. She shifted slightly, moving forward, and lowered her lips to meet his, kissing him fiercely.

Any feast, let alone a royal one, is apt to satisfy even the most voracious appetite swiftly after a lengthy fast, and Charles was no exception. He did not even complete the first course.

Willa lifted up to look at him with concern, then held his head in close against her bosom, stroking and rocking gently as if consoling a distraught child.

'It must have been a long time,' she whispered.

'I'm sorry... I couldn't help it,' Charles moaned dolefully.

She pushed away from him, forcing him to look at her, smiling at him. 'It's nothing to be ashamed of.' She kissed him tenderly on the forehead. 'Would you feel better if I told you I feel very flattered?'

'Not really.'

She shifted onto her knees and began to unbutton her shirt. 'No looking please, turn around.'

Charles made a rapid recovery. 'Do I have to?'

'Yes.'

She moved away and he rolled over, dipped his head under the water, wanting to speed up the recuperation period, and was happy to feel his vitality responding swiftly. He shook his head to clear the disbelieving thoughts that clamoured inside, gradually replacing them with the truth. It had really happened. He listened to the sounds of her struggle with the wet clothes, happy beyond his wildest expectations. 'Are you sure you don't need help?'

'Yes,' she said firmly.

She called to him from the deeper water. 'Come on, time for a swim.'

'Now it is your turn to look away.'

She laughed. 'Why? I've already seen it... twice.'

'Turn around.'

'No.'

With sudden bravado, he stood up, and she quickly ducked under, the dark cloud of her hair spreading wide.

He swam towards her underwater, seeing the hazy outline of her wonderful body as he came up close to put his hands around her small waist. She felt as soft and sleek as an otter.

Standing chest-deep, she held her head back and swept the hair from her face, smoothing it away with the long slender fingers as she had done the first time he had seen her, then she entwined her fingers behind his neck and swung her legs up to clasp him around the waist. She looked at him in astonishment.

'Already?'

He grinned sheepishly.

She closed her eyes and leaned back, smiling as his hands roamed the body he had dreamt about so often, sliding down, supporting her weight - guiding her.

'Oh, God,' she whispered. 'I knew this was going to happen. Mother forgive me... I knew it from the beginning... Oh!' She gasped, as Charles, still holding her firmly about the legs, fell slowly back and disappeared below the surface.

'Charles? What's wrong... why are you...?' She broke off to paddle furiously with both hands to prevent herself from also going under. Finally, he let go of her legs and she was able to stand.

'God, Charles!' she exclaimed as she dumped him, limp and gasping like a barbel, in the shallow water. 'I thought you were going to drown.'

'I'm sorry, Willa, I just can't help it. As soon as you come near me, I lose control.'

She clamped a hand over his mouth. 'No apologising, just be patient.'

Late in the afternoon, she lay sprawled on top of him once more, entangling him in her hair, and once again his hands had resumed their exploration, but with less urgency now that the feast had been given the attention it deserved and hunger satisfied. For both of them. That he had been able to give as well as take was an achievement of immense satisfaction for Charles, even rivalling that of his own pleasure, and the smile that threatened to become a permanent fixture on his face bore inadequate testament to his happiness. Most of it was hidden deep within.

Hunger has little to do with appetite though, and his eyes devoured her body unsatiated. And there was always the odd nibble to keep things going.

'No more, Charles, please.' She rolled off to kneel beside him, covering herself with her hair, suddenly shy. 'I really must go.'

She put on the clean blue dress from the basket while he grappled with his wet, and still unwashed, trousers.

He picked up the basket, intending to accompany her as far as possible, but she took it from him.

'No, Charles, stay until I'm gone. I only want to be alone with you here, in this beautiful place, nowhere else... please? And I don't think it's a good idea to visit the camp too often.'

You'll come again?'

She stood on her toes to kiss him softly on the mouth, giving him the answer.

He watched until the last flash of blue had disappeared through the bushes, then listened until he could hear no further sound of her departure.

It was dark when he finally left the pool. Dark and lonely, and by then, a vague sadness had stolen over him.

.From his despised seat on the lead wagon, Marthinus Steyn watched with concern as the storm built. Each day, for the past week, the clouds rising above the towering barrier of the Maluti mountains had pushed higher, their anvil-shaped heads spreading farther into the plain. Now their swollen bellies had turned the colour of ripe mulberries and rumbled continuously.

The final stretch of the day's leg was through five miles of open sandstone country that would give little protection from hail, so while the Zulu encouraged the oxen with whistles and whip cracking, Jurie and Timisani removed the canvas canopy from the second wagon and lashed it down over the supplies.

Aneline rode ahead, leading the way through

the tall, red-topped grass, her elevated position on the horse making it easier to pick out the safest route towards the bell-shaped hill that her father had pointed out as being their destination. She waited impatiently every few hundred yards for the plodding oxen to catch up, spending the interludes casting anxious glances towards the threatening clouds.

The past few weeks had been successful, though tiresome, with long, boring treks between destinations, and little for her to do except try to keep the contents of the three-legged pot interesting. She had been looking forward to the change of scenery the foothills would bring as they began the long trek home through the Caledon valley, but rains there could delay them, and she tried not to dwell to much on the consequences of not meeting the bank's deadline.

They reached the valley with barely enough time to outspan on the narrow track above the river when the storm broke. Timisani was still returning from having driven the oxen deep into the cover of the willow trees when the gloom was fractured by lightning, and he raced for cover, spurred on by booming claps of thunder.

Gusts of wind rocked the wagons and tugged at the trees, lifting the drooping branches high, then pushing them flat with powerful down-draughts that scattered the dead leaves below. It blew in a stinging gale under the wagons, causing the restraining brake-blocks to creak and squeal in protest.

Marthinus huddled his family together under a wagon, covering them with a sail, as the valley became hazy with dust and wind-drifted rain. Quabe and Timisani followed his example beneath the second wagon, their excited chatter finally stilled.

The wind stopped suddenly, and behind the ominous silence they heard the dull roar of approaching hail. The first stones began to drop around them, thudding solidly onto the wagons, and clanging against the exposed cooking pots and tools that hung on the sides.

It plopped in the river, like jumping fish, and clattered amongst the rocks and trees, growing in intensity until the individual sounds were engulfed by the stupefying clamour of the main column of hail.

Aneline squealed as a stone half the size of her fist glanced off a wheel spoke and smashed into her leg. Jurie pulled her in closer and she put her head under the sail, clamping her hands to her ears as above her the cooking pots began clanging like bells.

The hail passed as swiftly as it had come, moving down the valley in a dense, dark pillar, leaving behind a carpet of white, and swirling veils of light, cold mist.

The animals stood bewildered under the shredded branches of the trees, their wet hides strewn with leaves and flecks of grass. While the men checked them for signs of injury, Aneline climbed on the wagon under which they had sheltered and cleared the canvas cover, and also the pots, all of which had filled to the brim with egg-size lumps of ice.

Standing on top, she surveyed the ravaged splendour of the landscape in wonder, awed by the beauty and raw power that had created it. Like an apology from heaven, shafts of sunlight appeared, forming a double rainbow in the mist behind the retreating storm, glowing gold on the sandstone hills, and dazzling her as it reflected from the brilliant white on the ground below. The red-seeded heads of the grass poked through like bloodied spears.

She shivered and climbed down from the wagon to see what the others were doing.

Jurie was examining a dead vulture that must have been caught high in the boil of the clouds. He spread the wings to show her the size, stepping out three full paces from the tip of one wing to the tip of the other. Only a few stringy feathers remained.

'The poor thing must have been terrified,' Aneline cried.

'It's only a vulture, Anna.' Jurie used his big toe to prise open the viciously hooked beak. 'Look. Imagine him digging your eyes out with that.' He turned it over and prodded with his foot. The grotesque body was soft and pulpy under the grey skin, as if every bone was crushed.

'Stop it, Jurie. That's horrible.' Aneline shuddered with revulsion and turned away.

For the next two weeks the storms were a regular occurrence, coming every second or third afternoon, and although they suffered no more hail, her father insisted they outspan early each day where the willow trees were thickest and would provide the most protection for the animals. The first time they had been lucky, he said, with no injuries - apart from the bruise on Aneline's leg, and a few small cuts on the tough oxen - but he was not taking any chances. He had seen larger animals than oxen killed by hail.

As Aneline had feared, once they left behind the small settlement that had been their final call, their progress through the valley was frustratingly slow. The track ran on the muddy flats beside the river, and it was heavily veined by the run-off of water. The numerous streams that fed the swollen river were rough and treacherous, often requiring them to double-span the teams and pull the wagons through one at a time.

Nevertheless, despite the hard work, the oxen thrived on the sweet grasses, and Aneline was kept occupied by the abundance of game-birds available to test her culinary skills. And the swollen river itself, which was too hazardous to cross, even at the drifts, was a blessing. With two wagon-loads of valuable goods, and their own lives at stake, it gave welcome protection from the renegade Koranna Hottentots purported to be harbouring in the old Bushman caves on the opposite side.

Quabe glared frequently across at the sandstone cliffs, as if willing the renegades to appear so he could extend a greeting with his axe, but they saw nothing. Still, for almost a week, until they were well clear of the area, the fires were kept hidden at night, and Aneline was forbidden to ride out of sight. It was a restriction that for once she had no quarrel with. The grim-looking cliffs and stark red hills of the badlands gave her an uneasy feeling that lingered until well after they had reached the flatter country of the Orange River.

As they travelled south, away from the mountains, the storms lessened, then stopped altogether, although thunder still rumbled in the distance, and the sky at night provided spectacular entertainment as it flickered and glowed.

'The good rains won't be long now,' Marthinus predicted. 'Not more than two, maybe three weeks. It's been a long drought. Much too long.'

'We'll be home by then.' Jurie was confident.

Aneline hoped he was right. By her calculations, they still had eight days to go before they reached the farm. At least a week had been lost with the slow progress through the valley, and the date she had arranged with the bank for a payment had passed four days ago. It would be almost two weeks overdue by the time they arrived.

She said nothing to her father or brother, seeing no point in worrying them when she knew they were already doing as much as they could. But it would be ironic, she thought, if they were to lose the farm because of the rain, when it was the lack of it that had caused the problem in the first place.

They lost another two days at Colesberg, after off-loading and having to wait for a replacement load of timber and, fuming impatiently at the delay, Aneline decided to do something about it.

'Sorry, miss,' the clerk at the coach station told her when she enquired about a ticket to Hope Town, 'I have no seats available. We even have a waiting list.'

'Is there no other way?'

The clerk shook his head in apology. 'With new

diggers arriving every day you would think they'd put on another coach, but all they do is talk about it.'

Aneline considered riding ahead by herself, but that solution too, was denied her.

'Don't be stupid, Anna,' her father said. 'It's not safe for a girl on her own. Too many funny people about. Just be patient. A few more days won't make any difference.'

With no avenue left, she sent a letter to the bank instead, explaining the delay, and asking for a two week extension, then she tried to put it out of her mind. She'd done all she could for the moment. At least they would know what was happening. Delays were common in the transport business at the best of times, and these were definitely *not* the best of times.

The Hope Town branch of the Standard Bank was one of the few stone buildings in the town. Solid and ornate, it was the economic fulcrum around which the local agricultural community turned.

The new manager from Cape Town was proud of his elevated status as a leading citizen. His popularity had soared as the drought-stricken populace had sought to buy his sympathy. It had plummeted sharply, however, when, after accepting invitations to wine, dine and flirt with the womenfolk of the town, he nonetheless began to implement his new stringent policies. And with a most unsympathetic enthusiasm.

Aneline had to wait an hour before she could get to see him, and when he finally called her in, the news was not good.

'Of course, I sympathise with your predicament, Miss Steyn,' the manager said, allowing his eyes to wander candidly. '...and I do wish there was something I could do, but the bank has had to take a very firm position on these overdue loans. The way things are these days, well, I'm sure you understand how it is?'

'But I told you we were delayed by the weather,' Aneline protested. 'Did you not get my letter?'

'Ah...' He dragged his eyes away to leaf through the bulky file. 'Yes, there it is. Sent on the sixteenth. Well overdue, I'm afraid. If only you had contacted me sooner.'

'How could I?' Aneline was still too stunned by the news to feel any anger. 'We were in the middle of a trek. Anyway, I don't see why you can't just take our money now. I'm sure Meneer Visser would have agreed. We've been dealing with him for years. He knows us well. Why don't you ask him?'

'Yes, well, I'm afraid he is no longer with the bank, my dear, and things have changed since then. I have a big responsibility to the shareholders, you understand, and you are already five months behind.'

'Is there no way I can stop this... this auction thing?'

'Only if the amount of the loan is paid in full before that date. Let me see...' He checked the file again and scribbled a few quick calculations. '... two hundred and thirty eight pounds, twelve shillings and four pence, including interest.' He closed the file and placed his hand flat on the top in a gesture of finality. 'Are you are able to raise that amount, Miss Steyn?'

'No. If I could, I would pay you, wouldn't I?' She stood to glare down at him. 'My grandfather started that farm, sir. I don't see how you can take it away for such a little amount.'

The manager observed her thoughtfully for a few moments. 'You know, it could be a blessing, my dear. With the money left over from the sale you should be able to buy a nice little dress shop, or something of that nature, here in town.' He leaned back to cross his legs and smile at her. 'With my help you will have no difficulty in making a go of such an enterprise. And a pretty girl like you, Miss er... Aneline, should be enjoying herself in the town instead of trying to work a debt-laden farm, don't you think?'

Aneline swung away and strode to the door without answering. She slammed it shut behind her, shattering the fancy glass panels, and causing the customers and staff to start nervously and stare in shocked surprise.

Willa came every Sunday afternoon, and he was always there before her, sitting on the flat rock beside the pool, waiting.

She usually arrived after having spent a few hours visiting with Ouma Theron, either baking, or simply talking or sewing, and he suspected she used that as her excuse for getting away from her husband, but he never asked.

Only once did he visit the Therons' while she was there, and the atmosphere was so thick with subterfuge it embarrassed everyone. Thereafter, he visited Oupa on Saturday or during the week, to talk about hunting and diamonds, and to keep up with his language lessons.

On Sunday mornings, before Bally departed on his own regular visits to neighbouring Africans, they washed clothes, checked traps, or repaired equipment – tasks usually completed soon after sunrise, for they both rose early. The remainder of the morning he spent waiting by the pool, preparing the low-walled reed shelter he had erected there for added privacy, lining the sandy floor with the fluffy tops of freshly cut reeds. With a blanket thrown over, it made a wonderfully soft bed. On one of the poles he cut a notch for every Sunday she was there, and from it hung garlands of the yellow flowers – her favourite colour. By the time she arrived he was strung as tight as a whip-snare.

She used the pool often during the week when he was busy, tying a ribbon across the path so he would know she did not want him there. When he asked her the reason, she was obscure. 'I'm sorry, my darling, but can't we just leave it like that... please?'

He let her make the rules, and worked hard on his claim in an attempt to quench his smouldering impatience. And in some ways it was worth it, for the build-up of anticipation during the week exploded on the Sunday afternoons into a banquet of passion that left him deliriously contented for days.

By unspoken agreement, they never mentioned her husband, and he stayed away from their claim as much as possible. Not so much because she had requested it, or out of guilt, for he still felt little, but because he did not want to see her there with the man to whom she legally belonged. He had plotted every inch of her body, and could no longer look at the man who had possessed what he had come to believe was his own special domain. The mere thought of another's hands touching his wonderful preserve was enough to push him to the brink of violence.

She was his love and he wanted all of her, and the only time she ever became angry with him was when he took his hand from between her thighs and inhaled deeply on it.

Aghast, she struck his hand away, her eyes blazing, and cheeks turning first pale then pink. 'Don't be so disgusting!'

'What's wrong?' he asked, a little taken aback by the sudden outburst. He could not imagine how anything associated with her body could be called disgusting. 'It is perfectly natural. It's you.'

'No, it's not natural... and don't ever do it again. I don't like it.'

'Yes, you do,' he contradicted, a mischievous gleam in his eye, 'and I will do it again if I want to. You can't stop me.'

'Charles, I'm serious, I don't.... why are you looking at me like...' She broke off as he kissed her and pushed her down gently, but firmly. He started kissing her on the stomach, moving down quickly to the wiry dark hair, holding her down with a forearm as she started to resist.

'What are you doing? ...Oh, my God, Charles... Don't!' She pulled on his hair with both hands, trying to hold him back, wailing in despair as he ignored her entreaties and forced his way between her tightly clenched thighs. 'No, please!'

Suddenly she ceased struggling, her body relaxing, and he almost stopped, fearful he had gone too far. Then her body began to move in the way he knew, and he was surprised at how quick it was.

'Oh......Jesus!' she cried, her breath rasping.

She let go of his hair to cover her face, moaning softly behind her hands, and twice more her body responded to ecstasy before he released her.

He brushed the damp hair from her face and moved to kiss her, but she pushed him away.

'Don't you dare kiss me! God... I'm so ashamed! How could you do that to me?'

He grinned at her.

'Don't. God, you're disgusting!'

'You liked it, I could tell'

'It was... I don't know... Oh, Charles, I'm so ashamed!'

'Why? It's only natural. Isn't that what you said to me the first time in the pool?'

'No, I didn't mean that. It's never happened to me… like that.'

'Good.'

She had taught him everything, and it did much for his ego to know he had been able to do something in return. He had shared an experience with her that she had never shared with anyone else, and he basked happily in the knowledge.

Their lovemaking gradually took on a new and softer intensity, and there were moments when he was aware of her studying him when she thought he wasn't looking. When he caught her at it, her eyes and her smile were tender.

When nine notches had been carved on the pole, Charles decided that before he carved the tenth, he would ask her to go away with him. He wanted to be with her more than only once a week. He wanted to be with her all the time. He could think of no reason why she would want to stay with her useless husband. They had no children, and he had enough money to take care of her as she deserved.

Although she had never said it, he was sure that she loved him. Their lovemaking, and way she looked at him, could have no other meaning. They would go north, away from the desert and into the beautiful Caledon Valley Oupa Theron always talked about. They would buy a small farm and raise a family, and he would give her flowers every day. Yellow flowers;

her favourite colour.

'Coffee, dear?' Ouma Theron poised the jug over Willa's mug.

'No, thank you.'

'You look a little pale, dear, not feeling well?'

'It's this terrible heat. I wish it would rain.'

'Yes, we do need it badly, but when it comes, you'll be sorry you wished. It doesn't rain here… not like in the south. Here it comes like a waterfall, and when it starts to…'

'I'm sorry, Ouma... do you mind if I use your wash bowl? I think if I give my face a rinse...'

'Of course, dear, use some of the nice cold water from the cool-bag.'

Ouma fetched Willa a towel, then went across to the sorting table where Oupa was cleaning his rifles. He had cleared the table and laid them on a blanket ready for stripping..

'Where did you put my pull- through, Hettie?' he asked. 'I hope you haven't used it to tie up your flour bags again.'

'I think she is pregnant.' Ouma said.

'What?'

'I said, I think Willa is pregnant.'

'Ja? How come?'

'What sort of question is that? You know what I mean.'

'I mean, how come you think she is pregnant.'

'This is the second time she has visited in the morning and been sick. She is pregnant all right, I can tell by her eyes.'

Oupa looked up, frowning. 'What's wrong with her eyes?'

'Don't be a loskop, Danie. There is nothing wrong with her eyes. When a woman is pregnant her eyes somehow show it. Sometimes I wonder why I bother talking to you about these things, really.'

'Ja, well, you know how it is, Hettie. Why don't you just ask her?'

She probably doesn't know.'

'Oh, well then...' Oupa returned his attention to the rifles, shaking his head in bewilderment.

When Ouma questioned Willa, she looked blank. 'Sick in the morning? What do you mean?'

Ouma sighed patiently, then took one of Willa's hands and patted it gently. 'I mean, are you pregnant, dear?'

Willa looked at her for a moment longer, then

lowered her eyes. 'Yes,' she said quietly, I thought I might be. I'm overdue. I just wasn't sure.'

Ouma squeezed her hand. 'I'm happy for you, dear. It's what you wanted, isn't it?'

'Yes, of course...'

'Have you told him yet?'

When Willa remained silent, Ouma prodded further. 'I mean your husband.'

Willa's reply was barely a whisper. 'You know, don't you?'

Ouma Theron gave her hand a consoling pat then got heavily to her feet. She fetched the coffee pot and added a good slug of brandy to both mugs. 'Drink up, dear, it will settle your tummy and make you feel better.'

'I suppose it must have been obvious.'

'Yes, It was. Are you sure it is not your husband's child?'

'Yes. I know it isn't.' Willa chewed on her lip and studied her restless fingers. 'You have been so good to me, Ouma. I don't know what you must be thinking of me now.'

'I'm not blaming you, my dear, God knows, it is none of my business. Mind you, I can't say I approve either. It is a sin, what you are doing, but it is done, and is something you will have to live with.'

'Yes, I suppose I will.'

They sat for a while in reflective silence.

'I suppose I should feel ashamed, Ouma, but I don't. I feel guilty sometimes. I've never done this sort of thing before, and I know it's terribly wrong, but I don't think I've been this happy either... I just don't know what to think any more.'

'Oh my,' Ouma sighed. 'It's worse than I thought. Are you in love with him?'

'I think... at times, I'm mad about him. He makes me feel so... good.'

Ouma sighed again, more deeply. 'Oh, dear.'

'What can I do, Ouma? It has to end, doesn't it...?' her voice began to waver, 'he's younger than me, and I... oh, God, I wish this wasn't happening....'

Ouma stood up and moved to comfort her, pulling her close and patting her shoulder. 'I know dear, I know...' She gave her a hug. 'Come, you must think of the good things. You will have a lovely baby to care for, and you still have your husband to think of... here, use my apron.'

After Willa had dried her eyes, Ouma gave her a final squeeze and sat down. 'Tell me about your husband. Is he cruel to you?'

Willa shook her head. 'No, he's never been that.'

'Good. I can't stand a man who lifts his hand to a woman.'

'He didn't always drink like this,' Willa murmured. 'It's only because he feels such a failure. He's a very sweet person really, and it wasn't his idea to come here, it was mine. I thought it would be good for us. Everyone seemed to be so excited about diamonds, and as we had no children I thought it was worth a chance. I didn't think it was going to be so hard.'

'I think we all felt like that, dear. Fortunately for Oupa and me it doesn't matter, the children look after the farm now and we are just in the way. For us, it is something to do, but it is no place for a young married couple. Do you still love your husband?'

Willa shrugged. 'I don't know... I suppose so... in a way.'

Ouma was thoughtful for a moment. 'If you told him you were going to have a baby, would that make a difference, do you think?'

'You mean tell him... as if it was his?' Willa shrugged helplessly. 'I don't know if I could do that, Ouma, and what if he should find out?'

'What would he do if you told him the truth?'

'I'm not sure, he's not a very strong person, inside.'

Ouma took one of Willa's hands. 'It is

274

something only you can decide on, Willa, and it is not a decision I would like to make in your place, but you will have to do something soon, this is no place for a pregnant woman, and it is a very rough ride back to Cape Town... or even to Hope Town, for that matter. You could lose the child, and that would be a sad thing.'

Willa took a deep breath and let it out, as if coming to a decision. 'Yes, you're right, Ouma. We should leave right away. I won't tell Sandy anything until we get back to Cape Town. I have my family there… if anything should happen.'

'I think that is a very sensible thing to do,' Ouma agreed. 'Will you keep in touch with me? I'd like to hear how you get on. I'll give you my address.'

'I'd like that, Ouma. Would you let me know… about Charles...?'

'Yes, of course. Will you say anything to him, before you go?'

Willa sat for a long time, chewing reflectively on her lip. When finally she looked up, anguish showed in her eyes. Unable to speak, she simply shook her head.

'Good morning, meneer!'

Charles looked up from his gravel washing to see a khaki-clad, swarthy man standing on the bank above him, and the first thing to catch his eye was the blue insignia of the Cape Mounted Police on his sleeve.

'Can you help me please? I'm looking for a Mister Otherstone. Charles Otherstone.'

Charles returned the greeting and tried to smile with muscles turned suddenly wooden. 'It's Atherstone, what's wrong, officer?'

'You are he?'

'Ja, why are you looking for me?' He spoke in Afrikaans and the policeman relaxed visibly.

'Good. You can speak the language. My English is not so good. Man! But I have been looking for you everywhere. It is not so easy to find a person here. So many people, and all moving about. I need to speak with you on a very important matter.'

Charles handed the cradle over to Bally and followed the man to where two horses had been tethered in the shade of the trees near his tent.

The policeman introduced himself without offering his hand. 'Corporal Pienaar, Cape Police. Do you have a bucket for me to water the horses?'

Charles fetched a bucket of water, then offered the corporal a drink from one of the canvas cool-bags.

He gulped the water thirstily and nodded

appreciatively. 'Funny how those things work, isn't it? You would think it would leak out all over the place.'

Charles could stand the suspense no longer. His jaw was beginning to ache with tension. He had already made up his mind to deny he had ever seen the hunting party or their wagons. With luck, the corporal would not yet have spoken to Oupa Theron.

'What did you want to see me about, Corporal?'

The policeman adopted an official manner. 'It is the matter of a missing parcel, sir, given to you by a Mister er...' He removed a note book from his breast pocket and began leafing through it, and Charles felt the muscles in his jaw relax into a smile of relief. He decided to help. 'I think his name was Smythe.'

'That's it, sir. Do you know the gentleman?'

'No. I only met him once. He paid me to deliver the package to Hope Town. It was for a Mister Sylvester, I think.'

'I see... can you spell that for me please?'

Charles spelled it for him and the corporal wrote it down carefully.

'So, you don't have the parcel, hey?'

'No.' Charles explained what he had done with it, and the policeman looked resigned.

'I see, and you don't know what were the contents?'

'I never opened it. They were supposed to be important papers. Something to do with an inheritance. Why? What's happened to it?'

The corporal ignored the question. 'You mean like valuables and such?'

'I really can't say. Something like that, I suppose.'

'Would you be able to identify it?'

'Of course. It was bright red... has it gone missing?'

'I hope that is not the case, sir, but I will have to ask you to accompany me to Hope Town to try and clear up the matter.'

Charles was dismayed. 'But that is nearly a hundred miles away! Why don't you just ask for it at the post office? Anyway, it has probably been collected by now. It was months ago.'

The corporal seemed unimpressed by the argument. 'Ja... it could be the case, of course, but we don't believe it is so. We will require you to make a full statement about it.'

Charles was incredulous. 'You think I stole it?'

'I cannot say, sir, but you were the last one to have it, and we do not know for sure if what you say is correct. If you can prove that it was at the post office it will help to clear you.'

No matter what he said to try and convince the policeman it was not really necessary for him to go, the corporal was apologetic but adamant, and Charles realised he was not going to get out of it.

He was not worried about the parcel, or the veiled threats about stolen property. He remembered what the barman looked like at Pniel, and as soon as he could establish that it had been handed over, he would be in the clear. His main concern was that he was not going to get back before Sunday, and the thought of not being with Willa for so long a time sent him into mild shock.

While the Corporal was having a rest under the tree, he wrote a note to her and took it down to the pool to leave on the upright. Then, after thinking about it further, he retrieved the note and set out for their claim, but turned back before he was half-way when he remembered he would have to see her husband. In the end, he went to see the Theron's and told them what was happening.

'I can see how you must have been nervous,' the old man laughed. 'If it was me I most likely would have put my hands up straight away. What is this parcel thing all about?'

Charles explained and the old man looked relieved. 'I'm glad there is no problem, but if you want me to come with...'

'No, Oupa, but thanks. Just tell Willa what is happening, will you? She... they are expecting my help on a new dig.'

He borrowed the horse he had ridden to the pan, and promised Oupa he would bring back some tobacco and a new pull- through. Before waking the corporal, he removed the diamonds from the tin and put them in his money belt. It was a nuisance, but if he had to go, he may as well get the stones valued and make good use of a police escort.

Pniel had changed out of all recognition since he had last seen it. The number of tents had more than tripled, looking as if a large army had set up camp, and it was impossible to see how far it extended for the haze caused by dust and smoke from countless cooking fires.

The main street at six in the evening was so packed with people it was impossible to ride through, and they had to lead the horses around the back of the buildings, being careful not to fall in the holes. An extension had been built on to Jardine's hotel, and it no longer served as the post office. A separate building had been erected, a regular postmaster installed, and all the mail had been transferred there. It took some time to discover that the barman to whom Charles had given the parcel had since left, and no one could remember having seen a red parcel.

They bought an overcooked meal at one of the crowded canteens, then Corporal Pienaar suggested they ride upriver towards Hope Town and camp under a tree away from all the people. Policemen were not all that popular on the diggings, he explained, especially the Cape Mounted Police, who were not part of the new local constabulary. Charles had to agree with him, although he suspected it was not because of the people, but rather that the policeman did not want to let him out of sight. Thankfully, he had brought his bed roll. He looked at the stars for a while, then conjured up his favourite image of Willa and went to sleep with a smile on his face.

On the long ride to Hope Town he encouraged the policeman to talk of his experiences patrolling in the remote areas, and they spoke at length on hunting and animals, Charles cultivating the policeman carefully, and speaking only in Afrikaans.

The corporal seemed pleased by his many mistakes, laughing when he made them, and helping enthusiastically with some of the more difficult words, so by the time they reached the town, Charles was sure he had made a friend. He only hoped he was not going to need one.

Hope Town was almost deserted by comparison to Pniel. The buildings were more established and, because it was Sunday, nearly all closed. They rode through it to the Police Camp; an orderly collection of huts and corrugated iron buildings surrounding a parade ground and a flag pole. Limewashed stones edged the straight paths and dried-up flower beds. The corporal was leading the way through them, towards the stables, when Charles suddenly stopped. Several men, both black and white, were lounging inside a fenced compound guarded by two policemen with rifles.

'Are they prisoners?' Charles asked.

'Yes, why do you ask?'

'Just curious,' Charles replied, smiling. At least he would never have to worry about the three Irishmen again.

They spent the evening drinking and talking in the canteen with several off-duty policemen and members of a new militia, which had been formed, the corporal informed him, to patrol the badlands area of the Tulle river. The corporal seemed unduly interested in the militia, and Charles was not surprised when the policeman told him he had put in for a transfer.

'No offence meneer, but those bloody *rooinek* officers in Cape Town are a big pain in the bum. My sergeant is also leaving. He is going to be made the officer in charge, and I will become a sergeant. It will be good to get back to the bush.'

'They look like a tough bunch, corporal.'

'Ja, and they need discipline. When Erasmus takes over he will have them jumping around like ants in a fire.'

Next morning Charles gave the policeman a statement, including a description of Smythe, and all the details of the transaction as he remembered them.

At the Hope Town Post Office, the postmaster checked thoroughly, but could find no parcel waiting to be picked up that fitted the description.

'I'm sure I would have remembered,' he said, frowning, then called out to his assistant: 'Have you seen a red parcel at any time in the past few months, Martha?'

His question took the plump, pretty assistant by surprise. She had been staring at Charles over the top of a handful of papers, and she shuffled them hastily, dropping several to the floor.

They all waited patiently as she hastily gathered them up.

A red parcel was collected a few months ago, she informed them. She remembered it because it was red cloth and not paper. She did not know the person who picked it up.

Had it been registered, the postmaster explained, there would be a record, but no signature was required for picking up a parcel. Anyone could collect it.

'I think it is a dead end,' the corporal stated blandly.

After a few more questions, they left, and the policeman offered his hand. 'Thank you for your help, meneer. You are free to go. It seems we have been wasting our time.' He did not sound too disappointed.

Charles breathed a sigh of relief and went in search of a diamond dealer.

He went to three different ones, showing them his largest stone, then returned to the one who had given him the best valuation, handing over the remainder, and waiting nervously as each was meticulously weighed and scrutinised through a magnifying glass.

'River diamonds, by the look of them, Mister Atherstone. Quite good quality. Four thousand two hundred pounds is what I can offer. Of course, if you would like to try another valuation...?'

'No, I'll take your word for it,' said Charles, barely able to hide the excitement from showing. It was a full thousand more than he had expected. He was a rich man.

Charles took the dealer's promissory note

directly to the solid-looking stone bank across the road and opened his first account. He withdrew fifty pounds for running expenses, and buttoned it securely in the pocket of his shirt, patting its satisfying bulk into place at least once every minute as he waited for the paperwork to be completed.

He thanked the bank accountant who had taken care of everything, and was about ready to leave when a sudden bang and the sound of breaking glass made them both turn quickly.

A young woman strode angrily from the manager's office, past the gaping customers, and out onto the street.

'Good gracious!' the accountant exclaimed. 'Excuse me sir, I must see what has happened.'

The accountant hurried away, and Charles waited with a frown of concentration on his brow. He had only seen her back, but something in the purposeful manner in which the young woman had walked plucked at his memory.

The accountant returned. 'I do apologise for the interruption, Mister Atherstone, so unpleasant when these things happen.' He shook his head sorrowfully and shuffled the papers around unnecessarily on his desk. 'Now, where were we...?'

'I have a feeling I know that girl.' Charles said.

'Who is she?'

'You mean Miss Steyn?'

'Of course!' Charles smiled at the accountant's puzzled expression. 'I should have known. I just didn't see her face. What happened?'

'Very distressing business... the new policies at times like these. So unnecessary, I believe. Like many others they haven't had the easiest time with the drought.'

'Financial problems?'

'Well, I can't really say, but...' the accountant hesitated. 'I'm afraid the manager has seen fit to have an auction for their farm at the end of this month.' He sighed. 'It should go for a very reasonable price, if you are interested in attending.'

By his tone and expression Charles guessed he did not approve.

'Don't they own the farm?'

'Yes, they do, it's been in the family for a long time, but with the loans, and then the old man laid up for so long with his leg... the disaster with the vegetables... well, they have found it a bit difficult, to say the least.'

Charles was surprised. 'Marthinus must have borrowed an awful lot if he has to sell the farm.'

The accountant squirmed uncomfortably in

his chair. 'I'm afraid I'm not at liberty to disclose the details, sir, even though you know him. You will have to ask the manager.' He looked questioningly at Charles over the top of his spectacles. 'Would you like to see him?'

Charles sat thinking for a moment. 'If you could find out how much it is they owe, I would be obliged. They happen to be friends of mine, and I may be able to help in some way. I owe it to them.'

The accountant's gloomy expression brightened. 'It will be a pleasure, sir. One moment, if you please...'

He came back a short while later, looking decidedly peeved.

'I'm sorry, Mister Atherstone, but the manager says he is unable to see you for at least two hours.'

'Did you tell him why I wanted to see him... why I wanted a word with him?' Yes, I did, sir. Could you call later this afternoon perhaps?'

Charles stood up. 'No, I have to get back.' He shook hands with the disappointed accountant. 'Thank you for your help.'

Charles strode purposefully across the bank to the manager's office. A clerk was removing jagged pieces of broken glass from the half-open door, and moved aside hastily as Charles pushed past and went in.

A dapper, balding man sitting behind a large desk looked up with an expression of surprised inquiry. He opened his mouth to speak, but closed it quickly and shifted his chair back hastily when Charles put both hands flat on the desk and leaned forward to glare down at him.

'What did you say?' he demanded in a menacing tone, 'to upset my good friend, Miss Steyn?' He was not angry. The morning's successful events had left him in a buoyant mood that refused to be spoiled. Rather, he was finding it rather difficult not to smile at the man's frightened expression.

'Nothing!' the manager spluttered. 'I said nothing to Miss Steyn. Really, sir! I must protest at your... at this intrusion. I happen to be very busy at the moment.'

'So am I!' Charles thumped the desk with his fist, causing the manager to flinch and lean back even further. Since his involvement with Willa, Charles was not all that kindly disposed towards male bank personnel. 'How much is the loan?'

The manager glanced nervously towards the door as if hoping for reinforcements, but the clerk had closed it and made himself scarce.

'I really cannot disclose the...'

'How much?' Charles repeated mildly. He picked up a heavy stone paperweight and tossed it in his hand, glancing around the office as if looking for something worthwhile to throw it at.

'A little over two hundred pounds,' the manager blurted.

Charles looked at him contemptuously. 'You were going to sell the farm because of a small amount like that?'

'It is the bank policy. Naturally, if it was up to me, I would...' He broke off to grab clumsily at the paper tossed gently in his lap.

Charles walked to the door. It was not necessary to attract the accountant's attention. He already had it – and that of most everyone else in the bank as well. He beckoned him over with a crooked finger.

'Mister Jarvis,' he said pleasantly as the accountant hurried towards him. 'Would you be so kind as to remove sufficient funds from my account to pay Mister Steyn's loan in full?' He winked at the flustered accountant. 'I'll wait here with the manager until the transaction is completed.'

'With the greatest of pleasure, sir.'

Charles strolled casually around the office while the paperwork was being attended to, thoroughly enjoying every moment.

'One more thing,' he said, and they both looked up expectantly.

'I wish this to be confidential. I don't want them, or anyone to know who paid the loan. It does not have to be paid back, and you can make up any story you like. If at any time they need a loan in the future, you may use my funds as security.' He stopped pacing and raised his eyebrows at them. 'Is that clear?'

They both nodded, the manager looking pale and tight-lipped, the accountant smiling as though he had just won a prize.

Glaring defiantly at the manager, Charles laid a kindly hand on the accountant's shoulder. 'Take some time off, Mister Jarvis. See if you can find Miss Steyn and give her the news. I'm sure she will be relieved to hear it.'

Charles left them sitting there and walked out feeling as if he owned the bank. It was a good feeling. By far the most satisfying he had ever experienced.

Awkwardly encumbered by his sister's parcels, Jurie Steyn swore as the reluctant horse turned in a circle while he was trying to mount. With one foot already in the stirrup, he was forced into a clumsy hop, which turned into an embarrassing stumble when he tried to jerk his foot free after becoming aware that he was being watched by Christina Jarvis. She giggled.

He grinned sheepishly. 'Good day to you, Miss Christina.'

'Hello Jurie. I'm sorry, I didn't mean to laugh. How was your journey?'

He shrugged self-consciously. 'It was all right.'

'Have you seen your sister? My father is looking for her.'

Jurie nodded. 'She was angry with the bank manager and took off for the farm.' He held up the two bags. 'She left me with all her stuff. She has a temper, that one.'

Christina pulled a sour face. 'She won't have heard the good news then. I had better go and tell my father.'

'Huh?' Jurie looked at her with a puzzled expression. 'What do you mean, Miss Christina?'

'Jurie...' She blushed. 'You don't have to call me *miss* all the time, you know. We're friends.'

He shuffled uneasily and nodded, then suddenly remembered he had not removed his hat. He lowered one of the bags to snatch it from his head.

Christina smiled demurely, then became

thoughtful. 'If you're going back to your farm now, maybe *you* can tell her the news, Jurie.'

'Tell her what news, Miss... I mean, Christina?'

She hesitated. 'I'm not sure if I should be saying, but seeing as she has already gone and my father won't be seeing her...' She glanced around, as if wary of being overheard. 'Your farm won't be sold by an auction, Jurie. My father says the loan has been paid, and that Aneline should know right away.'

'I don't understand, Christina, what has happened? Has there been a mistake?'

'No.' She shook her head. 'My father is the accountant. He should know.'

'Know what?' Jurie was finding it increasingly difficult to follow.

'A friend of yours was in the bank when your sister had an argument with the manager, and he went straight in and threatened the manager with a good hiding, then he paid the loan.'

'Ja?' Jurie was incredulous. 'Who was it?'

Christina Jarvis shook her head. 'I don't know. Nobody has seen him before, and Pa had never seen him before either. He just came into the bank to open an account, Pa said.'

Jurie scratched his head and frowned. 'But we don't have any friends with money. There must be a mistake, Christina. Maybe I should go and ask what is happening.'

'No, Jurie, you can't. You'll get me into trouble... and Pa too. No one is supposed to know about it. Your friend said it was to be a secret and made everyone promise not to tell. I'm only telling you so you can let Anna know. You must promise not to say anything... do you promise?'

'Ja, I suppose...'

Christina nodded, then smiled coyly. 'Are you coming to the church picnic on Sunday? It's by the river, near the drift.'

'I'll try, Christina. I'll try hard to come. Thank you for asking.'

'You're welcome, Jurie.'

Aneline was also incredulous. 'She has probably got it all wrong and is telling you silly things because she likes you and wants you to like her back.'

His face brightened. 'You think so, Anna? She invited me to the church picnic on Sunday.'

'We're not talking about that, Jurie. What do *you* think, Pa?'

Marthinus nodded. 'I think you are right, Anna. We don't know anyone like that. It sounds to me like someone heard your argument and has started a rumour.

You know how they like to talk about everyone's business in the town.'

'Maybe it is someone who likes you, Anna,' Jurie ventured, 'and they want you to like them back.' He sniggered at his joke.

Aneline was not amused. 'Don't be dumb, Jurie, please.'

'Well, I think she is telling the truth. Christina wouldn't lie to me about such things.'

'Huh… little you know!'

'Oh, Ja? Well maybe I know more than you think. Like it was her father who was looking for you to tell you the good news himself, and he should know because he's the accountant.' Jurie gave her a smug look.

.Maybe you should go back in the morning and find out what's going on, Anna,' her father suggested, and Jurie's smug look changed to one of concern.

'You mustn't tell anyone that it was Christina who told us,' he said, frowning. 'It's supposed to be a secret.'

'I bet it is. But don't worry, Jurie, I'll keep your little secret. You will still be able to hold her hand at the picnic.'

Aneline could not bring herself to go directly to the

bank after her scene the day before. She found Christina alone at her home, baking for the picnic. After talking to her for only a few minutes, she was convinced that, although mistaken, Christina was telling the truth.

'And you're sure it was me your father was looking for?' Aneline enquired.

'Oh, yes. He asked me to help find you, and when I told him you had already gone he was quite disappointed. He was going to send a messenger, so I had to admit I had already told Jurie. I was expecting him to be angry with me, but he wasn't.'

'And he wouldn't tell you who it was?'

'No, he said it was none of my business. I spent all afternoon trying to find out, Anna,' Christina said earnestly. 'I even asked the new teller who has been calling on me if he could find out the name on the account, but he says it has been filed in the manager's safe.'

Aneline sat in troubled thought as Christina removed a tray of biscuits from the oven and then stoked the fire. She wanted desperately to believe. It would mean so much. But there had to be a mistake somewhere. Maybe it was someone else they were talking about, or the accounts had got all mixed up. Such things as strangers paying other people's debts simply didn't happen. At least not to her, it didn't.

'But it just can't be us, Christina. Did you hear anything else?'

'Martha Griel saw the man at the bank, and then the same man came into the post office with a policeman. She said they were looking for a red parcel, and the man spoke Afrikaans with an accent.'

Aneline was nonplussed. 'I don't know anyone with money, Christina, it all seems so strange. Did Martha say what he looked like?'

'Oh yes.' Christina giggled. 'She did that all right. She got all dreamy when I asked her. She said he was the handsomest man she had seen in a long time. You know what Martha is like. She probably means that day. He was about twenty-five, she thinks, and sort of tall, with dark hair and blue eyes. She said it made her legs go all wobbly just looking at him.'

Aneline laughed without conviction, her mind busy scanning all her acquaintances and friends. 'Well, I certainly don't know anyone like *that*!'

'Martha has been asking as many questions as I have,' Christina continued, 'but we can't find out anything. He left town on the Pniel road by horse yesterday, going straight from the bank. She said it was funny, but no one had seen the policeman before either.'

'I'll have to speak to your father, Christina. It

has to be a mistake. I don't know why anyone would do that for us without saying anything.'

Christina agreed with alacrity. 'I'll come with you, but I had better wait outside.'

Mister Jarvis was pleased to see her, but was also quite adamant. 'I'm sorry, Aneline, but it is strictly confidential.' He leaned back in his chair to smile at her. 'It seems that half the town knows about it. I've had several people ask me his name already.'

Aneline was still disbelieving. 'Are you sure there is no mistake?'

'No mistake.' He indicated once more to the cancelled loan agreement lying before her. 'Read it yourself. Your loan has been paid in full.'

'But surely, if our loan was paid by someone, don't we have a right to know who it is. Otherwise how can we thank him?'

Mister Jarvis looked at her for a while in silence, then he removed his glasses and polished them while he thought.

'I suppose there is no use trying to deny what appears to be common knowledge, but I cannot give you his name. I'm sorry.'

'Did he say anything at all? You know… about why he was paying it?'

'Only that he owed it to you. Surely you must know him from somewhere, Aneline?'

Aneline shook her head. 'I wish I did, sir.'

'He recognised you as soon as you came out of the manager's office.' He chuckled, almost wistfully. 'Rather noisily, if I remember.'

Preoccupied, Aneline continued to frown in thought, and the accountant leaned forward again to reassure her.

'Well, all I can tell you, Aneline, is that there is no mistake, and you have the papers to prove it. You are very fortunate to have such a friend.' He paused, suddenly remembering. 'Oh, yes. He also said that if you ever need to borrow money again he will guarantee the loan.'

Aneline was astounded. 'He will do that too?' She suddenly experienced the horrifying sensation of wanting to cry.

Harold Jarvis smiled with genuine pleasure at her expression. 'He was very... how should I say... determined, with the new manager. He insisted that I was to be the one to inform you, and I can tell you, Aneline, it has been one of the most pleasant duties I've ever had to perform. We have known your family for a long time.'

'Thank you, sir, you're very kind.' Aneline

stood to look at the accountant with a dazed expression. 'I wish I knew… I still can't believe it.'

He stood with her.   'Believe me, my dear, I would like nothing better than to be able to tell you his name. He was a most remarkable young man.'

Aneline rode home with her thoughts in turmoil, searching her memory for anyone she or the family would know who could afford to be so generous, but there was no one who even came close. It was a mystery.

She was still preoccupied an hour later when it began to rain.

Caught by surprise, her first thought was for the important document in her flimsy carry-bag. She removed her hat with the silly flowers and placed the bag inside, then she stuffed both down the front of her shirt. She looked around for somewhere to shelter, but it was already too late. She bundled the cumbersome skirt under her seat to free her legs, and that was the moment when she began to believe it was true. They owned the farm again. She had the document to prove it. Ma would not have to be with strangers. With an undignified yell of sheer exuberant joy, she dug her heels in and the startled mare took off at the gallop.

The rain pelted down hard, stinging her bare arms and face, blurring her vision, but she did not care.

Whooping with excitement, she raced through the puddles, screeching with delight as mud splattered her face. It was a good feeling. A truly *wonderful* feeling.

Fleetwood pondered the irony of his changed situation with a philosophical indifference that surprised even him. That his original idea of filling the wooden safe with valuables, then arranging for it to disappear in a puff of smoke along with himself, was no longer possible, did not bother him - the dust cloud created by those pressing would have been visible from the cliffs of Dover. What caused him more concern was the safe's raging success.

Its size and apparent immovability by unauthorised persons had attracted so much business that paperwork and security problems kept him awake for most of the night. But although its seeming invincibility may have convinced the unwary depositors, he knew better and, having considerable experience in such areas, worried that others would come to know as well.

He hired builders to replace the flimsy iron of his office walls with solid ones of stone, and had the redundant iron placed on the roof - sandwiching a thick layer of reeds.

The new building was not only cooler and more secure, but its imposing permanence amidst the ramshackle affairs surrounding it served to further enhance his reputation as a man of substance and foresight. As a direct consequence - and almost overnight - he discovered that besides being the most successful diamond dealer in Pniel, he was also in the banking business. Even the suspicious Ikey Hiam became a regular customer.

With an estimated five thousand diggers in the area and, not surprisingly, most not doing as well as they had expected, the collection of rings, watches, gold pins, and even photographs, had grown so large he had been forced to purchase two more safes to accommodate them. Prudently though, he went with the more conventional type.

As the business flourished, several offshoots appeared. From a simple depository, blossomed pawnbroking and short-term loans, which in turn led to an equally productive auctioning enterprise. Through loan defaults, he acquired a canteen, a store, several claims of dubious worth, and another diamond dealership.

Although he accepted the diamond agency reluctantly, it turned out to be one of his biggest triumphs, and the one that changed his thinking in a way he would never have thought possible.

Knowing nothing about diamonds - except that they were valuable - and wary of being duped by unscrupulous diggers and kopje-wallopers, he employed an expert appraiser and, after much persuasion by the crafty old Jew, reluctantly agreed to experiment with paying better and more honest prices than his competitors.

When the increase in business more than made up for the difference, Fleetwood was not only astonished, he felt betrayed. It seemed not only illogical to pay more than was necessary, it contradicted every basic principle of survival he had previously taken for granted.

Almost reluctantly, he came to the conclusion that there was more money to be made in being honest - and far less risk. He further discovered that he rather enjoyed playing the role of trusted benefactor - although he was still careful not to allow that to cloud his judgement.

His life had suddenly changed and, despite the heat, the dust, and the shortage of congenial company, he found himself happier than he had been in a long while. He extended the building further, installed a full-size bath, a four-poster bed complete with mosquito-proof canopy, and several other compensating luxuries. He could not have lived much better in Mayfair. He even managed to raise a toast to Toby Hollings one night after having had one too many.

But his most treasured asset was acquired the day a man and a woman came to see him about a loan.

As had become his custom with those who came begging, Fleetwood offered champagne, having found it was the most effective way to defuse nastiness when a loan was refused - which happened more often than not.

The man did not introduce himself or his ladyfriend. She sat upright with her elbow propped on her raised knee, holding the long-stemmed glass high and close to her lips. Although unseen beneath her full-length skirt, her legs were gracefully crossed, one ankle tucked behind the calf of the other. She wore several expensive-looking rings, but Fleetwood noted that none adorned her wedding finger.

Her male companion, dressed inappropriately in white, including the hat - which he failed to remove - also wore ludicrous silver spurs on the high heels of his riding boots. The ridiculous attire, and the over-manicured moustache with goatee beard, led Fleetwood to immediately assume he was American, but this was quickly dispelled when he spoke. After glancing at the label, the man refused both champagne and chair, and stood with legs astride and hands clasped beneath the tails of his coat, rocking on his toes. In an off-hand manner, he explained that he needed the money to cover a small gambling debt.

'I would not normally stoop so low as to ask for such a paltry sum as two hundred pounds,' he declared loftily. 'But a recent small misfortune has left me temporarily short of liquid funds, and being a man who believes that debts of honour should be settled promptly, find myself in the unfortunate position of having no choice in the matter. I'm sure, as a gentleman yourself, you understand how it is.'

'What misfortune?' Fleetwood asked bluntly. He had learned from experience not to overlook all the salient facts in a transaction - especially those glossed over and accompanied by so much folderol.

'Oh, nothing really.' He waved a deprecating hand. 'A small fire in a wagon while out hunting, that's all.'

'Oh yes, I heard about that,' Fleetwood said, shaking his head in genuine dismay. 'Such a tragic waste of good imported food and wines.'

'Of course, if you're worried about your money,' the man said with a belittling smile, 'you can hold my claim as security... cigar?' He removed two from the row in his breast pocket and held one up, raising an eyebrow in query.

'No, thank you.'

'Really?' He replaced it with a barely perceptable shrug and sniffed appreciatively at his before lighting it. He peered haughtily down through the smoke. 'It only happens to be one of the largest claims on the river.'

Fleetwood knew all about the man - and his claim was indeed one of the largest - but also no longer that productive. Nevertheless, it was still worth well in excess of two hundred pounds, and he would have seriously considered the request had the fellow not been such a boorish strutter. The only way he could see himself lending him the money was if he offered to put up his girlfriend as security instead.

So far, other than to murmur her thanks for the champagne, she had remained silent, and he suspected she was there only to impress. And, unlike her poseur escort, impress him she did. She had the sinewy, athletic look of a flamenco dancer, with sleek black hair swept severely back and tied into a bun with a red ribbon. As her companion talked she used her dark eyes freely, first taking careful stock of the tasteful furnishings, then observing Fleetwood with frank speculation over the rim of her glass.

Despite her olive complexion, Fleetwood suspected she was also a Londoner, but he was less inclined to be swayed by origin anyway, than appeal, and she appealed to him no end. And not only because he was desperate for female companionship. She would have struck the same chords no matter where they had been.

Although Fleetwood had made it a rule never to lend money to a gambler - which he believed was the equivalent of lending drink to an alcoholic - he was himself a bit of a punter, and with enough faith in his luck to take a risk when he thought the chances were better than even. And he was willing to bet there was something more behind her speculative glances than idle curiosity.

In any case, win or lose, he was not going to be intimidated by a man whose closest approach to being a gentleman was standing in the company of one.

'Sorry, old chap,' Fleetwood apologised mildly. 'But I don't lend for gambling debts, so I'm afraid it's no dice.'

The short, stunned silence that followed was broken by the woman. With becoming modesty she had turned away from Fleetwood's meaningful look and raised eyebrow, and was in the process of taking a covering sip when his apt rebuttal suddenly struck her. She snorted explosively into the glass, blowing a spray of champagne over her escort and, apparently, up her nose as well, for she collapsed forward, the almost full glass wavering precariously above her head as she coughed, spluttered, and emitted sounds suspiciously reminiscent of choking laughter.

Fleetwood was quick to rush to her aid. While her escort glared at her, frozen in outrage, he hurried around the desk to rescue the glass and thump her gently between the shoulder blades, changing it to a soothing - almost caressing - rub, as soon as she showed the first signs of recovery.

With a contemptuous snort of his own, the man in white threw his cigar angrily on the oriental rug and stormed out.

She did not follow.

While her former friend's cigar lay smouldering unnoticed, they shared the rest of the champagne, then popped another bottle. Before it was finished, Fleetwood kissed her fingers and led her, smiling and unresisting, towards his new four-poster bed.

Her name was Constance, and Fleetwood soon came to wonder if perhaps her previous boyfriend - who he later learned had sold his claim on the same fateful day and left the diggings - had been either impotent or otherwise inclined in preferences, for her sexual appetite was voracious. It was not long before he found himself having to visit Frankie's on an almost daily basis to gain inspiration from the magazines.

They made a perfect team. Released from the constraints of his predecessor's obviously tight rein, she took the bit between her teeth and streaked for the winning post, and Fleetwood was hard pressed to keep up.

He gave over the humdrum running of the several businesses to her, and she displayed a remarkable, if sometimes ruthless, talent for organising and extending them in the right direction. Furthermore, she had an eye for fresh opportunities

'What we need, Fuddy,' she said to him one morning as he sat exhausted on the edge of the bed, 'is another building. There are thousands of men here, and only a handful of women. That fat cow, Rosie, is making herself a fortune. Imagine what a pretty girl could earn.'

Fleetwood glanced at her suspiciously. 'Oh?'

'Don't worry, my little stallion, I am not that type, but if we had a building with enough rooms, we could bring some girls in from Cape Town and do it in style.'

Fleetwood was shocked. 'You mean a

whorehouse?'

'Don't worry, it will cater to only the best clientele. Leave it to me.' She pulled him back onto the bed. 'But you must promise not to sample the goods. It's not nice to be greedy.'

With more time on his hands, Fleetwood concentrated his efforts on filtering the remainder of the stolen diamonds into the business through the agency. He did not tell her about the waistcoat or the wooden safe, suspecting, for some unaccountable reason, that she would not have approved. He stored the now ruined waistcoat in the bottom of a trunk and, nostalgically, as if burying a part of his past life, sprinkled it with mothballs.

When rumours began spreading of diamonds being discovered away from the river at Colesberg Kopje, and the populace began mysteriously thinning, Fleetwood reacted swiftly. He went there with Constance in the crested barouche he had purchased from Hans Struben to see for himself.

The place was flat, dry and even more dusty than Pniel, but his Jewish appraiser -whose advice he had come to respect without reservation - had been enthusiastic about the quality of the stones there, and was of the opinion it would be the next big rush. That was enough for Fleetwood. He bought the options on as many claims as he was allowed, and purchased two of the best and largest buildings they could find in the dreary village.

One of them boasted an underground stone cellar that would make an ideal vault to replace the embarrassing wooden safe. The other had an upstairs floor, which Constance said would be ideal for the new venture she had in mind.

Fleetwood told Frankie all about it on his return.

'Ah, yes. I have been hearing a few things about it myself,' Frankie admitted. 'Truly amazing it is, sir, what you hear in this business.'

'You haven't heard the best part yet,' Fleetwood enthused. 'In my new building there is a nice little shop on the corner that will be just perfect for you. It is immediately below where Constance intends to install her um... ladies, and right next door to where I will put the canteen.'

Fleetwood dipped his finger into the bowl of shaving cream and sketched a rough outline of the layout on the mirror. 'If we put a back door to your shop there...' he dabbed a spot next to where he had shown the stairs leading up, '...it will provide a discreet entrance for those not wishing to be seen. With your magazines to stimulate temptation, Frankie, and alcohol right next door to water-down any doubts, business should be good all round, what? A nice little package. It was Constance's idea.'

'A very astute lady she is too, sir, a credit to you, I must say.'

'Well? Are you game?'

Frankie did not hesitate. 'Just tell me when we are ready to move, sir.'

'Good man!'

Frankie cleaned the mirror and studied Fleetwood's beaming face in it. 'You know sir, if you don't mind my saying so, it was a good decision you made about the moustache, even though it proved unnecessary. Without it, and with that touch of grey now above your ears, you look every bit the successful businessman. I must congratulate you on it, sir.'

'Yes, rather!' Fleetwood agreed happily.

'Care for a splash of that nice French lotion while you're here, sir?'

'God, no.' Fleetwood grimaced. 'It turns Constance wild.' He snorted with laughter. 'A man can only take so much you know.'

The shock of finding Willa gone had the same effect on Charles as when his mother had died. Numb disbelief. An emptiness where nothing existed other than breathing and walking; no feeling but the agony of loss. A disembodied sensation, as if he were outside of himself, looking down on a stranger.

He felt no hunger, tiredness, anger, or even sorrow. In his mind she was still there, lying on the flat rock with her hair spread out to dry in the sun, or curled up next to him in the shelter, eyes glowing with submissive warmth when she looked at him.

She had been his life and his passion. He knew her body as well as his own, had studied it in detail, and could not believe he would never again trace its silken curves, or smell the lemon in her hair.

Emotionless, he walked, and when it started to rain, he ignored it and continued on. Moving was preferable to being still, when the ghosts of the past would crowd around.

While walking he could think of simple things, such as avoiding obstacles or the feel of the rain on his head. He went nowhere in particular. He simply kept moving and stayed away from people. Even Bally was excluded.

For a long time he also avoided the pool. Too many ghosts lingered there, and that was where he wanted them to stay, but they constantly beckoned, and finally he weakened.

The flat rock was no longer visible, submerged under the rising water, and so too was the floor of the shelter, which had partially collapsed. The pool itself was a swirling mass of the reeds he had cut, floating in a tangled mat that ebbed back and forth where the beach had been.

He stood at the end of the path with the muddy water lapping his feet, strangely relieved that it looked so different. Without her it seemed only fitting that their special place should go too.

He saw the yellow ribbon as he was about to leave.

The garland of flowers through which it had been entwined had long since wilted and turned brown. He removed them and began folding the ribbon mechanically, realising with deepening melancholy that it was the only thing he had of hers that he could touch.

He almost missed the writing on it. The words were blurred, perhaps from the rain, and difficult to read, although there were only three: *Darling, I'm sorry.*

The Therons were concerned about Charles. They had seen him only once since his return, when he brought Oupa's pull-though and tobacco and asked for news about the Johnsons, and Ouma had suffered the unpleasant duty of having to inform him they had returned to Cape Town.

Ouma had foolishly insisted he stay for some of her special pheasant soup, and he had sat morosely toying with it, answering their questions about his trip in a desultory manner, then had left without drinking his coffee, in which Oupa had put a double tot of brandy.

'He's taking it much harder than I thought, Danie,' she said when they were alone.

'Ja, well...' Oupa sighed and picked up his pipe. 'Best we just leave him to get over it. There is nothing you can do.'

But they were not the only ones to be concerned. On the third evening, Bally had come to see them, reporting to Oupa that Charles was not eating and did nothing but walk around like a mad person, and he was sure that someone had put a spell on him. Maybe the policeman he had ridden away with, for he had seen that he hadn't wanted to go. Oupa had sent a message back inviting Charles over, but he had not come, or even sent a reply.

'I didn't think he would take it so hard,' Ouma confessed. 'If he's not careful he's going to get sick. Maybe I made a terrible mistake by interfering. I should have left them alone to work it out.'

'You were only trying to help, Hettie, that's all.'

'No, Danie, it was the same for Willa. I thought it was just a small thing... you know... like infatuation or something. Not a big thing like love.'

She started to weep, and Oupa went quickly to place a comforting hand on her shoulder. She dabbed at her eyes with the corner of the apron, then shrugged off his hand and went to the stove where she clattered noisily amongst the pots, and Oupa returned thoughtfully to his seat. He spoke to her back.

'I think we should ask him to come to the farm with us, Hettie. It is finished here now with the rain, and we should make a move before it sets in or we'll be stuck here. He can stay in the rondavel until he knows what it is he wants to do.'

She nodded without turning around. 'Yes, I want to go home now, Danie.'

'Good. That's it then. I'll speak to him first thing tomorrow.'

But when Oupa went to see him in the morning, only a forlorn Bally and a shivering dog were at the camp to greet him. Charles had already gone.

The bank clerk was apologetic. 'I'm sorry, sir, but we have no one here by that name. Have you tried the Colonial Bank across the square? They have a fairly large staff.'

Charles thanked him and left without bothering to explain that he had already been there and had received almost the identical answer.

It had been the same for the last six days. No one had ever heard of Willa or Sandy Johnson, and he was beginning to wonder if they had ever existed other than in his imagination.

When the banks had been exhausted, he called on the government departments, starting with the Post Office, and when those had proved fruitless, he walked the streets, going into every shop and salon, every shipping company and bar; even the hospital.

When he became tired of walking, he sat on the steps of the Town Hall and stared at the people passing by, hoping to recognise her by her hair or the way she walked. He took a room at a hotel, which had a balcony overlooking the main street, and he sat there in the evenings, looking down.

Several times he thought he saw her, and each time he suffered the same sinking sensation when it turned out to be a stranger.

And what made it worse, was that he knew she was there.

The Inland Transport Company had their names and arrival time written down neatly in black ink along with the other five - two weeks before.

The thought almost drove him crazy with frustration. She was there, somewhere close. More than likely flinching at the crash of the signal cannon at the exact same instant as he did, then watching the same startled pigeons circling the town.

By the end of the second week he was close to giving up. Only the thought of the journey back made him delay. While he was there, hope was alive. On the return would be only despair as he moved farther away from her.

He wished he could find the will to hate her, to feel anger for her leaving him with no word except the three on the ribbon that kept going around in his head. Anything that would fill the vast hollow in the centre of his being.

He stood on the same dock at which he had arrived a year previously, watching a ship preparing to leave for England. A brass band was playing lively but nostalgic English tunes, and gaiety, laughter and brightly coloured streamers floated in the air, tempting him, and for a moment he came close to capitulating. But that would be taking him even farther away from her.

Then, as he stood looking and wondering what he would do, he recalled a morning on a hilltop, watching the mist drifting, and the animals as they stood amongst the wildflowers. And he remembered the vibrant colours of the flowers; the red, the blue, the orange, and the purple.

But mostly he remembered the yellow - her favourite colour.

PART TWO

The San woman threaded each tooth of the bracelet with difficulty. The holes were small, and her fingers twisted and blunted from a lifetime of digging in the coarse sands of the desert. And she worked silently, for her mind was troubled, and the old man sitting beside her was also quiet; sharing her concern.

She tied the single strand of wiry elephant hair linking the teeth, then replaced the bracelet in the leather pouch that hung from her neck. To be the keeper of the bracelet had once been a great honour, but it no longer held much importance for her. The painter had been gone for many lifetimes, and none had come to take his place. More important now were the stories; of which she was also the keeper. They must be passed on or they too would be gone forever, and she feared she had left it too late. Those to whom she must tell them now lived across the great desert in the white mountains, and she had little strength remaining for such a long journey.

With her work on the bracelet finished, the San woman looked again at the painting of Eland on the sandstone wall of the cave opposite. A time had been when the red colour glistened like fresh blood in the morning sun, but careless fires had dulled and flaked it, so that now it had more the colour of blood that had dried.

In the big mountains she would go to was a similar painting of Eland, which she had last seen when still a girl. Would it be the same now as it was then, she wondered? Or would it too have shared the same fate? She sighed deeply with resignation. She would have to find the strength to see it once more and tell the stories. Only then would she be happy to join with her ancestors.

When the cave filled with shadows, the old San couple climbed stiffly to their feet and left the hills called Bracelet of the Morning for the last time.

Still showing dark wet patches from the birth, the elephant calf moved unsteadily through the trampled grass towards its mother, stumbling to a halt when it trod on its trunk. It stood swaying, glassy-eyed and uncertain, before tugging it free with a jerk that sent it staggering forward once more.

The cow waited patiently, moving slowly, and pausing often to look behind, helping her calf to rise each time it fell, and giving encouragement with gentle nudges.

The bull stood apart from the herd, ears wide as he listened to the sounds of their approach. As they came clear of the trees, he rumbled deep in his belly and moved to meet her, reaching out for her smell and running his thick trunk across her back before weaving it slowly above the new calf.

He led the way back to the herd and stood aside as the cows came up one at a time to touch the mother and scent the new addition, as if offering their congratulations.

Charles smiled and cautiously eased his numb buttocks on the branch. The sausage tree was solid but not that tall. With a new calf in the herd it was no time to be testing their protective instincts.

He waited for them to move on, squinting and trying not to breathe in any of the tiny flies that swarmed in a fine haze around his head and body. The idea of smearing himself with elephant dung to disguise his scent had seemed like a good idea, but he had not counted on the attraction it would have for pests.

It was another half-hour of torture before the herd was finally out of sight and he could climb down. He removed the satchel holding his paper and made a quick sketch of the baby elephant while the image was still fresh in his mind. He checked the drawing of the old tuskless cow again, adding a few more lines to the wrinkled skin that resembled oversize clothes, including a series of small arrows and notes to remind him where to add the emphasis when he did the final drawing. The unusual depth of the skin folds would look good if he could shade them right.

Back at the camp, Charles washed off the crusty

elephant dung while Bally, with his nose wrinkled and turned aside, took charge of the satchel. He placed it in the large food box along with the hundreds of other sketches and notes accumulated in the past year and a half.

With no food remaining in the box, it was the perfect receptacle. The luxuries of tea, coffee, sugar, and tinned meat had long since been used. So had the maize-meal and flour. Only a bag of salt remained, which had turned solid. For more than a year they had survived on fresh meat and fish, and whatever wild fruit and greens they could find in the bush. Thanks to Bally they had suffered no shortage of things to eat, and had fared well, although Charles had drawn the line at some of the more exotic grubs that Bally relished.

They had come to the Okavango because Charles had not known what else to do. The rains had settled in and the claim was unworkable by the time he had returned from Cape Town - not that he wanted to stay there anyway. And although the Therons had left a message with Bally inviting Charles to stay at their farm in the Clarendon valley, he was not sure if he was ready for that. He was still in the mood for walking.

Then Bally had solved the dilemma by asking if he could leave. He was rich now, he explained, far richer than he had ever expected, and he had the small matter of a wife to be taken care of.

At first Charles had been angry. Already despondent and feeling that his life was falling apart, it was not what he wanted to hear.

'You told me you had no wife,' he protested

'It is true,' Bally had replied, talking slowly, as if to a child so Charles would be able to follow without getting it wrong, as he usually did. 'I have no wife, yet she has been promised. I will give her father the money for his cows in exchange.'

'Go then,' Charles had told him curtly.

'I will stay if you wish it,' Bally offered.

'No,' Charles responded, instantly humbled by the little African's loyalty. 'You have told me there are many animals where you live. Is it true?'

'So many,' Bally replied enthusiastically, 'they could not be counted by one man alone. Nor even by a hundred men.'

'I will go with you then,' Charles said on impulse. 'I think I would like to see this wife you are going to buy.'

The next day he went back to Pniel and bought a small cart and another mule. They loaded up with supplies and ammunition, and Charles persuaded the owner of the *Diamond Field News* to part with a bundle of blank paper.

Four days after he had returned from Cape Town they crossed the Vaal river and headed into the wilderness of the Kalahari.

Three weeks later they arrived at Bally's village to discover that his promised wife had already become the wife of his cousin.

Charles had never seen Bally angry before, and was surprised by the ferocity of his verbal attack on the poor woman. Plump, and also very pregnant, she cowered on the ground as he stood over her and loosed a tirade with such vehemence that Charles began to fear for her safety.

Dressed for the occasion in the new clothes Charles had bought for him, Bally clutched handfuls of them as he raved, bringing her attention to them. He pulled a handful of pound notes from his pocket and shook them in her face. This action seemed to stimulate him to even greater efforts. He stuffed the notes back in his pocket and picked up a stick, and Charles had to intervene with sharp words of his own to save the woman from a beating.

Several curious children were bustled away by two older women, and an old man ran from one of the huts with an axe, but retreated hastily when he saw Charles, closing the door firmly behind him.

Bally shouted abuse at him, and the muffled replies seemed to infuriate Bally even more. He hurled a log of smouldering wood at the door, and followed it up with a collection of clay pots.

Charles pulled him away and bundled him onto the cart as shouts came from another group of huts a short distance away. Holding Bally firmly by the collar, he whipped the surprised mules into a brisk walk.

For the rest of the day Bally was sullen and refused to talk, whispering to himself at length, but next morning was his usual self, acting as if nothing had happened.

Charles tried to hide his selfish pleasure. Bally had become an extension of himself, and he had not been looking forward to the parting of their ways. And he would have found it difficult without the African's knowledge of the bush. In a perverse way, he was also pleased that Bally had suffered some of his own disappointment with women. He tried to make up for his treacherous feelings by teaching him how to shoot, but it was an undertaking he soon came to regret. Bally's prowess with weapons was strictly limited to things he could throw, and which did not make a noise or require the closing of eyes. It was impossible to tell who was the more pleased when the exercise was abandoned.

The hundreds of miles of swampland and waterways that made up the Okavango swamp teemed with such an abundance and variety of wildlife that Charles was kept busy sketching from dawn to dusk. In a year of constantly being on the move, he estimated they had covered less than half of the area, and in all that time the only white face he had seen - or what was visible of it behind the bushy beard and long hair - was his own, reflected in the still, dark water of the swamp.

It was only when the ammunition and the supply of sketching paper had run low that he began thinking of returning to civilisation. He was looking forward to completing the final drawings of the sketches, and needed somewhere to work that was close to a ready supply of materials.

He had considered Cape Town, but did not fancy the idea of being close to Willa without being able to see her - if indeed she was there. And worse, if he did see her, not being able to resume where they had left off. Although less frequently now, she still occupied his mind more than he would have liked.

He decided instead to call on the Therons and see if their offer was still open. They were the closest he had to family, and the old man may also be able to identify many of the species of game for which he had only the African names. He smiled when he thought of how envious Oupa would be. He had always talked about visiting the Okovango.

Giving Bally's village a wide berth, they headed east towards the Kgalagadi pans, and the stretch of desert that would lead them up to the high veld. Bally had suggested leaving before the pans became dry. If they left it too late, he explained, they would not be able to carry sufficient water in the barrels for both themselves and the mules.

The clay-pans were almost in sight when they stopped to make camp for the night in a grove of Baobab trees. Charles was removing the mules from the harness when the dog growled and Bally spoke.

'The San are here,' he stated calmly.

'What?' Charles looked about in surprise. He had seen nothing.

'It is the ones from the hills.'.

'Here?' Charles was incredulous. The hills where they had first seen the Bushmen were a good two hundred miles away.

Bally nodded towards the far edge of the grove, and Charles saw them sitting in the deep shade. 'We should ask them to join us,' he suggested.

Bally raised his hand high, palm outwards, and called a greeting to them in their strange tongue-clicking language, and they came without hesitation, as if they had been expecting the invitation.

Charles recognised them as they approached. The three men walked briskly with their hands held high in greeting, smiles creasing their faces, bows, quivers and leather satchels slung from their shoulders.

Behind them came the girl, a bundle of skin blankets on her head and her belly well rounded. Charles had been taken with her own child-like beauty the first time and had wanted to sketch her, but had not been sure if it would cause offence. He had still much to learn about the little nomads. Her skin was the colour and texture of wild honey, and although pregnant, still her naked breasts were small. She was probably older, yet looked no more than twelve, and it saddened him to think that in only a few years the harsh life in the sun and hot winds would have sapped her youth, leaving her body as wrinkled as a dried apricot.

He had not seen the old couple before, although Bally had mentioned their existence to him after the meeting at the hills. Both used sticks to lean on, propping up their bowed frames, their sparse hair like flecks of ash on their heads, and it seemed incredible to Charles that they could have walked the long distance from the hills.

When all the lengthy greetings had been

dispensed with, Charles tried to follow as Bally spoke to the men in the same strange mixture of his own language and theirs. The replies were unintelligible, a series of clicks interspersed with long pauses, and thoughtful grunts. The old couple and the girl sat aside, taking no part in the conversation.

'They are here to see you,' Bally explained finally, looking smug.

'Me?' Charles was sceptical. 'How did they know I would be here? Were they following?'

Bally shrugged. 'They know.'

Charles did not inquire further. If there was one thing he had learned about the Africans, it was that you had to accept certain things as they were. Further questioning usually led to an amused silence, as if no answer was required and they were waiting for you to continue.

'What is it Bally?' Charles asked, knowing by his manner that it was something of importance.

'It is the marks of the eland,' Bally replied. 'They wish for the old ones to see it.'

Bally always referred to the sketches as marks, there being no other word in his language to describe them.

'I will not let them touch it or look for too long,' Bally continued anxiously, mistaking the long pause for hesitation.

Charles put on a solemn expression. He had learned how important the big eland was to the Bushmen. Of all the animals, it was the one they revered the most, treating it almost as a deity. He had done a sketch of one after seeing a Bushman painting in a cave at the hills. Using a full page, he had sketched the outline of the stylised animal exactly, shading it faintly to give the impression of age and distance, then had superimposed the lifelike and much darker sketch of another eland over a part of it, as if one was the spirit of the other. The drawing was one of the few he had completed, and he had to admit it was one of his finest.

'Show them, Bally,' he said. They can look for as long as they like.'

The response from the younger members was much the same as it had been the first time they had seen it. They crowded around eagerly, clicking their tongues in amazement while Bally exhibited the drawing, keeping it well out of reach, and seeming to almost glow with paternal pride at their awed expressions.

The old couple had remained sitting patiently and silently together on the dusty ground, and Bally took the sketch to them, kneeling so they could see it without standing.

The response took Charles by surprise. After

barely more than a glance, the old woman covered her head with her arms and started to wail, while the old man stared with an expression of disbelief, his frail body rigid but alert, as if ready to jump away should the eland suddenly come to life.

No one attempted to console the woman as Bally returned the sketch reverently to the box.

Not knowing what to do in what seemed like a family tragedy of some sort, Charles sat down and leaned back against the wheel of the cart, wanting to be unobtrusive. Immediately, the four younger Bushmen followed his example and, to Charles's continued bewilderment, so did Bally.

Still no one spoke, and when Charles looked at Bally with raised eyebrows, Bally would not meet his gaze. Convinced that he had committed some unpardonable sin, Charles waited anxiously, picking at the dried scabs of scratches on his arm.

After a while, the woman stopped wailing. She rolled onto her hands and knees, then rose slowly and awkwardly to her feet. She hobbled stiffly towards where Charles sat and, with a weary groan, squatted before him. From a small leather pouch hanging from her neck, she removed a bracelet of what looked to be ivory beads, and offered it to him with both hands, one atop the other, in the same manner in which Bally had presented the diamond.

Charles took it from her tentatively, and the woman grunted in satisfaction, then began speaking to him at length in a thin wavering voice. She stopped abruptly and struggled once more to her feet, then rejoined the old man.

As soon as she sat down, the younger Bushmen broke into excited chatter, as if some momentous happening had just occurred, and Charles waited for Bally to explain what it was all about.

'It is the bracelet of the one who painted Eland,' Bally explained hesitantly, being careful to choose the right words. 'It is a very great honour.'

Charles studied the bracelet more carefully. It was much too small to go over his hand. The segments were yellowed with age, strung together with a single black strand of hair from an elephant's tail.

'It is made from the teeth of Eland,' Bally told him. 'It was given to the San woman by her mother, and her mother before, and as many mothers as the fingers of three hands before that again.'

Bally turned to the old woman and spoke to her for a while, asking questions, then he continued.

'The San woman says that the one who wore the bracelet was the last of the ones who did the paintings. She says that if you wear the bracelet, the same spirit that showed the way to the hand of the painter will lead your hand also.'

Charles was astounded. 'The same painter wore this?' He found it hard to believe. If what the woman said was true, the bracelet must be over five hundred years old -.maybe even more.

'It is what she has been told by her mothers,' Bally assured him.

'Why has she given it to me?'

'She says it has been her duty, and the duty of all those before her to pass the bracelet to one who could do the marks of Eland. Only those San who did them could wear the bracelet. She says that even though you are not a San, still you are such a one.'

Charles was touched. The bracelet obviously had great significance to them but, isolated as they were, they had probably never seen anyone who could draw. He felt that it would be wrong if he took it from them.

'There are many people who can do marks, Bally. And much better than I can. You must explain to them. They should give the bracelet to one of the San.'

Bally seemed reluctant, but spoke to the woman again.

'She has seen many pictures before,' he translated her reply to Charles. 'But all have been of

333

dead things, and there have been none of Eland.'

It seemed that he had no choice. He would have to accept the bracelet or risk offending them, and he had no desire to antagonise anyone who carried poisoned arrows.

'There is more,' Bally said, and Charles looked at him expectantly, hoping for a way out of the dilemma.

'The San woman says that you must be the one, or why else would you do the picture of Eland at the same time as her children were there to see it? They had not been to that place before. It is a sign that the spirit of Eland made them go.'

Charles could find no solutions in this strange logic.

'Tell the San woman that I am much honoured. And give them as much meat as they want. I'll shoot something again tomorrow.'

When Charles awoke at sunrise, he was surprised to see that the three men and the girl had gone, but the old couple sat huddled in their skin blankets next to the small fire.

'Why are they still here?' he asked Bally.

'They wish to return with us to the white mountains,' Bally answered conversationally, making himself busy with encouraging the dog onto the cart.

'Why?'

'It is where they wish to die. It was also the home of the one who wore the bracelet. If you wish, they will show you the last marks. It is close to where the Oupa lives.'

'How do they know we are going there? Did you tell them?'

'They can show us a better way,' Bally said evasively. 'They can take my place and I must walk.'

Charles had no choice but to agree. He could not simply leave them, and there was no good reason why he should anyway, particularly as they knew the way. He had the distinct feeling though, that he had been expertly manipulated by Bally and the Bushmen.

Martha Griel didn't recognise him right away. She was busy serving a customer when he walked into the Post Office, and it was only when she looked more closely at the tall man standing patiently waiting his turn behind Mevrou Visser and saw his eyes, that she knew. The beard was thicker and the hair longer, but the eyes were the same. There was no way that she would forget the eyes.

'I think you've given me too much change,' Mevrou Visser said.

'Oh...' Martha reclaimed the two extra pence. 'Sorry... thank you.'

Mevrou Visser moved away, clucking, and Martha put on her brightest welcoming smile as he stepped forward to take her place.

'I need to send some money to Cape Town,' he said. 'Is it safe to put it in a letter, do you think?'

'Oh...' She frowned, trying to gather her wits. 'A letter? Oh, no. That is, I think a postal note would be safer.'

He seemed uncertain. 'I have another problem, Miss. I don't have the exact address, only the name of the place. It's in the main street. They sell books and stationery.'

Martha was quick to oblige 'Oh, don't worry about that, sir. I can get the address for you easy as anything.' She gave him a blank form and a pencil. 'If you put the name of the shop and how much you want to send, I'll get the address and send it for you.'

He smiled. 'That's kind of you, Miss.'

'Martha,' she said.

He nodded absent-mindedly, already writing, and pink-faced, Martha watched as he wrote quickly in a bold, flowing script. He was obviously educated, even though he looked like a wagon driver....or maybe a hunter.

'Oh, and don't forget to put your own name and address at the bottom,' she said.

When he had finished, she took the money and wrote a receipt, and was dismayed to notice that her hand was shaky. She wrote faster to hide it, scrawling, then franked the note, forgetting to ink the pad first.

'Thank you,' he said. 'You've been most helpful.'

Martha felt the tingling reach her ears. 'You're very welcome,' she murmured.

She watched as he crossed the road to the bank, and saw him again when he came out and walked up the road and out of sight. She copied his name and address from the form onto a scrap of paper and put it in her pocket. Then she removed it and pushed it down the front of her dress.

She removed it again a short while later to memorise the details, wondering if she should keep it to herself, then she sighed with resignation. It was not the Christian thing to do. Impatiently, she waited for the lunch break.

Late in the afternoon, as Ouma Theron was throwing scraps to the chickens from the verandah, she saw the small wagon leave the track by the river and come towards the cottage.

'Danie, come quick!' she called excitedly. Visitors were not all that common. 'Someone is coming.'

Oupa Theron came out to stand behind her, and they watched expectantly as the cart and its two unknown occupants trundled up the hill past the orchard.

'Who do you think will be coming so late?' Ouma queried. 'Maybe I should make some more food.'

'They could be just lost, Hettie. Wait and see.'

The cart stopped next to the milkshed and a tall, bearded man jumped out and came towards the cottage, as they both went down the steps to meet him.

The stranger held up a parcel. 'Special delivery,' he called out. 'Chocolates and French brandy.'

Ouma Theron stopped short. 'God in heaven!' She clamped two hands to her cheeks. 'Charles?'

'I hope you have plenty of food, Ouma. I haven't eaten a decent meal since the last time you fed me.' He lowered the parcel to gather her into a hug, lifting her considerable bulk clear of the ground.

'Man!' Oupa exclaimed, shaking Charles's hand with both of his. 'We thought you had gone back to England.'

'Not me, Oupa. Too many bloody *rooineks* over there.'

The old man's eyes twinkled. 'Too many bloody *rooineks* over here as well.'

'When you two have finished swearing at each other,' Ouma interjected, 'you can move the little wagon into the shed and attend to the mules while I make the dinner. Tomorrow, Danie, you must clear all of your rubbish from the rondavel so I can clean it up for Charles.' She paused to look at Charles anxiously. 'You will stay?'

'I don't want to be a trouble to you, Ouma. If it would be all right for me and Bally to camp somewhere until I can...'

'No, you must stay in the rondavel. Bally can stay with the workers.' Ouma gripped Charles firmly by the arm and kissed him on the cheek. 'We are happy to see you again, my boy. We were worried. You must stay for as long as you like.'

'Ja, exactly,' Oupa agreed 'Welcome to Sani Kloof.'

The two circular thatched rondavels were set apart from the cottage, on a tree-covered knoll overlooking the river.

Constructed of sandstone blocks cut from the nearby cliffs, they had once been the original homestead, but as the family and the farm had grown, more suitable sites had been found elsewhere, and the rondavels had become the unofficial storerooms.

A thatched, open-sided walkway linked them together and doubled as a verandah, and the next morning Charles helped Oupa move the collection of old harness, broken implements and numerous boxes onto it, from where Ouma ruthlessly organised its further disposal via several labourers.

When the buildings had been cleared and the floor scrubbed clean, she had the good furniture moved back in, and the stone floors covered with lion and zebra skins.

'It looks good enough for royalty,' Charles complimented.

Ouma dropped a heavy rabbit-skin kaross onto the large table in the centre of the room. 'You will need this,' she advised. 'It gets cold here in the mountains. I'll get some wood sent down for the fire. You can eat with us.'

'You've done too much already,' Charles protested. 'I can manage.'

'Nonsense, man,' Oupa replied. 'We need the company.'

'I must pay for this,' Charles insisted as Ouma bustled off.

Oupa laughed. 'If you give me money, Hettie will kill me. Better you talk with her about it. Come, it is time to water the roof.'

Charles grinned, experiencing for the first time in his life the feeling of coming home after a long time away. 'I think you mean, wet the roof, Oupa.'

'Bugger the roof!' Oupa glanced around, searching. 'Now where the hell did she hide it... did you see?'

With the enthusiastic help of the old man, Charles set about turning one of the rondavels into a studio. Another table was found and placed by the window, which would provide good light, and the large table in the centre of the room was piled with the sketches from the trunk.

Seeing them, Oupa began sorting through, shaking his head, then called for Ouma to come and look. When he came to the one of the eland, they were both stunned into silence.

'Man!' Oupa finally exclaimed. 'Look at the way he is standing. I have seen them like that many times before. He wants to run, but his eyes and ears are saying no, wait a bit longer, it is still too interesting to run.'

'The Lord has given you a wonderful gift, Charles,' Ouma said in a hushed voice. 'Why didn't we know it before?'

Charles shrugged. 'Too busy looking for diamonds, I suppose.'

Ouma indicated the sketches that lay scattered across the table. 'These are your diamonds, my boy.'

When he told them of the Bushmen's reaction to the drawing, and how he had been manipulated into bringing the two ancient ones back with him, he expected them to laugh, but they remained serious.

'Ja, the San are strange people all right,' Oupa said thoughtfully. 'I can see how it would happen though. The eland is a big thing with them. Where are they now - these Bushmen? I didn't see them with you.'

'They left about ten miles down the river from here,' Charles said. 'We had to help them across the drift. I don't know how they're going to make it in the mountains. All they had was one blanket and walking stick each.'

'Poor things.' Ouma clicked her tongue in sympathy.

'They know what they're doing, don't you worry,' Oupa reassured. 'Many good caves in the area for shelter.'

Charles showed them the bracelet, and Oupa examined it carefully in the light of the window.

'It could be eland teeth, but they have been made round, so it is hard to say. It is a pity you didn't speak with the old woman some more.'

'I should have taken her more seriously I suppose,' he defended, a little surprised at the hint of reproach in the old man's voice, 'but we had a bit of a language problem, and when they said they would show me the painting if I brought them, I thought I was just being tricked into giving them a ride.'

'I don't know, Charles.' Oupa was dubious, 'I have known the San for a long time, and I have a feeling there is some truth in it. There is a story about a painting of an eland that looks as if it has been freshly painted, but I don't know anyone who has seen it. I always thought it was a bit of a legend, but now I'm not so sure...'

He looked at Charles with the trace of a smile. 'Perhaps it is the one they were going to show you, hey?'

'I'll ask Bally,' Charles answered lamely. 'Maybe there is something he hasn't told me yet.'

But when he questioned him later, Bally had not been able to add anything new, and Charles wondered if he would see the old Bushmen couple again. They had said nothing more about the painting when he dropped them off, and not much at all on the journey, for the most part remaining huddled silently in their blankets, even during the heat of the day.

Sitting alone on his verandah that evening, watching the sunset and waiting for the clanging of Ouma's pot to signal dinner, Charles reflected that he could not have chosen a more inspiring or peaceful place to work, and wondered if the mysterious painter had also been inspired by the view. The sandstone cliffs had turned gold in the setting sun, and the russet grass to liquid copper, changing sheen in the light breeze like the rippling fur of a moving animal.

But perhaps best of all, until that moment, he had not thought of Willa for an entire day.

It took the family of San most of the day to climb the steep mountain. The way was narrow and overgrown, slashed across with deep gullies and obstructed by fallen trees and rocks. In many places the younger children and the old couple had to be lifted bodily. But they were in no particular hurry, and their climb was interspersed with many rests while the area ahead was scouted.

As they neared the top the undergrowth suddenly thinned to a rocky knoll, and they entered a narrow fissure at its base, squeezing through to reach a shallow cave. On hands and knees they crawled to the back, then the leader of the group shucked his military-style coat and slithered forward over a ledge of rock to disappear into the gloom.

The others listened in silence to the diminishing sounds of his progress, and when they stopped, waited expectantly for his call. Finally it came, distant and echoing. 'He is well.'

A collective murmur of relief came from those waiting outside.

When the man returned, the old couple removed their blankets and passed them over the ledge, then followed, and the others came after, feeling their way in the darkness.

They entered the big cave through another fissure and stood blinking in the bright sunlight. With a word of warning to the children not to approach too close to the edge, the old woman went to the wide entrance and stood looking at the painting of Eland for a long time, remembering.

'Yes,' she pronounced finally with deep satisfaction, 'he is well.'

The painting was large, almost life-size, and filled the smooth sandstone wall of the cave opening. The deep russet colour looked fresh, the outline crisp, seeming to lift out in relief, as if Eland were poised to leap out of his cave. The remaining walls were unmarked, and the floor was clean, without the usual musty smell of small animals and their droppings, and showed no sign of human habitation. The old woman knew why no animals ever ventured into the cave, and it would be one of the stories she would pass on in the days ahead.

But the first thing she told them, was that no fire was ever to be made in the cave for fear of burning the hide of Eland, and that no animal, or even a snake, must be killed within one whole day of visiting the cave for fear of offending the spirits, and they all murmured their assent tactfully, as if they had not already known.

The cold food they had brought with them was eaten, and more news spoken of all that had happened since last they had met, many seasons before. And that evening, huddled together far back in the cave away from the bitter wind of the mountain, she told them the story of the bracelet and the white man who had brought them from the desert, and for the first time there was dissent.

'It is because of the white man, Old Mother, that

we are being hunted like the chicken-stealing jackals,' complained the man who wore the coat. 'Without them we would be free to hunt where the spoor takes us.'

'You speak the words of the tall black men,' she replied, 'yet you are not one of them.'

The old man spoke for the first time. 'If you live with the jackals, you will be hunted with them.'

'Must we run to the desert when the mountains are the home of our ancestors?'

'Our homes are many, and our people are few. Soon there will be fewer because of those who are killed for stealing cattle.'

'Yet they steal our land.'

The old woman held up her hand to stop the argument. 'We came to this place of Eland so our spirits can live in peace with our ancestors. Let us not anger them with our talk. It is they who spoke in my head and gave the signs that told me to give the bracelet to the white man. Is it not because of him we are here and the stories did not die with us on the journey? The bracelet is for him. When you see his marks of Eland, then you will know I speak the truth.'

'How will we see them?'

'You will see them,' she stated with finality.

At dawn, with the valley below still shrouded in mist, they waited patiently for the sun to clear the mountains in the east. When it came, bathing the wall with warm gold light, and shining full on the painting so it glistened like fresh blood, they sat in its warmth and the old woman told the stories that had been passed down to her.

First she told of the valley below, and how it was that no other large animals lived there, only birds, rabbits, snakes and the ancestors of Eland. No jackals, hyenas, or even leopards or lions ever went there. And she told of their own ancestor, the one who was the last of the painters, showing them the smudged handprint that was his sign.

On the day that the painting was finished, she explained, even before it was dry, he had leaned out to make his mark and had fallen from the cliff. His spirit returned each morning to renew the paint so it would always look fresh.

Many of the stories she told more than once, emphasising their importance, and she spoke particularly to the young woman with the child, whose duty it would be to pass them on.

She taught them songs from their ancestors, singing them in a thin broken voice, and answered their questions patiently, except when they spoke of things not belonging to the past.

For three days she talked and sang, and when it

was finished, when the time finally came for the young ones to leave, she watched them go without sadness, then sat with the old man looking out over the valley of Eland, content that it was now done.

On the morning after the family had departed, and for two mornings thereafter, the man in the military coat returned with food for the old couple, even though they ate nothing.

On the third morning he wrapped their cold and lifeless bodies in the skin blankets and rolled them gently over the ledge to join with their ancestors below.

44

Engrossed with her troubled thoughts, Aneline almost dropped the heavy package in fright as the bird exploded from the grass beside her. She swore under her breath, then watched with heart thumping as the pheasant beat urgently through the red-topped grass towards the cover of the trees by the river.

She waited until it disappeared, taking time to regain her composure, before hoisting the package higher on her hip and continuing on.

Once again the frown returned as she rehearsed what she would say to the man whose package she was delivering - the mysterious blue-eyed stranger that she had been waiting to meet for almost two years.

Unanswerable questions plagued her. Would he be angry that she had discovered his name? And why would he not want them to know? If only she could think of a reason why a perfect stranger - and a *rooinek* at that - would want to save the farm, she would know what to say and how to thank him.

The old woman, Mevrou Theron, had not been much help either, giving her no clue other than that he had been waiting eagerly for the parcel. She had expressed pleasant surprise at such good service. Usually, she said, they collected the mail themselves once a week from the store at Eland's Drift. Then the knowing smile when she said she would like to deliver the package personally to Mister Atherstone because she knew him. The silly old cow had got the wrong idea altogether.

The two rondavels appeared deserted. Aneline stood undecided on the verandah between them, wondering if she should call out. It was still early in the morning. He may be asleep. Yet the doors on either side were open, and when she edged closer, craning forward, she could see inside both rooms. One looked like a sitting room, the other was a bedroom. Both were empty.

She put the package on a chair beside her and knocked on the open door of the lounge. 'Meneer? Are you here?'

A dog growled from under the chair, and for the second time that morning Aneline started with fright.

'Dammit!' She stepped back quickly to peer under. A black dog with a grey muzzle and yellow eyes stared out at her, showing its teeth, yet she could hear its tail thumping against the floor.

'Stupid dog,' she muttered.

She walked around the building, then returned to the sitting area and stepped into the doorway. A large table stacked with papers dominated the room. Another by the window, with a jar of pencils and a stack of leather folders, looked as if it was used as a desk. Pinned to the wall on the far side were what appeared to be drawings of some description, but they were too far away to make out any details.

Aneline stepped out again and did another circuit of the building, listening for any sound that might give a clue as to where he was, but all she could hear was the thumping of the dog's tail whenever she passed close.

She hesitated for only a moment. It would be a waste to come all this way and still find out nothing

She went boldly into the room and dumped the package on the centre table, then flicked quickly through the papers. They were all rough sketches and notes of animals, and there seemed to be hundreds of them.

She moved quickly to the desk by the window, where the light was better, and opened one of the large leather folders, hoping to find some clue to his identity. She drew in a sharp breath of surprise when she saw a pencil drawing of an old elephant.

The deep folds of the animal's skin hung loose with age, the ears scratched and torn. The head hung low, the trunk resting on the ground, and the leaking tear ducts had made streaks through the dust on the cheeks. The forlorn old elephant was so detailed that it could have been a photograph.

Enthralled, Aneline studied each drawing in the folder carefully. She had lived all her life in the bush, and knew they were authentic in every detail. Whoever had done them must not only be a very clever artist, he must also have a deep understanding and love of animals.

She closed the folder and went to open the next one, but it was tied securely around with a yellow ribbon, so she left it and turned her attention to the drawings pinned to the wall.

They had not yet been completed, but even so, she could tell how they were going to turn out. The one that appealed to her most was also of an elephant, a baby that was standing on its trunk. The surprised look in its eye was so comical that she couldn't help but giggle.

'Do you like them?'

'Oh...!' For the third time that morning Aneline jumped in fright. She spun around, taking an involuntary step back, and bumped into the desk, knocking over the jar of pencils.

He caught the jar before it fell to the floor and replaced it, smiling apologetically. 'I'm sorry, I didn't mean to startle you.'.

'I didn't know... hear you coming,' she stammered guiltily. He looked vaguely familiar, something about the eyes, but she couldn't place him. He was standing close, wearing only a pair of shorts, and his sun-darkened body was lean and hard looking. She averted her eyes, feeling the blood tingle. 'I didn't want to leave it outside.' She pointed to the parcel on the table and made a move towards the door.

'Thank you, Miss Steyn.'

Aneline stopped. 'You know me?'

'I recognised the colour of your hair. It's most unusual.' He ushered her towards the door. 'Please, why don't you sit on the verandah? I'll put a shirt on and arrange for some coffee.'

He left before she could respond, taking her

acceptance for granted, and Aneline sat thankfully, glad of the opportunity to gather her wits. She leaped up quickly again and moved to the other chair when she remembered the dog, but it had gone.

'Damned fool,' she breathed. Things seemed to be getting out of control. She smoothed her dress and ran her fingers through her hair, pulling a few strands down to squint at the colour. She had never thought of it as being unusual.

He reappeared wearing a khaki shirt without sleeves. 'I'm sorry, Miss Steyn, but you caught me by surprise. I normally have a swim early in the morning. Bally will be here in a minute with the coffee.'

'Oh...well, actually, sir, I was...'

'Charles.'

'I beg yours?'

'My name is Charles. You don't remember me, do you?'

Given the excuse, Aneline studied him carefully. His hair was long, and his beard thick. It would be hard to recognise anyone behind all the hair, yet there was something about the eyes. Martha had been right. They would not be easy to forget.

'I'm sorry, but I can't...'

'Maybe you remember this.' He held up his bare foot and wriggled the big toe. 'You never gave me the chance to thank you for removing the thorn. I don't think you liked me very much.'

Perched primly on the edge of her chair, Aneline stared at the wriggling toe as if mesmerised by it. But it wasn't the toe she saw. Instead, she saw the *rooinek* leaning back on his elbows, smiling at her with his eyebrow raised as she pulled the thorn. She recalled the swollen nose, the puffy eyes, and the blotchy skin, and also how she had felt angry with him for allowing her to make a fool of herself.

And she remembered too the odd feeling as she held his foot. Strange men had been a rarity in her life.

She had been angry with herself about that as well. He was only a *rooinek* that couldn't look after himself. But he looked so different now. So much older and self-assured. She saw the same smile, and the same raised eyebrow, and although she fought against it, she felt the same odd tingle of excitement.

It was in her belly as she spoke, and she could hear it in her voice. 'You are that same *rooinek*?'

He laughed. 'You mustn't tell old man Theron that. He doesn't like Englishmen much.'

'Oh!' Aneline clamped a hand to her mouth, and felt the blood rush to her face once more. 'I'm sorry, meneer, I didn't mean...'

'It's all right, Miss Steyn. I've been called a lot

worse things before.'

Aneline was saved from further embarrassment by the arrival of a thin African with a laden tray. He bobbed and smiled at her, then talked to himself in a whisper as he unloaded the tray onto the table.

'Don't mind Bally,' Charles said, speaking in fluent Afrikaans. 'He always talks to things like that. He believes that everything has its own spirit and must be treated with respect.'

He broke off to speak to the African, using a language Aneline had never heard before, and she poured the coffee feeling clumsy and ashamed. She had called him a *rooinek*, yet he could not only speak her language, but that of the African as well.

Aneline became aware that they were both looking at her. 'I'm sorry, I didn't hear…'

'Bally was asking if you would like some breakfast. He fancies himself as a cook.'

'No... thank you. I really can't stay. My father will be waiting for me.' She smiled at the African and shook her head, and he left, looking disappointed.

'Marthinus is here?'

Aneline nodded. Her head felt strangely loose, seeming to go through motions that were beyond her control. 'He's waiting at the store.'

'I'll come with you,' he stated. 'That's one man

I would really like to see again.'

Aneline sipped at her coffee and answered his questions about the transporting business awkwardly, for the first time in her life unable to think of anything to say.

Only much later did she remember about the loan.

Standing in the small cluttered kitchen helping Mevrou Theron prepare food, Aneline listened with one ear as the old woman prattled on about her family, and with the other tried to catch what the men were laughing and talking about on the verandah.

The invitation to stay the night had come as a pleasant surprise. Her father and old man Theron had met once before, it seemed, and they had all been talking non-stop -mostly about hunting and diamonds.

The old woman had spoken about nothing but her grandchildren, and Aneline had tried to be polite and pay attention, but the stories of the men were more interesting, and she still hoped to find out more about the generous Charles Atherstone. When she had ridden with him to the store, her father had thanked him for what he had done, while she had stood like a dumb person, saying nothing, although she had been practising the right thing to say along the way. The finances of the farm had always been her responsibility, and she still felt a little resentful that her father had got in first. And what with all the talking and stuff, she had not found another opportunity.

Some of the stories she had heard earlier in the evening, as they sat on the verandah having a drink and watching the glorious sunset, had been fascinating.

The one of the baby elephant, whose picture she had seen on the wall, was marvellous. She could not imagine anyone covering himself with elephant dung. And the one of the angry honey badger that had chased a buffalo away from the water hole, then had pursued Charles when he tried to sketch it. The way he told it, she had laughed so much that tears had come into her eyes, and her father, with a funny smile on his lips, had given her a strange look. After that she had remained silent.

She had seen the scar on his foot where the badger had nipped him before he could climb the tree, and found it hard to believe that it was the same foot she had come so close to shooting off when he had been lying on her pillow.

'He's quite a remarkable fellow, isn't he?'

Aneline looked blankly at Mevrou Theron for a moment, not replying, then busied herself with the gravy that was close to burning.

That night, lying in the short bed that smelled

strongly of children, she suddenly remembered that she had still not thanked him.

Still later, as she was falling asleep, she made a firm promise to herself that she would find the right opportunity the next day. And that she would also try to stop acting like Martha Griel.

Fleetwood listened carefully as Constance gave her final opinion on the four men waiting in the main office to see him. It was an important meeting, perhaps the most vital he had ever attended, and although he had ample faith in his ability to negotiate even the trickiest of deals, he valued her judgement highly. Especially when it came to understanding the frailties of men. Although, in that area, she had considerable help from the girls on the upper floor.

'The one with the round face and the soft hands you don't have to worry about,' she instructed, giving a gentle tug to his tie. 'If you give him a pinch on the bottom he will probably double his offer.'

'God forbid,' Fleetwood murmured, shuddering at the thought.

'And the dark thin one with the floppy lips

likes to dress up in Maggie's clothes. You don't have to worry about him either. I've already told him I would like to make a present to his wife of the red and yellow dress he was admiring. I'm sure he will see things your way.'

'Is all this necessary, Constance? I mean, it all sounds so... you know… caddish.'

'Of course it is. Don't be such a stickler, Fuddy.' She examined and brushed at his side-whiskers. 'You must tell Frankie that in future I will put the grey on myself. The idea is to make you look distinguished, not fancy. And that thin bit on top needs to...'

Fleetwood pulled away. 'What about the other two? What nasty little secrets are they hiding from us?'

'Oh dear, we are getting testy.'

'Sorry, just a touch nervous. A million pounds is an awful lot of money.'

'Million and a half.'

'Yes, well…' Fleetwood was not at all sure that the syndicate would pay that much more for his mining leases. He could see a definite risk of the whole thing collapsing. They had already offered a million, which was nearly twice as much as Barny had, and if they thought he was being too greedy they could simply walk out. They must know he didn't have the money to develop and would have to sell sooner or later.

With a million, he and Constance could leave this dusty hole forever. He could sell the hotel and other interests for a tidy sum as well, and live in style back in England. He wasn't at all sure she was right this time. It was too big a gamble.

'What makes you so sure they'll pay the extra?' he asked, tugging nervously at the tie.

'Trust me,' she said, knocking his hand away and readjusting it the way it was. 'They need the leases urgently. They've spent too much already to pull out now, and if Mister Banarto hears what they're up to, he'll chop them off at the neck.'

'At the knees.'

'If you say so, dearest, now run along and tell them the bad news.'

Constance gave him five minutes, then instructed one of the barmen to deliver a bottle of champagne to the meeting.

'When you have served them,' she said, 'tell Mister Tucker that Mister Banarto is in the bar and would like to see him as soon as he is finished. Tell him quietly, as though it is confidential, but it is important that you say it loud enough for the others to hear.'

She explained it again so that he knew exactly what to do. 'Do you understand?'

The barman nodded. 'Yes, madam.' He looked

puzzled. 'I didn't see Mister Banarto in the bar.'

'Of course he isn't there,' she said curtly. 'But tell them he is anyway.' She turned to walk away, then stopped. 'Oh yes, when you have done it, come and tell me what happened. I'll be in the office.'

She went to the little office at the back of the hotel and waited, fuming at the foolish male convention that excluded her from the important meetings simply because she was a woman. If she were there they would pay the extra half-million and walk out laughing at how lucky they were. Fuddy must be getting soft. If they fell for it, the extra would be hers. She would insist on it.

When the barman returned, she tried to hide her anxiety by ignoring him until he knocked on the open door.

'Yes, what is it?'

The barman was perplexed. 'I did as you said, madam, and then Mister Tucker tells me quiet like, that I was to wait outside until he could think of a message for Mister Banarto. Then he calls me in again real soon to fetch more champagne, and says I must tell Mister Banarto as how he is sorry, but he is too busy to see him today.' The barman paused. 'Will that be all, madam?'

'Thank you, Jack.' Constance smiled broadly. 'Bring me a bottle as well please.'

'Speaking of champagne, madam, there's a gentleman at the bar who wants to know if we can sell him twenty cases of our best. I told him as how I didn't think we could spare that much, but he says it's important. He says he'll pay double the price if he can have it.'

'What does he want it for? Did he strike it rich?' Requests for champagne were common, but twenty cases seemed a lot.

'He says it's for a wedding.'

'Oh?' Constance was intrigued. Weddings were not at all common. 'Do you know him?'

'No Madam, he's not one of our local diggers. What shall I tell him?'

'Bring him here, Jack. And check our stores. We can't ignore such a generous profit.'

When the barman left, Constance jumped up from the chair and danced around the office, lifting her skirts high and kicking her legs, yipping with delight. She twirled several times like a ballerina, then plonked herself down in the chair, breathless and dizzy. It had worked! She was rich. She could return to England and thumb her nose at those titled snobs who had forced her to leave because she had married above herself. Well, she would show them who had ended up in the gutter.

She was still slightly breathless when the barman brought in her champagne, and the man who wanted to buy the cases. She smiled gaily and offered her hand and, apparently sensing her buoyant mood, he kissed it with a flourish, sweeping his bush hat low to the ground and bowing.

Constance laughed. 'Oh, my! A real gentleman, no less.'

He grinned. 'Charles Atherstone, at your service, my lady.'

'I do believe it is I who can be of service to you, Mister Atherstone. Twenty cases?'

'If you can spare them, I would be in your debt. I can't seem to get that much anywhere, and there isn't time to get it from Cape Town. The wedding is in two weeks.'

'Is it you that is getting married, Mister Atherstone?'

'Yes... please call me Charles.'

'My name is Constance, and you may have your champagne, Charles. We will have another shipment in by then, but there is a condition.'

He was thoughtful for a moment, then smiled. 'Before you tell me what it is, may I invite you to join us at the wedding?'

She curtsied. 'I would be delighted, kind sir,

and you have just won yourself some free cases for guessing what my condition is to be. I haven't been to a wedding in years.' She pushed the bottle toward him. 'You must tell me about yourself, Charles, but first let's drink a toast to the lucky...' she looked him up and down frankly, rolling her eyes. '...very lucky... bride.'

Everyone agreed that it was the best wedding ever to be held in Hope Town. The weather was perfect, with the scent of spring in the air, and a breeze cool enough to warrant the wearing of the finest clothes without fear of perspiring too freely.

The bride wore a gown of white satin, lavishly, but tastefully embroidered with white flowers, and wore a garland of orange Barbeton daisies twisted through the curls of her blonde hair. She arrived with her father in a coach and, when she alighted, drew gasps of admiration from the guests.

Besides an expression of vacuous surprise, the groom wore a green velvet morning coat with black tie, and waited self-consciously in the care of his best man, Jurie Steyn, and the Dutch Reformed Dominie, in the shade of the willow trees.

He held her hand as the local church choir sang a hymn prior to the marriage vows being taken, and when they were over and he kissed her on the lips, a sigh, like a sudden gust of wind, moaned through the audience and produced a sudden flapping of handkerchiefs.

The local dance band played lively Afrikaans folk music on their concertinas, accompanied by the popping of champagne corks, and the hundred guests descended on the mountains of food laid out in the marquee.

Martha Griel swooned when the groom hugged and kissed her full on the lips, then burst into tears when she realised what she had done, and Christina led her, sobbing, to a dark corner where she tried to console her.

'For goodness sake, Martha! Pull yourself together, You'll embarrass Anna.'

Martha wiped her eyes and nodded. She smiled weakly, then followed Christina outside to resume their duties as bridesmaids.

Charles walked beside his new wife as she introduced him to the guests, feeling dazed and speechless. Most of the people he had never met before.

His hand was crunched, his back slapped, and his cheek kissed so many times he began to wonder if he would survive the day intact. His jaw ached from smiling, and he had repeated the same thing so often that his voice had become hollow with insincerity. He could not remember a single name, and resorted to mumbling inane endearments such as friend, fellow or dear, whenever he bumped into someone he thought he had already been introduced to.

He knew the Theron family and the Steyns, and remembered Christina Jarvis's father from the bank, and Martha, the girl from the post office. He saw Corporal Pienaar, now a sergeant with the militia, who had kindly organised the marquee, and clung to him gratefully for a while, but he was soon hustled away. Then, in the background, under a plume of ostrich feathers, he saw Constance standing with an elegantly dressed man with a red puggaree flowing from his hat, and Charles took Aneline over to meet them, making suitable adjustments to his fixed smile of greeting on the way.

'What a wonderfully gorgeous wedding,' Constance gushed, giving Charles a moist kiss on the cheek. 'Is this the lucky girl? Oh, my dear, you're so beautiful... I can see why Charles fell in love with you. I've been so awfully jealous.'

'Anna, this is the generous lady I was telling you about who supplied our champagne.'

Meanwhile, her elegant escort stood back, waiting, seeming hesitant, and glancing around nervously as if searching for an avenue of escape. Charles observed him curiously. Although he seemed vaguely familiar, he was not one of those he had already met that day. He stepped forward, offering his hand and opening his mouth to speak, and the man suddenly lunged forward with a big smile and pumped his hand vigorously.

'Well, well, I see you made it, my boy... in grand style too. Good show!' He slapped Charles on the back and left him standing bemused while he bowed and kissed both of Aneline's hands.

'Fleetwood Erskine Tucker. Congratulations, my dear, you are quite the most beautiful bride I've seen.'

Aneline simpered modestly. 'Thank you for coming, sir, and for your generous gift.' 'Do you know Charles?'

'Of course, my dear. We are old friends. Will you excuse me while I have a word with him?' He winked at her. 'I shall instruct him on his marital duties.'

He took a puzzled Charles by the arm and led

him aside. 'Where did you find such a flower? Are you sure you are the same lad who walked from Brighton to... where was it again... Hycroft?'

'Hastings. I thought you said your...'

'Of course it was. Where they had that battle thing. I have such a terrible memory. It was only when I saw you a few moments ago that I remembered. Constance tells me you're an artist? Well now, I like a few paintings around, myself, you must allow me to buy...'

'I thought you said your name was Smythe?' Charles interrupted.

'Ah, yes, well, I apologise for that small deceit, but you see...' He lowered his voice, 'at the time it was necessary. A little matter of a woman, you understand, and her, let us say, well-connected husband. After my blood he was, Charles, and hot on the trail to boot. Had to leave town in a hurry the very next day, by God.'

Charles was getting the same feeling as when the San people had arranged themselves a lift.

'Oh? Then why were the police after the package you gave me?'

'The police? How do you know the police were after it?'

Charles could feel himself becoming annoyed. The package had caused him a great deal of trouble.

Had he not been forced to go with the policeman to try and clear himself, he would have been at the camp when Willa left. He may well have been able to talk her out of it.

'Because they came after me,' he said coolly. 'I was arrested and brought here to Hope Town. They told me it was stolen property.'

'Stolen...? My dear fellow, there must be some mistake. I had no...'

'As a matter of fact,' Charles interjected. 'That very same policeman is here now. Why don't we find him? I'm sure he'll be happy to have the mystery solved.' He looked around to see if he could spot Pienaar, and instead saw Constance approaching.

'Don't look so worried, Charles. If you are looking for your lovely wife, she was spirited away by three good-looking young men...' She broke off to look curiously at her partner. 'Are you feeling all right, Fuddy?'

'A trifle warm, that's all.' His lips twitched as he attempted a smile. 'I think we should be leaving soon.'

'Come now, Fuddy, we've only just arrived, and I'm having a wonderful time. You have to dance with me, and you mustn't keep Charles away from his duties. He has to give a speech.'

'What?' Her words brought Charles back with a rush. Meeting up with Smythe again - or Tucker, as he said he was - had been unexpected, but not so much of a shock as to hear he had to give a speech. He searched desperately for Aneline. The thought of having to stand unprepared in front of a hundred people without her support filled him with trepidation.

It was fortunate that by the time he gave it, most of the guests had drunk sufficient quantities of alcohol to immunise them against his clumsy efforts, and they applauded enthusiastically.

He was even more clumsy when it came to dancing, apologising for every step, and was relieved when the others joined in and Aneline was whisked away. But his relief was short-lived. First Christina, then Constance pulled him back. She tried to teach him, and he forced himself to concentrate.

'Relax and feel the rhythm with your body,' she advised. 'And take smaller steps, it is not marching.'

He tried to copy her, and was just beginning to get the hang of it when the music ended. She hooked a possessive arm through his and led him away.

'Fuddy told me about the package. He is very upset that you don't believe him.'

'He lied to me, Constance. He also gave me a false name.'

'Yes, he told me about that too. But I can assure you there was nothing in the package. I know Fuddy, and he wouldn't lie to me.'

Charles stopped to look at her. She was a striking woman, and he liked her straightforward manner. In some ways she reminded him of Willa, with the same dark eyes and hair, but she did not have Willa's softness. A determination showed in her chin that he would not like to test, and he decided he would rather have her as a friend than an enemy. He wondered if Tucker - alias Smythe - had told her about the husband he had been running away from.

'Did he tell you that I was arrested on suspicion of having stolen property?'

'Yes, he regrets that. The police were supposed to find the package first, that's why he made it red. You were just the delivery boy, Charles. There was nothing in it but old paper.'

Charles gave a wry laugh. 'So I was duped.'

'You had your fare paid.' It was a statement of fact.

He did not want to pursue it further, it was finished, and she was right. He had his fare paid and had been happy about it.

He wanted to explain about Willa. He had a feeling she would understand what he had gone through, and why he had been angry, but he remained silent. That was finished too. He was now happily married to a beautiful girl that loved him. He could ask for nothing more.

'Fuddy is a very rich and influential man, Charles. He can be of much use to you with that new project you were telling me about. In a few months we will be returning to England, and I would love to do some fund raising for the society.' She squeezed his arm to endorse her feeling.

'My ex-husband was one of those nasty people you described. I would feel as if I were making amends on his behalf. We may even be able to add the word Royal to the name.'

She unhooked her arm and studied him earnestly. 'Think about it, Charles. It's such a worthwhile cause, and Fuddy and I can't afford any trouble with the police at the moment.'

'Constance!' Charles pretended to be shocked. 'You wouldn't be trying to bribe me now, would you?'

She laughed. 'Don't be silly, my dear. If I was going to do that I could think of much more interesting ways to go about it.' She gave him a mischievous smile.

Charles grinned, his spirits lifting. 'You're a naughty lady.'

'Yes, I am, darling, and I must go before I

disgrace myself further. Fuddy is waiting.'

'I didn't thank him for the gift of champagne.'

'Oh, that wasn't his, that was mine.' She handed him an envelope. 'This is his gift to you.'

She kissed him quickly and spun away, then turned after a few steps to twiddle her fingers at him and blow a kiss. 'Bye, darling.'

Charles watched with the grin still fixed as she skipped her way gracefully through the guests, then he opened the envelope.

He was still looking at the contents with a bemused expression when Aneline came to join him.

'Come, Charles, we have to leave before our guests.' Then she saw his expression and the paper he was holding. 'What is it?'

He handed it to her and she read it. 'My, God, Charles, it's a promissory note for two thousand pounds!'

'Do you see who it is made out to?'

'The Cape Wildlife Society?'

He put his arm around her. 'That's us, Anna. You and me and anyone we can get to join us. Look after it well. It's probably the most important bribe we'll ever receive.'

Aneline liked things organised. With the two of them now working in the studio rondavel, space had become scarce. She had arranged more shelves on the wall, and replaced the desk by the window with the large table.

They worked together, Charles on his sketches, and the posters to be sent to England for the society, which Constance had promised to take care of, and Aneline herself on the letters that would accompany them. She recorded the address of each letter sent in a ledger, and in another made meticulous notes on all the finances and expenses. She also listed the donations and memberships that were beginning to grow at a steady and satisfying rate.

She loved the work. It was rewarding, and a pleasant change from having to juggle the money in preserving jars. And with Christina Jarvis and her accountant father now looking after the money side of the farm, she had only been getting in the way. It was now well on its way to becoming the largest supplier of trek oxen in the cape.

She had never been happier. Charles was the most considerate man she had ever known. So much so, that at times she had a perverse desire to make him angry simply to see what he would do.

His lovemaking was thoughtful, and she surmised he must have had considerable experience, for he knew things about women that not even she had known - or even heard about. Someone had taught him well, but she had no intention of asking. Some things were better left alone.

She had not been nervous about making love, she had been petrified. Some of the stories she had heard about men had all but convinced her that she would not enjoy it. She had been told that it was painful, and that men were demanding and interested only in themselves, but on their first night together, he had shown so much concern that she had become almost convinced he didn't want her.

After leaving the wedding, he had stopped the mule-wagon in the middle of the drift and taken two flowers from her hair, tossing them into the water.

'Like you and me, Anna,' he had said, taking her hand. 'We'll float over the rocks and through the rapids together.'

It was so romantically sad, she had clutched onto him and cried as they stood on the seat and watched the daisies bobbing along together until they were out of sight.

They had camped a short way down the river,

well clear of the town, in a pleasant spot under the trees, and in the evening had strolled hand in hand along the bank, talking in a polite, stilted manner about the wedding and what a success it had been.

It was the mosquitoes that finally provided the excuse for them to go into the wagon.

Her small bed took up most of the space, and she had to stand on it to undress and put on her nightgown while he waited outside.

He had taken a long time to come in, and her nervousness had grown by the second as the stories she had heard kept running around in her head. She was expecting the worst, but was determined to make the best of it and not let it show, holding grimly onto what Martha had said about it being the most wonderful experience in the world, like flying to the moon, she had said.

When he finally came in, she had pulled the blanket over her head to give him privacy, listening as he sat on the bed to remove his clothes, and when he climbed in beside her, even though she had been expecting it, still she had been shocked to realise that he was completely naked.

He had caressed her gently, although silently, for a long time before removing her nightdress, and her dry throat had clamped tight as his hardness pressed against her.

When it happened, she had flinched and cried out at the sharp stab of pain, and instantly he had pulled away from her and sat up. For a horrible moment she had thought he was angry with her, but he wasn't.

'I'm sorry, Anna, I didn't mean to hurt you…'

Surprised, she had sat up as well. 'No, it's all right… really, I'm just…'

'Maybe we should wait until later.' He had given her hand a consoling squeeze.

Suddenly alarmed by his emotionless tone, she had tried to gauge the expression on his face, but it was too dark.

'Don't you want me?'

'Of course I do. But I can tell you're nervous. I won't mind if you want to wait a few days.'

Determined, she had pulled him down again. 'I don't want to wait, Charles. Do you think I want to be a virgin forever? I promise not to squeal like a baby.'

Not answering, he lay beside her, caressing in a condescending manner, and her fear turned to sudden anger. 'Dammit, Charles! Just do it, will you… please?'

It was over soon, and she had kept her promise and not squealed, although her jaw ached and she had left red marks on his shoulders.

In the morning, while he was still asleep, she had

gently eased the sheet from under him and inspected it carefully for traces of blood, but found none. Vaguely disappointed, she washed in the river, singing quietly so as not to wake him. It had not been that bad, really.

Gradually the pain lessened, and by the time they reached Sani Kloof five days later, she felt hardly any, and was even beginning to enjoy it a little, although she experienced none of Martha's silly flying to the moon.

On the last day, they stopped at almost the same place on the Caledon River where she had sheltered under the wagon with her father and Jurie during the hail storm. Unlike then though, the weather was warm and sunny, and Charles suggested they spend the last day picnicking under the willows and swimming.

She spread a blanket on the bank then, feeling a shyness she could not hide, and forcing a confidence she did not feel, agreed to swim naked with him in the river.

She saw his body for the first time in the light, and was acutely aware that he was staring at hers.

'You're very beautiful, Anna... my wife.' he had complimented, and they had continued their exploration of each other on the blanket, her shyness finally giving way to excitement as he feasted his eyes on her and kissed her with real passion for the first time. And when they made love, the leaves and branches above became blurred and hazy against the sky, and she discovered that most of them had been wrong and Martha was right after all. Only it wasn't the moon she was flying to, but somewhere far beyond.

'I've never smoked in church before,' Oupa Theron confided to Charles as they sat together on one of the roughly hewn benches that served as pews. Around them, most of the male population of Eland's Drift was similarly occupied in reducing the visibility as they waited for the meeting to begin.

Charles fanned ostentatiously at the tobacco fog with his hat. 'It looks like the damned place is on fire.'

Oupa chortled. 'Ja, it's a good thing Hettie isn't here or she'd be giving us one hell of a sermon.'

Sergeant Major Erasmus of the Cape Mounted Rifles abruptly ended the buzz of conversation by rapping on the pulpit with the head of his swagger stick, and all eyes turned expectantly towards the imposing figure of the warrant officer.

'Captain Singleton will now address you,' he barked.

Several of the younger members of the community scrambled hastily to their feet as the officer entered, but were waved down impatiently by the sergeant major, who saluted the captain, then assisted him with pinning a large hand-drawn map to the back wall.

'It's the area between the Orange and Telle Rivers,' Oupa whispered to Charles.

Using the sergeant major's stick as a pointer, Captain Singleton indicated a circle drawn in red at the junction of the two rivers. 'Most of you chaps already know all about this thieving scoundrel, Murosi, and his supposedly impregnable mountain.'

An assenting murmur and several embittered growls confirmed it. Many of them had lost a considerable amount of stock to the renegade Korannas, not to mention murdered friends and relatives.

The captain waited patiently for the noise to subside before continuing.

'You are probably aware that the Cape Mounted Rifles have also lost several men in previous attempts to bring him and his rustlers to justice, so you can rest assured that the government is now more determined than ever.'

The assurance raised some derisive laughter.

'This time,' the captain went on, lifting his voice, 'we have been provided with two field canons, and with the help of volunteers such as yourselves, and others from Colesberg, we intend to put an end to his activities.' He returned the stick to the sergeant major. 'We will discuss the plan in detail over the next few days, once we have organised you into squads. Are there any questions before we take names?'

There were many, and while they were being asked and answered, Charles took the opportunity to observe the crowd. He was pleased to see his old friend, Corporal Pienaar - now wearing sergeant's stripes - standing at the back with several men from his unit. If he had to join the volunteers, which seemed inevitable if he was not to lose respect in the community, at least he would make sure to be part of the sergeant's group. For the most part, the men of the Cape Mounted Rifles looked as rugged a bunch of cut-throats and renegades as Murosi's lot was reported to be.

When the meeting was over and the groups were being organised outside, Charles sought out the former policeman and made his request, and Sergeant Pienaar agreed happily.

'Leave it to me,' he said. 'It will be good to have someone sensible to talk to for a change. Most of this lot came straight from Breakwater Prison , but at least they can shoot. Do you know how to work a cannon?'

'Haven't the faintest idea,' Charles confessed.

'Just like a bloody great blunderbuss, only noisier and you don't have to hold it.' He laughed. 'Don't worry, meneer, you'll soon get the hang of it, I think.'

Oupa was disgusted to learn that he was to stay with the older men of the community and guard the village in case of reprisal attacks.

'They think because you're old you're no damned good,' he grumbled. 'I know that badlands country around the Telle better than anyone.'

'Yes, but there is also no one better than you to look after our women, Oupa,' Charles reminded him diplomatically. 'Also your grandchildren.'

Somewhat mollified, Oupa nodded. 'Ja, I suppose there is that. Still, I don't think any of Murosi's men will come this far up the valley now with so many soldiers around. My bet is they will stick to their mountain.' He shook his head dolefully. 'I can tell you, man, I've seen that place. It's going to take a hell of a lot more than two cannons to blow them off.'

Dawn was yet to lighten the shadows in the room when the insistent tapping on the door finally woke Charles.

He lay still for a moment, wondering why

Anna was knocking, then realised she was still curled snugly against him. He carefully extricated himself and padded across to open the door.

Bally stood there, shivering in his blanket. 'It is the San,' he reported, foregoing his usual greeting. 'They are here.'

Charles peered at him, yawning, absorbing the information slowly.

'The San,' Bally repeated. 'They wish to be seen.'

'It is too early,' Charles muttered. 'Tell them to wait. I'll see them later.'

'They do not wish to be seen by others. Only by you. It is why they come early.' Bally hesitated. 'They wish to see the marks of Eland.'

Charles groaned. 'Again?'

Bally adjusted his blanket, giving himself time. 'It is not the old San from the Kgalagadi,' he explained. 'It is the other ones from the mountain. It is better that you speak with them.'

Charles felt a stirring of alarm. Only last night at the meeting they had been discussing the disturbing reports of Bushmen having joined forces with Murosi and his renegades. Hot lead was clean and quick, but the nightmarish thought of a barbed arrow slowly dispensing its vile poison into your body was enough to curdle the blood of any man. It was the main reason, many believed, that the small yellow men had been hunted almost to extinction by both black and white.

Although these San may not be a part of the rustlers, Charles did not exactly relish the idea of meeting with them alone. Maybe they had somehow learned of the imminent attack on the mountain and were employing a few tricks of their own. He had personal experience of how crafty they were.

'Do they have guns?'

'One has the gun, the other has the arrows.'

Charles's alarm grew. He wondered if he should wake up Oupa as a precaution. Maybe even send him to contact Captain Singleton.

'I do not think they will shoot the guns,' Bally said, not sounding all that convincing to Charles. 'They wish only to see Eland.'

Charles gave it some more thought. It sounded genuine enough. Had they wanted to attack they could have done so easily while he was still asleep. And with the way things were it was reasonable that they should want to remain hidden. Any Bushman or Hottentot could expect to be shot on sight. Even Bally was at risk.

'Tell them I will come,' he said finally, 'but only if they leave the guns and arrows in the bush and stand in the open by your hut.'

'I will tell them,' Bally said, sounding relieved, then added. 'It will be better if you do not bring the gun also.'

Aneline stirred as he was leaving. 'What is it, Charles? she murmured sleepily. 'Where are you going so early?'

'It's nothing, Anna. I'm going with Bally to show a sketch to some Bushmen. Put the coffee on and stay inside. I won't be long.' He left quickly, before she could ask any further questions.

He collected the drawing from its folder, then followed the path to where Bally had built his two small huts.

Three men and a woman with a small child were waiting for him. One of the Bushmen was of mixed blood, probably Hottentot, Charles surmised, with the same mustard colouring as the others, but taller and thinner, his steatopygia not so pronounced. He wore heavily patched and filthy European clothing, and held an ancient-looking rifle.

Another wore a military-style coat so large that it reached the ground. A bedraggled ostrich feather dangled from the crown of his mutilated bush hat. He held no weapon that Charles could see. Despite the cold, the other Bushman wore only a loincloth and a torn vest that showed some evidence of once being white. A short bow and a bark quiver filled with arrows were slung casually on his shoulder. The woman and child sat apart from the men, wrapped in skin blankets.

Charles stopped when he saw the weapons, suddenly regretting having not brought his own. He called sharply to Bally. 'I said no guns.'

'They do not understand all the words I speak,' Bally excused himself.

Charles observed the group carefully and decided to let it go. It was too late now anyway, and better not to make an issue of it. He went towards them with raised hand, palm outwards, his eyes cautious, but his step confident.

'I see you,' he called the traditional greeting.

Only the Bushmen with the long coat raised his hand, almost reluctantly, in reply.

Bally took the drawing to them. Except for the woman and child, who remained seated, they gathered around to look, talking animatedly amongst themselves, their breath steaming in the chill air.

Charles could smell the smoky odour of them from where he stood some five yards away. As pungent and strong as that of sweating horses, but definitely not as sweet.

The child stared at Charles, its attractively

slanted eyes unmoving. It was impossible to tell if it was a boy or girl.

He became aware that the group had fallen silent. 'What is it, Bally?'

Bally looked uncertain. 'They do not speak all the words I know.'

'Ask the woman if she understands.' Charles had been studying her and was struck by the similarity to the young woman from the desert. Perhaps she was from the same tribe. 'Also, show her the picture.'

She stifled a gasp of surprise when she saw it, quickly covering her mouth, but her face had brightened. She answered shyly when Bally spoke to her, and he grunted in satisfaction. 'She understands.'

'What does she say?' Charles prompted.

A three way conversation began between Bally, the woman and the men, then Bally translated back to Charles.

'They wish to know if you wore the bracelet when you did the marks.'

Charles thought before answering. Wondering where it was all leading. It was a relief to know that their main interest lay in the sketch and bracelet, and not in anything more sinister. The old Bushman couple had obviously told them all about it or they wouldn't be there, but their attitude gave him the feeling they harboured some resentment. And why would they ask him a question to which they already had an answer? The old woman had not given him the bracelet until after she had seen the drawing. There was a chance that Bally had got it mixed up.

Playing safe, Charles decided to evade the question. 'Say to them that the bracelet has much power. Tell them that when I use it the spirit of Eland is in my head.'

It sounded ridiculous, and he waited anxiously while Bally translated, watching them carefully for reaction, but although they listened intently, nodding in apparent understanding, they said nothing.

'Tell them also,' he instructed Bally, 'that it is a great honour to have it, but I am sad that it does not guide the hand of a San. If they wish, I will return the bracelet to them.'

Bally looked startled. 'I do not think it is a good thing to tell them this. It is a big honour.'

'Tell them,' Charles insisted.

Reluctantly, Bally spoke to the woman, and by the tone of his voice, Charles guessed that his offer was being heavily embellished with apologies.

After some animated discussion amongst the men, the Bushman in the coat spoke to the woman, and Bally gave Charles a smug, I told you so expression as he passed on the answer.

'The San wish it also, but they did not come for the bracelet, they came only to see the marks of Eland, and the one who brought the old woman from the desert, whose wish it was that you have it.'

Charles was surprised. It seemed he had guessed wrong. 'Where is the woman?'

'She is now with her ancestors.'

'How do you know this? Did they tell you?'

'They did not tell me,' Bally replied patiently, as if repeating something simple to a child. 'I know it by the way they speak that her spirit is no longer with her body.'

Charles was about to reply when he became aware that the men had suddenly fallen silent and were looking at something behind him.

He turned to see Aneline coming along the path, and felt a stab of irritation that she had not taken heed of his warning, but was relieved to see that she wasn't carrying her shotgun.

'Is anything the matter, Charles? Who are these people?'

'You shouldn't have come, Anna… be careful.' He spoke to Bally. 'Tell the San that my wife has seen them. Tell them a greeting that will make them feel safe.'

Bally complied at length, with many smiles, and the tension appeared to ease.

'Say to them,' Charles continued, wanting to get it over with, 'that the old woman San whose spirit is now with her ancestors came to me in a dream. She was holding a child such as the one they have brought here. I have a voice in my head that says they must bring this child to me and I will show it the way to make the marks of Eland.'

He had to repeat it to a puzzled Bally, but eventually it was passed on, although hesitantly, and when the woman heard it, she looked first at Charles, also in bewilderment, then down at the child sitting between her legs, as if surprised it was there. She made no effort to pass the message on to the men, and a long, uncomfortable silence ensued.

Charles explained briefly to Aneline what had happened so far.

'Do you have the bracelet?' she asked.

'In my pocket. I thought it might be good insurance.'

'I think your idea of giving it back is good. They don't look all that friendly, do they? I was a bit worried to see them here, they look like renegades.'

'I think they are,' Charles said.

'Give me the bracelet. I have a feeling they'll

be happy to have it back.'

Charles took it from his pocket. 'Let's hope you're right.'

Aneline took the bracelet and walked across to the woman. Smiling encouragement, she knelt beside the child, taking its hand. She slipped the bracelet over the small wrist, and the bewildered toddler stared at it for a moment, then returned its gaze to Aneline, apparently finding her the more fascinating.

The woman took the child's hand to study the bracelet, then she removed it and gave it back to Aneline. She spoke to Bally.

'The San woman says that her boy-child is much honoured,' Bally translated, and Charles heaved an inward sigh of relief when realising that the child may well have been a girl. Only men had ever been painters.

'She asks that you keep the bracelet of the painter until she returns with her son. Only when it is seen that he can make the marks will he be allowed to wear it.'

Excited questions were being asked by the group, and when the lengthy translations were completed, none of which were passed on to Charles, he said to Bally, 'Ask them if this is what they wish.'

Further lengthy conversation ensued between

the men and the woman, during which Aneline cooed and played with the child.

Bally looked relieved when he finally spoke to Charles. 'The San say that if it is what you want, then they wish it also.'

Charles was also relieved. 'And what of the woman and child?'

'At the time when the ashes of Eland fall on the big mountains, she will return with the child.' Bally adopted a stern frown. 'She has no husband now, he is with his ancestors, and I have two huts and much room for her. Also, I am rich. I will buy her from her brothers.'

'Charles grinned. He could think of no better outcome. 'Have you told her this?'

'Not yet,' Bally replied.

Aneline thought back over the past few days for anything she could have said or done that could have caused Charles to be angry with her. He had been a little annoyed that she had followed him to the meeting with the Bushmen, but only because he was concerned for her safety. They had laughed about it later, and about Bally's plans for the woman, and also how they had both automatically assumed that the child was a boy. It could have been embarrassing had they been wrong.

At first she thought it was because he was worried about leaving next day with the militia to Murosi's Mountain, but they had spoken often about it, and if anything, he seemed to be looking forward to going.

Then she remembered that it was after reading the mail that he had become moody and preoccupied. She had assumed at the time he was short with her simply because of her interrupting while he was trying to work, or that he had received some disturbing news, but he had denied it, and she was sure he would have shared any information with her if it involved business matters.

He had gone for a long walk by himself, something he had not done before, then returned late and busied himself in the studio, and she had gone through to confront him.

He was reading from one of the files, and hurriedly closed it before getting up and coming towards her. 'I thought you had gone to bed.'

'No, I want to know what's wrong, Charles. What has happened that you can't tell me about? Is it something I've done?'

He had placed his arm around her, leading her from the studio. ''I'm sorry, Anna. Of course you haven't done anything. I have a few things I want to clear up before leaving, that's all.'

'What things?' she had persisted, not convinced. 'Can't I do them?'

'Yes, of course, but not now. It's nothing you have to worry about. Come, let's go to bed. It's late, and I have to be away early.'

Aneline had wanted to insist that he tell her right away. They were supposed to share everything, the good and the bad, that's what they had agreed when he had thrown the flowers in the river. And it was only because there had been so much good in her life over the past months that she allowed herself to be persuaded. Still, she wasn't about to let him off that easily.

'You must tell me, Charles,' she had said firmly. 'First thing in the morning. Promise?'

Although he hadn't answered, she had taken it that he would. She heard him get up quietly and go through to the studio when it was still dark, but thought nothing of it, and when he came to wake her at dawn with a cup of coffee, he

seemed almost himself again, talking about what she

would do while he was away. He had cautioned her about locking the cottage at night and keeping the shotgun loaded and ready on the floor beside the bed, and he had arranged for Bally to sleep in the studio where he could be close. He had kissed her goodbye then, although too briefly, she thought now in retrospect, and had promised to return as soon as possible. He said nothing about what had been bothering him, and because he was leaving and she wanted things to be good between them, she had not persisted.

But later that morning, sitting alone at the desk and reluctant to put her mind to the tasks ahead, Aneline looked thoughtfully out through the window at the sweep of the long grass leading down to the willows, and wondered again about what could possibly have happened to produce such a change in his manner. He was definitely more distant, and despite his denials, she knew him well enough to know that something serious was on his mind.

She tried to remember what had been in the mail. There had been the usual letters addressed to the society, which she herself had opened, and two addressed to Charles personally, which she hadn't. Both had been from Cape Town, but she hadn't taken much notice, sorting through quickly, and couldn't recall having seen anything particularly distinctive about them.

Looking in the tray, she found one of them. It was from the Standard Bank, but contained no unhappy news. Quite the reverse, in fact. She couldn't find the other, and wondered if she should look through the waste-bin for the envelope, then she frowned at her suspicions and went through to make some tea before settling down to work.

It came suddenly after the first mouthful of the sweet brew, a queasiness, followed almost immediately by a burning in her throat. She clamped a hand to her mouth and rushed from the studio to vomit in the garden.

She stayed there for a while, her brow clammy, leaning forward with hands on her knees for support as she spat and, despite the bitterness, smiled.

She had suspected it. Now she was sure. She was going to have their baby at last.

Hettie Theron watched thoughtfully from the kitchen window as Aneline led her horse along the path to the shed. It was unusual for the girl not to stay and chat for a while over a cup of tea, and she hoped it was not because Anna was angry with her for writing to

Willa. But Charles would have explained, so surely she wouldn't blame her.

Willa's reply coming only a few days ago, after so long a time that she had already forgotten about it, had been an unpleasant surprise, but not as bad as the disturbing news that Willa had also written to Charles. He must have received the letter on the same day she had got hers, but had not mentioned it, so maybe he was angry with her too.

Hettie sighed and turned away from the window, once more regretting having contacted Willa. Danie had been furious with her.

'Dammit, Hettie!' he had stormed. 'What did you do a stupid thing like that for? Didn't you tell her that he's married?'

'I wrote to her the day he arrived. I thought she might be interested. How was I to know he was going to marry Anna? He hadn't even met her then.'

He had thumped the table and glared at her. 'Dammit, woman! You've really done it this time! Why must you always interfere? Do you see now what you've done? And what of Willa's husband, didn't you think about that?'

'Don't you listen to anything I say? I told you before, he left her when he found out the child wasn't his. She's been living with her parents.'

'Well, you had better go and explain.'

'Do you think he will blame me, Danie? I was only trying to help.'

He had pushed his chair back angrily, then stomped to the door.

'Where are you going? You shouldn't let Anna know. It is for Charles to tell her.'

'Ja, well, maybe you should worry instead that I don't go and shoot myself.'

Charles had been gone for over a week before Aneline discovered the file.

It was the same one she had seen on his desk the day she had met him, when she had delivered the parcel and discovered who he was. A black folder tied around with a yellow ribbon, and it was not simply her intuition that told her it was what she was looking for. She had not seen it in all the months they had been married, although she cleaned regularly and knew the exact location of every piece of paper. It was finding it hidden where she would never normally have looked that convinced her.

A stray swallow had flown in to the studio through

the open door and taken refuge on top of the wall, and it was while she was standing on the table trying to chase it out that she had seen the file wedged between the pole and the thatching.

She was also sure that it was the same one he had been working on the night before he had left, even though she had not seen the ribbon. She had thought his actions a little odd at the time, almost furtive, but her determination to confront him had overshadowed it.

Reluctantly, and also with some measure of guilt, Aneline took the file down and placed it on the desk. She observed it thoughtfully, wondering what could possibly be in it that he didn't want her to see. They had taken on a commitment to be partners, and the sense of sharing everything with him was something she had come to cherish greatly. It was not a duty, as it had been with the family, but something special, like having another self to care for. Secrets were not a part of it.

She was acutely aware that once she opened it, even if what it contained was perfectly innocent, like perhaps some financial dealings, something would be removed that could never be replaced. Sharing was like that. It could well be the end of the thread that, once pulled, would unravel the whole delicate veil of trust that she valued so highly.

She wanted to put it back unopened. To have everything the way it was, but it was too late for that now. With a sigh of resignation, she unwound the yellow ribbon and opened the folder.

The drawing of a woman looked back at her. A woman with long hair that almost covered the basket she had propped on her hip. She had a sensuous smile and dark eyes. It was a woman she did not recognise.

With a prickling feeling around her ears and neck, she turned the page and drew in a sharp breath of surprise.

The same woman was kneeling over a tub, apparently washing her hair, and from the waist up she was naked. Her head was thrown back as she swept the hair from her face, a pose that emphasised her large, perfectly formed breasts.

Aneline turned the next page with trembling fingers. Several smaller sketches of the same woman filled the page, all in different poses, and in all of them she was naked. Lying on a flat rock with the hair spread out behind. Leaning back on her arms looking up with eyes closed and an expression of bliss. Sitting cross-legged on a rock, blatantly exposing a small triangle of dark hair between her thighs. Showing well-rounded buttocks as she stepped gracefully into a pool.

Aneline was flabbergasted. Pictures of a naked woman had been the last thing she had expected. She wasn't sure if they were what they called dirty pictures or not, as she had never seen any before, but she had heard that some men kept them, and that they were even in magazines, but she would never have expected Charles to have them. Maybe she didn't know him as well as she thought.

They were wonderfully drawn, with every detail shown, as only Charles knew how, leaving no doubt as to the woman's beauty and sensuous body. Her breasts made her own look like mosquito bites by comparison.

She studied the drawings with a deep feeling of resentment. Wondering about them, and the woman. Had she posed for them? Had he made love to her? And why would he still have them?

Of one thing she was almost certain though. The pictures could hardly be the reason for his behaviour. Unless... and the thought struck Aneline like a physical blow. Could it be that he kept them because she couldn't satisfy him? Was he dissatisfied with her body? She knew she had a reasonable one. It was firm and had a good shape, and he often commented on her nice legs, but it did not compare with that of the woman in the sketches. Could that be the reason he had been looking at them on their last night together… why he had made love to her as if he had considered it a duty?

Another thought struck her, and it was even more horrifying than the first. Did he have to look at the pictures before he was able to make love to her at all? And who was he thinking of when he did…?

With the shocking questions flooding her mind, Aneline turned the last page almost absent-mindedly, and saw the envelope she had been looking for. Also a letter.

It was on a single sheet, opened out, and the writing was small and neat; a woman's writing. But it was the first words that caught her attention like the sudden clanging of alarm bells. It began: *My darling Charles.*

Aneline stared at the words and knew with certainty she had found the reason for Charles's distance. It *was* another woman.

With a sensation of approaching doom, Aneline pulled it slowly towards her and began to read.

My darling Charles,

> *How you must be wondering why I write! It has been such a very long time. Do you still remember me? I haven't forgotten you, Charles. How could I? We shared so much together on those wonderful Sundays by the pool, with the sunshine and*

the yellow flowers. Oh, I do miss them so!

Can you ever forgive me for leaving without saying goodbye? I could not have left if I had seen you again. I loved you so much it almost broke my heart. I thought it was the right thing to do by my husband, but it wasn't. I was so confused when I discovered that I was pregnant. Yes Charles, I should have told you. I hope it's not too big a shock for you, but we have a beautiful daughter. She has your lovely blue eyes and my black hair, and her name is Charlotte. I named her after you, my darling.

How could I ever forget you when I see you every day? She's so much like you that I sometimes want to cry. What have I done, Charles?

Sandy left me when he found out that it wasn't his child. Poor Sandy, it was just too much for him. Charlotte and I have been living with my parents at their winery near Constantia, and although we don't have much money, we are not poor either and there is always plenty of food. I'm only telling you this so you will know that I am not asking for money.

I could not believe it when Ouma wrote and told me you were there, and I would have replied immediately, but I did not get the letter until a short while ago. My father had kept it from me as he did not approve of what I had done, and I thought you had gone back to England for ever. I should have known that you wouldn't leave Africa. I remember how your eyes used to shine when you spoke of the animals and the bush.

I have not been seeing any men since Sandy left, it's strange, but I feel more married to you than I ever did to him. I think it's because of Charlotte. Do you know that you were the last man I made love to?

If you want to see me again, Charles, will you write to me?

I love you,

Willa.

Aneline held the letter in her hands and stared at it unseeing, with unending disbelief. Unwilling to absorb what she had just read. Wishing it not to be true. Wanting to put everything back the way it was before she had read it.

She looked at it for a long time, seeing only a blur in front of her, then she put the letter back and closed the folder, and she knew that she had just turned a page in her life that she could never turn back again. The fairy tale was over.

Now she understood everything. All the small mysteries suddenly became painfully obvious. His distant attitude towards her - especially over the last few days - his occasional moodiness, even his overly considerate lovemaking - which was obviously reluctance - all pointed to only one conclusion. He didn't love her. He could never have loved her, and the knowledge filled her with shame.

And the Therons, whom she had thought of as friends, had known all along about the woman and had never told her. Ouma had even written to tell her that Charles was here. How could she have betrayed her like that?

Aneline rose woodenly and, feeling as if she was in a trance, went through to the bedroom and changed into her moleskin trousers, a shirt and her riding boots. She threw some clothes in a blanket and rolled it up, then picked up her saddle and shotgun from the rail on the verandah. Struggling under the load, she left without looking back.

She saddled her brown mare and rode off downriver, through the valley and along the foothills of the mountains and sandstone cliffs. She did not care that it was not the safest route. She only cared about getting home soon, away from the shameful lie she had been living, and this way it would save a whole day in travelling. She hadn't seen her family or spoken to her mother since the wedding. It was time to speak to her again.

She let the mare choose its own pace as far as the drift, some five miles downstream from Sani Kloof, and she stopped there to dismount while it drank.

Where were the flowers Charles had thrown in the river now, she wondered? How far had they travelled before becoming stranded or torn apart?

She cried hot, angry tears that burned her cheeks, then wiped her eyes and continued on. What a fool she had been. Well, he could go back to his married bitch and his bastard child. She no longer cared.

Angrily, she dug in her heels and the startled mare grunted, then bounded forward into a run.

Murosi's flat-topped mountain loomed starkly over the Orange River like a vulture waiting for unwary prey to stumble past. Rising in a wilderness of rocks and jagged peaks, it was a forbidding, yet still spectacularly beautiful landscape in the mellow glow of the late afternoon. It was the perfect stronghold for the chief of the Phuthi people and, looking at it from across a barren, rust-coloured valley scarred with deep ravines, Charles could see that Oupa Theron had been right. Even with the cannons and additional hundred volunteers Captain Singleton had been able to muster to support his militia, it was going to be a difficult and hazardous task.

The mountain was steep and rimmed around below the flat summit with seemingly unscaleable cliffs. The few ravines that broke through the sheer wall were dense with thorny scrub and, no doubt, easily defended. The river itself, flowing dark and sullen through a layered sandstone canyon, was a major obstacle, and once across, the besiegers would be exposed and in range of sniper's bullets, poisoned arrows, and rocks. Any approach would have to be made at night and, Charles thought, thankful not to be included, a dark one at that.

The first assault was to begin the next day.

Slowed by the rough terrain and heavily laden supply wagons, it had taken five days to reach their present position, and Captain Singleton was anxious to launch an attack before the undisciplined volunteers initiated one of their own. Scaling ladders were in the process of being assembled, and the cannons sent from Colesberg had been positioned on small fortified hillocks, one at either end of the mountain's length, where the steep trajectory of the barrels would be less likely to cause casualties amongst his own men due to overshoots.

Despite the barrier of the river and the open ground though, it was the squads spread out on the opposite side of the mountain that proved to be in the most hazardous position. Although the rugged country, with its myriad rocky ravines and sandstone caves afforded plenty of protection, this also worked in favour of the many renegades that were apparently not prepared to sit and wait for the attack.

Showing unexpected daring, they launched raids of their own, setting up ambushes in the caves and along the complex labyrinth of bridle paths linking the mountain to the surrounding countryside. Several men had already been killed and wounded, some with poisoned arrows, and their pitiful cries, heard clearly in the surprised silence that usually followed after an ambush, were often accompanied by distant goading laughter and cheers drifting down from the summit. Still, the captain had no shortage of volunteers to lead the assault.

It began in the late afternoon with a bombardment from the cannons.

Working on one of the guns with Sergeant Pienaar, his ears stuffed with rifle-cleaning cotton, Charles loaded a shell every ten minutes - which was about the maximum they could fire without overheating the steel barrel. The second cannon at the other end of the mountain followed suit, and for five hours the two roared intermittently into the night, lobbing their deadly projectiles onto Murosi's flat-topped stronghold.

The cannonading ended when Captain Singleton's red skyrocket arched high into the air above the mountain, and Sergeant Pienaar left Charles and another volunteer to stay with the gun while he rushed off to join his men for the final assault.

Under the covering fire of the cannons, the militia and volunteers had already reached the base of the cliffs with the scaling ladders, and began climbing the moment the rocket was fired.

Sitting beside the cannon, watching the firefly flickering of muzzle-flashes against the dark bulk of the mountain, and listening to the sporadic clamour of the battle raging all around it, Charles had no way of knowing what was happening. Only much later, long after the firing had ceased and the false dawn was beginning to lighten the sky, did the men return, exhausted and with sweat streaking their blackened faces, to tell of the disaster that had occurred.

Every attempt to reach the top had failed. It seemed Murosi had more men and weapons at his disposal than had been anticipated and, aided by a clear sky and reflected moonlight, the soft-leaded bullets and arrows of the defenders, often fired at almost point-blank range, had caused havoc among the men on the ladders. Fourteen had been killed, over thirty wounded, and three had been captured, including Sergeant Major Erasmus who had been leading the attack. And the number was expected to be even higher once all the reports were in from the squads on the far side. It was more than a disaster, it was a major setback.

Then, adding insult to the failure, shortly after dawn they received a further blow.

Chief Murosi, accompanied by several of his men, led the three bound captives to the edge of the cliff where they were in full view of the militia below. One of the captives - who turned out to be the sergeant major - was thrown to the ground and, in a gruesome act of defiance, decapitated by Murosi himself.

The headless body was tossed contemptuously over the cliff, and the head clearly displayed near the edge, spiked onto a pole. The two remaining captives were led out of sight, and some hopeful speculation suggested that they were to be kept as hostages, but this was soon dispelled when, a short while later they reappeared after having been stripped of their clothes. One at a time, they were simply pushed over, still alive and bound, to crash on the rocks below.

Coming on top of their resounding failure, the bizarre exhibition was yet another humiliating blow for Captain Singleton and his forces, but it was also possibly the chief's first mistake, for it served to anger the men and strengthen their resolve, including that of Charles.

Until then he had been remote from the fighting. He had not known any of the men killed, or even seen their bodies, but watching the grotesque performance on the cliff-edge through a pair of field glasses loaned to him by the sergeant, brought him sickeningly close to the reality of it.

Like most, he was keen to resume the attack immediately, but the captain demurred. They needed to wait at least another week for the moon to wane completely, he informed them, and they would need more supplies from Colesberg.

A small, fast mule-wagon was also dispatched to Eland's Drift with two bodies, and Charles volunteered to go as part of the escort. It would give him a chance to see Aneline, and perhaps explain about the letter from Willa that had weighed so heavily on his mind. He had been given plenty of opportunity to think about it, but had still not been able to come to terms with the fact Willa still loved him, and that he was a father.

He would have to see the child, that was certain, and by doing so would also see Willa. He had no idea how he would feel when that happened. He did not know if he still loved her, or even if he loved Anna, for that matter. All he knew was that he was confused. But Aneline was his wife and deserved to know the truth. They had vowed to share both good and bad, and so far he had fallen short with his side of the bargain. No matter what the consequences, or what happened after, it was time to even the scales.

The first day of travelling through the Caledon Valley did not bother Aneline all that much. She had her anger to sustain her, and it was the same route used by the men on their way to Murosi's Mountain. She felt reasonably sure that no renegades would have lingered there.

The first night though, was one of the longest and most miserable she had ever experienced.

With no fire for company, and with her anger sufficiently cooled to allow depressing thought to take its place, sleep was all but impossible. Even the joy of her pregnancy failed to comfort her. She had wanted a child so much, but now it would be nothing but a constant reminder of Charles's deceit and her own shame.

At one point during the night, close to dawn when her spirits were at their lowest, she had considered returning to Sani Kloof, to await his return so she could confront him with his treachery. Maybe he would have a good excuse, and Charles was not the sort of man to abandon her, even if he did love another woman, and at least the child would have a father and a secure future.

She came close to capitulating, but finally could not. She knew herself too well. She would never be able to share him, and it would be a lie to stay with a man who did not love her. No matter how considerate a person he was, she would be better off without him.

Aneline led the mare from their hiding place in the willows at dawn, and studied the track hopefully for signs that militia, or perhaps even a wagon, had passed during the night, but no one had. She was alone.

Dispirited, she continued on, cautiously at first, walking the horse, then as the sun rose to bathe the peaceful valley in gold, her confidence returned and she coaxed the mare into a steady lope. If she kept a good pace, another day would see her past the badlands area and onto the coach road to Colesberg, where she could expect to be reasonably safe. With luck, in two days and nights she would be home.

She heard the solid slap of the bullet as it struck the mare in the neck, and was already falling when the sound of the shots exploded in her ears.

Instinctively, she threw herself sideways to avoid falling under the horse, and hit the ground hard, knocking the wind from her body and grazing her hands and arms as she skidded over the rough surface.

She lay stunned, gulping for air. The mare lay kicking feebly a few yards away, shivering in spasm as it died. She stared at it, shocked and uncomprehending.

Then, faintly at first, becoming louder as she regained her senses, she heard the excited shouting of approaching men. Korannas!

Aneline's paralysing shock gave way to instant panic. She scrambled on grazed hands and knees towards the mare and her shotgun. It was trapped under the body and she could not pull it free. With a wail of despair she left it and ran towards the nearby river. With no adequate cover now along the bank, beneath the surface of the brown water was the only place she could think of.

She was halfway down the bank, stumbling and sliding in her awkward boots through the lush water-weeds when they caught her.

One of them dived on her from behind, knocking her down, then they dragged her back up the bank by her arms, gleefully ignoring her struggles and futile demands to be freed.

They dumped her at the top and gathered around, laughing breathlessly, prodding suggestively between her clamped legs with their rifle barrels, holding themselves lewdly and making jokes. Six sweating and happy Koranna Hottentot renegades.

Aneline closed her eyes to shut out their grinning faces, and with her body tense and shivering with terrified expectation, prayed that it would be quick, and that afterwards, they would kill her.

55

Charles frowned at Oupa Theron in bewilderment. 'What do you mean, she's gone?'

The old man shifted in obvious discomfort on the saddle. They had met some twelve miles from Eland's Drift, going in opposite directions. Charles travelling with the four men escorting the bodies in the mule wagon, and Oupa Theron accompanied by two old friends from the village. Charles had been a pleasantly surprised to meet him there, but that soon vanished when he discovered the reason.

'Two days ago, soon after lunch,' Oupa said. 'Bally reported her gone. At first we thought... that is, Ouma and me did... that she had only gone to stay with someone in the village, but when I checked, no one had seen her there. Then Hansie here,' he indicated to one of the men alongside, 'said he saw her going through the drift the day before, coming this way.'

'Ja, man,' Hansie said earnestly. 'Both me and the wife seen her. Going like hell, she was, and I said to Marie right then that there was something...'

'This way?' Charles uttered the words reluctantly. No one had passed them going either way, Oupa and his friends were the first, but now, with a sudden premonition, he remembered the dead horse they had passed a few miles back, lying a short way off the track.

He had not looked closely at the animal himself. One of the other men had investigated and reported that the horse had been shot. It was not too unusual an event. The saddle and bridle had been removed, and they had naturally assumed the horse had become blown or had broken a leg. But now, although he tried to convince himself otherwise, Charles knew that was not the case. It had been a brown horse. The same colour as Aneline's mare.

Charles looked silently at Oupa and his friends, reluctant to face the obvious, and Oupa edged his horse closer to speak confidentially.

'I should tell you, Charles. When Ouma was looking in your studio she found the letter on your desk... you know, the one from Willa... and also the drawings you did of her.' He shook his head in disbelief.

'Jesus, man! What were you thinking, leaving that stuff lying around?'

Charles continued to stare silently at Oupa, but with dawning comprehension, and a sick feeling in his stomach.

'She took some clothes,' Oupa continued, 'and a bed-roll.' He paused to look anxiously at Charles. 'Are you sure you didn't see her? Maybe you missed her last night, hey, in the dark.'

'No.' Charles shook his head. He did not want to explain that they had camped beside the track, ambushing it, and no one had passed in the night. He turned his horse aside and walked it to where the escort was waiting a short way ahead.

'That dead horse,' he enquired of the man who had inspected it, 'did you notice if it was a mare?'

'It could have been, I didn't look. Why?'

'How long do you think it had been there?'

The man frowned in thought. 'A day or so, I'd say. It was stiff, but not too bloated yet, although the vultures had been at it… is something wrong?'

'You fellows go on,' Charles said. 'I have to go back there with the old men and check a few things.'

Two vultures hopped away as they approached the dead horse, then flapped heavily into a nearby tree. Charles dismounted to inspect the animal. It was a mare, but he was unable to identify it further. He had not known the horse all that well, and the birds had been busy, particularly around the head and eyes.

What he did notice though, with a sinking feeling, was the bullet hole in the neck. No one would put a horse out of its misery by shooting it there. Also, several chunks had been cut from the carcass while it had still been fresh, no doubt for food. It seemed unusual. The surrounding ground was hard and showed little sign other than scuff marks where the saddle had been pulled clear.

'What do you think, Charles?' Oupa enquired tentatively.

'I can't tell. Let's have a look around.'

It was one of Oupa's friends who found the first clear sign that something out of the ordinary had occurred. He called them over to have a look.

A sapling that had been stripped of its bark The sap was dry, and the pale skin of the exposed wood had turned brown, but not dark. It could not have been peeled much more than a day ago.

The signs they had hoped not to find were in the soft soil of the riverbank.

Charles stared morosely at the small prints of a woman's riding boots. They had been overlaid in places by much larger prints, and also a few heavy scuffs and grooves, as if something had been dragged up the bank.

Widening the search, they found a trail of footprints leading away from the river. The deep imprint from the sharp heels of the boots were unevenly spaced, sometimes close together and erratic, as if whoever had worn them had been staggering.

They followed them into the hills cautiously, not for fear of being ambushed - that was something Charles was almost hoping for - but because with the hardening rocky ground the marks were gradually becoming less defined. And they were more than a day old, blurred by the wind, and did not follow any clear path that would enable them to push ahead with any sure knowledge they would eventually pick up the spoor again farther along. Painstakingly, they had to confirm it as they went, then, with the lengthening shadows of evening, they finally lost them altogether.

'What now?' One of Oupa's friends - an old rancher who had tracked cattle through the hills for much of his life - voiced the question Charles had been asking himself. 'It is hopeless in this country. We should get the militia and more trackers to come and search.'

'Impossible,' Charles answered shortly, unable to hide his frustration. With the lost tracks went his only sense of contact with her. 'They can't leave that bastard Murosi now. Wait here and rest with the horses. I'm going to climb this hill. Maybe I'll see a fire or something.'

They offered no objection, sitting thankfully to smoke their pipes, and Charles, with a sense of purpose that he already suspected would be futile, pushed himself hard up the hill.

As expected, little could be seen from the top. No smoke and no light. Only a depressing shadowy wilderness of more jagged hills and thorny scrub, and the emptiness of it spread to engulf him as well. He fought to control the feeling of hopelessness with anger and determination. He had no doubt it was Anna. It was no time to weaken. She needed him.

Oupa and his friends had accompanied him willingly so far, and he knew they would be prepared to go farther, but he could not expect them to continue indefinitely into renegade country without support. It had been foolish enough to come as far as they had. It would be better to send them home with his horse and continue alone, when he would be less likely to be seen.

But he knew he did not have the skill to follow. The four of them, all experienced with tracking, had already lost the old spoor on the stony ground, and to lose it completely would be to lose Anna as well. He could not take the chance. It had already been too long.

That single thought was as far as Charles would allow himself to go. Beyond that lay the unthinkable.

The freshly peeled bark that bound her wrists had begun to dry and shrink, cutting into the flesh to swell her hands and turn the fingers numb. The inside of her forearms, grazed from when she had fallen from the horse, stung where they pressed against the trunk of the sapling around which they had been tied. With her legs spread on either side of it and also bound at the ankles, she could neither stand nor lie down, and her back ached from the strain of sitting in one position.

The inside of her moleskin trousers were stuck to the drying blood of her grazed knees, the injury made worse by the many falls she had suffered during the rough hike, and her feet were blistered and swollen in the tight boots, which were not designed for walking long distances.

She had no idea of where she was. They had twisted and turned through the hills, following no defined path that she had been able to see, stumbling with her hands tied in front, around thorny bushes that ripped at her skin and hooked at her clothes. It had been a relief to stop, even though she had felt safer on the move.

They spoke only in their own language, so she had been given no clues as to what they were going to do with her. At first she had been a little surprised that they had not raped and killed her at the river. It was what she had expected from their actions and taunts, and for a while she had clung to the hope she was going to be held for ransom.

But as the day progressed her hope had faded. Their lecherous manner had not changed. They still grinned and prodded too often for her peace of mind, and she had come unwillingly to the discouraging conclusion that she was simply being removed to some safer place. Their shooting may have attracted attention. They wanted to take their time and enjoy themselves without fear of interruption.

And they had stopped in such a place. A level clearing against a steep hill, protected on two sides by dense thickets and with a view down the slope where anyone approaching could be seen. Three of them had rifles, and one her own shotgun. The remaining two carried spears and knives.

She had expected it to happen right away, as soon

as they had stopped, but they seemed in no hurry. One of them, a half-caste with pale eyes and crinkled reddish hair that betrayed a distant white side to his ancestry - and whom she guessed was the leader because he was the biggest - had untied her hands, then made her sit while he retied them around the sapling, allowing no time for the painful circulation to be completed, and showing no sympathy for her gasps of agony. He had stared at her, his light eyes without expression as he bent to chew off a length from the bark on her wrists to use on her ankles.

When completed, he had moved to stand behind and slide his hands down the front of her shirt, roughly fondling her breasts, and chuckling as she hunched her shoulders and attempted to bite his arm. He withdrew his hands and sauntered off, making some joke to the others, who immediately showed interest in feeling for themselves, but he waved them aside with some explanation that seemed to Aneline like a postponement, for they obeyed too happily. One made a small fire while the others sprawled in the shade, then they sat around the coals to roast and gnaw on the chunks of meat they had cut from her mare.

Aneline watched them surreptitiously, thankful that she had not been offered any. They all wore European-style clothing in various states of disrepair.

Probably looted, she thought miserably, from unwary travellers like herself, for one was wearing her bush-hat, and another had claimed the jacket from her blanket-roll.

When they had finished eating, they began playing some sort of noisy card game, exclaiming and slapping at each other good-naturedly as each drew a card in turn from the pack. The half-caste was apparently excluded, for he held the deck and disagreed authoritatively when it was suggested he have a turn as well.

But it was a short game, and when the half-caste stood to stretch, then swaggered casually towards her, grinning vacuously at the snide-sounding jokes of his comrades, Aneline realised with sudden dread what the game had been all about. They had been drawing for their turns, and the leader was to be first.

It was approaching dawn when Charles, Oupa and his two friends reached Sani Kloof.

Charles went immediately to wake Bally in the studio, feeling the tight rein on his emotions beginning to slacken as the little African, his face wrinkled with concern, dressed quickly and without question. It was made no easier for Charles by being in familiar surroundings, with the sense of her presence in every corner, especially the bedroom, and he left quickly after checking for himself that she had taken some of her clothes and the thick blanket.

Oupa and his two companions had insisted on accompanying him and Bally back to where they had found the dead mare, overcoming his protests by explaining that someone would have to return with his and Bally's mounts.

While Bally helped Oupa and his friends round up fresh horses, Charles assisted Ouma as she bustled around the kitchen, making a large breakfast and putting together a food parcel.

Ouma made no attempt to hide her distress. She wept openly, blaming herself for what had happened, and brushed aside Charles's subdued efforts at reassurance.

'Everything would have been different had I just minded my own business,' she lamented. 'I should never have written to her.'

'No, it's my fault for not telling Anna. I kept putting it off because I didn't know what to say. You were only trying to help.'

'And what good did it do? That poor girl... what

she must be going through.' Ouma looked at Charles through swollen, miserable eyes, lip trembling, and he put a comforting arm around her shoulders.

'I'm sure she'll be all right, Ouma. They took her with them, so it probably means they'll keep her for ransom. They do that quite often, apparently. And remember, she met three of the renegades when they came to see the sketch. I'm sure when they find out who she is they'll release her.'

Ouma nodded. 'Yes, I'm sure you're right.' She dabbed at her eyes with the corner of her apron, then returned to her stove, jabbing vigorously at the coals with a poker. 'I'll never forgive myself if anything happens to her or the baby, Charles. Never.'

Charles stared at Ouma's back, not sure if he had heard correctly. 'Baby?'

'Oh, dear...' Ouma laid down the poker with a sigh that culminated in stifled sob.

'Anna is pregnant?'

'I'm sorry... she was so looking forward...'

The rein suddenly snapped and Charles sat down heavily to hold his head, fingers gripping into his hair. 'Oh God, Ouma...'

They arrived back at the dead horse in the early afternoon.

Nothing much remained of it now except scattered bones, shreds of hide, and a ripening smell. While Oupa and his friends lit their pipes and rested, Charles helped a painfully stiff Bally dismount, somehow finding a weak smile at the comical look of relief on his face. It was the first time Bally had ridden a horse, and by the precarious manner in which he had bounced and swayed it seemed a miracle to Charles that he had managed to stay on.

'If you ever leave,' one of Oupa's friends commented to Charles. 'You can tell that little bugger he can work for me. I could use a good man like that.'

'That'll be the bloody day,' Oupa growled. 'Bally's not going anywhere.'

Hearing his name mentioned, Bally paused in his grimacing and stretching to grin at them and straighten up, misunderstanding their interest, then he hobbled away to read the signs on the ground for himself, apparently not prepared to trust such an important task to amateurs.

He was back before Oupa had finished his pipe, and held up six fingers, indicating the number of men. Then, frowning, he raised another finger on its own. 'Missy Anna,' he said.

Any shred of hope that he and the others may somehow have been mistaken and that Anna was

428

staying with a friend vanished for Charles. He picked up his rifle and shotgun, and slung the light pack containing their food and blankets. No further talk was necessary - or desirable.

They parted with a brief exchanging of solemn nods. Only silence could adequately convey their feelings.

Stooped over, Bally followed the all but invisible tracks at an erratic jog, whispering constantly to himself as he unravelled the story of the trail. He stopped occasionally to feel the ground with the back of his hand, gauging the texture, or to peer closely at something that looked out of place, getting to know the habits of those that had passed and unknowingly left messages on the earth.

Charles followed a few steps behind, keeping as sharp a lookout on the surrounding country as his gritty eyes would allow. He looked down only to check his footing, trusting all the tracking to Bally, confident that he would miss nothing of importance and that eventually he would lead him to her. He refused to think beyond that, trying to keep his troubled mind free and his dulled senses alert.

Once they were deep into the hills the direction of the trail changed, heading south, and Charles was undecided about whether to be pleased or concerned. In that direction lay Murosi's Mountain, and he would find reinforcements there, but also more renegades. And the trail was now three days old. When the group they were following had passed this way the cannons had not yet begun firing. They may not even have been aware of the impending siege and could possibly have been ambushed by militia, when anything could have happened.

Charles gave up worrying about it, finding some consolation in the knowledge that surrounded as it was, the mountain would be inaccessible to the abductors. At least Anna would be spared from falling into the clutches of Murosi.

It was late afternoon when Bally stopped suddenly and raised his hand in warning.

Charles jerked to a halt close behind him, lifting his rifle in readiness. He strained his eyes and ears for whatever it was that had alerted Bally, glancing at him for a clue, but Bally remained still, his head to one side, listening intently.

'What is it?' Charles whispered, his anxiety getting the better of him, and Bally waved his hand impatiently. He moved forward slowly, his hand still held out behind, poised for further communication.

He walked on the edge of the faint trail, where

the grass was short and would make no sound as they passed. Then he suddenly turned off the path to follow a trail of bent grass, stepping carefully through it towards a thick tangle of scrub.

Charles crept behind him, hands sweating, his breath short and shallow with tension.

They came into a small open area where a fire had been lit. Bally approached the ashes and felt them, pushing his hand deep. He withdrew it slowly. The ashes were cold.

They found the saddle and two of Anna's oldest shirts under a bush, and Charles examined the clothes anxiously, but could find no clues. They did not appear to have been worn. He stuffed them into his bag.

Searching farther afield, Bally found a few short lengths of knotted bark that had obviously been used to tie something, and recalling the peeled sapling at the river, it was not difficult to work out what that something had been. A small tree nearby with dried blood on both sides of the trunk low down and, clinging immediately above, a few long strands of blonde hair, gave further disheartening clues. The earth around the tree was scuffed and the few tufts of dry grass flattened, as if someone had rested there for some time. Drag-marks and footprints were all around, including those from Anna's boots.

Then Charles saw her khaki shirt.

It was lying balled- up beside a clump of dry grass, its colour blending, and it was stained with blood. He stood looking down at it with a sensation of deep foreboding.

Reluctantly, as if someone was holding a gun to his head, he knelt to pick it up. Blood had splattered and smeared the material, both inside and out. A few buttons had been pulled off, but it was not torn and showed no bullet or bayonet holes. He sniffed it, burying his nose deep, and the strong, familiar scent of her was like a sudden jab in the hollow of his gut. He held it against his face for a few moments, painfully savouring the sense of her presence, then handed it silently to Bally, who went through much the same procedure except the sniffing before returning it, also without comment. None was needed.

It was not something Charles could simply discard. Neither could he stuff it indiscriminately into the bag. After some agonising hesitation he folded it neatly and placed it inside his own shirt, tucking it into his waistband and pressing it flat against his stomach.

He sat brooding beside the bloodstained tree where she had been tied, while Bally continued the search alone, unwilling to participate for fear of what else he may find. It could only be her blood on the inside of the shirt, and how it came to be there was something he was not sure he wanted to know.

When Bally whistled softly from the bushes at the edge of the clearing, catching his attention then signalling urgently with his hand for him to come and see what he had found, Charles could not bring himself to go. He remained sitting, heart thudding, and Bally was forced to come closer to avoid calling out.

'Missy Anna,' Bally whispered, pointing to where he had been standing a few moments before, and Charles could only stare at him with his own blood turning to ice.

The half-caste leader freed her ankles, not bothering to untie them, but slicing through the bark with his hunting knife, and Aneline fought to control her trembling as he did the same with her wrists, but she could not. Suddenly her body seemed to have a will of its own. She glared defiantly at him though, with all the contempt she could muster.

Once she was free he moved quickly behind to drag her clear of the tree, and Aneline began struggling, kicking and punching with her swollen hands, bucking violently as he forced her down and sat astride her.

He struck her face hard, the blow catching her partly on the nose as she thrashed about, sending lights flashing through her head and causing her nose to bleed, but she did not cry out or stop her struggling, determined to keep fighting even if it meant being beaten senseless.

It was not necessary. Five willing helpers came quickly to subdue her.

Laughing and giggling, they began to strip her.

First her shirt, which they pulled up over her face, ripping off buttons. Her arms were outstretched above her head and clamped together at the wrist by strong hands. Her feet were likewise held fast. The half-caste began tugging on her tight moleskin riding breeches, edging them with difficulty over her hips as she strained in return to hold them hard against the ground. She knew they would not come off completely while she still wore her boots, and prepared herself for kicking out when they came to remove them.

Then suddenly they stopped.

For several moments nothing further happened. Although she was still being held, all movement had ceased. So had the breathless giggling. Two of the men were standing, and all were staring in the same direction, at something she could not see.

Then she realised they were not looking at anything. They were listening. She had not heard anything, but suddenly hope flooded into her. Someone must be coming. Maybe the militia. She took a deep breath and screamed.

It had little effect. The half-caste muttered angrily and clamped a hand over her mouth, then he pulled it away again with a mild exclamation of disgust at the blood on it. He reached for her discarded shirt and wiped his hand, then tossed the shirt contemptuously over her face, effectively cutting off the glare of hate she had been directing at him.

Then Aneline heard the sound herself. The boom of a distant cannon.

A few of the men ran for their rifles, their exclamations of surprise tinged with panic, but the half-caste stopped them with a few sharp words. They spoke animatedly, their tone questioning, and Aneline realised they must be ignorant of the attack on Murosi's Mountain.

But she knew, and grasped thankfully at her secret knowledge, her resolve to continue struggling refuelled. Charles had been with a cannon squad. It may even have been he that fired it. And it did not sound all that far away. If she could somehow escape she could easily reach the mountain and the militia.

When the cannon sounded again the men pulled her to her feet and, with painfully fumbling hands that felt as if they were encased in thick clay, she hastily pulled up her breeches. They gave her no opportunity to pick up her shirt.

They shoved her towards the tree, still speculating excitedly, their lust for the moment forgotten, and Aneline sat quickly, hugging the tree without being told. It was not being submissive. She doubted if she had sufficient strength in her legs to stand a moment longer, let alone run.

They did not bother to tie her, but stood listening to the continuing cannonade for a while, twitching - much to Aniline's satisfaction - at every shot. The half-caste issued a few brusque orders. Some of the men argued vehemently, apparently not agreeing with them, but soon changed their minds when he caught one by the shirt and threatened with his fist.

They began packing up the camp. Her spare clothes - other than those they had already distributed amongst themselves, including her blanket - were discarded along with the saddle. It seemed they were to travel light.

It also appeared obvious to Aneline that they believed she would not be needing anything, and the disturbing knowledge forced a decision. She would go willingly only if they went in the direction of Murosi's Mountain. If not, she would try to escape by diving down the first steep hill or cliff they came to. In the dark she would have a chance, and maybe they would be wary of giving away their position by shooting.

But even if they killed her, which she was sure now they intended doing anyway, once they had used her, at least she would have deprived them of that small pleasure.

Two Renegades went ahead, presumably as scouts, and Aneline was made to walk in front of the ones following.

It was easier with her hands free, and she gave no cause for them to be tied, complying swiftly to whispered instructions, and submitting without complaint when gagged with a pair of her own ripped-up underpants, lulling them into a false sense of security.

Free hands would also make running much easier if that became necessary, and for a while she thought it would be, for although the direction they took was not away from the steady booming of the cannons, neither was it towards them, and she kept a sharp lookout in the increasing dark for a likely place.

Then gradually they began swinging around, following defined trails and, although their progress became slower, with many a cautious pause to listen, each step was taking her closer to safety and increasing her chances of escape. She guessed that the renegades were probably also unaware that the mountain was surrounded by militia. There would be patrols and ambushes. She still had a chance.

It was well into the night when a rocket suddenly soared high into the sky ahead. The men dived quickly into the undergrowth, leaving Aneline alone on the path.

The bright rocket had startled her too, and spoiled her vision, but seeing it so close - only a few miles - then hearing the men diving away, prompted her to run.

But she had hesitated too long. She gasped as the half-caste caught her by the hair after she had gone only a few paces. He jerked her back, tripping her with his foot, and as she fell he cursed and struck the back of her head with his rifle barrel. Fortunately it was only a glancing blow, and her hair absorbed most of it. He called angrily to one of his men, and once again she was bound, this time her feet as well, and with her wrists behind her back, using her bootlaces, which cut into her flesh even more cruelly than the bark strips.

They left her sitting on the path in the open while they moved into the bushes nearby, obviously alarmed by the rocket and the gunfire that had followed. The two men sent ahead returned, running, and more excited chatter and gesticulating followed.

Watching apprehensively, Aneline suddenly realised that she had become a part of the discussion. It seemed to have something to do with her skin, and her assumption was soon proved correct. Three of them came to remove her breeches.

She kicked out, but with little effect. Seeming nervous and hurried, not making the usual lewd jokes, they held her down and, not bothering to untie her feet, simply hacked through both her breeches and blue underpants with a knife, quickly removing them and tossing the remnants aside. Then they left hastily to join the others in what she assumed was an ambush position.

Apparently she, completely naked now except for her socks, and with her pale skin clearly visible to anyone approaching on the path, was to be the bait.

Feeling vulnerable, yet also relieved, she lay on her side with knees drawn up against the cold, shivering as it crept over her exposed skin and seeped into her bones. For a while her exhaustion allowed her to doze fitfully, and she found some comfort in the sound of the attack and the thought that Charles was there, only a few short, frustrating miles away, but as the dark hours passed and the cold increased, even thought became impossible, and she lay chattering in a state of frozen stupor.

It was dawn when the shooting finally stopped, and the extended silence brought her fully alert. The same two men who had scouted ahead before reappeared, accompanied by another man. They paused in surprise at seeing her there, one of the men calling out anxiously, then exclaiming with relief when the half-caste answered sleepily from his hiding-place.

They entered into a lively whispered discussion, then a short while later the stranger came to look at her, and Aneline experienced a surge of hope when she recognised him. She sat up stiffly to ensure he could see her clearly, nodding at him in an attempt at collusion, even managing a tight smile beneath the gag in the hope its appeal would show in her eyes. Surely they wouldn't harm her now. When he informed the others who she was, and what Charles had done, they would release her. No need for them to take chances. Somehow she would get across to them that they could simply untie her legs and leave her there. She would find her own way.

But he gave no sign that he knew her. After observing her nakedness silently for a few moments, he left, returning to talk with the renegades.

Still hopeful, Aneline watched intently for some

indication that he was telling them about her, but they appeared to be discussing the battle, gesturing towards the mountain, and when he left on his own a short while later, not even glancing in her direction as he came back on the path, she gazed after him in disbelief, a chill coming over her that had nothing to do with that of the early morning.

She watched until the dark grey of his military coat blended then disappeared into the gloom, feeling a loneliness such as she had never known descending on her like a shroud, and she sank under the weight of it.

It came as no surprise when, as the men gathered on the path and began to follow in the wake of the Bushman, the half-caste detached himself and came towards her, cocking his rifle.

This time she could not find the will to glare her defiance. She sat woodenly, feeling a slight dizziness, watching without interest the haphazard meandering of an ant on one of her tucked under legs.

She did not flinch as he placed the cold muzzle against her temple, but did at the sudden, sharp exclamation from one of the men. Enough to cause her to glance up. The man was pointing, first towards the mountain, then to his ear, cautioning that a shot would be heard.

The half-caste grunted an acknowledgement and

laid the rifle aside. He withdrew the hunting knife from its hide sheath on his belt. He was not in a hurry, and she sensed his pale, predator's eyes willing her to look at him, but she would not give him the satisfaction.

As if she was no more than a sack of maize, he casually placed a foot against her shoulder and pushed her over.

Even had she wanted to, Aneline could offer no resistance as he rolled her onto her stomach and placed a heavy knee in the small of her back.

But a long, involuntary groan escaped her lips as he took a fistful of her hair and pulled her head so far back she thought her spine would snap.

With her vision already blurring, she caught a brief glimpse of steel as the knife passed under her chin, and closed her eyes. She offered no prayer that it would be quick. She knew it would be.

'Missy Anna,' Bally said patiently for the third time, drawing a circle around the clearly defined imprint of her boot with a stick. 'She go there.' He pointed in the direction she had walked, going away from the camp.

Charles stared at him with dawning understanding,

the clammy sweat on his brow warming as sudden anger replaced his sickening fear.

'You stupid little bugger! Why the hell didn't you say so the first time?'

Bally looked startled at the unexpected outburst. He frowned in bewilderment and pointed again with his stick. 'Missy Anna,' he repeated. 'She go there.'

'Are you sure?' It was a rhetorical question, something to give himself time rather than reassurance, for he could see the prints clearly.

Bally looked hurt, and Charles relented, relief quickly overcoming his anger. 'Never mind, keep going, it will soon be too dark to see.'

They ate Ouma's syrupy cakes alongside the trail they had been following, then slept, separated and well away from it, in thick, thorny undergrowth where they could not easily be disturbed. Sleep was essential if they were to remain alert, and despite his concern for Anna, two day's worth of exhausting activity had taken its toll. It seemed only moments before Bally was shaking him awake.

The tracking became more difficult. The signs were getting older all the time, and it soon became clear that Anna had been near the front of the group, with the result that many of her prints had been obliterated. When they did find a few together that hadn't been overtrodden though, her steps were evenly spaced, indicating that she had been walking strongly, and could not have been badly injured as Charles had suspected. It gave him new hope.

His spirits were further uplifted by the direction in which they were going. They were moving steadily towards Murosi's Mountain. A fact confirmed throughout the morning by the sound of sporadic firing directly ahead, and getting closer. The militia was apparently continuing with their campaign of ambushes. It was quite possible that the renegades they were following had walked into one. If it had been in the daylight, Anna may already have been saved.

When the flat-topped mountain finally came into view at the top of a rise, and Charles estimated the distance at about two miles, he cautioned Bally to move slowly, but the warning proved unnecessary. They were already barely moving. The trail had become a confusing jumble of tracks going in both directions, so that even Bally was having trouble deciphering them. For long stretches at a time they saw no sign of Anna's small distinctive heelprints.

Then they could find none.

While Bally searched like a retriever, doing everything but sniffing, Charles waited, undecided, in the sparse shade of a bush from where he had a view of the path ahead and could offer Bally protection. They were so close now that walking into an ambush or patrol - which could belong to either side - was a definite possibility. The broken country of ravines and caves where many skirmishes had taken place at the beginning of the siege was only a short distance ahead. He could no longer take the chance of Bally walking into one. He could easily be mistaken for a renegade and shot without warning.

After an hour of fruitless searching, Charles came to the painful decision that they had no option but to alert the militia by firing signal shots and hope they would come to investigate. The sporadic shooting from the mountain had gradually eased as the morning had progressed, so the chances of their signal being recognised were reasonable, and by now the militia should be in control of the surrounding countryside, at least during daylight.

He calculated that Aneline and her captors were still two days ahead, maybe even more, as they may have travelled at night, whereas he and Bally had been forced to stop. Trying to track her now, after so long a period, and with the increase of fresher traffic on top, was obviously a waste of time. He could only hope that she may already have been rescued, and he clung to the unlikely possibility like a drowning man would clutch at a length of sodden timber, for it was all that remained.

The patrol arrived early in the afternoon, finally answering his repeated groups of three evenly spaced shots with a few of their own.

As soon as he caught a glimpse of movement in the bush ahead, Charles called out the password, not wanting to give away his position until he was sure. 'What score in the first innings!'

'Two hundred... and three... not out,' came the tentative reply after some hesitation. 'Show yourself and be recognised.'

The number increased by odd amounts each day, and Charles was not sure of the number himself, but the English accent was pronounced. He stood up. 'I have a tracker with me, don't shoot him.' He signalled Bally to stay close beside him and they moved onto the path.

'You're taking a big risk being out here alone,' the corporal in charge of the ten-man patrol said after Charles had introduced himself. 'Are you lost?'

'No, we've been tracking my wife. She was abducted by Korannas three days ago. We managed to follow this far, but...'

'Your wife?' The corporal's tone was disbelieving, but his frown was one of genuine concern.

'You haven't seen or heard anything, have you? I was hoping she might have been found. Maybe a patrol... or ransom demand...'

'Sorry, mate, I'm sure I would have heard. Your wife. Good God.' He shook his head sympathetically, then called to his men. 'Any of you chaps hear of a woman being seen around here?'

His query was met with an exchanging of confused looks, head shaking, and a few predictable sniggers that were quickly silenced by the corporal's scowl. He turned back to face Charles with a helpless shrug and more sorrowful head shaking. 'Sorry, mate, maybe the Captain will know.'

Walking with the patrol towards Murosi's mountain, Charles could not escape the morbid feeling he was leaving Anna behind to fend for herself. Together with the guilt he already suffered, his sense of betrayal increased with every step. Had they found her body it would have been easier. Then he could simply hate himself. But not knowing was like living with a venomous snake around his neck. Hoping, but never sure if it would suddenly bite.

Charles was not aware that they had left the broadening path and were detouring around until the dead-animal smell hit him.

'Dead body,' the corporal explained. 'We don't

bury the buggers. Leave 'em there for their friends as an example.'

'It's his friends what did that one, though,' said a man behind. 'Did us a bit of a favour, like.'

'Should be a bit more of it, I say,' another commented. 'Nothin' like an arrow in the head to settle a good barney amongst friends.'

'In the throat, it was, I'm sure.'

'Nah, I seen it…'

'When?' Charles asked.

'On the way up, when we was coming to meet you. Lying right on the path it is, and stinking somethin' awful, as you can smell for yourself.'

'Mind if I have a quick look?' Charles asked the corporal. It was obvious the body must have been there for a few days - about the same time that Anna would have been in the vicinity. He had to see.

'Not if you don't mind us getting down wind first,' the corporal replied. 'Not much to see though. Been a bit chewed-up and spread around.'

There were no other volunteers. Charles took Bally with him, using one hand over his nose to quell the sickening stench, and the other holding the rifle to wave off stray flies.

He approached the dismembered body alone, Bally occupying himself with checking the surrounding area, and when Charles saw it, the hand covering his nose moved shakily to also cover his eyes, which had closed tight in blessed relief. The body was that of a man. And the cockney was right. The arrow had penetrated deep though the ear.

Charles turned and retraced his steps, light-headed and thankful to be moving away. He looked for Bally and saw him standing a short way off the path, examining what appeared to be a length of cloth in his hands, and something in the small African's demeanour caused Charles's pulse to start hammering.

'What is it?' he called softly, and when he received no answer, he went to him, moving on legs that seemed full and heavy as cannon balls.

'What?' he repeated, and Bally handed him the several pieces of cloth silently, his face so screwed and wrinkled with emotion that Charles could almost believe he was about to cry.

'Belong Missy Anna,' Bally whispered, then turned away, and Charles stared at what was left of her moleskin breeches and underpants with a heart so empty and broken he wanted to die.

With the willing help of the corporal and his patrol the area was searched thoroughly, but only one other sign of Anna's presence there could be found, and that was yielded guiltily to Charles by the cockney soon after they began searching.

'I'm sorry, mister,' he apologised. 'I didn't know they was women's boots. I thought they was maybe stolen from a kid, so I took 'em for mine. They was lying right there on the path. You won't be reporting me to the Captain now, will you?'

Charles shook his head. 'Don't worry…' Resignedly he put them in his pack with everything else he had collected of hers, except the bloodstained shirt, which he could not bring himself to remove from inside the haven of his own. Having her laceless boots as well did little to alter his state of numb acceptance, except the certain knowledge she would not be able to walk far without them.

But even more disquieting was the knowledge that he now had all the clothes she had been wearing. Anna would have nothing.

Awkward in their sympathy, the men of the patrol were silent in his presence and avoided his company - even Bally - and he remained isolated in his misery until they reached the mountain and Captain Singleton's headquarters.

When the details had been recounted, tongues clicked, and heads sympathetically wagged, Charles was quick to change the subject to a less discomforting topic.

'When do we attack?' he asked the officer.

'The bombardment will start at dusk and continue for thirty six hours,' Captain Singleton informed him with some relief. 'Much longer this time. The ground assault will commence at around midnight tomorrow with the waning of the moon.'

'Good. I would like to go with it.'

The captain demurred. 'Look, old chap, I appreciate how you feel, but in the circumstances, I don't think that would be such a good idea. Why don't you take some time? We have an additional fifty men in the militia now, and more than enough volunteers. No need to…'

'No. I'll stay with the cannon until tomorrow, but after that Sergeant Pienaar can find someone else.' Charles did not mean to be insubordinate, and his tone did not suggest it. He simply spoke with the quiet determination he felt. A cannon was too remote for his mood. He wanted their blood on his hands, and if it couldn't be that of Aneline's abductors personally, their friends would have to pay. As many as possible. 'I'm sorry, Captain, but one way or another, I'm going up that mountain.'

Captain Singleton did not take offence. After twiddling distractedly with a pencil for several moments in silence, he looked up with an expression almost of sadness. 'Very well, Mister Atherstone... Charles. Work out the details with the sergeant, and if you change your mind...' he paused, then stood to offer his hand. 'I know how you feel. We have a few scores to settle ourselves. Be careful... good luck to you.'

Aneline woke to the insistent trilling of a guinea fowl somewhere in the distance. Dawn had broken, but inside the cave it was still dark, and she lay snug and warm in the fur kaross, listening to the familiar sound.

The ground was hard, her neck stiff and sore, and the fur smelled strongly of uncured leather, wood-smoke and stale sweat, but she had never felt more comfortable.

There had been times in the night when she had woken, gasping, convinced she was dying, and so strong had been the sensation that, even after coming fully awake, she had not been able to resist putting a finger to her throat to reassure herself that it was not really cut through.

Even now, lying there awake, safe and secure,

she was aware that her hand was couched under her chin, her knuckles resting on the rough surface of the scab that she knew would leave a scar - a constant reminder of how close she had come to death. A racing heartbeat away, and she marvelled yet again, with a sudden shiver, at the miracle of her life. Never again would she take it for granted.

The thud of the arrow striking him in the head was a sound she would never forget either. She had thought it was her spine snapping. The sudden release of pressure, then her face striking the ground with his weight behind it. Warm blood running from her nose and seeping onto her lips through the gag. The roaring in her ears before she fainted. All had led her to believe she was dying.

Then coming around again as she was being lifted, catching a hazy glimpse of the half-caste lying with an arrow sticking from his ear, herself being jostled onto a naked shoulder, her breathing cut short by the jarring run.

She did not know she was being rescued, and had accepted her life reluctantly. All she had wanted was to be left alone to die, to be returned to the comfort of oblivion. She couldn't take any more of being alive.

Only after her bonds and gag had been removed, the blood carefully wiped from her face with a wet cloth, and her nakedness covered with the coarse military coat, did she become aware of what was happening. She gulped at the cool water given to her in a calabash, tasting the mustiness, and feeling her strength flowing back.

The pain came after. First her hands, then a sharp stinging under her right ear beneath her chin. She sat dazedly as the ripped underpants used for a gag was tied around her neck to stem the trickle of blood. She tried to judge the extent of the wound, but her thick, insensitive fingers could feel nothing.

She had thought there was only one - the man in the coat - but he had two companions, also Bushmen, although she was unable to tell if they were the same who had come to Sani Kloof. Both carried bows, so it was one of them, she surmised, who had killed the half-caste.

Understandably, they had been in a hurry. They urged her to stand, lifting her under the arms and supporting her on clumsy feet, but her woollen socks had given some protection from the leather lace used to tie her ankles, and together with the roomy buffalo-hide moccasins they provided, she soon managed on her own.

Walking soon became easier than it had been in her tight boots, which was fortunate, for they walked steadily for the next two days and much of the night.

Food was provided, for the most part, in the form of wild fruit and reptiles, thankfully charred beyond all recognition, and she ate what was presented to her with gusto and a closed mind, smiling in genuine appreciation. Freedom had given her a ravenous appetite.

The difference in attitude between the Bushmen and the Korannas was marked. No one stared, even when, in the heat of the day, she tied the arms of the heavy coat around her waist, leaving most of her legs and her upper torso exposed. It was only their colour that was different, she excused herself. Female Bushmen went bare-breasted all the time.

Communication had become remarkably effective, considering it comprised only signals, nods and smiles. The old one, whose coat she wore, cut a leafy branch for her to carry as protection against sunburn, and she had laughed - a strange sound in her ears - as she flicked away insects and made foolish comparisons between herself and the Queen of Sheba.

They had taken a circuitous route, seeing no one, heading deep into the hills before turning north, away from Murosi's mountain and, Aneline guessed, roughly in the direction of Eland's Drift. But they had not gone there. Late in the afternoon of the second day they stopped at the base of a steep mountain where they met with the young woman and her child.

It was like coming home. Teary-eyed, she hugged them both, then, carried away by her emotion, and much to the men's obvious discomfiture, she hugged them as well.

The woman had provided the kaross for her to wear and the coat was returned to its owner with effusive thanks. They had sat around a fire eating real meat, Aneline with the child on her lap, where he seemed content to remain so long as she kept feeding him, and she had fallen asleep there, still sitting up.

Next day they had toiled up the mountain, through an oblique slash in the cliff-face, then through a dank rock passage at the top to the cave. A sanctuary.

When Aneline woke again bright sunshine flooded the mouth of the cave, causing the painting of Eland there to glisten and shimmer as if freshly painted.

She studied it again, as she had the first time, marvelling at the vibrant colour, and the crisp outline that showed not a single blur. It would impress Charles, as it had awed her. Perfect except for the small imprint of the artist's hand at the bottom. Its outline was smudged, but he would have had to reach out over the sheer edge of the cliff to put it there.

Aneline threw aside the kaross and went to join the woman and child in the sun, donning the skimpy loincloth she had fashioned from scraps, including the former gag. It left little to the imagination, but with the men gone it didn't matter, and she had come to enjoy the sensual freedom it gave. She wondered what Charles would think of her fast developing all-over tan.

'A lovely morning,' she greeted cheerily, and the woman returned a demure but equally unintelligible greeting of her own, smiling shyly and shifting to make space for her on the blanket.

The valley below was streaked with mist, giving it a fairytale look, and beyond the next hill the sandstone cliffs glowed orange. The same cliffs that she and Charles could see from the verandah of home. She had been surprised at how close they were. She would bring him here to see the cave and painting. He would like that. It was so high and peaceful. Like a church in the sky.

Aneline sat carefully, arranging the scrap of cloth modestly, then placed a hand on the child's head. 'Moro, Xai-Xai,' she said, clicking her tongue twice in rapid succession to pronounce the difficult name. The child looked at his mother for confirmation before responding, and when she nodded her encouragement, he returned his gaze to Aneline and solemnly passed on the nod. Both women laughed.

'I do wish I could understand more,' Aneline said with a sigh. 'There is so much we could talk about, isn't there?'

Both had been trying to learn, passing the hours as they waited for the men to return by exchanging words and practising them, but about the only thing they both understood were their names - Hunna for Aneline, and something that sounded like the clip-clop of hooves on cobblestones for the woman. Giggles invariably followed her clumsy pronunciation of it.

For some reason that she could not understand, they often ate, but never cooked in the cave, which would have been much easier, alleviating the need to crawl through the narrow passageway between the boulders, but at least it gave the opportunity of attending to her toilet needs in private.

The fire was well concealed and small, and the men had left a supply of water and the remains of a small buck - fast deteriorating in its wrapping of leaves and hide - buried under a rock.

Sitting in the mouth of the cave with the woman and the child, knowing she would soon have a child of her own, admiring the painting and basking in the morning sun, Aneline was at peace with herself. She had learned much about the fragility of life in the past week, and vowed she would never again allow petty emotions to take control of her.

With her dangerous predicament constantly on her mind she had given little thought to her troubles with Charles, but now she thought of him often, and of the short span of life they had shared. Happy times full of love. And she recalled the misery and loneliness she had felt when tied to the tree and lay naked and vulnerable on the path, expecting death, and believing she would never see him again. No threat, justified or unjustified, from the dark-haired woman, could compete with that.

The anger she had felt seemed so trivial now after what she had suffered. She had always been headstrong, but this time she had also been stubborn and foolish. What did it matter if some woman he had known before they met loved him - even felt married to him - and had given him a daughter? She loved him too, and *was* married to him. It was the other woman she should have felt sorry for instead of herself.

Even if he left her for the woman she would still love him. She accepted the fact, but she also accepted she would not give in without a fight. Only this time she would choose the right weapons. Understanding instead of jealousy, and love in place of anger.

A sound like that of distant thunder broke the stillness of the late afternoon, and Aneline looked to the south for the dark clouds, but the sky was clear, streaked only with the pale lemon of a setting sun, and she and the woman exchanged knowing glances. The cannons had started again at Murosi's Mountain.

They were still thundering away when Aneline woke late next morning to see Bally sitting with the woman and child in the sunny mouth of the cave. She sat up quickly to look around, her heart taking a leap when she noticed a dark bundle against the opposite wall, then slumping in resignation when she saw it was only the military coat. The Bushmen had evidently returned, apparently bringing Bally with them, but must have left again.

Then she noticed a smaller bundle of clothes had been placed beside her, and she smiled. Her nudist days were over.

Bally greeted her like a boisterous puppy when she joined them, bobbing around with the beaming smile on his wizened face interchanging rapidly with frowns of concern as his eyes touched on her many scabs and bruises.

He whispered her name, 'Missy Anna', several times, as if unbelieving, then rushed to fetch her a package of food he had brought from her kitchen at home: a tin of stale scones, a jar of her home-made gooseberry jam, and one of Oupa's discarded brandy bottles filled with cold tea.

'For Missy Anna,' he murmured, arranging them carefully on the blanket at her side.

'Thank you, Bally,' Aneline said huskily, her smile of appreciation distorting somewhat under the strength of her emotions.

Knowing she would be unable to swallow, she scooped jam onto a scone with a piece of stick and passed it to the child. 'Mmm,' she encouraged, and was grateful when he took it. She did the same for the woman and Bally. A real tea party.

'Mister Charles?' she asked Bally, nibbling on a few dry crumbs and vowing once again to learn his language.

He pointed in the direction of the thundering. 'By Murosi.'

She nodded, then, with her eyebrows raised in question, pointed to the military coat and hat. 'The men San?'

Bally pointed to the west, holding his arm high with bent wrist motioning down, indicating distance. 'Go Kgalagadi,' he said, and Aneline nodded again. It was good news. They would be safer in the desert.

'What about us?' She pointed to the four of

them and again raised her eyebrows and shoulders in question.

Bally spoke briefly to the woman before answering. 'Missy Anna eat tea, us go Sani Kloof.' He paused to grin. 'See Oupa.'

Aneline matched his grin. Surpassed it. 'Damned show-off,' she muttered.

Ouma Theron was placing a bowl of dough on the kitchen window-sill to prove in the warm sun when she saw them. They were on the path to the shed, coming towards the house, and the bowl slipped from her fingers to crash on the floor as she clamped both hands to her face and let out a shriek. 'God in heaven!'

With his back turned and a tin mug full of hot coffee halfway to his lips, Oupa was in no position to absorb such a surprise. The mug jerked upwards, hurling its steaming contents onto his arm, and eliciting a further yell before it also clanged to the floor.

'Oh, my God, Danie, it's her!' Ouma's voice rose to culminate in another shriek. 'Quickly, man!' She rushed for the door, and Oupa clattered after her, kicking aside the fallen chair.

'Who... what the hell is it, Hettie?'

'Anna. It's Anna, Danie! Oh, thank you, God.'

'What?'

'Come on, man, quickly! She's here…' Ouma thumped down the steps, shrieking with delight, and ran heavily along the path to meet them. 'Anna! Anna!'

Aneline detached herself from the group and hastened to meet her, and they clung to each other in tearful joy. 'It's really you,' Ouma wailed. 'You're safe… oh, God, Anna, how I prayed…'

'Dammit, Anna,' Oupa intervened gruffly, pushing between them to hug her. 'Man! You don't know how good it is…'

'Yes, I do Oupa,' Aneline sniffed. 'Yes, I do.'

'Hell, man, Anna… are you all right? We thought… when Bally returned without Charles… they tracked you for days, you know. Hell, man, when they found your things…'

'I'm fine, Oupa. A few scratches, I was lucky.'

'And Bally? How come he…?'

'The Bushmen brought him to me last night… at the cave. That's their sister… going to be Bally's wife… I think.'

Oupa relinquished Aneline to the clutches of Hettie and transferred his attention to Bally. 'You little bugger,' he rasped, placing an arm around his neck in a stranglehold and rubbing his head. 'Man! You little bugger, you…'

Lying snug in her own bed, with the lingering scent of Charles still on the pillow beside her, Aneline smiled with contentment. It had been a happy day. And more would follow when Charles returned, she knew.

She tried to estimate how long that would be. Oupa and his two friends would reach the mountain with the good news early tomorrow, and if all went well, and there were no delays, Charles should be home the day after. At most by late afternoon. She and Ouma would arrange a special homecoming dinner. A feast.

The cannons couldn't be heard from the valley, and she wondered drowsily if they had stopped and what he was doing. At least being with the cannons he would be safe. It didn't matter that he knew about the baby. Nothing mattered anymore, only love, and she had enough for both of them. She would share…

Speed in the attack was crucial. The moon did not wane until close to midnight, leaving only four hours of darkness to negotiate the formidable slopes at the base of the cliffs with the heavy scaling ladders, manoeuvre them into position against the sheer face, then fight their way to the top. If caught in daylight they could expect a similar lively reception to that of the first debacle.

Three of those vital dark hours had already gone by the time Sergeant Pienaar and his men reached their position at the base of the cliff, and they were the first of the three advance squads to arrive.

A different location had been chosen to scale the final barrier this time - a place on the eastern slopes known as Bourne's crack - but either the rugged steepness of the terrain, or the superhuman effort required, had been underestimated.

With their blackened faces streaked by sweat, the men sprawled in the deep shadow against the wall, exhausted even before the battle had begun.

Still, apart from cuts and bruises, they were fortunate to have arrived that far unscathed. The diversion tactics, particularly those created by the volunteers positioned around the mountain to keep the renegades separated and occupied - hopefully until the advance squads had reached the top - seemed to have worked.

Captain Singleton had wisely chosen not to signal the beginning of the ground assault by firing a single skyrocket. He had fired three. The first had been launched late in the evening, followed by the others at half-hour intervals, the cannons remaining silent for twice their normal cooling period between rockets to lead the renegades into believing the attack was commencing.

That it worked was made evident by the sudden outburst of random firing from the cliff-tops soon after each rocket had extinguished itself in a shower of sparks. It not only kept Murosi's men confused, but also gave away their main defensive positions to the diversionary groups, who returned fire enthusiastically, creating so much noise that the advance squads with their cumbersome ladders were able to reach their own positions undetected.

It was a short rest. A low whistle from the darkness signalled that the adjacent squad was ready, and Sergeant Pienaar answered it before clambering to his feet with a groan. The men did likewise, forming into a line in the order in which they would ascend the ladder, fidgeting nervously with their equipment.

Charles tested the sling of his rifle once again, ensuring it could be slipped from his shoulder quickly if needed, but was not so slack as to become a hindrance when climbing. His loaded shotgun was slung across his back.

As a proved marksman, he and two others were to follow the sergeant up and secure the top while those below provided covering fire if needed. A duplicate operation would take place on the other ladders.

'Remember,' Sergeant Pienaar cautioned in a hoarse whisper. 'No more than four on the ladder at a time, and keep your weapons safe or you may shoot the man above in the arse. And good luck, hey.'

An answering mumble came from the men and the sergeant gave Charles a nudge. 'Okay, man, let's go get the bastards.'

Charles wiped his palms on the seat of his trousers. 'I'll be right behind you, Jannie.' As far as he was concerned the sooner he reached the top the better. He did not enjoy heights, and the cliff was a lot higher than it had looked from a distance.

They climbed cautiously at first, trying to maintain a steady rhythm, but it was hard and tiring work with the weight of their equipment and ammunition, even more so than on the treacherous slopes, and the higher they climbed the worse the ladder bounced, despite it being held secure at the bottom.

Then, to make it worse, shouts came from above, followed by firing to the side of them, from one of the adjacent squads. It seemed they had finally been spotted. The steady ascent suddenly became an uncoordinated scramble.

Exposed on the ladder, Charles pressed hard on

the sergeant's heels, with the two men behind pushing close on his, and it soon became evident that the sergeant was holding them back. Overweight, and already exhausted from climbing the slopes, he puffed and wheezed like a leaky steam engine, his warm sweat splattering down on Charles.

Clinging to the bouncing ladder that gave the impression it was about to snap and send them plunging to their deaths at any moment, Charles paused briefly to look past the sergeant to the top, and realised with dismay that they were only halfway. Then when he saw movement at the top, and the men below started firing over his head, he knew if he did not do something soon he would either lose his nerve on the unstable ladder, or be shot.

'Move over, Jannie,' he panted, 'I'm coming through.'

He did not wait for confirmation, but clawed his way past, and the exhausted sergeant had no option but to allow him passage.

With his way clear, Charles climbed rapidly, finding his own rhythm and pace, the ladder bouncing less as he neared the top, and given further encouragement by the buzz and crackle of bullets. When a rock the size of his head smashed on the ladder above, narrowly missing him as it bounced away, he paused to catch his breath and unsling the shotgun, hooking his leg through the rungs to hold him.

He could see the edge clearly now, less than five yards away, and continued climbing with one hand, holding the shotgun pointed at the break between the solid mass of rock and the starry sky. When another solid object the size of a head appeared, he fired.

The recoil threw him sideways. Off-balance, and holding the shotgun with only one hand, he clutched wildly, his foot slipping through the rungs and the shotgun clattering against the upright, almost knocking it from his grasp.

Hanging precariously on the side by one arm and one leg, but still holding the gun, he glanced up to see that the head-like object he had shot was attached to a falling body. It struck the ladder two rungs above, flopping past him, but landing squarely in Sergeant Pienaar's arms directly below. Charles heard the crack as Jannie's arm broke.

It was only the sergeant's brute strength, and the support of the man close behind, who saw it coming and gripped hard to the supports, that prevented him from being knocked off. He removed his arm to let the body fall, then roared at Charles. 'Keep going, man!'

Charles needed no urging from him, he was getting plenty from above - from a seeming avalanche of boulders. He all but flew up the remaining rungs. Fortunately, most of the rocks were being thrown from somewhere behind the ledge, out of sight, and they either went wide or bounced overhead. He fired the second barrel blind, hooking on with his leg and raising the shotgun high to clear the top.

He reloaded quickly, the two cartridges already gripped in his teeth, then tossed the weapon ahead and scrambled after it, both hands scrabbling for a grip on the loose surface as rocks pelted, sparks flew, and bullets whined and buzzed around him like a swarm of angry hornets.

He rolled, snatching up the shotgun, and saw the muzzle flashes coming from a low stone wall. He also saw that no cover existed between himself and it.

A sudden calm took hold of Charles. He didn't care. These were the swine who had taken Anna from him, were now trying to stop him from reaching her. They would pay.

He stood up and roared the Zulu war challenge remembered from Quabe. 'Bekizwe!' He fired both barrels in quick but calculated succession at the flashes then, still standing, he flicked the lever to break open the breech and reloaded with shells from his pocket, feeling strangely detached from it all.

He strode purposefully towards them - to the men

who had taken Anna, ripped off her clothes, violated her. He didn't care how many there were. He wanted them all.

Sergeant Pienaar bellowed from the top of the ladder. 'Charles! Get down, man!' Then urgently to the men behind. 'Push me up for Christ's sake!'

Charles paid no heed. Other men shouted too, some close, some distant and confused, a babble of words, and he paid them no attention either. Words meant nothing, he wanted their blood.

A sudden blow to his left shoulder sent him staggering back a few steps, but he caught his balance and continued his determined advance. They would not stop him. His left arm felt oddly heavy, reluctant to hold the stock. He let it hang and tucked the shotgun under the crook of his right arm, gripping the slender neck firmly with finger on the trigger. He was close now, only a few paces away, and he held his fire, wanting to be sure.

Two shadowy figures jumped up from behind the wall, close together with weapons raised, and Charles fired between them without aiming, the gun kicking high, but the spread of shot hurling both renegades back. Another scampered away on hands and knees, trying to stay low behind the rocks, and the second blast, fired from directly above, flattened him into a sprawl of outflung arms and legs.

A fourth man lay writhing with hands clutching at his face, the victim of stray pellets, and Charles dropped the smoking shotgun for the rifle. Holding it in one hand he leaned over the wall and poked the man with the barrel.

'Where? What have you done with her, you filthy bastard?'

The man screeched and pulled his hands from his bloodied face to hold them up in appeal. 'No shoot! No shoot!'

'You rotten swine,' Charles said coldly, and shot him in the head.

At the ladder, the men of the squad were piling over rapidly, hoisted up by the two on top.

His breath rasping, Sergeant Pienaar stumbled to where Charles sat on the wall loading the shotgun, gripping it in his knees. 'Jesus, man… what the hell…'

'Over there, Jannie,' Charles said calmly, indicating with his head. 'On the mountain. More of the bastards coming.' He slung the rifle and tucked the shotgun under his arm. 'I'll get these… our men need help on the ladder.'

He placed two spare cartridges between his teeth, then strode away into the darkness, towards intermittent firing some fifty yards away on the cliff-edge, where another ladder had been positioned.

'Hey, where do you think you're going?' the sergeant shouted. 'The squad is not all up yet.'

'Uh huh.'

'Jesus, man...' He broke off to bellow at his men. 'Come on, you buggers, get a move on!'

Charles smiled at the sergeant's ranting. His thinking was clear, his senses sharp as a blade. Bullets couldn't harm him. They would pay for Anna and his child. Oh God, the child too...

It almost unnerved him, his step faltered, but only for an instant. He could not let them down. He quickened his pace, following the haphazard line of crude barricades and defensive cairns that had been erected close to the cliff-edge.

The sky was beginning to lighten in the east, the stars fading, but it was still dark on the mountain. He could see muzzle-flashes clearly now, coming from the edge where the ladder would be. A shadowy figure detached itself from the barricade ahead, moving to the edge, staggering under the weight of something heavy... a boulder.

Charles continued on without slowing, staying erect until he was directly behind them, then he sat down amidst a jumble of pots, tins and blankets. He exchanged the shotgun for the rifle and rested the barrel on the stones in front.

He could see their dark outlines lying along the edge, at least five on either side of the one with the rock. The man was sitting now, leaning back on his elbows and pushing the boulder towards the edge with his feet.

Charles shot him before the rock went over.

In the surprise and confusion that followed, he killed another two, clamping the rifle with his knees after each shot to work the bolt. Then he left the rifle and picked up the shotgun as bullets smacked and splattered into the makeshift wall before him, showering him with fragments of rock and hot lead.

They still seemed reluctant, shouting and gesticulating, urging each other, then finally one man ran towards him, shooting wildly, and another two followed.

Charles waited until they were close, until he could see the desperation in their eyes and hear their gasping breath, then killed all three with two blasts.

The remaining renegades fled along the cliff as Sergeant Pienaar and five men from the squad flung themselves down beside Charles and opened fire and, caught in the open between the barricade and the edge, the Korannas had no chance.

'Move that rock and help those men on the ladder,'

Sergeant Pienaar yelled to his men, then turned angrily on Charles. 'Dammit, man, what the hell do you think you're doing, hey?'

'We should check the other ladder.'

'It's been cleared. Do you think you're the only army around here? I've a bloody good mind to have you charged for...'

'Save it for later, Jannie... give me a hand with this, will you?' He unbuttoned his shirt and slid it off his shoulder, exposing the wound in the top of his arm.

'Hey, man, you've been hit!'

'Can't feel much.'

'Ja, that's how it is, but you will... let me see.' He pushed aside Charles's probing fingers to look. 'Gone clean through. Lucky it wasn't a soft-nose.'

'Bind it with this.' Charles tugged Anna's bloodstained shirt from the warm sanctuary of his waistband.

Sergeant Pienaar examined it briefly. 'No, man, we can't use that dirty old rag. Hollings can put a field-dressing on.'

'It's not dirty, it's my wife's.'

'Even so, I think...'

'It's hers, Jannie. Anna's blood.' Suddenly he felt exhausted. Weary beyond all measure.

'Jesus in heaven, Charles...that's why you're

doing this, man, isn't it?'

'Press it on, Jannie.'

'First some sulphur, then Hollings can do it. I also have only one hand.'

'Yes, sorry, I forgot. Get him to put on a splint.'

'Yes, sir. Anything else, sir?'

Hollings attended to both injuries as the men from the second and third ladder began arriving, and a man from the sergeant's squad came to report that the renegade reinforcements were being held back.

'Time for the fireworks,' Sergeant Pienaar instructed, and a few moments later a rocket hissed its way skyward to the accompaniment of cheers. The position was secure. The main force could ascend safely.

With no need for caution, and with visibility increasing rapidly, the advance squads vented their relief at being there with breathless and excited chatter. Several came to gape at Charles, whose exploits had been recounted with enthusiasm, and no little awe.

'My, God,' one man enthused. 'I thought we were goners. They had us pinned on that bloody great ladder so we couldn't move. I'd like to shake your hand for what you done, sir. You saved our lives… and you being wounded and all.'

'Bloody good show, sir,' another called amidst a

rumble of assent.

Sergeant Pienaar gave Charles a wry grin and shook his head. 'You crazy bugger...'

When Captain Singleton arrived with the bulk of the militia, a cordon was thrown across the width of the mountain and the sweep began.

For Charles the battle was over. Having heard of the account, the officer likewise came to shake his hand and offer his thanks. 'A medal in this for you, I shouldn't wonder, Charles,' he said. 'We could have lost a lot more than only four men.' He smiled. 'I'm glad I allowed you to talk me into it.'

'Do they give medals for stupidity, Captain?'

Captain Singleton laughed. 'Of course they do. Nobody in his right mind risks his life, do they? But you're not taking any more chances with yours, old chap. We'll have more than enough wounded by the time this is over, and it's going to be one hell of a job getting them down. I have a few volunteers working on slings right now. You can be one of the first to test them out. Have the doctor at the camp look at your arm... and that's a bloody order.'

'Don't worry, sir,' Sergeant Pienaar growled, lifting his heavy service revolver. 'If he makes a wrong move I'll bonk him on the head with this.'

Charles did not argue. His arm had begun to throb

painfully, and he had no objection to being lowered down the cliff in comfort. The mere thought of having to climb down the bouncing ladder was enough to break him out in another cold sweat.

To take his mind off the throbbing, and while the sergeant gave unwanted advice to the volunteers on how to sling the stretchers, he strolled along the cliff, past the grotesquely sprawled bodies of the Korannas, to the so-called Bourne's crack. It was nothing more than a jagged cleft jammed with fallen boulders and dry, gorse-like thorny scrub. Mister Bourne must have had a hard time getting through.

It was a sombre view. The sun was up, though still unseen behind the higher mountains in the east, and he remembered the last time he had stood this high at dawn. Then it had been to see the placid herds of game and the palette of flowers around the pan - the day he had made the decision not to leave this wild, cruel land; shouting it from the hilltop like a lovesick fool.

It was different now. No herds or bright flowers here, only the dark forbidding hills through which he had recently searched in vain. As bleak now from a distance as they had been then. A fitting backdrop to the sounds of war.

A loose boulder lay close to his foot and he kicked it savagely over the edge of the cleft, hearing it bounce then crunch through the spiky grey bushes as, sick at heart, he turned away.

The bullet struck him low in the back, ripping upward into his chest with the goring force of an angry buffalo horn, lifting him off his heels and hurling him forward, and he lay looking at the ground, wondering in hazy surprise why it was so close. Then he heard the shot echoing in the cleft behind and lowered his head, smelling the raw dust, and listening to the clamour of battle in the distance... to the sounds of death.

The woman holding the child on her hip lingered in the passage until it was clear, then tentatively opened the door with the strictly no unauthorised entry sign and peered in.

The room was gloomy and smelled of death, a heavy smell. The only light came from a shuttered window on the far wall.

It had only four beds, all in a line. The first contained a man whose head and most of his face was covered by stained bandages. He was snoring softly, and the woman held a cautionary finger to her lips to warn the child as she went in, quietly closing the door behind. The second bed was vacant, and the third occupied by a canvas kit bag, a bush hat with the insignia of the Cape Mounted Rifles, and an open box containing personal effects.

The fourth bed, at the end nearest the window, was concealed behind a heavy white curtain, and she approached it with her finger still held to her lips, peeping cautiously around the screen to ensure it was him, and that he was asleep, before going closer.

She looked down on him. He was older, with grey tingeing his hair, but still the face she remembered. His pallid cheeks were sunken and etched, and dark shadows, like old bruises, ringed his sunken eyes. His breathing was faint and sawing. Iodine-stained bandages swathed his entire upper torso and one arm, and a network of tubes protruded, linking him to a complicated array of bottles suspended on a stand beside a chair and table. A woman's paraphernalia littered the table. His wife's.

'Why are you crying, Mama, is he dead?'

'Shush... you must be quiet, Charlotte... please!' She put her down to rescue the bunch of yellow chrysanthemums dangling from the small strangling fist, placing them in an empty tumbler on the table and filling it from an enamel jug of water. She cleared a space and arranged the flowers where they would get some light. A touch of sunshine in a sad room.

She leaned over to kiss him gently on the brow. 'Goodbye, my darling.'

She scooped up the child and left quickly, not pausing at the door to check the passage was clear, walking swiftly along it with head bowed, not noticing the blonde woman who looked curiously at her as she passed. And unaware that the woman had turned and was hurrying after her.

It had been three months since Murosi's Mountain. Short enough to remember well, but long enough for the easing of pain.

Forty-three troopers had been killed and eighty-four wounded in the affray.

Five hundred of Murosi's renegade rustlers, many of their women, and all of the chief's sons had died. A few, including one of Murosi's sons, had escaped by taking the desperate gamble of leaping from the cliffs and rolling down the slopes to the Orange river, but most were killed, and his son was later found in a cave beyond the river, his thigh broken, and dying of wounds.

At five thirty in the morning - five hours after the assault began - Murosi's head replaced that of the unfortunate sergeant major's on the pole. His storehouse containing seven tons of ammunition and gunpowder was blown-up, and most of the primitive fortifications destroyed.

Three Victoria Crosses were awarded for gallantry.

It was a perfect day for the showing of colours. One of those warm summer days with a cloudless sky and a soft breeze to unfold the red, white and blue poised halfway up its freshly limed pole.

In the surrounding gardens the blooms displayed their less formal colours in brilliant array; as gay a showing in the bright sunshine as the summer dresses and parasols of the ladies gathered on the lawn.

Even a few wildflowers had gatecrashed the ceremony, standing in defiant clusters along the edges of the well-ordered beds.

Amongst the proteas a Cape Sugar Bird put on his own display for a seemingly disinterested female, its long, yellow-spotted tail undulating as it swooped and dipped in a circle around her, while from deeper in the bushes an outraged rival voiced its disapproval in an odd, gobbling chatter.

A good day to be alive, and for honouring both the living and the dead.

'Hello,' said a small voice, and he turned stiffly in the chair to smile a welcome.

'Hello, Charlotte. You look very pretty, today.'

'Are you better enough so we can do some more drawing now?'

'Later, after all those important people have said their speeches. Maybe we'll draw the governor in his funny hat.'

'Do you still have bandages... can I see?'

He loosened a few shirt buttons to show her a glimpse of white and she came closer to peer eagerly.

'Do you think you could pick me some flowers?' he asked.

She nodded vigorously, confident, and he pointed to a cluster of wildflowers nearby. 'Over there... choose your favourite colour.'

She squatted to pick them, choosing indecisively, but he was not surprised when she returned with a fistful of yellow ones.

'Perfect. They go well with your hair. Do you mind if I put some in?'

'Umm...' She gave it a few moments of serious

thought, then nodded.

He nipped off the earthy roots with his nail and threaded the stalks carefully into her dark hair above her left ear. 'There… now you are the most beautiful girl here.'

'Can I go now? I have to see the magicians.'

He pondered this for a moment. 'Ah, you mean the musicians. You'd better go then. Where's your mother?'

'Ummm…' She turned to scrutinise the growing crowd, then pointed jubilantly. 'There!'

He had already seen her, standing watching, her arm linked with that of Captain Singleton - an introduction he himself had arranged with the enthusiastic help of his wife. They waved, and he lifted his hand in response.

'Goodbye, darling… and don't run, you'll fall.'

The raised dais had been placed in the shade between two large oaks, facing the rows of chairs on the lawn, and the students from the new Cape Town University Choir, dressed in white, were already taking their positions beside it, in front of the military band.

'You certainly have a way with females, don't you?' said another voice behind.

He started to turn, but she stopped him with a caressing hand on his cheek. 'Will it be the same with your son?'

'What makes you so sure it will be a son?'

'Ouma told me. She said she can tell by my eyes.'

He chuckled. 'Of course. How foolish of me. Where is she and Oupa?'

'With Pa and Jurie. We were having a look at the medals… especially yours. They're on display in the hall. It's bronze, with a crimson ribbon, and the citation...' She paused, adopting an official tone. 'for gallantry and conspicuous bravery…' Her tone changed, becoming husky. "There's more, but I can't remember… I'm so proud of you…'

He laughed softly, favouring the wound. 'More conspicuous than brave, my love. It's you who should be getting it. Now you had better help me over or we'll miss it all.'

'You're reading my mind again. Must we share everything...even our thoughts?'

'Especially those.'

'Always?'

He remained silent,placing his hand over hers, then moving it from his cheek to his lips.

Printed in Great Britain
by Amazon